PRAISE FOR 'TI

"*The King of Rhye* takes the reader on a journey through mischief, despair, and triumph in the land of Rhye. The lore and unique characters incorporated in the worldbuilding brings colour to the story. A solid debut novel for Mulhall."

— *Nicholas Brown, critic, Whistler Independent Book Awards*

"Fantastical, fictional creatures spill from the mind of author Craig Mulhall, onto the pages of his Faery book, *The King of Rhye* … an unparalleled imaginative journey. Anything is possible in this Faery tale."

— *Judith Flitcroft, author of* Walk Back in Time

"A story that trusts its audience … you'll find something rather grand and original here."

— *James Aron, author of* Testing the Waters

"A sweeping, grand, quirky, whimsical, romantic, epic tale in every way … PLEASE, for the love of all that is wonderful, READ THIS BOOK."

— *Melissa Battles, Goodreads*

"A gripping, complex tale of love, loss, redemption and finding a better world."

— *Michele Kurlander, Amazon*

"Dramatic, funny, irreverent, sad, silly, heartbreaking, grand and complex."

— *David Young, Amazon*

ABOUT THE AUTHOR

Craig Mulhall is a Medical Oncologist from Queensland, Australia. He is also a published author, releasing his debut fantasy epic, *The King of Rhye*, in 2022 through Sid Harta Books & Print. A suite of song lyrics followed, with Craig writing an entire album of material for French band *Fat Bottomed Boys*. This album became the original soundtrack for *The King of Rhye* (2022), making way for further songs, including *Rock of Ages*, released in 2023.

Craig proudly presents and discusses his own work, and the legacy of Queen, everywhere from his own rural township to far-flung regional France.

FOREWORD

W riting *The King of Rhye* was the actualisation of a dream. I began producing the story fragments that would eventually become that novel at the turn of the century. Only in 2019 did I realise what I was trying to do – to tackle the daunting task of piecing together a mythology for Rhye, based on Queen's music. By that time, writing some of these characters felt like sliding back into an old, well-worn jacket. But dovetailing them with the scintillating scraps of lore left behind by Freddie Mercury seemed all at once both cathartic and fraudulent: how dare I handle the delicate pieces of an iconic rock legacy, let alone sully them with creations of my own?

And yet, here we are.

For many fans of Queen, the characters and events that populate *The King of Rhye* are somewhat prescriptive. Everyone expects there to be mandatory inclusions such as an Ogre Battle, Black and White Queens, a Fairy King, Seven Seas and so on. Because of this, constructing my debut novel became less about creating something and more about finding an entertaining way to make the pieces fit. The early albums (which the book chiefly celebrates) are so densely rich with usable fantasy references, the main challenge was giving every element a natural time to shine.

Writing *Metropolis* has been an entirely separate experience … and, I say unreservedly, a more rewarding one in almost every way.

As the saga progresses, I decided to shift my focus chronologically; to focus on the 'middle years' of Queen, with the bulk of inspiration coming from those records between 1976 and 1985. Not exclusively, but enough to spotlight perhaps the most eclectic and thrilling years for the band, both on stage and in the studio. Triumph and controversy, in spades.

But where are the fantasy references in those songs? Where is the story? Well, that was the rewarding part: the slate was a lot cleaner. The path no longer obvious. I had the freedom to truly create a tale that would meander in unpredictable directions. My characters, already established, suddenly had room to breathe – to talk to each other, argue, fall in love and more.

Still, if you're prepared to truly look, the themes and aesthetics are right there in Queen's output. I see albums like *Jazz* and *News of the World*, hear songs about Emerald Bars and waltzes, and pulp sci-fi heroes and machines, and my mind goes to the interwar Art Deco era and the dieselpunk movement. The wonder of silent film. The ominous build-up to atomic warfare.

Other fascinating works of art, culture and philosophy also helped me write this book. If you are familiar with Faust, or the concept of heterotopia, or *Mercy's Dream* by Daniel Huntington, there is much to find between the lines of this book, as well.

Thus, a new adventure is born. Within *Metropolis*, you will find darker, deeper themes than before. You may also find the seedling from which could sprout a dream of hope.

Best wishes,

Craig Mulhall

CONTENT ADVISORY:

Adult themes.

Recreational drug use.

LGBTQIA+ content —

Sapphic romance, mild spice.

Trigger warning:

Suicide.

TABLE OF CONTENTS

For Beatrix Harriet,
who arrived during the
writing of this book,

and

For Charles William,
who departed.

THE STORY SO FAR

A Prophet's words from Ages past condemned the land of Rhye,
He told of war and roiling floods, a storm-beleaguered sky.
A song could turn the tides of fate and wrest away their doom,
Sung by nascent monarch born of blessed noble womb.

The strangeling, unsuspecting, led a life so laissez-faire;
Until he swallowed cinnabar, he lived with little care.
Embroiled now his friends and he in perils left and right,
A race across the land to find the forest set alight.

Beneath the eaves of Banwah Haunte, the lies of history found,
Along with poison's cure came a meeting most profound.
Ignited by his mother's love the strangeling then took flight
Through mountains, battles, plagues and death, the hero brought
his fight.

Upon a shining parapet, a saviour made his stand
And with exultant harmony, his gesture saved the land.
As sunbeams split the earth from sky and broke the endless night,
The godforsaken armies watched a boon of holy might.

Music rang from mountaintop all down the ruined vale
And in that moment, Time did stop — the blessed King prevailed.
Blinding brightness vanquished shade and bore our souls away;
Delivered then, both safe and sound unto this brand-new day.

His will made real upon the land, with flash and thunder-fire,
Atop a stately hillside rose a bold and wondrous spire.
All we knew was darkness and a never-ending strife;
Now we marched back to the light — a second chance at life.

The Seven Seas are joined as one, a unity divine;
May every nation thrive in peace, until the end of time.

The sacred Voice
The honoured Drum
All banners march in time to kingdom come.

With rousing Strings
And lively Horn
We praise the King of Rhye in a New Dawn.

A WORLD SO NEWLY BORN

A door burst open in Ackley Fahrenheit's mind, and he stepped through it.

The Prophet, Khashoggi, no longer stood beside him. An instant earlier, the two men had gazed upon the searing brilliance of the Pillar of Rhye, lit by the breaking of a new dawn. Now, such illumination filled his vision that Fahrenheit felt he must stand within the Pillar itself.

The truth would prove ever more extraordinary: in this moment, the land of Rhye ceased to exist; it also waited to be born anew.

Music hung in the air — a chiming, jangling phantasm. The source of the sound defied location, for it came from everywhere and nowhere, all at once. The ether rang with the sound of bells, while underneath, swirling like currents of an invisible stream, flowed a symphony fit for the Pantheon.

Fahrenheit squinted, edging forward, lest his bedazzled eyes fail to notice some object in his path. Sprites of an otherworldly song tantalised him, beckoning him on. His shoes met the reassuring firmness of a ground he could not see.

Ahead, almost obscured by brightness, he spied the grey silhouettes of two figures. One, a massive hulk perhaps nine feet in height, dwarfed the other. The shorter of the two struck a figure no less commanding, for it stood as if braced against a solar wind: hands on hips, feet apart, long hair dancing upon its shoulders.

A strange voice pierced the veil of light. It did not reach Fahrenheit's ears, but instead formed inside his mind; a telepathic voice, which caused the man to jump. It carried the whir and clank of a well-oiled machine.

<*Sire ... your First Citizen approaches.*>

Fahrenheit spun around, expecting to find someone – or something – behind him. If a world existed, the luminous mist concealed it. The mechanical voice must have referred to him.

The shorter figure threw its arms wide, in a sweeping gesture. As it did, vast wings sprouted at its back, their span casting a glorious, feathered shadow.

'It's about time!' cried a true voice, so new and yet so familiar that Fahrenheit felt the hot welling of tears. A laugh followed – one that could belong to only one individual.

Mustapha, the King of Rhye.

Through the enigmatic Khashoggi, Fahrenheit knew of Mustapha's evolution, from strangeling pariah to hallowed seraph: the creature who vanquished War and Death. He had known Mustapha only briefly; yet his heart stirred now, with the whisper of devotion.

Clad in white raiment, with gold circlet upon his brow, the King forged in flame welcomed him.

Fahrenheit stumbled forward, parting the veil. On instinct, he used his careless momentum to take a knee, but Mustapha grasped him in an embrace, hauling the human to his feet. Now, the two figures materialised in front of him.

Mustapha indicated his giant companion with an open hand. 'Yosef and I were just discussing how splendiferous a new Rhye could be – brand new cities, natural wonders and such. We could use the imaginative spirit of a human like you! You're just in time to help.'

'Time?' replied Fahrenheit. He offered Torr Yosef a dumbfounded look, recognising the golem as another fairy tale creature made real. 'Khashoggi told me that time is only a place, or something similar. I can't quite recall how it went.'

'Ah,' said Mustapha with a warm grin, 'so this time is Here, do you think? Marnis told me that this place is Now ... so I suppose that makes it Here and Now. How prosaic.'

<Certainly, we will need a better name for it than that,> said Yosef.

'Yes, yes of course.' Mustapha gave a dismissive wave. 'The land itself will always be Rhye; but in this place, we plant the first flag of a new civilisation. We shall know its name when we see it.

'So, Fahrenheit: on what ground do we create our new world?'

The human tried to rally his dizzying thoughts. Nervous energy churned within him, blossoming into wonder. 'Create a new ... you want me to—?'

Mustapha grinned. 'I insist! It is the decree of the Pantheon, at any rate. Onik, the God of Time himself, is waiting for us to get on with it ... and I suspect his patience is dwindling.'

'Why yes ... of course,' said Fahrenheit. He had scarcely seen the war-ravaged wastes of Fenmarck Haunte; had only a short while to contemplate the beauty of the distant Pillar in its glory. *Now ... another place?* 'I choose to honour the land in which you found me,' Fahrenheit said. 'My spirit felt at ease in Brighton-Upon-Sea ... a place where my God's own country rolled to meet the majesty of the waves.' He smiled. 'Yes, that's it. I do like to be beside the seaside.'

'Beside the seaside?' confirmed Mustapha.

Fahrenheit grinned wide and nodded. 'Beside the sea.'

'So it shall be,' declared the King of Rhye, reaching his hands into the air. Nobody knew quite what to expect, but they did not wait long to find out.

Like the morning fog rolls back from a misty moor, or a desert squall finds its peace, the blinding illumination parted before them. Sunbeams shot through cumulus cloud, dancing across a land that did not exist only moments before. Every ruffling blade of grass, handsome oak and glistening drop of dew simply winked into being, yet appeared to be in its rightful place.

A verdant dale, kissed by the light of Adatar the Sun, beckoned them down towards a bejewelled sea, perhaps a league distant. The land embraced a broad harbour, above which a lone kestrel soared. The bird, a tiny speck against azure and white, described lazy circles over a promontory near the shore.

Mustapha peered into the air, focussed on nothing in particular, his face pinched in concentration.

<What is it, my Lord?>

'Hmmm … that sound. I can hear…'

<Do you hear music?>

'Not exactly. I hear bells tolling. A welcome. Do you hear the bells?'

<Alas, I do not.>

The King of Rhye shrugged. The bepuzzled frown on his face soon fled, for the land all about them seemed a paradise.

Fahrenheit absorbed none of it. He stood apart, clutching his head.

'Forgive me, friends,' he said. 'A strange feeling came over me. For a moment, I was something other than myself. Now it passes – and I see the beauty of the new Rhye.'

The golem's blank countenance studied the human. If a thought came to him, he did not express it.

Mustapha reached for a pocket within his spotless jacket. 'There, upon that promontory circled by the falcon, I will place my home.' He drew out his fist and opened it. Within, cradled in his palm, sat a single white stone; the mineral shone, whiter than bone bleached by a desert sun. 'I will honour the legacy of my mother, the White Queen, with a beautiful tower. A spire to inspire ... my window on the world, from which to survey the land and its people.

'As we gaze into the future of Rhye, may this new tower celebrate a bold and bright future, as well. Citizens from all over the land will come to marvel at its reaches, and dwell in the shady respite of the finest gardens ever seen.'

A question from Yosef broke through the King's embellishment. <*How do you perceive the many peoples of Rhye will unite under the banner of one King, my Lord?*>

'It is time to put racial factions to rest,' replied Mustapha. 'The notions of segregation and discrimination are a thing of the past. The seat of my rule will be a place where all mingle — both low-born and high. All shall have a voice, and all voices shall speak the same tongue.'

The near promontory began to rumble and quake. Upon it materialised a violet cloud, a massive shadow cloaked within.

Only once Mustapha heard the clangour of bells once again, did he notice the chalk white of Ackley Fahrenheit's face. The human wore a worrisome frown.

'What troubles you, Fahrenheit?'

'I've heard this story before, Lord. The vision of a perfect society. A tower to unify all peoples, under a law spoken in a single tongue.'

'Truly! And what of it?'

'It did not end well.'

7

For a long moment, the King of Rhye rubbed his chin. In the distance, the pinnacle of an elegant spire rose towards the sky, as if the enormous structure had been buried within the rock from which it sprouted. Plumes of violet billowed outwards from an edifice birthed from the very ground.

At last Mustapha gave an assured grin. 'My city shall be different,' he said. 'Tell me: what was the name of your doomed metropolis?'

'Babel, my Lord. The tower was named Babel.'

Those seraphic eyes flashed. 'The Pantheon is on our side. We will take this unfortunate human name and make of it something magnificent. Just as you have done with this wondrous landscape, I will honour the quaint township across the Seventh Sea, which brought us together and granted me this new life. The seat of my Sovereignty will be named ... Babel-On-Sea.'

'Babel ... On ... What?'

'Yes — just Babylon! That's even better.'

Fahrenheit groaned in anguish.

<My Lord. A township appears at the foot of your new home.>

Indeed, clusters of dwellings emerged, as fungi after a teeming rain. Soon, neighbourhoods nestled at the foot of Babel. As the trio watched, shanties and huts evolved into bungalows. Green avenues and laneways interlaced the growing harbourside citadel.

As the township blossomed, all eyes remained fixed on Babel itself. From the will of the seraph and the mind of the human sprang a structure more grandiose than any of them had seen before.

They beheld a tower with scalloped cornices and a fluted motif, glistening with new glass and golden girders. Lower terraces spilled over with lush greenery — succulent fronds of fern burst forth from tiered gardens, while creeping jasmine climbed the foundations of white stone.

Mustapha glanced at his palm which had held the Creator's gift.

It was empty.

<In the name of Marnis,> remarked the golem.

'In the world of my birth, Babylon was a city of ancient splendour,' explained Fahrenheit. 'This structure reminds me of that long-lost wonder; but also, of the most futuristic cities. All clean lines and elegance.' Despite the ardour of his topic, trepidation edged Fahrenheit's voice. He stared, unblinking, at the newly formed edifice.

Mustapha placed a gentle hand upon Fahrenheit's shoulder. 'I see your apprehension. I know the weight of it. I felt it too, when I learned of my role in the Pantheon's plan. To create, and to govern, are hefty responsibilities. I can't face it alone.

'The new Rhye is born of my passion and your imagination. Within it, we will combine the greatest elements of our old worlds. Fae races will live alongside Mer Folk, sylphs and humans. Even the Wilden tribes will find their place. There is no need to be afraid.'

Fahrenheit nodded, with an introspective gaze. The golem spoke next.

<Lord, you speak long when it comes to flesh and blood. What of pistons and rivets? Does one such as I grow obsolete, in this new, idealist Rhye?>

Mustapha shook his head with vehemence. 'The last golem will not exist in vain, my friend. No! We have learned much about the destructive power of machines ... yet through the wonder of technology, we also advance. The Mer Folk knew it and so did Khashoggi; they will need your help. So will I.'

The new civilisation swelled. Whimsical Fae bungalows sat alongside human cottages, which in turn shared neighbourhoods with sylphic keeps, jutting skyward like shards of translucent crystal. Vibrant pavilions with dome-topped roofs sat waiting for returning Adept. The eclectic quilt-work hugged the hillside in terraced rows, right from where the companions stood, down to the headland on which the tower overlooked the sea.

Across the whole panorama, an eerie stillness reigned. The metropolis lacked bustle.

'Oh, Yosef?' said Mustapha, surveying the rooftops of Babylon. 'It's time to bring our people home.' The seraph's face beamed. To have this new citadel bloom with life would see his destiny realised … though the sight of certain faces motivated him most of all.

Torr Yosef brought his great palms together. In the minds of the two mortals, words of prayer hummed with sanctity.

> *O Holy Sun.*
> *You greet us at the waking of the world.*
> *Your sacred rays from throne on high*
> *We shout your praise from newborn Rhye*
> *Behold! Your faithful people gather here.*
>
> *O Blessed Love.*
> *Our King anointed in your cleansing fire.*
> *We live as one now through your grace*
> *To open hearts you turn your face*
> *And lo! Your gloried power conquers fear.*
>
> *O Divine Creation.*
> *Guide us as our land is made anew.*
> *With flesh and bone, and mercy dreams*
> *Through industry, we pledge esteem*
> *We honour you in voices loud and clear.*

Only a whisper of breeze could first be heard, barely troubling the lighter boughs of nearby camphor on the city's verge. Presently, there came a distant rumble – not an encroaching storm, but a terrestrial sound, from somewhere over the trio's shoulders. They turned around.

Beyond the reaches of Babylon, the undulating forest floor soon faded into a vast, white void. From a place outside this cradle of Rhye's rebirth, a broad shadow loomed. A thundering, crawling mass with a multitude of feet.

The tumult grew. Shapes emerged within the shadow: heads and shoulders of myriad beings; the tall, the stout, the birdlike and the serpentine. Mer Folk came rattling their accoutrements, the jewels of the sea. A flood of Adept, their garb a multicoloured river flowing through the immense crowd. Humans of all shapes, sizes and stations – some in the finery of courtiers, others the simple tunics and cloaks of provincial villagers. An exotic tide of Wilden Folk poured forth, many shielding their eyes, unaccustomed as they were to any brightness. Sylphic wings flared, ruffling at the backs of innumerable avians. In the midst of the snaking populace lumbered beings of great height – forest trolls and cave wights jostled forth from the void.

<I present your populace, my Lord.>

Mustapha did not reply. His eyes swam, glistening in the heavenly morning light. Though millions of creatures now made their pilgrimage towards him, he saw only the figures at the head of the column.

Two cheerful pixies, arm-in-arm as they gambolled into view.

A slight Fae woman, cloaked in a feathered mantle, her head adorned with an antlered crown.

An elegant sylph, beaming brighter than the light from whence she came.

And at their centre, a sturdy human – dressed as a farmer, but with the look of far places about him.

Mustapha strained to maintain a dignified pose, his regal demeanour faltering. He almost stumbled forward over his own boots.

Torr Yosef remained stock still. From somewhere within his shell, countless souls poured into their living, breathing vessels.

Neither of them noticed Ackley Fahrenheit, who cowered to one side of the forest path, quaking in fear.

PART ONE

WHEN LANDS
WERE FEW

CHAPTER ONE

THE BELL THAT RINGS

For the sake of her clansfolk, the kobold ran. If she paused for even a moment – for breath, for rest, or to adjust the candle fixed to her head – it might cost the lives of her entire crew.

Flying feet scurried up yet another flight of stone steps. On any given day, the sprightly creature would tackle the ascent without a moment's thought. Today, every new stair felt like a cruel taunt.

So many steps! Why didn't we install a lift when the engineers offered it?

She hurried on. The sunlit districts of Above lay just beyond a near corner. Ahead, a winding, subterranean tunnel revealed itself by the flickering light of innumerable candles and the reflective luminescence of scrallin. In a moment, the brightness of day would reveal the exit.

An immense network of galleries and caves riddled the underbelly of Babylon. Layer upon crypt-like layer of warrens drove deep into the chthonic heart of the new land. Mustapha had possessed presence of mind enough to will veins of scrallin into existence, for not all inhabitants of Below were accustomed to a life in such dreadful darkness. A curious few, like the kobolds, had developed adaptations: they lived with candle stubs melded to their heads. They had thrived beneath the soil and detritus of Banwah Haunte, lawless forest of the old world, hidden from predation.

'Move over!' she cried, for the dark passage swarmed with Wilden Folk. Dozens of tiny motes bobbed like fireflies in the dark, accompanying the burble of startled creatures. 'I said, move over!' Another titanic rumble shook; ominous trembling echoed from below. Satyrs, hobgoblins and fellow kobolds threw themselves against hovel doorways, as pebbles and grit crumbled from the earthen ceiling.

'Hey, hey, hey!' shouted a voice above the hubbub. 'Clear the way!' Bewildered onlookers did not need to be asked again. Many pairs of beady, nocturnal eyes watched as the frantic kobold dashed towards the upper world. She made no effort to acknowledge the helpful voice – to do so would be wasted breath.

She exploded into sunlight, racing beneath the vaulted arch that linked Below and Above. Beyond the threshold, Adatar's rays nearly blinded her. She had last surfaced several weeks before – since then, her eyes had become unaccustomed to daylight. Once or twice, she stumbled, scrambling. Sheer urgency drove her back to her feet.

I am the fastest of my clan. This message is mine to give.

As the dazzle of sunlight faded, the winding streets of the Urban Quarter materialised before her. Pebbled carriageways, lined with topiary and neat wrought-iron fences, presented a captivating maze on any given day. Today, tidy terrace houses leaned over her, as if to hamper her progress. A multitude of vibrant awnings stared garishly down at the desperate kobold as she ran.

Wild hair, the colour of burnt umber, flowed about her runtish form. Such a great mane – typical of her people – showed little of her swarthy skin beneath, save for the sinewed legs that propelled her ever closer to the King.

Perhaps he will know of our strife before I reach him ... but then, he does have an entire kingdom to watch! Oh, I hope I am in time!

Her nakedness did not trouble her. Clothes irritated the average kobold, covered as they were by a cloak of hair. Besides, almost no-one bore witness to her mercy dash. The humans of Babylon observed a monthly day of rest and prayer, leaving the streets deserted.

Only one or two window blinds snapped open as the curious creature passed in a flash.

Urban streets snaked up an incline towards the promontory's crown. There, she would find the grand portal to the Tower, known as Babel. Already, she saw the Tower itself, rising far above the roofline and the canopy of trees: lofty, wondrous, a true marvel of the new world.

In her haste, the kobold took no time to admire it.

The road forked before her, at a leafy place marked with a shrine to Oska, God of Fortune. To the east, a labyrinthine forest of Fae dwellings. To the west, the orderly patchwork and pruned hedges of Humankind. Both ways would lead to the promontory, though one promised to be the more circuitous, by far.

With nary a break in her pace, the kobold veered west.

Cottages, townhouses, bungalows and mansions: the men and women of Old Sontenan seemed determined to recreate a microcosm of Via, their once proud city. Most humans had been forced from their homes by floods and pestilence, driven on a perilous march across the doomed land. Here in Babylon, the survivors re-established their cosy environs, as if snubbing their noses at the recent, apocalyptic past.

17

The kobold hugged a wide corner, emerging onto the Corniche. A paved concourse wound around the lower reaches of the promontory, as a banister would skirt a curved stair. The Corniche commanded a staggering view of the Babylonian harbour, where ships bobbed like apples in a barrel of glittering cider. Dozens of craft packed the Marina; amongst them, the leviathan known as the *Khonsu*. A vast break wall – a veritable pair of giant's arms – created a safe haven for the vessels, and a gateway to the great blue beyond.

The Bay of Marnis.

The break wall itself housed yet another teeming civic centre: the hydraulic citadel of the Mer Folk.

From the Corniche, the kobold shot a glance towards the ocean. The azure expanse to the west beckoned and forbade with every change of the tide. Try as one might to view the horizon, it disappeared in a shimmering haze.

Feet flying, the kobold registered little of the beauty around her. *Almost there. Oh, I pray the foundations hold!* Her bestial features – not quite rodent, not quite dragon – scrunched in desperation. The ever-present candle atop her head guttered, but did not extinguish.

At last, blessed relief. She rounded one final corner, tackled one last uphill stretch. A desperate sprint took her along a broad avenue of stately golden gingko trees: within their leaves rested the homes of Fae notaries. Beyond the stand of gingko yawned the wide portico she sought.

She burst into the forecourt of Babel, shouting at the top of her voice. 'Help! I seek the King! The Caverns of Below threaten to collapse!'

A large dais, flanked by elegant columns, greeted all who approached the entry to Babel. Upon the dais congregated numerous figures. The usual contingent of sentries held their positions, at either side of the entrance. Today, they were Fae knights, liveried in green and gold. A vibrant huddle of cloaked forms stood upon the portico itself. Most were clad in Violet, though in their midst flashed a bright White robe. The Archimage, first amongst the Adept. He appeared embroiled in conversation with a coven of Warlocks.

Heads turned, as the kobold bolted towards them. 'I need help!' she cried, flustered, attempting to take the steps two at a time. She tripped on the top step, sprawling and skidding to a stop by their feet.

The huddle broke, to accommodate the downed Wilden creature. In a flurry of tangled hair, her snout and frantic eyes appeared.

The handsome Archimage knelt beside her. He spoke in a warm, even tone.

'What troubles you, little one? What of Below?'

The kobold drew ragged breaths. 'An accident … in the Caverns. Tunnellers, digging a new burrow … they struck a column. The ceiling is caving in … hundreds trapped. The King! He must come quickly!' She coughed, on the verge of losing consciousness.

A deep wrinkle of concern marked the Adept's brow. 'Your warning reveals much, good creature. We were just discussing the concerning rumbles from beneath the ground. Perhaps you have arrived in good time.' He stood and turned from the huddle of worried faces. Turning his face skyward, he looked to the soaring pinnacle of Babel. Then he spoke – his words emerging in an amplified voice, potent with layers of theurgy.

'My Lord: Strife befalls the Caverns. The foundations of Babel are threatened.'

His attention returned to the exhausted Wilden creature at his feet. Pallor blanched her face.

'You must fight, little one! Stay with us. You will have a place to rest within Babel. Through your efforts, many of your kinsfolk can be saved! I am the Archimage, Timbrad. What is your name?' He spoke gently, his rich voice drawing her back from the brink.

The kobold's heart hammered. Names held great power amongst the kobold clans; certainly, Timbrad recognised the bolstering effect of asking for hers. Still, darkness crept at the borders of her vision. The image of the friendly Adept grew dim.

'Godgifu,' she breathed. Her eyes lolled, and she fainted.

Her passing thought, before consciousness slipped away, cast her mind into torrid doubt.

An image of great stanchions holding up the earth, rising in the gloom of a deep cave … and upon one of them, an inscription she could not understand.

Mustapha already knew the plight of the Caverns.

The Windows rarely showed him a vision of misadventure in the depths of Below. For almost ten years, the peoples of subterranean Babylon had lived without incident or conflict, to the surprise of many. At first, the very notion of an entire Wilden community dwelling in the roots of Babel caused the members of his Court to twitch; in time, their concerns had proven needless.

The King's gesture paid dividends. Largely, the Wilden Folk accepted his olive branch. The surliest and most deviant creatures remained on the petulant fringes of society, too maladjusted from their lives in Banwah Haunte to ever fully assimilate. Meanwhile, the majority relished a change from the corrupted madness of the late Lord Ponerog. Most Wilden, under a promising sky and a benevolent ruler's hand, turned to craft and industry, in the warrens they now called home. The underground world known as Below became a populous hub of civil culture — earthy, vital and proud.

Until today.

No fewer than four hundred and one Windows adorned the majestic opulence of Mustapha's inner sanctum. They did not, as one might expect, line the geometric walls; but instead, drifted slowly, as if upon a concentric series of invisible cogwheels. An immense, conical layer cake of Windows, spinning in silent perpetuity, in the centre of the King's Pavilion.

At any given moment, most of the Windows were closed: the King of Rhye did not deign to stare upon the private moments of his citizens' lives. But when a new corner of the land came into being — or, when events threatened the sacred harmony of his kingdom — a Window opened, bestowing at once a vision of events abroad.

The *clack* of shutters, slamming open on a gilt-framed portal, showed Mustapha all that he needed to see.

An excavation gone awry.

A cave-in, deep in the Caverns of Below.

He did not need the Windows' revelation to feel the ominous quaking, emanating from beneath the roots of Babel.

Even as Timbrad's voice resonated in his ear, his great wings were unfurled.

People on streets below would describe an angel's descent. Aloft on buffering thermals, which curled like tendrils around the Tower, the King came to earth. An eagle's span carried him with stately grace, sunbeams dancing on feathers of ivory and gold, tanned skin and dark, tousled hair.

Outwardly, the music played; layered voices, bearing him earthward. In his mind, it was always the bells. The aural signature of Marnis, as far as he knew. This time, as with many times recently, one miss-chime struck a false chord. A sense of wrongness.

It came from deep underground.

Beneath his line of flight, the myriad homes of Babylon sprawled, a mottled canvas of dwellings, draped across the promontory and surrounding woodlands. Were it safe to plummet directly into the mouth of the Caverns, he would have done so.

With a word from his lips, the Adept gathered in the Tower forecourt. Timbrad alone stayed with the brave kobold; the brace of Warlocks took to the air, falling into formation beside Mustapha.

In a swooping, billowing array of Violet cloaks and sun-kissed wings, the King and his entourage streaked over terraced gardens and onion-tipped pavilions, skimming low enough to rattle shingled roofs.

The mouth of Below gaped wide below them. As they circled it, surveying the throat-like passage, a muffled *boom* reverberated from the depths. The earth coughed out a tremendous column of dust.

Exchanging a wordless glance, Mustapha and his Warlocks plunged below the surface.

Debris and desperate cries choked the air. The smudged light from thousands of candles bobbed in erratic patterns, as swarms of kobolds hustled for the exit, intermingled with their Wilden neighbours. The grind and crunch of rock upon rock brought another frantic wail from the populace, desperate to escape the gloom.

The seraph led his Adept against the tide, flying above countless heads. Grimy faces turned upwards in surprise and wonder.

'Deeper,' called Mustapha. His voice bounced off tunnel walls, making it an indistinct bellow, though to each Warlock it came with clarity. 'Beyond the crowd: a stanchion is down. I can feel it.'

No reply came from the Wearers of Violet, shadowing his every twist and turn. They knew the situation as well as he. Every robe cloaked the theroid form of a delve; a creature beholden to the earth itself, equally at home below the surface as upon it. The delves had aided their King to craft the grand sprawl of warrens through which they now raced. They knew the caverns and burrows around them as an extension of themselves.

Chaos ruled the depths. Slower creatures wandered without direction at the tail end of the crush, dazed by the fray. The only unifying motivation appeared to be escaping a tumble-down wall of rock, emerging like a behemoth from the darkness.

The crush of Wilden shapes issued a unified gasp as Mustapha and the Warlocks soared overhead, bringing new light to the claustrophobic scene. Describing a golden arc in the cave, the King directed his charges to land with him, at the place where a massive stone column tilted like a felled tree against its neighbour. All about lay earthen fragments of all sizes, for the fallen stanchion had brought the ceiling down with it.

Of their own initiative, the delvish Warlocks began a reconnaissance of the site. Probing here, testing there, they let instinct guide them around the perilous rockfall.

Mustapha picked his way through the wreckage. As he neared ground zero, he encountered a pair of kobolds laying in the grit. Nearby, the mangled and gore-soaked hindquarters of a satyr poked from beneath a fallen keystone: all that remained of their supervisor.

From behind the collapsed rock came the anguished wailing of many creatures.

Already stupefied by the sudden devastation around them, the kobolds did not register the presence of their King immediately. As realisation dawned, the candle stumps atop their heads flared; in the flickering illumination, the shocked pallor of their faces showed. With sluggish movements, they attempted to express fealty.

'Never you mind that,' said Mustapha. 'Stay as you are — we will fetch more help. Are you injured?'

After cursory self-examination and a glance at each other, the dazed kobolds shook their heads. 'No, my Lord,' replied one.

'The gallery...' replied the second. 'It was to be a new resting place. For our elders. Our crew were told to dig ... but you see, there's a dark place, behind the wall. We didn't know. The roof caved. We're sorry ... we didn't know!'

'A dark place?'

The kobold stared at Mustapha for a moment, then pointed to a gash in the tumbled rock, through which came cries for help.

'We shall dig your work crew free,' assured the seraph. Already, the brace of Warlocks gathered by the obstruction; Violet robes were cast aside, showing hunched backs, all bristles and nobbled spines. Large paddle-hands tipped with claws set to work, without the need for an order.

Trembling aftershocks, followed by tendrils of grit from above, marked the delves' labour. With every juddering of the precarious rockfall, the cries of entombed creatures grew more panicked. The excavation crew, likely consisting of kobolds, cave trolls and the odd satyr not averse to work, were accustomed to darkness and cramped places ... hence, something other than the gloom itself stirred their dismay.

Something in the mysterious void brought them fear.

Despite the innate mettle of the delves, work of clearing the debris moved at a treacherous crawl. Occasionally, proceedings ground to a halt, as bodies — or parts thereof — were cleared away.

Every creak and groan from the earth overhead came laden with peril.

When Mustapha offered a wordless tune, the stricken wailing subsided. His soothing countertenor sounded throughout the wracked cavern. Rather than trigger collapse, the sound shored up teetering columns, as if his voice becalmed the foundations themselves.

'This would be easier as a band,' he said in a moment's respite, referring to his trio of dearest friends. 'The others haven't joined me in a while ... but today, I might be enough.'

The King's voice fortified the tumbled stones. With a final effort, the delves broke through into the would-be tomb of Wilden labourers. Relief howled from the blackness within; several diminutive creatures shot from the slim fissure, heedless of their rescuers in the rush to be free.

Cries for help still emanated from behind the collapsed rock. Mustapha, no longer singing, reached for a fractured shard of scrallin. The luminescent mineral cast a pinkish glow, which he pushed towards the new opening.

'My Lord, should you be...?' questioned a Warlock, at his back.

'Me first,' confirmed Mustapha. 'You widen the hole.' With an effort, the seraph squeezed his wings through behind him, and disappeared from view.

Thus began the rescue effort in earnest. While the cavern held, the delves worked with feverish pace to clear the debris.

Behind the wall, a pitch-black hell crowded at the edges of dusky scrallin light. The echoing *trip, trip, trip* of water droplets conjured images of stalactites in an immense subterranean hollow – a place the Wilden Folk and other dark dwellers had no knowledge of.

Mustapha had no knowledge of it, either.

There came, all at once, that miss-strike of a bell. He knew no others would hear it: that harbinger of wrongness, like a glitch in creation. *All in my head.*

Yet from the recesses of his mind, there emerged another sound. A steady, rhythmic pounding. It drew reminiscences of a fever dream flight; of cold sweats and chilling threats and a gnawing, existential dread.

'Begone!' he shouted into the darkness, and the pounding subsided.

Fresh exclamations of fear burst from nearby creatures.

'I'm terribly sorry, good people,' cried Mustapha, spinning to face dozens of pairs of eyes – some great, some small, all glinting in the light from his flameless torch. Labourers who remained trapped, desperate for freedom, still too large – or perhaps too injured – to make their way out. 'Tell me, who is hurt and who is whole? There is no need to fret. My delves will have you out of here in a moment.'

Many, many moments elapsed – an interminable string of them. The delves worked in shifts, replaced by relief from the districts above. The opening grew steadily wider. One by one, the bruised, battered and shocked labourers were retrieved from their dread annexure, into the care of waiting Apothecaries.

The King stayed with his subjects – sharing songs, stories and prayers; whiling away the miserable hours, helping them forget the hunger, the chill and the vast unknown beyond their paltry pool of light. Only when the last troll reached the relative safety of the Caverns, did he leave his place, making for the exit.

The toe of Mustapha's boot met a small stone. The stone skittered away, some distance into the gloom.

Then it bounced.

It bounced again.

The stone bounced several more times … as if tumbling down a stair.

Mustapha shuddered. *Am I going crazy? Why is there a staircase back here?*

He edged towards the sound, hoisting the scrallin torch. Feeble beams of light were soon swallowed by the fathomless space; yet they found the thing he sought, disappearing into the void.

The ancient staircase began only a few yards from where he stood, and led downwards beyond sight. Mustapha knew it to be ancient, for the rounded stone edges suggested centuries – millennia? – of cave water, in runnels, traversing down to oblivion. Mustapha frowned.

This new Rhye, of my creation, is barely ten years old.

He sidled onto the upper landing of the staircase. His torch still failed to illuminate the distant walls of this enigmatic vault in the earth, but it did reveal other, less natural wonders. In this place, as with the subterranean Caverns, there stood enormous stanchions, carved from the native rock. These were of a very different design, hewn with simplicity and function in mind. A series of them ran alongside the descending stair. Neither top nor bottom of them could be seen for the shadows; though without a doubt, civilised creatures had shaped them, to support the vast underground space. Mustapha resolved to question the delves about them.

The nearest stanchion had words engraved on it.

Mustapha edged further forward, descending the first few stairs. He came near enough to study the writing, yet this only fuelled his puzzlement. The characters he knew, but the words he did not.

FUGIT INREPARABILE TEMPUS

His frown deepened.

A practised hand had chiselled stately capitals into the stone. The serifs, once crisp, were worn down by the relentless passage of draught and damp.

To himself, Mustapha sounded out the words. They meant

27

nothing. The alien phrase reminded him of another time — a land, long away — when an unintelligible word had unlocked the salvation of Rhye.

A faint grin played about his features. He dared not attempt singing these words, not here; lest the wrath of Nature bring the cavern down upon his head.

This is one for the Astrologers too, I think.

He turned for the exit, guided by his scrallin torch, leaving behind the sepulchral place full of darkness and menace.

CHAPTER TWO

BE NOT GONE

The blanket of night cloaked Babylon. In pockets where denizens gathered in nocturnal revelry, lights twinkled and boisterous sounds swirled on the summer air, to be snatched away into the great beyond. But most of the vast urban labyrinth lay swathed in indigo, as the populace slumbered.

From the luxuriant enclave at the foot of Babel, a single voice arose; drifting, soaring, swooning, it carried a poignant lyric into the night, accompanied only by the crisp chorus of katydids.

'Father, Do You Hear Me?

Another night falls
Just like the night from which you never woke
Now my heartbeat stalls
Can't set aside those final words you spoke

Father, do you hear me?
The hammer fell by my own fated hand
Father, do you hear me?
That grievous night I'll never understand

The tolling of bells
With every ring, the wheels of progress turn
In my private hell
See everything, through windows watch it burn

Father, do you see me?
I kneel before you cloaked in leaden sorrow
Father, do you see me?
That I may play the game again tomorrow

A plea for sweet release
The battle brought you peace
But will the raging tempest ever cease?

Father, can you help me?
Is this a doom or glory I've created?
Father, can you help me?
Give me the strength to see it elevated
With you inside my heart I feel elated
Could I have saved you, had I only waited?

Father ... Father ...'

Bastian Sinotar, the great sylphic General Prime, did not respond.

His marbled eyes offered only a dead gaze towards the prostrate figure upon the flagstones below him. That stony countenance, once so animate – impassioned, fearless, righteous even – marshalled not the slightest flicker of empathy. The light of Anato danced upon gold filigree, wound through his hair and inlaid on his clothes. The raiment ruffled, frozen at an exquisite moment in time. Yet even the lustre of gold could not imitate the fire that once stirred within him.

Even beneath a skilled mason's hand, a cold block of stone would never do justice to the memory of Mustapha's father.

The seraph knew this. Still, to sit and pray at the foot of Sinotar's memorial brought him inner stillness.

Anato's silver light still beautified the night sky, the same way it had before everything changed. Stars glittered in a plum-coloured firmament, framed by the foliage of an expansive garden: the Garden of Remembrance. A fragrant and leafy demesne, resplendent with canna and honeysuckle. By day, it hummed and fluttered with insect life. By night, every silvered leaf coaxed a dream, while every mottled shadow concealed a nightmare.

Beyond the garden, and the wall that enclosed it, lay the ever-growing, ever-changing conurbation of Babylon. Responsibility. Governance. The garden grew and changed too, though it asked nothing of Mustapha, except that he surrender himself to it.

In this place, away from prying eyes, Mustapha built the memorial. Seven statues, each a sculpted cynosure for reflection, stood in a broad arc amidst the garden's living enticements. Oberon and Titania stood together, an icon of unified strength. The form of Torr Enoch loomed darkly, limned in moonlight. Lord Rogar, the Archimage Benjulius and Lord Neptune all rose larger than life above the greenery.

In place of the beleaguered Lord Ponerog, Mustapha produced the enchanting figure of Lady Maybeth Giltenan. Maybeth flanked

Bastian Sinotar, her graceful features angled towards the same point on the flagstones where Mustapha knelt by his father's feet.

The gentle weight of a hand on his winged shoulder took the seraph by surprise. In his reverie, he had missed the approaching footfalls.

'Hey. Even the fairest in the land needs his beauty sleep.' The hand's owner spoke, with a voice like a rural spring morning.

Mustapha tilted his head and gave a half shrug, brushing his cheek against the comforting hand. 'Can't. I have a headache.'

Will frowned. 'That's the oldest excuse in the book.'

The seraph replied with a resigned huff. 'You're right ... it isn't just that. You know how it is when ... the anniversary comes around.'

'I do. Ten years, can you believe it? Once you disappeared inside that Mountain, I felt sure I'd never see you again. Another whole decade by your side has been a boon I never expected. But ... I haven't heard that song before. I don't know whether I should be awed or troubled.'

Mustapha rose from the flagstones, turning to face his late-night companion. The human, broad-shouldered and substantial, stood almost a head taller than he. The open face, writ with concern, belonged to a man more comfortable outdoors than in the Ministry chambers. He wore his nightclothes, his feet thrust into boots and a warm cloak thrown about himself. Beneath sideswept blond hair, burnt-honey eyes gazed down at the seraph.

'You know, Will,' said Mustapha, 'as King, I can order you to return to your quarters.'

'I would accept my banishment with honour and grace, my Lord. Still, your side of the bed grows cold. What is this about a "private hell"?'

Mustapha grimaced, torn between the hurt of sharing private

worries, and the greater hurt of holding onto them. His lover stood watching, waiting. His open face receptive to even the darkest torments. A sigh escaped the seraph.

'Creating a new Rhye isn't all glory and sunshine. It isn't a perfect world, by any measure. Rifts will occur...'

'The perfect world doesn't exist,' said Will, in his ever-pragmatic way. 'Especially not when you throw so many divergent cultures into one crucible, previously existing in separate corners of the land. Remember, it took all of Year One for the sylphs to recognise that not all Wilden Folk are inherently evil. And we've all had to adjust to Yosef's ventures with Khashoggi and the Mer Folk.'

'I enabled him. One way or another, technology is progress.'

'Maybe it is, but that isn't my point. If you expect a perfect world here, you set yourself an unattainable standard. You can't control it all.'

The seraph's shoulders slumped in acquiescence. 'Wagoner' Will, once an unassuming gourd farmer in Old Sontenan, brought a steadying sense of realism to the turbulent world of Mustapha's thoughts. He took the human's hand, and together they wandered deeper into the garden. The shrill chorus of cicadas mingled in the night air with the fragrance of blooming gardenia.

'There aren't only societal rifts to be concerned about,' confided Mustapha. 'The land itself is still in its infancy. As I imagine them, new territories sprout from nothing. Beneath our feet, the bedrock of the land moves, ever shifting as Rhye grows. Today's incident in Below was beyond my control ... and it shouldn't have been.'

'If it lay beyond your control, you need not castigate yourself for it.'

'They're my subjects, Will. Many Wilden could have died ... or worse, been buried alive.'

'And yet, you brought everyone out alive. Mustapha, I say this truly: Show yourself even half the respect the citizens of Babylon have for you. In their eyes, you aren't just a King. You're a legend.'

Mustapha spun towards Will; his face pallid in the silver light. Desperate eyes searched his lover's, wide and glinting with a silent shout.

Will saw through the seraphic glamour; past the blessings of Ophynea and Lhestra, and the towering persona he created for himself, to the fragile creature within. Will remembered the prancing sprite who beguiled him in the southern reaches of Petrichor — somewhere within the King of Rhye, the essence of that callow babe-in-the-woods still shone. The outer physique more commanding now, yet still limber, in the way of an acrobat or jongleur. His hair still lustrous black — as yet no trace of grey — but shorter. Almost as short as Will's, who had cut it for him. The seraph had changed, yet was still the vulnerable, vivacious vagabond. Without question, the change had come through responsibility: he now bore the weight of a whole new kingdom.

Beneath the vim and valour, uncertainty reigned.

'I made this place, Will, but somehow I am not entirely the master of it,' he said.

'This land is brimming with all of the diversity of the one that came before it, crammed into one enormous civilisation. Did you expect to have a handle on everything at this point?'

'It's been ten years—'

'—A respectable term in our eyes, but a mere blink to the God who stepped aside for you. Has Marnis offered you guidance lately?'

The Creator. The enigmatic and beguiling deity who had bestowed this immense task upon the seraph. Mustapha shook his head. 'Marnis doesn't speak to me in words these days. Only the chimes of bells ... whether he applauds or laments my efforts, I can't tell.

'Will ... I feel some sort of disconnect. Some part of this picture doesn't make sense. On one hand, I've been granted the power to see into small details of Babylonian lives; to see when new developments might disrupt the harmony of life in Rhye at large. That's more power than any one person should have. Yet there the Windows were, from the moment the Tower of Babel was created. I assume they were a gift from Marnis himself.

'On the other hand, there are whole regions of the land that I can't even see. For instance, why can't I see into the west—'

'Mustapha—'

'No, Will. The Milky Sea is a thorn in my side. The Western Way is a giant blind spot that refuses to be uncovered. But it is proof enough that my power has limits: on this little promontory of ours, I'm omnipotent. But beneath our feet, a cavern collapses, and suddenly I find an ancient civilisation has been there. I can know in a moment what new device Khashoggi is inventing down by the harbour, yet I can't cast my sight beyond the horizon.

'There's something wrong with this picture.'

Will exhaled. Mustapha had delivered this diatribe before. Whilst the seraph knew how to dramatie, this particular vexation gnawed at him in a fundamental way. Will's gentle exasperation came from a place of true concern.

'You don't have Mher to help you cross the sea this time,' said Will with a thoughtful look. The Ogre, by decree of the Pantheon, had helped Mustapha traverse the Seventh Sea ... by swallowing it up. 'If you want to explore the Western Way, perhaps it's time you sent Khashoggi on a voyage of discovery? I do believe he has an itch that needs scratching.'

Mustapha pursed his lips. The action came whenever his thoughts wandered to silent places; concealing the overbite that marred his regal countenance. To Will, that pearly white smile represented the youthful *joie de vivre* he had fallen for.

The seraph pursed with self-conscious assiduity.

'Khashoggi ... hasn't visited me,' he said at last.

'By the light of Anato – literally! Have you invited him to court?'

'Well ... no. No, I haven't. He's always so ... busy. So am I.'

Will's eyebrows arched high enough to support the heavens themselves. 'We're all busy, Mustapha. You appointed me Minister for Agriculture. Trixel oversees Conservation, and Leith long since assumed your father's mantle. The administration of the land consumes us all ... but there must be more to life.

'Do you give the same excuse for neglecting the others?'

Mustapha did not respond immediately. Heat flared behind his gaze, and in his cheeks; it may have been ire, an admonition, or even defensiveness. As quickly as it came, it died away. The seraph's features softened.

'It has been a while.'

Will waited.

'The years do march on, don't they?' continued Mustapha. 'Several years since we last played together, I'd say. Everybody sort of moved on. Harold has his Archive, of course. Dique must be off doing his own thing. We haven't really needed to come together. I could have used their help today, though: sorting out that mess in the Caverns was an ordeal. Shaping the land was so much easier when we played as a group. The power those instruments still hold ... it's undeniable.

'We got the job done, but the work is far from over. There's something down there, Will. Something old. Something impenetrable ... I can't unmake the bedrock with my songs. The delves excavate madly, though it may still take weeks...'

And so, it went. Will let the seraph have his head – he was talking, at least. Sometimes, the floodgates just needed to be nudged open.

The couple continued their circuit of the garden. They crossed the lawn while Mustapha nattered, skirting close to a row of hydrangeas in full bloom. Shades of violet burst forth amidst the lush herbage.

Beyond the hydrangeas, wild, twisting creepers climbed a wall of stone. The wall bordered the entire Garden of Remembrance, rising above the height of a golem. None could see in, and none could see out. Overhead, the constellations made their endless migration, joined by the beatific face of Anato.

Here, the King of Rhye found his peace.

Will chanced an interruption of his lover's stream of consciousness.

'I know you've been navigating some deep thoughts, Mustapha,' he said. 'There's a well-worn track around this garden's edge. But I never knew so many issues bubbled under the surface.'

Mustapha stared into space. 'I guess I'm a bit of a duck...'

'How so?'

Their eyes met. 'All calm on the surface, darling. Plenty of thrashing going on underneath.' He gave a wink. 'Quack quack!'

Will grinned. 'You're one tough duck, in that case. Must have hatched from a hard-boiled egg.'

Completing their perimeter stroll, Will and Mustapha returned to the courtyard, where the arc of stone Sovereigns stood, sentinels of remembrance.

They paused at the feet of Bastian Sinotar.

'I want you to promise me something,' said Will.

'Anything, darling.'

'Promise me you won't bear these burdens in silence. Even a king must share the load. It will make you happier.'

Mustapha glanced upwards once more, into those lifeless, marble eyes. 'All the sharing in the world won't bring him back.'

'Mustapha—'

'I know, I know. It isn't my fault. I pulled the trigger, but it was a mercy killing, right?' The seraph's eyes glistened. 'I mean … he chose to give up the fight, didn't he? I sent his soul to a better place … didn't I? Anyway, what good is a soul, if the only point of having one is that you can choose to give it up?'

For long moments, Will did not reply. The calm passivity of his face suggested that he also recognised the questions as rhetorical. Unanswerable, even. Mustapha didn't need his father back. He didn't even truly need to hear that Bastian Sinotar would never blithely *give up* his soul. Mustapha needed an ear … and the strong arm of support.

Eventually, when the heat of the moment subsided, Will did respond. 'You can't carry this guilt around forever, my love. My Lord. The hand of fate has seen you succeed him – seen you succeed every Sovereign here.' Will cast his hand in a wide circle, at the monumental figures all around. 'It's time to divest yourself of this dark cloak, and start celebrating your great victory for the land. Ten years is upon us. The Ball is just around the corner—'

'The Ball!' exclaimed Mustapha, slapping palm to forehead. His face betrayed something other than joy at first – something more akin to the unravelling knot of nausea he had held in his stomach. He fought to turn the grimace into a weak grin.

'Don't tell me you, of all people, had forgotten an upcoming party?'

'Nope. No. Hadn't forgotten it. It just … came around so quickly.'

Will ruffled the dark, wavy locks upon Mustapha's head. 'Then you had best get in the festive spirit. The celebrations are only weeks away, and the people need their King to be in the right frame of mind.'

Mustapha turned to Will, his back to the sculpted General Prime.

In the nocturnal glow, his eyes glinted beneath a dark brow. His lips curled in an impish smile. His teeth flashed.

'Let it be fabulous,' he said.

CHAPTER THREE

THE EMERALD BAR

L ike clockwork, the nightly circus repeated itself.
The same old show, over and over again.

Well before dusk, the gilt-edged doors, with their panes of transparent crystal, would swing open. First to arrive would be the working class — or rather, those who had abandoned work early. Skiving satyrs often initiated proceedings, bringing their boisterousness, tawdry humour and a promise of drunken brouhaha.

They usually chose Rhye whiskey (straight from the barrel) as their poison of choice, or drank moonshine from flasks, secreted in jacket pockets.

Next came the players of games; those who ensconced themselves in dim niches to discuss philosophy, play checkers and quaff nectar or gin. These were the dragonflies, humans and the odd Astrologer. Self-proclaimed thinkers, who frequented the gnarled boughs of the Repositree.

As the gloaming of dusk became evening, small hordes of pixies, fauns and hobgoblins spilled in from the street, swarming tables freshly laid with smoked meats and cornbread, dripping with golden butter. The proprietor's treat: the food helped patrons imbibe more, before passing out in a stupor.

The Fae, as creatures of habit, wanted nothing more than a bottomless chalice of drowseberry wine or a mug of amber lager. Most nights, the hubbub of revellers gave way to the bouncing, melodic jive of the house band. A quartet, sporting a trumpet, strings and skins, had taken up residence at the establishment some years prior. To the swinging sounds of these merry tunesmiths, Fae, Adept, Wilden and more would raise a jovial riot as hours passed. Rumours told that the band were blessed by the hand of Phydeas, God of Providence; honouring, as they did, the miracle of the King and his men at the hour of Rhye's crisis.

That other quartet had not been seen together in quite a long time.

In the shadow of midnight, the gilded doors would open once more, to admit the elite amongst all clientele: the veterans. Those who had been *there*. Defenders of the land at the last, when the darkness of Valendyne loomed, amidst the stark flicker of dragon-fire and the chilling machinations of Anuvin, also called War.

The company would enter shoulder-to-shoulder — mostly fairies, occasionally joined by several battle-worn sylphs, or sometimes a Warlock. Upon arrival, they would invariably need to splice their way through a throng of inebriated groupies. The cloud of clamouring patrons lent the latecomers an air of celebrity, though the air was ill-desired.

The veterans sought respite, not adoration. Peace had come to the land of Rhye — King Mustapha's Age of Harmony had begun. Many of them sought to disengage from the waking nightmare of battle, either in the conversation of their peers, or in the bottom of a crystal decanter.

They would make a beeline for the deepest recesses of the Bar –
away from the shimmering motes of light, scattered like splinters
by the massive chandelier, with its innumerable scrallin shards.
Away from the polished floors and the glint of brass furnishings.
They would convene in a far booth, from which most starstruck
patrons kept a respectful distance.

One of their number would peel away, heading for the barman
– as she did right now – to place the order for her companions.
Always the same drink: absinthe. The mesmerising green liquid
promised equal parts inebriation and vibrant, hallucinogenic
oblivion.

An alluring forest sprite, eyes dark with kohl, sashayed her way
to the glossy walnut counter.

'Green Fairy, please,' she said, through a wisp of a smile, 'and
eight goblets.'

A night like any other, at the Emerald Bar.

Across the counter, Sammy suppressed an eyeroll with great
effort. The hiss of a sigh still managed to escape his lips. Only
twenty inches of varnished countertop – and years of failed
ambitions – separated him from a life less ordinary.

With detached efficiency, he reached for the bottle of green
spirit. The glassware. A silver tray. Within half an hour, the Fae
would have embarked on their languid odyssey, a wormwood-
fuelled bliss, surrounded by the feverish tonal forays of jazz. In
due course, one of their number would return, to dutifully pick up
the tab. The night would descend into a haze of drunken stumbling,
dishevelled goodbyes and the debris of another bacchanal.

The glitz and glamour would be replaced by the reality of closing
time, yet again.

Sammy felt a meaty hand upon his shoulder, and shuddered.

'I don't know what you think passes for broom-work these days, sweetling, but it ain't this. I had to kick the trash from under my hooves just to reach the door at opening time.'

The rasping female voice breathed rank tobacco into his olfactory organs, and misery into his heart. His wings drooped.

Without turning, the butterfly mumbled a response. 'I-I'm awfully s-sorry, ma'am. All those other chores took a little longer than I expected, and I only just—'

Rapid-fire tongue-clicking tripped him up, mid-sentence. 'Tsk, tsk, tsk. I don't want to hear that you were too busy, honey bunch. Oh, no-no-no. I only want to hear that it won't happen again. You trying to get yourself kicked out on the street? Because you know, it ain't that simple.' The final words were delivered with a teasing, sing-song lilt.

Just over Sammy's flittering left wing – well within his bubble of personal space – stood a corpulent satyr. Fanny owned and managed the Emerald Bar, clopping about the boards on a substantial haunch, swinging her decolletage in a buxom display of wiles. To Sammy, she epitomised everything gaudy about the place. The apple might have a shiny skin, but the gloss belied the rotting fruit inside.

Sammy tasted bile. His face burned. *Can't this wait until after the Bar is closed?* In front of him, the place still heaved with patrons. Glaring at him.

'Yes, Fanny. I mean ... no, Fanny. I'm truly sorry. Never again.'

'That's better,' purred the ashen drawl of the Emerald Bar's proprietor. 'Repeat after me: *My place is here.*'

'Fanny—'

'Say. It.'

Sammy gave a quavering sigh. 'My place is here.'

'*I'm no good for anything else.*'

The butterfly gulped, his face pale. Patrons drummed impatient fingers on the bench top, absorbing every moment of his exquisite humiliation.

'I'm ... I'm no good for anything else.'

'Right. Now stop daydreaming and get back to work! These precious people all need their glasses filled! I'll be seeing you later.' The satyr gave his shoulder a nauseating squeeze, and moved off at last.

Sammy had never stood out in a crowd, and he was extremely comfortable with that.

He hatched in near anonymity nineteen years before, breaking free of his chrysalis one sunny morning alongside five thousand of his nearest relatives. The annual Emergence, a joyous event in the Monarch Quarter of Dragonfly Hollow, saw the arrival of the latest flood of vibrant insectoids.

Living amongst crowds is part of a butterfly's upbringing from the very earliest stage of its life. Caterpillars have a myopic sense of personal space. Then, in their pupal phase, they dwell in motionless hibernation, seeing nothing and learning even less about the world around them. As such, when they emerge at last from the cocoon, they have acquired no ability to give each other the necessary room to spread their new wings. Every single year, the Emergence is a wonderfully chaotic affair (for the spectator), with a kaleidoscope of swallowtails, fritillaries, morphos and of course the self-aggrandising monarchs, exploding onto the scene in a sort of whimsical mid-air brawl.

Butterflies know two things instinctively. The first is that their lives will be brief, frivolous, and cut shorter still the minute they decide to mate. The second is that each must complete the migration as a rite of passage or suffer the ridicule of a thousand vacuous relations.

Those same primal instincts buzzed in Sammy's mind as he burst from the chrysalis. He also suffered a fateful half-second of hesitation, in which he allowed his neighbouring brothers and sisters to start the fluttering stampede ahead of him. As he tried with a frantic effort to unstick his tangled wings, he copped several dozen elbows and knees to the face.

'Raaaaah!' he cried, tearing free of the shredded cocoon and fighting through the battering armada of colourful wings. He felt a rip, heard a tearing sound, and in a heart-rending moment he knew: he had torn his own wings, in careless haste.

Sammy had time, while spiralling to earth from the bough where he had hung fastened, to contemplate such things as misfortune and consequence.

His despairing thoughts were truncated by the swoop of a great net, that entangled him in a snare that tightened against his escape. He offered a weak struggle, until the drawl of a female voice interrupted him.

'Don't you wrestle with that net, sweetling. There's a good butterfly. It's there for your safety, see? Without it, you'd have fallen — crushed on the ground! Can't have that now ... can we?'

Sammy twisted in the confines of the net, until his rotation brought to view a satyr of voluminous proportions, dressed like a tart and showing him a theatrical grin. 'W-w-won't you let me down?' he asked.

'But of course! You're no good to anyone in there!' Sure enough, she pulled a few loose threads and Sammy came tumbling the final few feet to earth.

The satyr cast a huge shadow. So large was she that he could barely see past her significant hindquarters; in a narrow glimpse of sky, he could still see the flittering mass of his fellows, disappearing as a rainbow swarm into the daylight. His head drooped.

'See here now, sweetling,' continued the satyr. 'You can't go fluttering off in that state! Look at those wings, all tattered and torn.' With a glum look at the holes ripped in the shimmering blue membranes, he knew she spoke the truth. 'I can mend them though, you know.'

'You ... you can?' Hope welled up in his eyes.

'Oh of course, my dear little flutter-by! You just need to come along with me. I can help you out now, but I need you to help me out a little too, see?'

'Oh? With w-what?'

'Never you mind. Just a few tasks back at my lodgings. How about this, now: as a gesture of my goodwill, I'll even mend your wings first. You can do a spot of housekeeping for me, and we'll call it square.'

'I ... I guess—'

'Excellent! Tell me, sweetling. Does a charming young butterfly like you have a name?'

'S-Sammy.'

'Well, Sammy! My name is Fanny. They almost rhyme ... how adorable! Now ... chop-chop! Along with me.'

Sammy followed Fanny through the forests of Petrichor. They walked and walked and walked, covering what seemed to the butterfly an absurd distance. More than once he questioned his decision to follow the rotund satyr as she clopped along overgrown pathways; more than once he considered speaking up, but thought better of it. She had offered to fix his wings, and that was that.

Fanny's lodgings turned out to be a cosy little public bar, in a Fae town that Sammy had never visited. A sign above the door announced it to be the Oak & Barrel Inn. She bustled him inside, and closed the door behind them with a *click*.

'Wait here,' said Fanny. She vanished in the rear of the

establishment for just a few moments, reappearing with what looked like a bolt of blue silk and a sewing kit.

True to her word, she set to work right away. Setting Sammy on a stool, she brandished a needle and commenced the delicate task of patching the holes. While she worked, she chatted over his shoulder, a syrupy tone that both soothed and unnerved.

'Tell me about yourself, Sammy sweetling. Does a butterfly like you have plans? Dreams, goals, ambitions?'

Sammy frowned, thinking hard. 'Well, I'm ... I'm supposed to be migrating. With the others. That's ... about it.'

'Migrating? That's about it?' Fanny gave a hearty laugh that shook her jowls like jelly. 'You don't dream of anything else?' Her fingers continued the swift work of stitching.

'N-no.'

'Tsk, tsk, tsk. Isn't there anything more you wish for?'

The butterfly strained for something more profound. 'Well, I do want to travel. You know — not just to the other end of the forest. But ... travel takes time. I don't have a lot of time, so ... I wouldn't mind living a little longer, I suppose.'

Fanny spun him around on the stool. Her eyes glittered. 'Sammy my boy, have I got good news for you! First of all, those mighty fine wings of yours are as good as new. Second — and this is one you must keep between you and me, you hear? — I just might be close to a solution for your other conundrum, as well.'

'Truly...?' More time seemed a dream beyond reach. *Could it be...?*

'Of course, sweetling! As it turns out, I rather like the idea of more time myself. I've been saving up my precious coins ... when I've got enough, I'll make a journey to see the Adept in Aerglo. They have spells for all kinds of splendid things! Perhaps they can help us both!'

Sammy marvelled, lost in the glamour of the idea. *Adept.*

Aerglo. How magical. It still seemed out of reach, but the satyr's sly confidence got the better of him. He nodded. 'Th-that sounds like ... yes, please.'

'Wonderful. Now, I have a little work for you. Help me here at the Inn, and I'll save the money that much faster.' She reached for a broom, leaning against one end of the dilapidated bar. 'Here – you can start with this.'

Sammy swept. Then he mopped. Then he mended and polished and varnished and tidied, until his arms and back were sore. Hours became days; Fanny provided him a tiny room upstairs, for he had nowhere else to go. Days became weeks. Sammy often enquired how the finances were looking – how close they were to their goal, to set out for Aerglo. No matter how much he worked, the earnings always just fell short of what they needed. Then came the expenses, apparently – inns don't run themselves for free – and the money would dwindle again. So, Sammy worked harder, longer, forever clinging to the dream of having more time.

Eventually, it seemed that Fanny would never have enough money. The trip would never happen. Her attitude towards him became disparaging. 'You need to stop asking, honey bunch,' she would say. 'Your place is here.' She wheedled more from him, even when he thought he might fall down where he stood.

His ambitions were whittled away, but he never quite forgot the remnants of his dream. Travel. Adventure. A nice long life. Sammy followed Fanny through the New Dawn – what else could he do? – to her new abode at the Emerald Bar. The glitz inspired him, stirred a passion of sorts ... though in essence, his situation had not improved.

Time passed.

Pull the tap. Till the coins. Wipe the bar.

Repeat, *ad infinitum.*

And remember: *The patrons tell the barman* their *life story, not the other way around.*

Somewhere in the boozy haze — Sammy lost track, for his mind had gone upstairs, to the bedsit he called home — the patrons began stumbling for the exit. The crowd thinned. The band's clattering jive gave way to a mellow warble, intended to diffuse any potential late fisticuffs.

Closing time. He made the call, and released his sixty-first sigh for the night. Sammy ambled from behind the bar, collecting armloads of sudsy jars and empty flutes on his way to the galley.

Next came sweeping. The broom handle, worn smooth, felt all-too natural in his hands.

On his nightly tour of the Emerald Bar's floors, Sammy offered timid nods to those few patrons who still clung to the shreds of another exuberant evening. He struggled to muster the temerity to sweep any stragglers towards the door. The veterans, he knew, would be gone already; seldom did they stay long enough to be shown the exit.

As he swept, his eyebrows perked: in the rear most booth, two figures still hunched over goblets of drowseberry wine. The butterfly began summoning the wherewithal to offer a polite suggestion that they maybe leave the bar for the night, *please and thank you.*

The pair did not carry the languor of drunkenness. Rather, they murmured in social tones, heads bowed in earnest discussion. Pixies both, by the look of it, but otherwise dissimilar. The one with a thicket of dark brown curls wore a pastoral tunic and jacket. His heavy eyelids betrayed him as being awake past his usual bedtime hour. The other, with a shock of blond, held a gleam in his eye and spoke with the rasp of a cheroot smoker. The blonde wore a distinctive multicoloured coat, displaying a vibrant array of hues and motifs, reminiscent of banners once used to represent the various realms of Rhye. Now, they all flowed together, many coloured standards on one garment.

With furtive glances, Sammy studied the pair. The twang of something familiar plucked at his mind. Their faces? If they were regulars, they certainly didn't often stay late.

'Six!' exclaimed the blonde one, just loud enough for the butterfly to hear, though certainly not for his benefit. 'By Ophynea's big, buxom bosom! Why six?'

Sammy pushed his broom just a little closer.

Dique shrugged. 'She must want enough kids to enable three fights at once.'

'Good gracious. You're making me tired just thinking about it. How do you do it?'

'Well, Meadow, when two pixies really love each other—'

'I know how kids are made, Dique. I mean: How do you decide to walk away from it?'

Dique looked across at his companion over folded arms. He could only surmise that Meadow's perpetual boyishness came from eluding the burden of fatherhood. As for Dique, a trace of grey had begun to tease his thick brown hair. Above ruddy cheeks, laugh lines traced a permanent course towards his pointed ears. The twinkle in his eye still shone, though for a moment, Meadow's question threatened to snuff it out.

'I don't belong in a war zone,' said Dique. 'I lost myself there for a while. The darkness, the confusion. The blood. So much helplessness, all around. If Mustapha hadn't come back when he did, the Gods know what might have become of me. I was still trying to make sense of it when we got here, from the other side of that light.

'Then, along came Roni. Life made sense again. Now, I've got it all boiled down to just four things: the treehouse, tinkering, cheese and music.'

Dique's father had owned a fromagerie. The business had belonged to his father's father before that. Dique would have inherited it, if he hadn't met a wayward strangeling with a compulsion for thievery. At that very moment, back in the forests of Petrichor, his life had changed.

Dique wasn't sure if it had changed for the better.

Meadow's eyes widened; he gave a gleeful grin. Dique could keep his cheese. 'Music, eh?' he said, with a devious wink. 'Do you still play, then?'

Now, Dique smiled. For a moment, he had a thousand-yard stare.

'Sometimes, I do. These days, just for Roni and the kids. We sit by the fire. Roni dandles one of the kids on her knee – they all fight for a turn – and I go to town on the Zither. It's a real rockin' time.'

'But if Mustapha wanted to, would you—'

'In a heartbeat,' said Dique. 'Play a little, that is. Local jaunts only ... a small tour, perhaps. Just no dragons, this time.' They both laughed; glasses clinked.

'What about you? The Drum?'

Meadow rubbed his chin. 'As it happens, I've been practising here and there. Mustapha said he might get us to play together at the Ball.'

'Really?'

'Really. He doesn't seem too enthusiastic, though. Something's a bit off about him.'

'What's the matter?' asked Dique, his eyebrows providing the question mark.

Meadow leaned forward, lowering his voice. 'It's like this: he's found himself a problem with drums lately, you see. Can't stand the sound of a beat, for some reason. I don't get it.'

'Strange.' Dique interrupted his own thoughtful frown, to drain the last drowseberry wine from his goblet. 'Do you think he's just got a lot on his mind?'

'Oh, for sure and certain. Life in Babel just got real wizzy.'

'Wizzy?'

'Yep. *Weird* and *busy*, but at the same time. Everyone's a touch nervous, with the Ball just around the corner. Dignitaries coming from all over.'

Dique gave an appreciative nod. 'Dignitaries, you say? Who's coming?'

'Well,' said Meadow. His eyes darted over Dique's shoulder. Then, in a baffling turn, a complete non-sequitur: 'I says to him, I says, "to be frank, I'd have to change my name!"' and he slapped his thigh, throwing his head back in mirth.

Bepuzzlement creased Dique's brow. He offered Meadow a blank look, soon undone by a bleat of laughter from behind him. Dique turned, to find a sheepish butterfly standing there, two hands clutching a broom, a third hand clamped over his mouth. The eavesdropping insect had given himself away.

'So,' said Meadow to the butterfly, in the tone of a lion addressing an antelope, 'Why don't you sit with us? Then, you won't strain your earholes so much.'

Emptied of patrons, the Emerald Bar bespoke both grandeur and ribald frivolity. Sleek wall panelling and flared columns flaunted shades of green – the same shade as the verdant potion within a bottle of absinthe. Fan-shaped sconces cast their light upon scattered chairs and upturned stools, forlorn and silent.

Sammy sat with Meadow and Dique, his demeanour one part awe and two parts earnestness. The shackles of apprehension were cast off: Fanny would have waddled from the premises hours ago, leaving him to slave over the task of clearing away the mess.

Forever serving, then cleaning. Perpetual mediocrity. He now rubbed shoulders with legends. It had taken him a few moments to assimilate that curious sense of familiarity; an instinctive pricking of his antennae. He had seen these two faces before. Another bar. Another lifetime, perhaps. Moreover, they stood amongst the hallowed of Babylon. The band of brothers who, in the face of apocalypse, had saved the land with song.

He sat with Zither and War Drum – a sonic volcano. *Look at me now!*

Meadow belched. 'Not a bad place, this,' he said, waving his hand about in a vague gesture. 'It isn't "Smokies", of course, but it has its charm.'

'Ah … *Smokies,*' said Dique, with a sage nod and a wistful gaze, as if this were confirmation of an established fact. Observing the butterfly's questioning face, he assumed the role of raconteur.

'That watering hole kept Reed on the map,' he said. 'Great, sudsy jars by day, raucous forest shanties by night. 'Course, rumours told it was a front for some shady business of Mayor Scaramouche's, but the regulars didn't care. We'd queue halfway down the Fernly Strip to get in there.'

'The queue was half the fun!' rejoined Meadow. 'I had whole relationships, standing in that line.'

Sammy's features had drooped, from blank into sullen. His antennae sagged.

'Why the long face?' probed Dique.

Sammy drew breath over a quivering lower lip. Every facet of his eyes shimmered, dozens of mirrors into his pitiful soul.

'I don't … like bars anymore.'

'Why not?'

The bottle of weltschmerz was thus unstoppered.

'She's had me since the cocoon, don't you know? These wings

— I grew them myself. Watched all of my brethren use theirs to catch the spring breeze and disappear on the great migration — these wretched, patched-up wings, I don't know why I have them; trapped, as I am, on the wrong side of the bar, away from the brass and the jazz and the dances; I've never known what it is to close that door behind me and skip my way home — to my very own home, not a grim and dusty attic; not an upstairs dungeon, where the last of my waking hours are spent in service to Ms Fanny ... but why wouldn't I? I'm no good for anything else.'

Silence ensued, in which the pixies appeared as stunned as mullets. Perhaps processing Sammy's soliloquy or perhaps bludgeoned into a stupor by it. They exchanged a wordless look. Dique blinked.

'Look here,' said Meadow, after a while, 'your word salad could do with some vinegar and croutons on it.'

Dique frowned. 'Come on, Meadow, that's not fair. The fellow has just vented his spleen—'

'I mean it, Dique. Young Sammy here is watching the world pass him by. He needs a good nudge out of the doldrums, or his wings will never take him anywhere.' To Sammy, he said: 'What would you do? Where would you go if you left this place?'

The butterfly replied in an earnest tone. Clearly, he had considered his answer to this question many times.

'I am aware that a butterfly's life is short. It is often spent carelessly, I'll concede. Thrown away as if it had no value.

'I just don't want to be one of the faceless multitudes. If it is at all possible, I want my time to count. To matter! I want ... to make an impression. A butterfly who is remembered shall live much longer than his kin.'

'Well, well, whoever heard of an ambitious butterfly?' said Meadow, with glee.

'What you need is a station,' surmised Dique.

Meadow nodded, on the same mental track as his friend. 'We're not here to make a legacy for you, but we can set you in the right direction. If you want something important to do, you could present yourself to Babel. There's a demand for able bodies, what with the ceremonies just around the corner. The Tower needs staffing. Talk to the footman, and ask to see Leith Lourden. She'll give you something meaningful to do.'

'Really? You think so?' cried Sammy.

'I'm sure Meadow can put in a word for you,' said Dique.

A moment later, Sammy's face fell. He waved his arms about, in a hapless gesture towards the dishevelled Bar.

'What about all of this?' he fretted. 'I need to set the Bar in order. I can't just walk out of here, can I? Not without doing the chores. Fanny will be mad ... I must see to her needs, as well. The hour is very late—'

Meadow shooshed him to silence. 'This is your chance,' said the liveried pixie. 'It might be late ... but it isn't too late for you to make a brand-new start. Not yet.

'I have a lot of friends who drink here. Influential types. They'll be only too eager to hear about this Fanny. Once they do, I bet they'll be finding somewhere else to get sozzled.

'The Emerald Bar is finished ... and you're finished with it.'

CHAPTER FOUR

WE COULD FLY

The pursuit always felt this way: the delectable hunger, tempered by frustration and the need for patience.

The best things in life might have been free, but they often required phenomenal restraint. Such restraint only caused desire to heighten; the desire of a hunter, chasing her prey.

Hunger and restraint raged in the mind of Trixel Tate, flat on her belly in the undergrowth, hunter's crossbow laid beside her. Senses attuned to activity within a dense thicket some thirty yards away, her right hand hovered over the weapon. She hesitated, assessing the sounds and scents that drifted in her direction.

That's not a qilin. Too small.

Her instincts proved true, as a badger raised its inquisitive head, beady eyes darting about. It sniffed the air once, then twice; then it plunged over a thicket of butcher's broom and vanished.

Only once the beast had gone, did Trixel exhale – a near-inaudible puff.

A feathery whisper sounded close to her ear. 'Why did you

56

let it go?'

Trixel scowled. *Because I usually hunt alone, and you're a supreme distraction.* 'Because it's bad luck to track and capture a badger. Qilin? They're good luck. According to Cornavrian, or Fae superstition ... or both. Besides, qilin are much more fun to chase.'

Leith Lourden contemplated this, with a delicate crease marking her brow. 'I'll take your word for it. In Old Rhye, most of my hunting took place in the Vultan Range, where the wildlife was generally large and unfriendly. Nothing got a free pass for being "bad luck", or else it would chew your face off.'

Both women knew the struggles of survival. Before the New Dawn, they had dwelled upon vastly differing frontiers. Now that Mustapha's new vision of Rhye brought them together, the greater sense of displacement belonged to the sylph.

The pair ventured into Eleuthervale on an errand from Babel, happy for a refreshing break from officialdom. The potent combination of human wonder and seraphic willpower – plus a blessing from the Pantheon – had wrought a kind of paradise to the east of Rhye's premier city; a corridor of resplendent greenery, bursting with vivid floral colour and teeming with wildlife, reminiscent of Old Sontenan. Eleuthervale provided an arterial route for caravans and trade routes to settlements on the fringes of the fledgling land. Leith and Trixel had two such settlements in their sights; the travel would not be arduous and Trixel insisted they would have time enough to indulge in some forest sport.

Leith still felt strange without her armour.

Ten years, no war. Sure, minor conflict stirred from time to time. The entire population of Rhye had jostled for position in the new land – one expected some abrasive exchanges. But with Anuvin – God of War – safely boxed away, major conflict failed to ignite. Mustapha, in his grace, had managed to conjure up a worthy abode for all creatures, great and small. An eerie peace reigned. The ex-Vrendari still wore ceremonial attire, though the days of tramping around in battle-ready armour were over.

The sylph shifted her weight. Leaves crackled under her prone form. Trixel Tate, silent as an assassin, scowled again.

'You'll shoo away every creature this side of Hiraeth, with that racket,' she murmured.

'Sylphs aren't made to crawl in the undergrowth,' retorted Leith. 'We belong in the air, remember? Anyway — I had another question.'

The fixie — half fairy, half pixie — shook her head in resignation. Verdant fronds of hair, the ultimate forest camouflage, swayed side to side. 'Now that we're chatting ... what is it?'

'Why did it take you so long to ask me to come hunting with you?'

Trixel made a point of continuing to study the middle distance. Violet-grey eyes darted in response to every whispered breeze and avian chirp. 'I'm fine out here by myself. If you track game in the wilderness for centuries, you get used to your own company. It's a lonely old world, being a fixie ... but even loneliness can become familiar.'

'Ah.'

'Besides, you're a tough one to pin down. Do you remember the last time we were both free to run through the forest together?'

'You make a good point,' conceded Leith. 'As it turns out, Ministries are a lot of work. For a land without large-scale war, the Security Portfolio keeps me on my toes. Between extra detail for incoming guests next week, and extra shifts to keep intruders away from the Oddity, I've rarely been busier!'

Trixel turned from her vigil, face suddenly bright with curiosity. 'Of course! I had almost forgotten about that. What did they find down there? How far do the stairs go? Is there more mysterious writing?'

Leith smirked. 'I'm not at liberty to say.'

'No more of that jazz, Lourden. I know you – terrible at telling lies, and even more terrible at keeping secrets.'

'I'm the Minister for Security!'

'Still terrible.'

'Am not!'

'Are so.'

'Am not!'

'Are so. What is the "Oddity"? Or I'll poke it out of you!' An advancing finger wriggled towards the sylph's ribcage.

'Stop it! I'm not telling you anything!' Leith erupted into laughter, squirming away from the teasing fixie.

The jovial outburst triggered a jangling roar from the depths of the nearby forest. This first sound was soon joined by several others, a melodic bellowing of unseen beasts. Stomping hooves and the crisp snap of trampled saplings underscored the din.

Leith and Trixel gasped, in unison.

'Qilin!' cried the fixie. She sprang from their hiding place; stealth forgotten, for the advantage had now been lost. Leith, taller, long legs and folded wings cramped in the underbrush, scrambled to join her.

A broad fire trail cut a grassy path through the forest – Mustapha's safeguard against a repeat of the holocaust that marred ancient Petrichor, claiming the lives of the Fairy King and Queen. Trixel and Leith burst onto the trail, which angled down a long descent, into the flourishing embrace of the valley below.

From the opposite side of the trail exploded a herd of wondrous creatures. Elegant, regal and wild, the rare qilin appeared, amidst the threshing of foliage and a chorus of startled roars. Atop leonine heads their manes rippled; from the lustrous hair forked the antlers of a stag. Deerlike, too, were their bodies, leaping over knoll and fallen branch with fluid form. As they emerged into sunlight, the rays of Adatar reflected from gleaming rows of scales upon their flanks.

To see even one such creature could be considered a treat — elusive as they were, like the pterippi of Marnis.

Swift as the wind, a dozen qilin thundered onto the trail. Spying the hunters, they veered on sure hooves down the hillside, following the fire trail.

Leith sprinted, angling across the path of the fleeing creatures. Stowing her crossbow between her wings, she instead drew the compact net launcher from her belt. The device, from the mechanical mind of Torr Yosef, enabled a non-lethal means of capturing game. The sylph switched weapons in the blink of an eye, never breaking her long stride.

Somehow, the fixie ran faster. Trixel Tate, bred of the forest, sped past the sylph in a flash of Fae dynamism.

'First to down a beast alive is the victor!' cried Trixel, wielding her own net launcher as she sped by Leith.

'The stakes?'

'I'll decide when I win!' laughed Trixel, over her shoulder.

Leith doubled her efforts, loping after the Fae and the haunches of stampeding qilin.

East of Babylon, Mustapha had wrought a sanctuary fit to satiate a boundless imagination. In this endeavour he enlisted Ackley Fahrenheit: a human from a strange, alternative world, who came with him to Rhye when the land lay vulnerable. As Marnis the Creator had foretold, the unbridled awe of the human dovetailed with Mustapha's seraphic gift, turning wondrous mindscapes into real and idyllic landscapes.

From the forest byways of Eleuthervale sprang several paths, winding through the dappled light to distant reaches. To the south, beyond thicket and burbling brook, the vegetation parted to make way for a place of great learning — a single tree, to rival the splendour of old Oberon's Yew. A giant sycamore, crowned in myriad green and gold leaves.

The Repositree.

Beneath creaking eaves, immense in their reach, the denizens of Rhye could sit and absorb every truth and every tale of the world. The word of the land adorned every leaf in delicate print, telling the stories of time immemorial. A vertical labyrinth of ladders, lifts and pulleys ensured that even the uppermost canopy could be explored — though many visitors were content to sprawl amidst gargantuan roots, and simply read the leafy tales as they fluttered to the forest floor.

Within a few wingbeats of the Repositree, the curious and the learned of Rhye dwelled in verdant commune. Most zealous among these were the dragonflies. They had opted to refashion their beloved Dragonfly Hollow just exactly as it had been, prior to Valendyne's fiery desecration. Amidst them still lived Harold, Dragon Bane and Horn Wielder. There too dwelled covens of Elementals, effulgent in raiment of Gold.

Further still, beyond a glen of silver birch, stood the gilded village of Papilion. Here, Mustapha realised a home for the butterflies. The vibrant insects — whimsical though they were — enjoyed a neighbourly friendship with the remaining dryads and forest trolls of Arboria.

Leith Lourden's errand this day took her to Dragonfly Hollow, to visit the Dragon Bane himself. Harold had invested much in the orchestration of the upcoming Ball; Leith, who had stayed very close to him in the years since the New Dawn, took it upon herself to discuss final preparations with him. Most others in Babel — including Lance Sevenson, 'Wagoner' Will, and Archimage Timbrad — remained entrenched in their ministerial responsibilities.

This current flight of fancy might have been a pleasant distraction, though it wasn't exactly leading her towards her objective.

The rumbling thunder of hooves rent the tranquil forest air. A certain majesty flowed through the bounding, galloping qilin; the devout of Rhye believed Marnis had produced them as an antithesis to that other elemental beast, the dreaded manticore. Like all other terrestrial creations, the qilin had since been protected by Cornavrian.

Without doubt, the power of Nature coursed through the animals that stormed along the fire trail. Glossy manes shone in the midmorning sun. Powerful haunches propelled the qilin on, eluding their pursuers. Bellowing calls sent flocks of squawking lorikeets into the sky.

To down a qilin, a rope or net about the antlers provided best leverage. The challenge lay first in lassoing a beast in flight; then, to overcome its wild strength and bring it to ground.

None held the audacity to slay these creatures, nor did they have any natural predators. But to conquer a qilin, offer a prayer and release it again, caused the heart of a hunter to leap.

Leith's heart pounded. Her feet flew along the trail. Passing years had made of her an even stronger sylph. Her muscles thrummed; her joints knew no complaint.

Still, she struggled to cling to the rear of the galloping herd. Though her wings swept back behind her, she knew they only dragged her back. She needed to gain ground, if she were to cast her net within range of her quarry: a creature at the herd's rear. Ahead, the fixie darted and weaved, jockeying for position. So close to landing her prize. Her taunt spurred Leith on.

'I'll decide when I win!'

Not if I have anything to do about it.

Trixel Tate ran as if she were the hunted. The adrenaline surge came as much from the challenge she had issued as from a desire to conquer one of these magnificent beasts.

Her instincts focused. She knew exactly which of them she intended to subdue.

The creatures ahead and to either side of Trixel leapt into the air. She followed suit, soaring over a massive log that lay tumbled across the trail and dusted with moss. On the far side, dozens of hooves pounded the earth with a rapid-fire *chonk-ch-chonk*. Clods of dirt sprayed from qilin footfalls as they careened down the vale. They sensed the huntresses in their midst; one so close she could touch them, the other not far behind.

Trixel's diminutive size belied the speed of her pursuit. Centuries spent honing the predator's art, with the Mother Forest itself fuelling her vitality. To track, and to dominate, were in the fibre of her being. Closing in on her quarry, she brought her net launcher to bear, sabre-sharp gaze locked onto one of the bounding beasts before her. The supple, dragon-scale body, glinting ultramarine and gold. The flickering swatch tail, lashing to-and-fro in the qilin's wake. Too short to reach the bobbing splay of antlers upon the mighty head, Trixel needed to adjust her target. A lash about the unguligrade hind legs would work just as well.

In a single, wild moment, she unleashed a whoop of joy. She braced the launcher in the crook of her arm, steadying it as she ran.

She pulled the trigger.

The snare shot forth and captured the void, for the scarpering qilin was no longer there.

A bolt from above, a swooping flash of azure and ivory, descended upon the stampeding beasts. In a blur of motion, the regal head of Trixel's chosen quarry snapped to one side, dragging the qilin bodily from the fray ... and away from her snare.

Panicked, roaring cries rang from the herd. With much swerving and jumping, the qilin dodged around their fellow, frantic to resume their flight. Some dashed for the cover of the forest; others sped deeper into the heart of the vale.

The felled beast, wrenched by its antlers to the ground, slid to a halt, in a cloud of dust and shredded greenery. A defeated yowl issued from its maw.

Atop the qilin's conquered form, still gripping its antlers with white knuckles, crouched Leith Lourden. Sweat plastered platinum hair across her brow. Her skin glistened with exertion. Toned shoulders heaved with every breath. Her broad wings, cast wide and luminous beneath Adatar's light, fluttered down against her back.

Grunting, she launched herself from the downed qilin, falling to a knee beside it.

Trixel Tate skidded to a stop. Eyes wide, she fought to master her own bounding pulse.

'Wings beating is straight cheating!' she panted.

Leith's smile carried a vague sense of mischief. 'I don't recall seeing the rule book.' Turning to the qilin, she enacted a hand gesture, evoking a prayer of the sylphic people. The creature raised its bewildered head, terror receding from its gaze. Leith whispered in its ear, a devotion to Cornavrian.

Trixel watched, head tilted to one side. To see such a lordly beast overcome, and then to respond with silent deference, caught the words in her throat.

After a few moments, the sylph rose to her feet. The qilin, wary but unafraid, regained its hooves. The grace of the wild imbued its every movement. Hesitant at first, it pawed the ground, studying its winged vanquisher. The realisation of merciful freedom dawned on it then; with a final bellow, the qilin darted for the blanket of countless trees.

Trixel Tate stood with hands on hips. 'I am impressed, lady sylph.'

'You ought to be,' grinned the sylph, brushing damp tresses from her face and twirling them in her fingers. All around them, the tranquillity of a summer morning settled one more. 'Truly, though … thanks. I've been needing a break from official duties. We sylphs aren't made to spend our days in stuffy chambers and offices. It's nice to stretch my legs.'

Trixel tapped her foot, in mock disapproval. 'And your wings, apparently.'

'And my wings, yes.'

The sylph turned to leave. Her errand took her to Dragonfly Hollow; they had passed the southward road some hundreds of yards back along the trail.

'We'd best stay bound to our tasks,' she said. 'Good luck with Fahrenheit.'

'Wait,' called Trixel, to the retreating figure. 'You bested me, after all. Stakes are stakes. What is your prize?'

Leith stopped. She chewed her lip, stalling for time. After an endless moment she turned, a flustered look tangling her features. Then, her face dipped. She eyed Trixel from beneath her platinum fringe. Words were caught in her knotted tongue.

Trixel shrugged. 'Look, I—'

Leith held up a finger. At last, her words tumbled out in a rush. 'You owe me one dance at the Ball.' Then she spun on her heel and strode away up the trail, without looking back again.

If Eleuthervale buzzed with convivial forest life, Hiraeth stood apart as a natural ode to solitude and otherness.

Mustapha had never intended it this way. But in every civilisation, in every realm, in every Age of the world, it would be the same: the outcasts and fringe-dwellers would find their place, away from everyone else. An air of exquisite melancholy settled over the region, a veil of solemnity. League upon beautiful league of shadowed copses, rolling hillocks, and dales blanketed in spectral mist, were interlinked by many a twisting path or roadway.

To this place, far from the melting pot of Babylon, had Ackley Fahrenheit retreated.

The change came over him only a few years after the New Dawn. For him, there had been no subtle fade from prominence. One week, he stood at the fore of a new frontier, watching in awe as the fog of oblivion rolled back from the new land of Rhye. The next week, he appeared a frayed wreck, wanting nothing more than a life of seclusion.

Powerless to change his mind, the King of Rhye had, with much dismay, granted the otherworlder's request. A new home, where the serenity would cradle his fractured soul.

A serenity bordering on ghostliness.

Trixel stumped down the path. A thin layer of fog swirled about her boots. The purplish hues of dusk began to wash across the sky. Visions of beautiful sorrow met her eye at every corner: from the resigned droop of a weeping willow, to the accusatory fingers of granite that stabbed skywards, at odd intervals across the landscape; all painted in that glorious hue of golden hour. At the same time, the gaze of hidden watchers prickled the hairs at the base of her skull. In Hiraeth, a traveller was never far from a hamlet of outcasts, or the den of a hermit ... though nobody rolled out the welcome mat, or placed a friendly tea-kettle on the fire.

This suited Trixel perfectly. She had enough to think about.

The sylph had blindsided her – not once, but twice. First, with her victory at forest sport; then, with her chosen prize. To be bested at a hunt did sleight her pride, though Trixel could soon move past that. *Just a game, after all* ... and the pair had been no less than sisterly since the Battle for Rhye. Or had they?

You owe me one dance at the Ball.

There, the problem lay. Waves of instinct railed against the idea, causing Trixel's gut to churn. Centuries of instinct – that inner part, not quite intestinal, not quite emotional – rose to close protective ranks about her.

Centuries.

Sylphs live about one hundred years, if they aren't killed on a battleground first.

Trixel frowned. Heat bloomed behind her cheeks. *Does she even know what she's asking me?*

In the tumult of her thoughts, Trixel almost stamped headlong into the dark figure that materialised on the path ahead. Just in time, she saw it – the spindle limbs, the bell-shaped body, the lambent eyes. She stopped, in the glow it cast before it upon the path.

Compressed air moved past cane reeds within the creature's metallic throat. It had the melodic voice of a bassoon. 'Please halt. Passage is restricted. Who goes there?'

Trixel glared. 'It's me, you musical mailbox. Do you have your eyes in today?'

A mechanical being, no taller than the fixie, waddled forward. As it left its gloomy post, waning sunlight glinted from a burnished copper shell. Bezel-rimmed eyes focused on Trixel, scanning up and down.

'One moment. I am assimilating—'

'Arundax. It's Trixel Tate. Again. Now stand aside, or I'll have you sent back to Torr Yosef ... one hinge at a time.'

The automaton gave a submissive warble and stepped aside.

Upon the crest of a hill, by a stand of whispering fir trees, stood a sturdy log cabin. It hugged the very edge of Hiraeth's enchanting undulations, peering through a natural alpine window to a vast wasteland beyond. Trixel could have been standing before the dilapidated hovel of the Seer, Lily. This abode told a different story, for it had been built only a handful of years before; maintained with diligence, imbued with a sense of care. A warm glow emanated from within.

'Lady Tate,' said Arundax, 'I must advise that Mr Fahrenheit is not at home right—'

'Nonsense. He's always at home.'

Arundax offered only a disconsolate *whirrrr*. Trixel stalked past, muttering something about a *soulless tin pot*. She continued up the forested path towards the cabin.

'I'm not at home,' came a voice from within, in response to Trixel's third attempt at doorknocking.

'It's me, Ackley. Trixel Tate.'

A momentary pause. 'You, and who else?'

'Just me. I even left your sulking sentry down the path a way. It didn't want to be complicit in my reaching your door.'

'You chose not to heed it.'

'That is correct. I need to see you — it's important.'

'It always is.'

Under her breath, the fixie counted to ten. So far, she had managed to keep a measured tone. Her next words, she pushed out between clenched teeth. 'I come with tidings from Mustapha. He remains, as ever, your friend; but he is also your King. Are you going to let me in?'

Another pause. Lengthier, to the point where Trixel considered turning away. Then came the slow scrape of a chair, the *chink* of crockery, and the sound of ambling bootsteps, approaching from the inside. Several bolts snapped back in their housings.

With the barest creak, the door opened.

Ackley Fahrenheit had aged well beyond his years. Though a full head of hair still graced his crown, not a strand of it remained the rich brown of his past life. The silver mane and matching beard, well groomed, framed the cragged features that peered out at the fixie.

'You've lost more weight,' she observed. At least, she thought it to be true. Fahrenheit had long since discarded the clothes he wore, when leaving his old world behind. His voluminous robes — common amongst the humans of Rhye — seemed unlikely to conceal a figure of any great substance. 'The traderlings still deliver your supplies?'

Fahrenheit gave no answer. He looked beyond her now, eyes scouring the forest. Seemingly satisfied, he cleared the portal, gesturing for Trixel to enter. He closed the door directly after her, leaving it unlocked.

'You are lucky I was always a royalist,' he said to Trixel as they entered his home. It consisted of just two rooms, appointed in handsome fashion: an open space that doubled as kitchen and living quarters, and behind it, the hermit's bedroom. 'As for the traderlings,' he continued, 'they do their thing. Deliver and leave. I must admit I thought little of Yosef's creations to begin with. The genius of them is now apparent — no frivolous requests to socialise.' He gave Trixel a meaningful look, though it held no ire.

Her attention wandered about the hermit's abode. As on previous visits, it gave the impression of scrupulous care. Homeliness. Pots, jars and utensils stood aligned on kitchen shelves. Surfaces gleamed, devoid of any settling dust. Even a stack of firewood by the hearth appeared more orderly than a stack of wood had any right to be. No debris gathered in the hearth itself; the cabin's illumination came from a series of oil lamps, placed about the room.

No smells of cooking, or evidence of eating, were apparent. A single earthenware cup stood on a sill by the door.

The only sign of industry lay upon a writing desk, illumined by a front window but not near it. Reams of paper, writing implements and inkpots covered the desk; though not untidy, Fahrenheit had clearly been active there.

He had not invited Trixel to sit. She stayed on her feet, in the centre of the room. As ever, a subtle sense of intrusion niggled at her. She began to wish that Mustapha could make his own trips out to check on the man's wellbeing, though of course it was an indulgence his schedule could ill afford.

Either that, or Mustapha's guilt kept him away.

'What tidings do you bring, then?' questioned Fahrenheit.

The fixie scratched her nose, collecting her wits for the exchange to come. 'The anniversary is near,' she said.

'It is.'

'It will be ten years, this year.'

'It will.'

Trixel took a breath. Held it. 'There is going to be a small gathering—'

'No.'

'I haven't even invited you yet!'

'You don't need to.'

She exhaled, softly. 'It would mean ever so much if you made an appearance.'

The hermit's face showed tolerance. 'Lady Tate. You and I both know that Mustapha — *the King* — does not do "small gatherings". I find it difficult to believe that he would do so, for such an occasion as this.'

Truth. The fixie nodded, in glum acceptance. With little else to try, she threw out the bait. 'Khashoggi will be there.'

Fahrenheit only nodded. He gave no sign of considering this information, though the men had developed a camaraderie in years gone by. A shared love of adventure.

Until he, Fahrenheit, had drawn the shutters of reclusiveness.

A kindness softened the obstinacy of his face. 'I value your kinship in making the effort to come out here,' he said. 'The automatons make the half-day journey without complaint or regret, of course. I wouldn't fault a flesh-and-blood being for feeling differently.

'Hiraeth is my home. I choose not to deal with suffocating metropolitan life any longer.' His steady voice quavered over these last few words. The Adam's apple bobbed in his throat. Trixel watched as he produced a kerchief from somewhere within his robe, and dabbed his mouth with it.

'So!' he cried, with a sudden change of tone. 'Now that is settled, what other news of the world?'

The fixie grimaced. 'The world stopped expanding.' A pointed barb.

'Oh, I still marvel and wonder at it all,' said Fahrenheit, as if to reassure her. 'But this simple otherworlder is capable of restraining emotions, too. I need not venture to new frontiers any longer. My heart lies with parchment and stylus — Marnis knows, I've had a lifetime of tales worth writing down.'

Trixel tried another tack. 'They found something. In a collapsed cavern, underneath Babel. I don't know what it is — apparently, that's on a "need to know" basis — but there's a gravid air around it. Security is tight, and the mood is ominous.' She knew the old man's curiosity could still kindle a flame within him.

Indeed, his brows lifted, if even a fraction. 'You mean to say, something is down there that Mustapha did not create?'

'I do mean to say that.'

'How very intriguing. Do you know nothing more?'

Trixel smiled inwardly. *Is this how I lure him out?* 'Only a little more; of that little, it brings more confusion than answers. Hearsay, passed on by a kobold who brought word to Babel of the rockfall.'

'I'm listening.'

'An inscription, on a stone column beneath the earth. The words mean nothing to anyone, but have become the buzz of the Tower.

'Into the ancient stone, someone has chiselled *"Fugit inreparabile tempus"*.' The sounds felt strange in her mouth.

Fahrenheit stared out of the window. As Trixel spoke these words, his gaze hardened. He looked, with intense focus, to be counting the leaves on the trees outside. After a while, he offered a non-committal grunt. 'I'm sure the King has his best experts on the matter.'

Trixel slumped. 'I assume he does, yes. As for me, I'm kept busy on other errands.'

The hermit moved closer to the window. He peered out through the pane, up beyond the tops of trees. Daylight failed; the chorus of night insects swelled in the dusk air. The fixie knew what he would say. His home was not suited to accommodate overnight guests.

'The sun has set,' he said, 'but Anato turns her full face towards us. The way will be well lit. If you travel quickly, you can clear the depths of Hiraeth before the night beasts come about.'

The fixie glared at Fahrenheit's back, willing some other response from him. When none came, she capitulated with a huff. 'You're right. I'll be on my way. Nice to see you, Ackley. Keep well.'

He held the door open. 'Lady Tate,' he said with a respectful nod, as she traipsed past him into the night.

Trixel stumped down the path away from Fahrenheit's cabin, in much the same way she had approached it only a short time before. Surely enough, he had met her expectations; a wily recluse, afraid of the world.

She cast a look skyward. It mattered little to her, what time of day or night she regained the Tower. *I don't need your concern, silly human. I've managed to look after myself in the wilderness for hundreds of years. Just me.* Even as she thought it, Trixel felt a pang of something uncomfortable. *Damn you!* She refused to look back over her shoulder.

Had she done so, she might have seen the thoughtful expression worn by Ackley Fahrenheit, as he watched her go.

CHAPTER FIVE

BACK TO MACHINES

Two days before the Ball, Khashoggi sat on a strip of pristine white sand, pantaloons hitched at the knee, gentle waves lapping at his outstretched legs. The sea glittered like a dragon's hoard beneath temperate sunshine. Offshore, the waters lay becalmed, protected as they were by the hulking landmass known as 'Levi' – the Leviathan, several leagues distant.

Levi's tree-cloaked slopes dominated the horizon from Khashoggi's vantage point. He knew – better than almost anyone in Babylon – that beyond the mountainous island, the great, blue expanse engulfed all … and there may well have been no end to it.

Even on this most leisurely of days, Khashoggi exuded a kind of restless energy; that of a man forever on the move, engaged in some industrious undertaking. At the same time, he managed to maintain an air of astute worldliness. At any moment, he might fling himself from the sand, impatient for the next adventure. Such energy belied his elder status: the cliché of the gnarled old soothsayer hung about him like an ill-fitting cloak. The exalted blood of a Seer flowed in his veins, keeping the creep of dotage at bay. Still, most knew of him as a prophet – *the* Prophet – augur of a long-distant Age, who left a Song like a trail of breadcrumbs and then returned triumphant at the land's final hour, bringing with him the King of Rhye.

Quite the résumé ... though even Prophets need a day at the beach.

The white noise of rolling breakers, knee-high to an adult human, came to the ear as a pleasant rumble. The only other sounds to grace the morning were the high-pitched calls of kestrels, hovering overhead in their search for breakfast. The birds had established rookeries hugging the cliffs; they could be found here at Khashoggi's chosen beach, southwards beyond the Ogreshrine, and as far as Crueladaville. Not often were kestrels seen out over the water – this lone avian made the exception.

Khashoggi's gaze roved across the bejewelled turquoise sea. Just beyond the breakers, a compact, seagoing craft sat moored, bobbing in the swell. The twin-hulled craft, topped by a sleek passenger compartment, looked less like a tender than the tail of some great crustacean. Oversized propellers fanned out behind it, in an aggressive spiral shape.

The old man eyed the craft, his face full of scrutiny. It represented a prototype for a much grander vessel.

A shadow below the surface weaved around the bobbing craft, headed for the shore. In the shallows, a series of ripples marked the place where, with the barest sound, a figure emerged from the surf.

The woman – feminine, yet inhuman – rose with uncanny grace, moving as one born from the waves themselves. An undine: spirit of the marine element, steward of Cornavrian's law upon Rhye.

Khashoggi, half-reclining on the sand, watched the undine stride from the shallows. A delicate membrane of foam clung to her body like a sheer gown. On her shoulders, finely scaled, water droplets glistened beneath the sun. Her face, ageless as the waters themselves, belied the countless seasons of her aquatic dominion.

She offered him a serene smile as she sauntered up the beach.

'Bijou of the sea,' murmured Khashoggi. 'Your beauty remains a mystery ... fresh for me to unravel, every time I see you. Oh, how you have been missed.'

The smile broadened. She rolled her eyes. 'Calm your feeble human flattery — I took a short dip only.'

'Salacia...'

The undine knelt beside him, leaned close, and kissed his mouth. To Khashoggi, the brine upon her lips carried a unique sweetness. He marvelled now, as he had marvelled at her first kiss. It had cost her much to stand by him after the New Dawn; yet in him she saw the echoes of salt and wisdom, and to those attributes had she been drawn.

'The years melt from me,' he said to her. 'The water still calls to these ancient bones; yet they offer a more boisterous refrain, now they know the water's love in return.'

Salacia sat, legs bent, piscine eyes gazing across the tranquil stretch towards the Leviathan. 'It is to my fortune that you meet me here, where I may still hold power enough to resist your charms.'

'Ah ... you would resist?'

Something wistful shaped the undine's features. Hers was the beauty of untamed nature; the eerie calm at the eye of a storm. She looked beyond the great crags of Levi, to a place too far for the ships of mortals to reach. Khashoggi knew that she also looked back, to an age-old love ... a love lost to battle and raging tempest.

'Ophynea grants us each a chance at renewal,' she said at last. 'It gladdens my heart that we are united with the sea's majesty as our witness.' Her tension washed away, and she gave the Prophet a more embracing look.

Khashoggi grasped her cool hand, feeling the thin webs between her fingers. 'No finer place in all of Rhye than this place we make our rendezvous.'

'The King is generous in his provision,' said Salacia, before a smirk flashed across her lips. 'Or perhaps he would have been, if he knew the lone purpose with which we imbue this beach!'

'Salacious, indeed!' cried Khashoggi. He leapt to his feet, eyes a-twinkle, and lifted the undine into his arms. Together they danced, a lively sway in honour of shimmering seascapes and stolen moments.

Out on the water, much further than Khashoggi's mechanical craft, a small flotilla of other vessels traversed the strait. Most of these were sailing vessels — smaller yachts and larger caravels, at the mercy of the ocean breeze. Those heading north usually rounded the nearby headland, an immense artificial bulwark that sheltered the Bay of Marnis. Southbound vessels crossed the mouth of the Serpentine, before entering more treacherous waters. From the place of the Ogreshrine, great cliffs rose to meet the limitless ocean. There, merchant traders brought goods back and forth, from the distant reaches of the known land.

Collapsing against each other, Salacia and Khashoggi watched the vessels drift, left to right and back again, as far as the eye could see.

'Would you go with me, if I went?' asked the Prophet.

'My love?'

'Out there ...' he gestured, past the traffic in the strait, to the greater unknown.

'If you are on the sea, I am always with you,' replied Salacia. 'I am of the sea!'

'You know my meaning.'

The undine blinked. Khashoggi watched her gills expand and

contract several times, before she answered. 'A strange feeling eddies within me,' she said. 'A current of doubt, as once only the Seventh Sea stirred. All other waters of that vast world yielded their secrets to me, but for that one. This feeling is similar – the ocean to the west beckons, with the promise of discovery … but there is something else. A forbidding power. I knew nothing like it, in the old world.'

Khashoggi nodded. 'You hesitate, at the idea of voyaging the Western Way.'

'So should you, who survive the ocean's malice only if your fanciful schooners remain upright!'

The Prophet stroked his beard. 'The King toys with the notion. I'd wager the crafty seraph plans to send me.'

'And what is your desire?'

'To serve the one who rightfully sits on the throne of Rhye. By my own gift, I knew of his coming. Against odds most dire, he salvaged hope; to honour his wish is now my duty—'

'Your tongue does run on, human.'

'Fine. The sea calls to me … I have been preparing.'

'The Mer Folk know of your preparations.'

'More than that, my Lady. The engineering prowess of the Mer has been of substantial aid.'

<Pardon my intrusion, sir, but the timing seems prudent.>

The jarring insertion sounded like a hydraulic engine in Khashoggi's mind. Though Salacia could not hear it, she knew from the sudden change on her companion's face that he received a telepathic interjection.

The Prophet sighed. Reaching into the pocket of his pantaloons, he withdrew a small device, consisting of two thumb-sized copper probes, and a curved band to join them. He placed the device on his head, the probes against his mastoid bones.

Salacia stared at him. 'Never a truly private moment?' she asked, folding her arms.

Khashoggi gave her an apologetic look, though his words were directed elsewhere. 'Yosef: your timing is both prudent and dismaying. What news?'

<We may have solved the issue of lost power to rear starboard and port engines on the Khonsu.>

'Indeed?'

<There is much energy loss through overheating of the exhaust manifolds on both sides. It appears that both catalytic converters have been blocked. An impure fuel source – it is a wonder the engines have kept from stalling altogether.>

'And the solution?' Salacia scrutinised Khashoggi's face as he spoke, privy to only his fragments of dialogue.

<The Mer Folk know how to clear the converters, though this is only a temporising measure. We have the Sorcerers to thank for a more sustainable solution.>

'The fuel itself?'

<Well done, sir>, whirred the golem's mechanical speech. *<As it transpires, the amradite core you were using is less efficient than previously calculated. The Wearers of Sky Blue devised a rapid-decay strategy, by which the amradite is reduced to a new compound. They wanted to call it "Khashoggium". I disagreed, explaining that humans have a word for that sort of thing: "twee". The as-yet-unnamed compound forms a core that is much cleaner and more stable as an energy source.>*

'Brilliant,' said Khashoggi. 'Is it easy to produce?'

<So, it seems.>

'By what magic have they done this?'

<If I knew that, I would be a Sorcerer, sir.>

By this time, Salacia had taken to drawing idle shapes in the sand, with a finger. When Khashoggi caught her eye, she returned a patient smile.

'Are we in readiness?' he said to the golem.

<The Mer await only your command for a test run.>

'I will be on deck inside the hour.' With that, Khashoggi stripped the device from his head.

Salacia rose to her feet. 'And thus ends our seaside rendezvous?'

The Prophet pretended not to hear the teasing note in her voice. 'The pinnacle of many months' hard work, my dear. A true collaboration of races, in the name of technology. Advancement! An opportunity to explore your beloved ocean; to discover her secrets!'

'Certainly, a cause to celebrate,' the undine conceded. She did adore Khashoggi's fascination with the great blue beyond. 'You had best go. But do hurry back … the sea is a restless maiden.' She winked, and welcomed his tight embrace. Within moments, Salacia watched the spry figure of the Prophet wading out to his moored seacraft.

She recalled another time, when a lover had left her standing on a beach. *At least this time, the news is good*, she mused.

Khashoggi's craft knifed through the water, like a nautiloid skimming the surface at high speed. Sheets of spray, churned through the giant propellers, fanned aft for a dozen yards. The craft leapt forward with a deep, throaty roar, responsive to the lightest touch of its controls.

The water remained as smooth as glass. Khashoggi wondered if Salacia had a hand in this. More powerful than most undines, she possessed a stronger-than-usual ability to affect the marine environment in her vicinity.

Swift passage caused the Prophet's grey mane to stream behind him. Beard whipping back over his shoulder, he stood firm at the helm. One hand gripped the wheel; the other nudged the throttle, coaxing even more from the marching pistons behind him. Like a marine thoroughbred, the machine beneath his boots lunged forward.

Far to his left, the Leviathan still dominated his view. The shelter it gave no doubt maintained the relative calm of the strait. On his right, a new elevation rose: the cliffs along the southern coast of Babylon. From the picket line of green-fronded palms some fifty feet above the water, the land tumbled down to meet a series of scalloped beaches. Khashoggi flashed past them, mind and gaze fixed on the way before him. With a spin of the wheel, he veered around a ponderous sailboat, giving it a wide berth.

Ahead, partly obscured by the salt-mist, loomed The Works.

Rising from the sea at the mouth of the Bay, an immense construction of stone and gleaming metallurgy formed a partial barricade against the sea's ravages. Honeycombed within, a dizzying network of chambers, galleries and laboratories were linked by interconnected passages. There, the *hiss* of steam and the *clank* of machinery forever rang out, in accompaniment to that cornerstone of life in New Rhye.

Industry.

From industry, the shining beacon of innovation.

The King of Rhye decreed that the Age of Harmony would also be an age of enlightenment. The darkness would be pushed back in more ways than one; the New Dawn would prove symbolic, as the peoples of Rhye forged a greater understanding of their world.

A greater mastery of it.

The Mer Folk inherited this mantra with enthusiasm. They saw it as an extension of their old culture, in which technology and advancement fused perfectly with the world around them. Creatures of the Seven Seas, they learned to harness the one commodity that swirled about them in limitless supply: the oceans themselves. Their ancient home, Artesia, grew as a testament to the science of hydraulics.

The Mer relished the task of replicating this feat in a new world. This gateway – and the small network of islands beyond – became a clear stage for the aquatic peoples to set their vision into motion. While the Mer Folk toiled at creating The Works, the undines established their craggy cathedrals, in places where bedrock rose above the waves.

Closer to the headland, the sea developed a turbulent chop. Whitecaps tossed the craft into a series of hops, spray exploding each time the hull smashed back against the surf. With a practised hand, Khashoggi wove his way amidst the increasing traffic of wind-powered vessels. Sailors, fishermen and day-trippers alike leaned over gunwales to gawk as he rocketed past.

As he neared the Bay's entrance, turbulent swell forced Khashoggi to steer to port, heading towards the centre of the strait. Giant breakers rolled to smash against the megalithic roots of The Works. Even a state-of-the-art vehicle, such as his own, could be obliterated upon the foot of the edifice, if collected by the roiling seas.

The soaring construction rose like a fortress above dizzying cliffs. Atop the wall of stone, a structure in steel alloy and glass windows faced west, towards the ocean. An intricate façade swarmed with the chittering, clattering forms of automatons; many hundreds of them, engaged in the task of cleaning residue from portholes, and larger observation windows.

Further still, billowing shafts of steam poured from slender stacks into the sky, to be ripped away on coastal breezes. The perpetual signs of industry: inevitable markers of an advancing civilisation.

Khashoggi gave an involuntary grimace. He had heard of Figaro the Ploughman, industrialist and pawn of the Black Queen; engineer of deathly machines. He knew what the ambition of Humankind could lead to. He only hoped that the steadying hands of the Mer Folk – and Torr Yosef – could steer progress away from a destructive replay of history.

A broad starboard turn took Khashoggi and his craft beyond the headland. In a few moments, the chop settled; open water grew calm once more, and he entered the sheltered Bay of Marnis.

On any given day, dozens of ships traversed the Bay, where rough conditions were rare. Today proved no different: with a predominance of azure sky and scant, white clouds, the usual array of craft had been set free from their moorings.

In the distance, directly ahead, the crowded promontory and vertiginous spire of Babel dominated the skyline. The Tower never failed to awe Khashoggi, who had seen and done much in his generous lifetime. Today though, his goal lay much nearer, just off the starboard prow: the Marina.

There, amidst a small flotilla of proud, seaworthy vessels, lay berthed his pride and joy – the jewel of the Bay.

The *Khonsu.*

He borrowed the name from that other world – the place where he found Ackley Fahrenheit. There, it related to an ancient deity, representing the moon. It also spoke of wandering and discovery. *The Traveller.* Aboard the *Khonsu,* Khashoggi had borne the King of Rhye from across the Seventh Sea. This phenomenal vessel made the one voyage so many others had failed – a journey across time and space.

At just over two hundred feet in length, with a twenty-four-foot beam, the *Khonsu* dwarfed all other ships, in or out of the water. Elegant lines described the shape of a cigar, with a pointed prow like an arrow. The hull, a deep-V below the surface, curved in lines of startling beauty above the waterline. A shell of ivory white shone like polished marble in the afternoon sun, embellished with exuberant geometric designs in gold. Only a narrow deck, and several rounded balconies, featured on an otherwise fully enclosed superstructure. Two sleek stacks arose, reminiscent of sawn-off shark fins, from the rear portion of the ship. From each of these, lazy white tendrils drifted skyward.

Khashoggi considered this beautiful behemoth his 'other mistress', and gave her a respectful nod as he approached. With practised skill, he steered his powered seacraft alongside.

On cue, a hidden panel hinged open – a hatch on the side of the *Khonsu's* hull. The portal it created yawned wide enough for the compact runabout craft to be drawn inside. Indeed, from within the portal emerged a mechanical device like a small crane, piloted by two kettle-shaped automatons.

'*Greetings, Captain!*' announced one, in its reedy voice.

'*Please keep arms and legs inside the vehicle,*' advised the other. The automatons busied themselves with a series of cranks and levers, whereby a giant grapple lowered towards the idling craft. With great proficiency, the grapple took hold of prefabricated attachment points, and lifted the much smaller vessel from the water.

Khashoggi had only to sit and watch, as the device hoisted him – sea water streaming from his dangling craft – towards the belly of the *Khonsu*.

'You're new,' said the Prophet, eyeing the pair of cuprous deckhands who helped him aboard. They pootled along behind as he strode, at a clip, through the dim passages of the cargo hold. Along the bulkhead, wall lamps brightened to reduce the blinding contrast with dazzling sunlight outside.

'Commissioned just this morning, sir,' the two replied in unison. 'Our tasks were embedded prior to our activation,' one continued. 'We are to be your personal assistants.'

'I don't require personal assistants,' snorted Khashoggi, 'unless you can pack a pipe and draw a hot bath without being asked.'

'Both objectives achieved, sir.'

The Prophet eyed them again, this time through narrowed lids.

'Torr Yosef imparts that you are an elder creature of flesh and blood, sir,' reported the first. 'Perhaps, with your increasing frailty, we may be of greater service.'

'The tin pot retains a sense of humour,' gritted Khashoggi, fists clenched as they swayed, a pair of brusque pendulums by his sides.

The trio climbed an iron stair and stepped through a utilitarian doorway. Beyond, a passageway of generous width revealed the true interior opulence of the Khonsu.

Polished timber boards returned a reassuring *thunk* beneath Balmoral boots and mechanical feet alike. Spotless white bulkheads featured stylish scrallin lamps at even intervals – the latest design, powered by stored sunlight gathered from the ship's exterior. Trim of finest chestnut and fittings of brushed steel, ornamented this main thoroughfare along the Khonsu's spine.

Numerous rooms branched from the passageway. This level contained offices and a library. To the left – the fore of the ship – a further stair rose to the Bridge. Aft lay Khashoggi's stateroom; a private sanctuary, appointed to his most discerning taste.

Khashoggi turned right, then spun back to the pair of automatons on his tail. 'A man needs no great assistance to bathe,' he declared. 'Find Torr Yosef. Tell him I am aboard. Presently, I will meet him on the Bridge; we shall have a demonstration of the Khonsu's latest upgrades.'

'*Aye, sir,*' the mechanical creatures replied, then made to scuttle away.

'Wait,' said the Prophet. Two burnished faces, with luminescent green eyes, turned back to him.

'How do I summon you? Do you have names?'

The pair gave a simultaneous bow; a quaint yet formal gesture. '*My name,*' said one, '*is QTW2771766.*'

The other stepped forward. '*My name is QNOTW2771—*'

'No, that won't do,' said Khashoggi, with a shake of his head. He tweaked his moustache, indulging in a moment of thought. *So many years, so many acquaintances.* Myriad faces passed as a blur in his mind.

'I have it. You,' he pointed, 'are Mack; you,' to the other, 'are Mandel.'

Mack and Mandel exchanged a look. Artificial eyelids clicked, in a shared blink.

'*As you wish, sir,*' they said together, then headed fore along the passage.

Khashoggi made for his stateroom, eager to refresh ... and then to learn of the *Khonsu's* prowess from Yosef.

The Prophet intended only a short soak, though even this was interrupted by a blast of telepathy, like a klaxon in his brain.

<KHASHOGGI: *a matter of great importance. The Bridge – as soon as you are able.*> The golem's tone suggested something unexpected.

Khashoggi did not bother reaching for the bone conduction headpiece, sitting on a low cherrywood table beside his bath. He leapt from the water, sloshing suds halfway across the room. In scant moments, he dried and dressed; a bespoke transformation in a finger-snap. He swept along the passageway, threading through a jostle of busy automatons. Many were headed the same direction as he; were they capable of emotion, he might have seen excitement in their frenzied movements.

He bounded up the stairs two at a time, arriving on the Bridge with a flourish.

'Well then!' he cried, 'what is this commotion?'

<Captain on the Bridge.> At the golem's announcement, a menagerie of metal creatures – some two dozen of them – arranged themselves in perfect rows, standing at attention.

A vast port, crystal clear, replaced the entire forward bulkhead; through it, the prow of the *Khonsu* pointed forth as a giant wedge. Before the port stood a sturdy instrument panel, covered in dials, switches and neat labels for all. The helm, a vast wheel half buried in the deck, occupied the centre of the room.

The giant figure of Torr Yosef hunched by the instrument panel, unable to stand upright beneath the ceiling of decorated panels. He shuffled to face Khashoggi.

<You might like to step outside, sir>, said the golem. *<The sight that awaits is most ... unanticipated.>*

A side door, and a spiral stair, lead to a broad Observation Deck, perched atop the Bridge. Khashoggi followed the lumbering creature to this new vantage, where a light afternoon breeze ruffled his beard, and brought the tang of marine salt to his nostrils. Khashoggi took to an ornate railing at the fore of the deck, absorbing all he saw.

Adatar's golden rays illuminated a bank of cumulus clouds, which scudded across an otherwise pristine sky. Flocks of seabirds circled, swooped and dived upon the waves, questing for school fish.

Beside the *Khonsu*, on the Marina, hundreds gathered: humans, Mer, Fae, sylphs and Adept. Even the occasional Wilden creature had ventured to the spot, joining an amassing crowd. The dull roar of many voices, chattering away, wafted up to the Observation

Deck. One and all, the denizens of Babylon craned their necks, nudging one another and pointing to the sky.

Shielding his gaze from the sun, Khashoggi peered heavenwards ... and caught his breath.

In the middle distance, looming larger by the minute, flew an astonishing aircraft. An immense array of propellers and fins directed the flying machine from the rear, while a great air bladder and stubby wings kept it aloft. A passenger compartment, shaped like a galleon, hung suspended from the bladder; the nose of it featured a conical window. From the craft came the distant whir of engines.

There could be no mistake: as the flying craft drew nearer, it lost altitude. In keeping its bearing, it would drift over the Bay of Marnis towards the promontory ... and the Tower of Babel.

<It arrives from out of the west>, observed Yosef. Perhaps the lofty peaks of the Leviathan had shielded its approach.

Khashoggi did not respond.

Yosef turned to face him. <I've never seen anything like it ... have you?>

Still, the Prophet said nothing. The strange contrivance swelled in the sky, now almost directly overhead.

Khashoggi stared up at it. Deep within his whiskers, his lips drew into a taut line.

CHAPTER SIX
....

SECRET HARMONIES

From the Highlands, where bounteous soil put forth everything from barley to corn to pumpkin vines, came Crispin Crabapple, Custodian of the Northern Provinces. The former Nurtenean's convoy, ten large wagons, were hauled by draught automatons. Every wagon brimmed with lush produce: swollen gourds, orchard-fresh citrus and the plumpest drinking grapes. He arrived two days early, in time for the regular Babylonian Bazaar — half of the produce to be hawked there, the other half a gift for the King.

From the Southern Provinces came the three Governors: Grigory Sharles, Vladimir Flaye and Lucius Rintaaken. These esteemed men brought the finest textiles, spices and minerals the land could offer. Each Governor rode a fine thoroughbred, flanked by a noble entourage, provincial pennants snapping in the breeze.

From the woodlands of Ardendale, where pheasants nested in mottled glades and wild hares ran in abundance, came Erinfleur the Elemental, and her coven of Neophytes. They bore a haul of succulent game meat (kept fresh with a simple enchantment), as well as smoked fish from the clear waters of the Bottomless Lake.

A contingent of Fae and dryads – led by Harold, Dragon's Bane and Horn Wielder – made the journey from the forests of Arboria. They brought the gift of story and song; raconteurs rehearsed in the finest tales from the Repositree, and jongleurs from amongst the tribes of satyrs. Harold came cradling his Horn, said to now yield the boldest sound an instrument ever produced.

Over a period of days, these travellers arrived in the great city of Babylon, invited guests of the King of Rhye. Caravans of well-wishers followed them, streaming from near and far into the land's premier city. Steady traffic filled the arterials – the Babylon Road from the south, the pass through the Giltenan Ridge from the Highlands, even the forested byways of Eleuthervale – as countless creatures great and small flocked to celebrate the milestone of New Rhye.

Mustapha's trusted advisors, 'Wagoner' Will and the tireless Lance Sevenson, headed the Diplomatic Taskforce for the event. Amongst their responsibilities, the accommodation of special guests and their entourages, within the Tower of Babel. The two humans had moved through dozens of suites, allocating every available chamber, den and room to a visiting outlander.

Nobody had accounted for the arrival of the airship.

Mustapha wandered, as he so often did, in the Garden of Remembrance. Will found the seraph there, pacing along a broad terrace, over which spilled an enormous fringe of ferns. To walk beneath the verdant growth gave the sensation of entering the tube of a giant, green wave. The run of ferns extended beyond the King's Garden, around the skirts of the entire building, hanging over the heads of passers-by, outside the Tower's perimeter.

Mustapha waded amongst pressured thoughts. He paced with taut movements, a strained expression on his face. His wings sat high upon his shoulders, partly unfurled. The great well of his confidence threatened to run dry; the vitality with which he emerged from the fires of coronation seemed to resonate more faintly with each passing day. He knew not why.

He longed to hear from the Pantheon.

'Mustapha, my love,' called Will, catching up with him. 'You must know what has transpired.'

'I do know, yes. I hear it ... I feel it.' He turned a haunted face to Will as the human fell into step beside him; a visage darkened by dense, uncustomary stubble.

Will spoke. 'Did you know that Khashoggi and Yosef had progressed to developing a flying machine? I mean, I presume—'

'They did not contrive that machine.'

'No? It has all of their hallmarks. The intricate gearing systems, overwrought mechanics and a bombastic shape ... all slung beneath an enormous balloon. I thought they must surely have had a breakthrough. Something more to celebrate at the Ball. You think it has come from the provinces, instead? Who, then?'

Now Mustapha did stop, summoning the strength to put voice to his trepidation. 'This contrivance has not arrived from the outer provinces of Rhye, Will. It has flown from out of the west.'

Will stumbled in his astonishment. 'How—? Did the Windows show you?'

'A Window opened just this morning, yes. It showed me the ship, the sky and the empty sea beyond. But I already knew, Will. A sound has haunted me, for days now. Drawing nearer.'

'The bells? I've often heard you speak of those.'

The seraph shook his head. 'No, no, no. This is the sound of drums. An awful, rhythmic, throbbing sound. I haven't lied to you about recent headaches; the tumult comes nearer. It seems to have reached a crescendo with the arrival of this airship. I don't know how the two are linked, but I'm certain of it.'

'I see,' replied Will. 'Yet – you had an aura of drums some weeks ago. You haven't been yourself since. Is this one and the same?'

'It is ... yet different, as well.' Mustapha frowned, his mind going to that deep cavern below the earth. 'It came to me when I first found the staircase leading to the Oddity. Then, it gnawed at me, but it was more ... unsettling, I suppose. Now, it's nauseating.'

'So ... you think there is a connection, between the Oddity and this airship?'

Mustapha stared back along the terrace, without offering a reply. A shimmer in the air caught his attention, like a shrug of the atmosphere. A sudden finality.

'The ship alights ...?'

'Torr Yosef has a crew of his mechanical offspring preparing to anchor the craft to the Balcony as we speak,' said Will with a confirmatory nod. 'Leith and Timbrad scrambled – with honourable haste – to assemble a welcoming party, of sorts. All are in place ... awaiting only the attendance of the King.'

Mustapha had already begun moving back along the terrace, at an ethereal pace that Will struggled to match. 'Then we must greet our guests ... invited, or otherwise,' he said.

The pilot of the strange, sky-going contrivance could have chosen no finer a place for a sensational arrival.

A broad turn, where the Corniche angled up a grand stair to the avenue of gingko trees, created a wide platform of marble flagstones, known as the Balcony. Only the Tower itself commanded a greater view of the Bay of Marnis.

As the airship crossed the Bay, crowds surged through the streets of Babylon, worrisome eyes turned skyward, anticipating the place at which the ship touched down. While they were used to the sight of winged Fae, sylphs and insect folk taking to the sky, this vision came altogether unfamiliar to them.

With sylphic efficiency, Minister for Security Leith Lourden dispatched a contingent of Officers — numerous races among them — to clear the Balcony and create an organised arrival berth. Likewise, Archimage Timbrad detailed a cordon of Mages, to secure the on-ramp leading from the Corniche. Within a short time, a crush of onlookers crowded the roadway for a quarter-mile, craning for a glimpse.

A broad, stone balustrade hemmed them in, saving hundreds of citizens from a fatal fall: beyond the Corniche, and the Balcony itself, the promontory dropped away in a sheer precipice. The glittering waters of the Bay lay one hundred feet below.

An array of automatons, directed by Yosef, stood in readiness upon the Balcony. Many wielded coils of rope or cable, fitted with grapple hooks. Behind them, a greeting party from Babel waited in formal rows: a contingent from each department of the Ministry. They assembled in two groups, with an aisle between.

At the head of the stair, accompanied by Will and Lance Sevenson, stood the King of Rhye.

The airship cut its engines, looming in vast silence overhead. Testament to the pilot's skill, it drifted within a few yards of the Balcony. Short expulsions of compressed steam, from outlets positioned about the hull, kept the ship stable in the air.

The golem's voice clanked in Mustapha's mind. <Do you see them from upon the stair, my Lord? Figures move within.> Mustapha eyed the large, forward port — and a series of flanking ports — and found Yosef to be correct.

At that moment, with an explosive whir, several cables shot from the belly of the ship. Each gave a sharp *fwip-crack*, as the ship's own deployed grapples fastened to the Balcony. The row of automatons, waiting nearby, leapt back in unison.

To the grating sound of rachets, the airship crept close enough for an ornate door in the nearside hull to open, creating a wide gangway between the ship and the flagstones.

The visitors had arrived.

Visitors from the west.

For some moments, silence reigned. Even amongst the gathered denizens of Babylon, a collective hush fell.

Mustapha did not know silence. The rumbling rhythm of drums persisted, an ominous roll that both beckoned and warned. Still, his stately face displayed the calm confidence of monarchy. *All calm on the outside, all chaos underneath. Just like a duck.* Against an inner tide of uncertainty, he descended the stairs to the platform below. The two humans followed.

TOM ... TOM ... TOM ... TOM ...

At last, four figures appeared at the door atop the gangway. As they emerged from the belly of the airship, the drumming that plagued Mustapha now came to every creature present, with ears to hear.

TOM ... TOM ... TOM ... TOM ...

Four individuals, human in appearance, marched a formal procession down onto the balcony. White robes, fine but simple, adorned their bodies. Loose sleeves hung from pallid forearms, while a simple cord cinched each figure's robe about the waist. Wide-necked cowls rested upon shoulders, revealing the newcomers' faces.

Three men and one woman. Their faces maintained a polite neutrality, their eyes roving the assembly with a manner neither warm nor hostile.

Each bore a drum slung about their torso, and struck a beat in time with their solemn footfalls.

TOM ... TOM ... TOM ... TOM ...

Mustapha approached them, down the aisle.

Further figures spilled from the craft; sixteen more, all clad in similar white attire. With such robes, they could have passed for a distant branch of the Adept. The true Adept amongst the assembly stirred, at the sight of so many wearing the privileged shade of White.

Six amongst them, not carrying drums, shared the burden of a large package between them. A large oblong box of considerable heft, given the way in which its bearers moved, stooping and shrugging taut shoulders as they marched.

In the midst of the procession walked a woman who, by virtue of her grander garments, distinguished herself from the rest. Fine hem-work lined the sleeve and foot of her robe, while her belt, a broad sash, carried an array of letterings. Her aged face conveyed wisdom, couched in serenity.

The drummers ceased their march midway along the aisle. They stood two to a side, creating a small passage of their own, and dropped their arms to their sides. The others behind them fanned out, making way for the central figure to come forward. Those bearing the giant box set it gently upon the ground.

Mustapha breathed an internal sigh of relief. A brief respite from the psychic clangour. It allowed him to study the woman before him more closely.

Her manner blended elegance and humility, touched by the strain of power. She wore her age gracefully, for a human. Without doubt, she led this baffling troupe of sky-farers, though in what capacity, he could not be certain. Something in her eyes told Mustapha that she answered to another.

The woman fell to a knee before him, then promptly regained her feet. A strange bow, unlike any used by the humans of Rhye. She spoke then, in a voice that carried to the bystanders upon the platform.

'We honour you, King Mustapha of Rhye. May you know

boundless prosperity in your time, and may this new land thrive in harmony by your hand.

'My name is Lady Mercy. I present to you my company: Acolytes of the Order of the Unhomed. In our realm, I am known as High Priestess of the Order.

'We come bearing this gift of our people, in the hope that it will unite us, across distance, race and creed. We also carry the hope of celebrating this historic moment in the Ages of the land – the loftiest of occasions since the time of the Winged One.'

Though she spoke with clarity, Lady Mercy's voice carried a slight waver. Perhaps the timbre of age. Perhaps she felt a moment of nerves, in the presence of the seraphic King.

Somehow Mustapha managed to navigate good grace, lordliness and warmth. It nonetheless presented a challenge – an alarming air hung about the entire scene. *Winged One? Who is that?* He felt as if he were meant to know.

He executed a florid bow. 'I bid you welcome, good Lady. You and your Acolytes shall find generous greetings and fair custom amongst the people of Babylon. Excitement stirs the populace, for it is the eve of our tenth anniversary in a land reborn; a new world under the light of Adatar.

'Already, you give knowledge of this momentous occasion. I pray, be among us, for tomorrow night this kingdom shall come alive with dancing and song.'

As Mustapha waffled niceties, his mind raced. He wanted, more than anything, to unleash a torrent of questions on the High Priestess. He knew it lay within his power to do so. Surely, wherever the Order called home fell beneath his jurisdiction? *Why do I not know of it?*

He had also learned much of diplomacy, from the likes of Lance Sevenson, former Advisor to Lord Rogar Giltenan. He corralled his questions, but they gnawed at him still. These delegates from the Order of the Unhomed – *what meaning does such a name conceal?* – already demonstrated a civilised command over technology. In all of Rhye, the winged creatures ruled the air. None had yet to create a machine capable of flight, though Khashoggi had spoken of achieving it for many a year. He wondered what other surprises lay behind the Order's sensational entrance.

Their gift had an innocuous shape, concealed within its haulage crate. Perhaps it would yield more clues as to the outlanders' intent.

In his peripheral vision, Mustapha could see the massive form of Torr Yosef. The golem had turned from the assembly and studied the moored airship. For once, Mustapha hoped for some telepathic interjection, though for now, Yosef remained silent.

The seraph expected Khashoggi to also be drawn to the incredible flying machine. For the time being, the Prophet could not readily be seen amongst the crowd.

This mental journey passed in the blink of an eye. Without missing a beat, Mustapha returned to the High Priestess, Lady Mercy. With a paltry smile, she was accepting his offer of hospitality and merriment.

'Wonderful!' declared the seraph. 'My Chief Advisor, Lance Sevenson, will arrange for porters to escort you and your Acolytes to your lodgings. May you find Babel a comfortable home at this festive time.' His words were met with a voluminous cheer from the bystanders within earshot. During the roar, he drew nearer to Lady Mercy, a sharpness in his eye. 'Perhaps this evening, you would grace me with your presence for dinner. I would hear of your travels, and the place you call home.'

'An honour, Your Majesty.' The waver remained, though the woman appeared relieved, as if their encounter had been some kind of test.

The King of Rhye often dined late. Chefs and servery staff found themselves scouring the pantries and sculleries of the Residential Parlour at all hours. The culinary requests were rarely indulgent, though the seraph valued a touch of luxury.

For the audience, Mustapha chose a handsome drawing room, set apart from his private suites. He harboured no intention of displaying the upmost Pavilion to his unexpected guests – that sanctum in which revolved his Windows upon the world. This room, by contrast, lacked extravagance, though the elegant furnishings encouraged a certain decorum.

Upon a low-set table were laid several platters and trays. Portions of roast duck, rarebit melted to perfection and fruits poached in spiced syrup appeared, borne by discreet Fae wait staff. Next came fine drinking crystal and a decanter of rich, red wine, courtesy of Crispin Crabapple's premier parcel of grapes.

Setting the platters and accompaniments on the table, the green-clad Fae vanished beyond a plain oaken door.

Mustapha offered a congenial gesture towards the repast, encouraging his guest to avail herself.

Lady Mercy did not attend the audience alone. A pair of dour companions – Acolytes of the Order – sat one to either side of her. In curt tones, they introduced themselves as Brother Michael and Brother Aaron. The seraph wore a quiet smile as they heaped plates with food, glaring at their surrounds from beneath heavy brows. Something in the way they shot dark glances back and forth suggested that they reserved some special ire for one another.

Anticipating the High Priestess's escorts, Mustapha had invited friends of his own to dinner. Minister for Security, Leith Lourden, chewed on a roast duck leg, managing to make the indelicate task appear elegant. Archimage Timbrad brought a welcoming warmth, even playing down his own ceremonial use of white robes for the occasion. The ochre stole he wore, over a simple white tunic, only enhanced his swarthy handsomeness.

At first, small talk burbled in the quiet space. As each ate their fill, the two parties exchanged banal pleasantries. Lady Mercy commented on the grandeur of Babel. In return, Mustapha described the surprise and delight of the Order's arrival. Friendly sharks, circling the purpose for their meeting.

At length, the seraph took the initiative, with a good-natured wave of his wine crystal. 'Your aircraft, Lady Mercy — it's splendiferous. Can you tell us about it?'

The High Priestess gave a stilted laugh. 'Yes, well ... I'm in no way an engineer, but she is certainly an impressive ship.'

'*She*? The aircraft is female?'

'Oh no, Your Majesty — a figure of speech, only. My people have a habit of giving gender to inanimate objects ... especially machines.

'Where we are from, nobody has yet managed to grow wings.' With a subtle nod, she acknowledged both Mustapha and Leith. 'The craft is invention born of necessity. The journey to Babylon — the tenth anniversary of New Rhye — marks her maiden voyage.'

Leith sipped her wine. 'And was it ... a long voyage?'

Again, the mild chuckle. Lady Mercy licked her lips. 'It was but a simple journey. We count it not in days, my dear. A journey consists not of time, but of a home, a destination and the adventure in between. As a wise man once asked me, "What is time, but the space between——"'

'Forgive me, my Lady,' interjected Brother Aaron, though his stern glance sought no such pardon. 'Your Majesty — Minister Lourden — time is, in fact, of fundamental importance. By her good humour, the High Priestess downplays the reverence we offer to Onik, alongside the Creator, at the head of the Pantheon.' Brother

Michael nodded, as if this was the one thing on which the pair could agree.

Lady Mercy gave a dismissive titter and a wave of her hand.

Mustapha blinked. He had not deemed the oafish Acolyte capable of two individual sentences, let alone stringing them together.

Brother Aaron continued. 'We anticipated a voyage of six days and eleven hours, Your Majesty, though we were obliged to break and renew our supplies with an interceding island community.'

Mustapha fought to keep the perplexed creases from his face. Were these people unaware of his covenant with Marnis? Had he not forged the rebirth of Rhye, from his own imaginings? What did the human, Ackley Fahrenheit, know of these island nations and far-flung civilisations? He resolved to confer with Fahrenheit at the earliest opportunity.

Surely, he will be present at the Ball.

Well ... hopefully.

Mustapha searched his brain for the right question, sliding his plate aside and leaning forward. 'Talk to me about the Order, Lady Mercy. The Order of the Unhomed.'

The Lady nodded. She flicked her eyes left and right, seeming to challenge either Acolyte to interrupt her again. She downed the last of her wine; Timbrad smoothly refilled her crystal.

'The Order's mission is to address a long-unmet need in the land,' she began. 'To this end, it has existed for nigh on one thousand years.'

A soft gasp burst from Leith Lourden. Timbrad offered a low whistle.

Mustapha maintained a vice-like focus. 'An unmet need ... unhomed creatures?'

'Creatures, great and small,' confirmed the High Priestess, with a pious nod. As she continued, the Acolytes shifted in their seats, meals forgotten. To them, this subject resonated, as something much more than mere conversation. This lore served as their gospel.

'Throughout every Age of Rhye, conflict has ravaged the land. The earth itself has borne the scars of offensive magic. The scorch marks of conflagration. The God of War saw fit to even level a mountain in the name of vengeance.

'Through your valour, the land itself is born anew. But there are other scars; memories of conflict too often overlooked, which persist as a stain upon the legacy of our rulers. As the One King, this stained legacy now rests with you … Your Majesty.

'I speak of those who are dislodged by the act of war. Those whose homes were destroyed or overrun; who found themselves ragged and destitute, in Rhye's darkest hours. Others have had their homes stolen, usurped by higher powers. Relentless greed leaves them at the whimsy of the wilderness. Alas, the wilderness knows little of mercy. The Unhomed are left to die, or wander indefinitely, ill-equipped for the task of rebuilding, and too numerous to be readily sheltered within the wracked settlements around them.'

Leith jolted, her face haunted by memory. 'Two-Way Mirror Mountain …'

Another sage nod. 'You understand, Minister Lourden. Perhaps you recall a vast sea of innocent souls, cowering on the edge of battle, praying for their lives. You recollect the filth. The starvation. The helplessness.' She turned back to Mustapha. 'After the battle, and the victory, and the New Dawn … those souls had no place to call their own, Your Majesty. Therein lies the chief mission of the Order: to send forth our Acolytes, to see the innocent accounted for.'

Mustapha frowned, his face growing ashen. 'Did I not provide for every soul …?'

'Aye, you did provide,' answered Lady Mercy. 'But these are *the Unhomed*. Having slipped between the cracks of time, they find their own place, for there is no home for them in Babylon.'

The King of Rhye sank back in his seat, mouth open.

Archimage Timbrad stepped into the breach. 'And so, your Order has undertaken this – this ministry to displaced beings – under the noses of Rhye's Sovereignty, for one thousand years.' His words came as a confirmatory statement, rather than a question. His customary humour had been replaced by a visage of stone.

'Indeed,' replied Brother Aaron.

'One thousand years,' said Brother Michael.

'Hmm.' The Adept said nothing more.

Mustapha regained himself. 'I grasp your mission, High Priestess. It seems at once both humble and virtuous. But there are details that still baffle me.

'Where have these Unhomed been for much of the past millennium? Do they remain the "Unhomed" if they have found a new society, fostered by the Order? And where are they now, that they dwell beyond my knowledge of Rhye?'

The benign smile remained plastered to Lady Mercy's face, though her eyes danced a jig. First, they slid across to Archimage Timbrad; then to her peripheries, where her gargoyle Acolytes crouched.

When she spoke, she sounded almost relieved, as if she had been handed a kind of opportunity. 'The answer, Your Majesty, is at the crux of our journey here. We come not only to celebrate a momentous occasion, but also to ask for your help.'

This admission eased the tension of the room by a shade, though Brothers Aaron and Michael continued to bristle. If anything, they leaned further towards their High Priestess.

'Our ancient forebears founded the Order to aid the First of the

Unhomed. Only twenty in number, they represented the survivors not of war or plague, but of something far stranger. They named themselves wanderers, from a place so far away, it may well have been another world. With no way back the way they came – and conflict arising amongst themselves – those who found the wanderers saw that they desperately needed respite. In the forest wolds of Nurtenan, a band of humble northern folk gave rise to the Order, and anointed the first High Priest from among their number.'

All were now leaning in around the table, lest they fail to catch Lady Mercy's words. Her Acolytes leaned in, too, though this tale already lay at the source of their faith. With intent eyes, they watched her.

'It is as I have said,' she continued. 'With the passage of years, refugees of every kind found their way to the Order of the Unhomed. I suspect many Sovereigns did indeed know of our work; though finding it just, they interfered not in our mission.

'Now, at the last, we encountered the forgotten souls of Rhye's greatest crisis: the innocents, who found themselves caught between chaos and miracles. Death and life. For those who live still, a safe haven was needed. A place that has stayed beyond your percipience, O King … until now.'

Mustapha, now deep in contemplation, murmured his question. 'What would you have me do?'

Lady Mercy's voice still carried the strange, wavering quality. A full minute elapsed before she spoke again; when she did, the waver persisted, buffeting her words like a breeze through autumnal boughs. 'Recognise them,' she said. 'If you cannot create for them a home, return them to the one they knew before. Your Majesty, the work of the Order reaches its culmination. For true Harmony to exist in this Age, restitution must be brought for the Unhomed.'

For the second time, Mustapha dropped back in his seat. Now, the tension truly did lift: even the Acolytes seemed at peace. Brother Michael returned to his wine. Several wait staff materialised to clear empty platters away.

The pinnacle of Lady Mercy's narrative left her shrunken and pallid, even beneath the parlour's warming ambient light. Mustapha determined that she had felt a great weight upon her, and little wonder – the request she made took root in a time long before any of them were born. The magnitude of this meeting now sat with him.

He mustered a tone of clarity; of authority, and reassurance. 'I have heard you, Lady Mercy. From the moment of Rhye's rebirth, I have known the gravity of the task before me. This – this, I did not anticipate. But I will consider the plight of the Unhomed. I must deliberate, and confer with my Ministers. The response you deserve shall be forthcoming.

'For now, I must insist: it is a time for celebration. Tomorrow, we join as one people. Let us rejoice, that you are here to witness it.'

In the aftermath of his pronouncement, solemnity mingled once again with a more convivial mood. Mustapha sang, Leith offered stories, and the Acolytes spoke of their home – a place not unlike Babylon, yet still a place of inevitable contrast. Eventually, yawns and weary words – feigned or otherwise – saw the audience disband in the small hours.

Mustapha did not retire to his bedchamber.

His bones ached with both tiredness and duty. Though the comfort of cotton sheets and eiderdown awaited him, he instead stopped in a dim, deserted passage behind the kitchen. His energy drew both Timbrad and Leith Lourden to his side. Will, recognising the tension on the seraph's face, joined them.

'That's enough excitement for one day,' Mustapha declared. He kept his voice so low that the others had to close in, almost to the point of contact.

'The corridor is secure,' said Leith, though she also spoke in a whisper. 'What do you make of it all, my Lord?'

'Honestly? I have no idea. We are presented with a genuine plea, yet I cannot shake the sense of something brewing beneath the surface. We have not heard the full story. What do you think, Archimage?'

The Adept had not shown good humour since his exchange with the Acolytes. Here in the passage, by the muffled glow of scrallin, shadows clung like condemnation to his chiselled features.

'You are right to be concerned,' he said. 'A distinct sense of wrongness shrouds our new ... acquaintances. Fear emanates from Lady Mercy. I do not understand it. Still, there is something more.'

'What more?' asked Will.

'She is goaded,' replied Timbrad, 'or something similar. She wants to convey a message, but cannot. A forbidding force restrains her words.'

Mustapha's lips grew taut. Behind the darkened growth of his neglected facial hair, his face pinched. 'I know this one. A hex of silence. She is kept from revealing some truth, on pain of death. Do we suspect the Acolytes are something other than they appear?'

'My senses are not augmented by any mystic power,' said Leith, 'but even I grew suspicious of them.'

To Mustapha's surprise, Timbrad shook his head. 'No ... this is something different. Almost unfathomable. I am awed to even contemplate it, my Lord. But I sense the hand of the divine, in this.'

Mustapha's brow furrowed. Leith made a sylphic sign of piety, her eyes wide in the semi-darkness.

'The Pantheon?' asked Will.

Now Timbrad nodded. 'The High Priestess acts at the behest of a power beyond any of us.'

'The Ball?' questioned Leith. 'Will there be danger? Shall we call off the event?'

Mustapha waved her concerns aside, his resolve firm. 'No. We must not show that we suspect sinister play. At any rate, if a God or Goddess is involved, then it is likely our fates are already determined.' His thoughts flashed to the small box, within which resided two tiny, black grains of sand.

If not either of you two, then whom?

The sylph shuddered. 'The Ball proceeds?'

'The Ball proceeds,' confirmed Mustapha. 'The show must go on.'

<h2>CHAPTER SEVEN</h2>

MUSIC & LOVE EVERYWHERE

Leith allowed the stream of cool water to gently pummel her upturned face. It found its way, in soothing runnels, over her shoulders and down her body. A cascade of droplets drummed on the stones beneath her feet. She hoped it could wash away the nervous tension in her muscles; or at the very least, quell the buzzing swarm of thoughts, like hornets in her mind.

Somehow, she did manage to keep her wings dry, having just spent a precious hour preening them. *An hour I could have spent triple-checking everything, for the fifth time.*

She reached for the lever, shutting off the flow of water. Wrapping herself in a ready towel, she moved from the washroom to her bedchamber.

A squalid mess of discarded tunics, leggings, belts and boots, strewn across the polished floor and every available surface, met her in the main room. On any given day, the space would be a haven of perfect order. Today, the sylph ignored the mayhem, staring at one item, laid with deliberate care upon the bed.

The ballgown.

She wrinkled her nose at the alien garment. Never in her life had she faced the prospect of wearing one of these. Not in Babylon, nor in Via … and certainly not in Wintergard.

The swarm of hornets continued to buzz, as she dried herself.

Twenty-two thoroughfares, in or out of the city. Twenty-three, if I include the Balcony, which now seems to double as an aerial landing platform. Sentries to welcome and guard at each: sylphs for the high roads; Mer for the harbour and grottoes; humans, Fae and Warlocks for everywhere in between.

Her towel fell to the floor.

Nobody in or out of Below for the next seventy-three hours. The Wilden Watch are covering that duty. Nobody within three vertical shafts of the Oddity.

She shimmied into her undergarments.

Recruitment of extra patrol staff for Babel went surprisingly well. I must thank Meadow for identifying so many able-bodied volunteers … who would have thought the bars and slums around town could yield so many dutiful souls, and not a drunkard amongst them? That butterfly gave an astonishing account of himself. A butterfly! So diligent. What a find.

Leith stepped into the gown, drawing it up until she could slip the halter strap over her head. At the back, her gown plunged to the base of her spine, leaving her skin bare, wings tucked against her body.

As for Mustapha – His Majesty – he has kept himself out of the way – scarce, I mean – since this morning. Will says he needed time to prepare … no, "beautify" himself. Honestly, he's handsome enough already. He and Will make such a striking couple.

Ah … couples.

A hook here, a fasten there, and the ballgown hugged Leith's form like a winter glove. She slipped her feet into elegant, heeled boots, all but obscured by the glittering hem of her gown. A few paces to one side, and she stood beside a full-length mirror: a gift from Mustapha, who lamented that she hitherto had no way to appreciate the beauty of her own self.

A mirror is the very last thing I wanted. Oh, well ... at least I can ensure I look respectable in a ballgown.

The bodice clung to her athletic torso, accentuating her lean angles in a sleeve the gentle pink of dusk. Halter straps lead to a neckline that dived between her breasts. Upon her hips sat a generous ruffle, beneath which a sweeping skirt fell in a grand silhouette, right to the floor. Towards the hemline, the colour deepened, from pale dusk to deepest magenta. Twinkling stars bejewelled the bodice and skirt, with a map of constellations. Leith knew that Mustapha had created her gown; she wondered at his inspirations. He seemed to know her measurements with precision.

The sylph stared into the mirror, and saw only one thing: the vacant space beside her.

I am six kinds of idiot.

What possessed me to ask Trixel for a dance? She doesn't dance. She doesn't do anything of the sort. She lives her life alone, managing the land's conservation, and she loves it. She's got no time for a doe-eyed sylph. Now I have to face her at the Ball. What a calamity! I will be the first sylph in history to survive the fields of battle, only to die of shame instead.

Leith gave her wings a furious ruffle. It helped to dispel a modicum of her frustration. It also served, in a flurried instant, to dry her platinum tresses — a talent all long-haired sylphs possessed, and many long-haired humans envied.

She clenched her teeth, fixing a delicate band around her wrist, and an ornate clasp about each pointed ear.

Time to face the music.

At the soaring peak of Babel, the King's Pavilion sat, a crown of petal-shaped facings and gilt-edged arches. Beneath it, the Residential Parlour formed the collar of the great spire. Within the Tower itself, a grand, spiralling passage connected floor upon floor of sitting rooms, treasuries, armouries, vaults, libraries, chambers, bathing rooms, kitchens and dens, for all manner of staff and visiting guests. Towards the very base, just above the wild vinery and ferns of the Hanging Garden, a grand ballroom consumed almost an entire lower floor.

Leith surveyed the cavernous hall from near the foot of an ostentatious stair, which poured onto the parquetry from the mezzanine level above. A vast, polished floor gleamed beneath a trio of chandeliers, dripping with scrallin. The last shafts of luminous sunset also spilled into the room, from an outer wall consisting almost entirely of towering windows. A fine iron framework laced through each floor-to-ceiling portal, creating giant jigsaws of soft-hued panes.

Scrallin-light, and the fading rays of Adatar, fell on a series of imposing statues, overseeing the crowd of guests from stone plinths set around the room. Eleven statues in all, each a minor shrine to a member of the Pantheon – the Sun, the Moon and all their children. Well, almost all: Anuvin and Valendyne were excluded. The King of Rhye saw no place for them, in this haven of celebration.

The splendour of the room did not register for Leith, who studied the mingling dignitaries, notables and other visitors from across the land. Hundreds of creatures of all kinds wandered and chatted, a microcosm of life in Babylon. Fairies greeted humans, undines embraced goblins, pixies joked and sylphs laughed their silvery laugh – all bedecked in their evening finery. The Adept seemed to drift and cluster without aim, having struggled more than most to integrate within the new society.

White-clad Acolytes of the Order also appeared at loose ends. Many others buzzed about them, attempting to create a welcoming vibe; still, the Acolytes clumped in stolid groups, most of them casting a wary eye from upon the mezzanine. Lady Mercy, her face nearly as white as her attire, stood by Torr Yosef, as if to use the golem as a shield against her own kind.

Amidst the crowd threaded a small army of service automatons. These kept glasses brimming with punch, nectar or drowseberry wine; others hefted kegs of lager, filling thirsty mugs without the spill of a single drop.

Leith's ears twitched. The air, suffused with the hubbub of polite revelry, lacked a certain something.

I wonder where those—

'Hey! Look who I've found!'

A jovial cry cut through the general clamour, and a trio of pixies burst from the crowd to Leith's left. In their midst came Meadow, cloaked in a lavish mantle shot through with reds, yellows, blues and greens, his blond hair coiffed to a mischievous point at the back. Each arm he had slung about the neck and shoulders of a fellow pixie. On one side Dique, wearing his finest silver-grey dinner suit; on the other, Dique's rosy-cheeked wife, Roni. Roni's gown, the yellow of melting butter, featured blooming garlands of sunflowers and poppies.

'At least you're putting the "fashionable" into "fashionably late"!' offered Leith, with a relieved grin.

'Tuning the Drum takes time, you know!' retorted Meadow.

'Actually, he spent most of the time doing his hair,' said Dique, in a stage-whisper. Dique clung tight to his treasured Zither. The instrument, refurbished with care, glinted beneath the scrallin-light.

'We had to organise great-aunt Myrtle to babysit all the kids,' explained Roni. 'Myrtle doesn't like being organised in a rush.'

111

Leith craned her neck, eyes darting over the crowd. 'Harold is already here,' she said, pointing to the stage. 'He's been fiddling about up there for hours already.'

Meadow scoffed. 'I don't know why he bothers. The Horn is always ready to go!'

'You two should be ready to go, too – hurry up!'

The pixies threw mock salutes to Leith. As Meadow dragged them away towards the stage, Roni called over her shoulder. 'You look beautiful, Leith. Enjoy the Ball!' With a squeak, she disappeared in the crowd.

The sylph gave no reply. During the exchange, her roving eyes had picked out a vision in midnight black, topped with lush, forest green.

Trixel Tate meandered through the maze of guests, stopping on occasion to offer a word or a smile. Her gown, a tight bodice with sleek-lined skirts, swathed her in a style befitting a warrior maiden. She wore not the antlered crown, but a stylised headpiece with swept-back prongs, containing the wild fronds of her hair.

A wave of heat coursed through Leith's face, and she turned away. All of a sudden, the room contained so many meaningful duties.

Evening fell. The last burnished rays of sunset were replaced in full by the ambient light of chandeliers. As night descended, strains of music began to drift through the room. For a moment, voices quelled; gasps of pleasure, and murmurs of 'It's them!' greeted the sound of Zither, Horn and Drum.

A multitude of faces turned to greet the opening refrain from Harold, Dique and Meadow. In a tide of shuffling bodies, the eaters and drinkers flocked to the edges of the floor, making way for those who would dance. No instruction had been given; all understood the power of the band's thrall. Soon, the introductory grandeur gave way to a merry pomp. The night's gaiety took full swing.

In a far corner, by a table laden with delicacies, Leith spied three figures who did not dance ... or socialise, or make any attempt at frivolity whatsoever.

Well, I'll be...

On instinct, the sylph left her post, gaze locked on the trio making a beeline for the refreshment table by which they huddled. In the meantime, dozens of guests had swarmed the dance floor, cutting off her direct route. She found herself swept amidst the waltzing couples.

Leith weaved and threaded her way through the joyous tangle, with many a 'Sorry!' and 'Beg pardon!' Still, despite her best efforts, she found herself jostled into several partner swaps, and fending off several more.

Stumbling clear of the dance floor, she almost collided with an automaton and found a crystal of nectar thrust into her hand. She mumbled her thanks and approached the disconsolate knot of figures, who remained rooted to their spot. Two were well-dressed men. One declared himself a dandy in coat-tails and waistcoat; the other appeared staid, in fawn and ivory, a dining jacket and formal tunic. The third figure exuded all the pelagic beauty of an undine.

Salacia gave Leith a cordial nod, studying the sylph with silent approbation.

'Surely the belle of the Ball!' declared Khashoggi, as Leith entered earshot. 'After you my dear, of course,' he added, with a wink to Salacia.

'You are over-kind,' replied the sylph; then, acknowledging the third figure, 'Good evening, Mr Fahrenheit.'

'Where is he?' hissed Ackley Fahrenheit, his face stern, his cheeks taut. 'The *King*. This is his Ball, is it not? He asked me to be here. Sent Trixel to do his dirty work, of course. Where is he?' The human stood so close to Khashoggi and Salacia he crowded the pair.

Leith attempted to placate him. 'Mr Farhenheit – Ackley – it is a delight and an honour to have you join the celebration. The people of Rhye are indebted to you, for assisting—'

'Where is he?'

Leith flinched. She could hear Fahrenheit's breaths, sucked between clenched jaws. Keeping hooded eyes locked on her own, he held an empty beer mug out to one side. A passing automaton filled it from a keg and moved on.

Fahrenheit chugged it.

'I am certain he will be among us presently,' said Leith. 'I spoke to His Majesty only this morning. He has long awaited the chance to welcome so many to Babel.'

'You don't understand,' grated the human. His beer mug arm drifted into refill position again. 'I don't want to be here. I can't be here. Mustapha has to arrive soon.' A haunted light flared in his eyes. Khashoggi touched his arm, muttering inaudible things, in a tone meant to soothe. The beer keg rounded once again.

All about them, dancers spiralled, to the surge and flow of music. Lady Mercy flashed by, on the hand of the dashing Archimage; dizzying steps snatched them away. A sylph and a pixie replaced them, followed by a human couple. The great wheel of revellers revolved to the enchanting waltz.

Leith gave a gentle shrug, unsure of what to say. 'All in good time.'

Fahrenheit shrieked, a wild laugh. 'How ironic! Time, you say? It escapes, irretrievable time!'

The sylph frowned, puzzled. Fahrenheit raised his mug in a quivering hand, suds spilling over the side. The look he wore spelled panic.

Horn and Zither swirled, in relentless peaks and eddies. The Drum marched on. Dancers turned in ever more frenzied circles. Overhead, twinkling lights seemed to flare brighter, in a migrainous crescendo.

Monotony became cacophony.

Then, in another instant, all of the lights blinked out.

Confusion erupted. A sea of startled cries filled the room. Dancers clung to each other; glassware tinkled and smashed, dropped from unsuspecting hands. Beyond the windows, the light of day had long gone. The silvered shafts of Anato fell upon the silhouettes of guests, mingling with the warmer glow of firefly lanterns upon the terrace outside.

Another heartbeat, and bedazzling light banished shadow to the far corners. Splinters of refracted luminescence danced upon the floor and every wall, even the ceiling. The giant chandeliers flared white and the gathered crowd gasped anew.

'Good evening all of you, beautiful people!' boomed a numinous voice, from atop the stair leading to the mezzanine. 'Citizens, denizens and other beloved riff-raff of Rhye, let me welcome you!'

Every head turned, to the place where scattered light now coalesced. A sorcerous cloud of gold and purple mist swirled upon the landing; from within it stepped the winged form of Mustapha. He stood, legs akimbo, one hand on his hip, the other thrown wide in an all-encompassing gesture. The blinding light caught his spreading wingtips, making of him a celestial wonder to behold.

White trousers and boots clad his figure below the waist. A scarlet sash ran his hips around, matching a flamboyant red jacket, in a style worn in green by Fae infantry of Old Rhye. His hair he wore shorter than ever, and in his eye shone a disarming gleam.

On the stage, Harold and the pixies huddled.

'Are you seeing what I'm seeing?' said Meadow, with a quizzical stare.

'Dear friends, I do believe the time has come,' said Harold, standing tall and proud.

Dique sniggered. 'You're right, Meadow. Did he shove a tuber down his trousers?'

'I mean it, boys — this is our moment! After ten long years!' huffed the dragonfly.

Meadow pointed. 'And is that ... a moustache?'

The pixies stifled laughter. Exasperated, Harold grabbed them each by their coat collars. 'Listen up! We haven't been together like this for the longest time. All four of us. What better entrance could we give Mustapha? I ask you ... shall we play?'

Dique shrugged, wearing an approving grin.

Meadow twirled a drumstick in his fingers. 'Couldn't hurt, could it?'

As Mustapha positioned himself atop the stair, a raucous drumbeat filled the room. A moment later, Dique began picking out a tumbling run of low notes on the Zither, fed through an amplifying device Torr Yosef had helped him create.

Mustapha tossed them a wild smile from his elevated platform, and started bobbing to the music. By the time Harold added a wailing note from his Horn, the seraph held every eye in the room.

His voice rang loud and clear.

Our life is a song and your world is a stage
To tell you this story, we've waited an Age
It's time to go crazy, it's time for a show
Get out of your seats and go — go — go!

Stomp your feet and punch the ceiling
Sing it with me and give it feeling!

The seraph thrust his arms out over the enraptured crowd, stabbing the air with his finger. As he did so, the statue of Ophynea sprang to life. Startled shouts and screams rose from the crowd; the naked Goddess of Love leapt from her plinth, landing amongst shocked onlookers with more grace than a block of sculpted marble had ever displayed. The staff she carried became a spinning baton, the ends of which exploded in flame.

The icon of Ophynea became, at the whimsy of the King, a fire-twirler.

Listen to the Rock of Ages
Right across the shining Seas
Can you hear the Rock of Ages?
Shout it out now, if you please

We'll play you the hits and we'll play you best-sellers
We'll smash it to bits – but we're no Fairy Fellers
Don't stop us now 'cause we'll conquer the land
Surrender your fears, come along with the band!

More brazen posturing; more wilful gestures. Animated by the force Mustapha's desires, Floe, Augustine and Phydeas also lurched from their foundations. The portly statue of Phydeas, God of Providence, waddled over towards a table laden with food. Augustine, wielding a symbolic chalice, began refreshing the drinks of wide-eyed guests ... with emerald absinthe.

Mustapha threw his hands in the air. In a burst of kaleidoscope colour, the very chandeliers transformed. One moment, they cast a stately, warm-white scrallin glow; the next, a carnival array of red, green and gold shimmered overhead.

Stomp your feet and punch the ceiling
Sing it with me and give it feeling!

Listen to the Rock of Ages
Right across the shining Seas
Can you hear the Rock of Ages?
Shout it out now, if you please...

The tune thundered on, driven by a frenzied performance from Harold and the pixies. Floe threw wild cartwheels and somersaults amidst the slack-jawed crowd, who shrieked and cowered from the horrifying sight of airborne marble. Ophynea twirled and danced with her flaming baton, weaving a path across the floor. All the while, the dumpy, kettle-bellied automatons bustled about their duty, platters, kegs and drink carafes balanced on their heads.

Hundreds of mesmeric faces stared all around at the dizzying spectacle. Most of the faces shone with enchantment, watching a miracle revisited; others, less certain, offered their bewilderment. Murmurs rumbled beneath the cheering.

King ... but also troubadour?

This is not what we expected!

Is this what happens when they play together? I suppose ... we were not there.

Lady Mercy wore a strange, vulnerable look. Surrounded by festivity on all sides, yet somehow alone. Her Acolytes, now more than ever like gargoyles, watched from the upper balustrade. As the music ramped to a febrile peak — Meadow pounding an allegro beat, the dragonfly's Horn a siren's wail — the Brothers and Sisters of the Order held an insidious calm.

Without warning, Mustapha leapt from the mezzanine.

Somebody screamed. For a breathless instant, the King hung in the void, suspended over a multitude of astonished guests. With a casual beat of his wings, he grabbed hold of the nearest chandelier.

And began to swing.

'This wasn't in the script,' shouted Dique to his friends. 'What do we do now?'

'Just keep playing,' replied Harold. His eyes followed the pendulous trajectory of the seraph, bellowing and whooping as he dangled overhead.

Leith Lourden's head swam. The heat of ensorcelled scrallin light flared upon her brow. The song, boisterous and majestic in equal measure, pulsed against her eardrums. The sheer sensory attack stretched her focus thin; she found her attention snatched between the careening statues, conspicuous visitors, and the ridiculous sight of Mustapha.

Though her remit called for screening potential security threats within Babel, the task seemed at once both exhaustive and redundant. The seraph could look after himself. He had wrought this beautiful chaos, after all ... the sylph imagined Mustapha remained somehow in control of it.

I need a breath of fresh air.

She elbowed her way through milling bodies. An ornate double door, paned with glass, stood open; it beckoned to her, as a way to escape the tumult for the open-air terrace. Close by the door stood a table, piled high with victuals – choice cuts of cold meat and smoked fish, morsels of delectable taste.

Something for my stomach, perhaps. There's an idea.

As she approached the table, Leith leapt back aghast, for the food began to writhe. There, from beneath the canapes, poked the animate, marble face of Phydeas. A stone arm waved at her.

With a disgusted frown, Leith pushed through the doorway,

stumbling empty-handed into the night.

The broad terrace, paved with ivory flagstones, gave immediate reprieve from the escalating madness inside. Only a few other guests, alone or in pairs, sought to embrace the beauteous summer evening.

Leith walked a dozen paces, across the terrace to a stone wall, four feet high. Beyond the wall, a series of colossal planter boxes contained an abundance of thriving greenery, which flowed in supple vines and stalks over the concourse below. From there led a stairway to the Balcony; further still, the glittering sea winked back with mysterious charm.

Tendrils of honeysuckle scent drifted to the sylph's nose, fragrance drifting on the sultry air. Darting fireflies and will-o'-the-wisps leant their golden luminescence to the silvery spell cast by Anato. Here, the clamouring sounds of the Ball gave way, just a little, to the chatter of cicadas and the rumble of distant waves.

Leith exhaled.

'You're tougher to track down than a blasted qilin, Lourden.'

Leith inhaled, with such force that the breath whistled through her teeth. She whirled, turning her back to the stone wall. There stood Trixel Tate, not ten feet away. The fixie's head lay tilted to one side, bright violet eyes studying the sylph.

'No-one but no-one can creep up on me like that,' said Leith. 'Well ... no-one but you.'

'Best tracker in the land,' replied the fixie with a shrug, and a slight dimpling of her cheeks. 'You needed to get away from it all, as well?'

Leith nodded. 'It's a wondrous Ball. The atmosphere gives me such a thrill! To see so many guests from across the land ... I'm still trying to work out the newcomers, though. Timbrad is especially worried about them, but I've seen no trouble. I'm more worried about...' she trailed off, lowering her face.

'Mustapha?'

'Mhm.'

'So, he's trying a new look. It explains his secrecy in the past day or so. It was definitely time to lose that wild mane – I'd say he's much more regal, now.'

Leith threw a hand towards the ballroom. 'Trixel! He's swinging from the chandelier.'

'Blowing off steam,' replied the fixie. 'He hasn't flexed his creative muscles for a while. I thought the lighting change was an exciting touch. I only hope he knows what the exertion of power might be costing him.'

Leith made a non-committal sound. The frenzied music had died away; blessedly, a gentler, more graceful sound now wafted from within. They could still hear the King's seraphic voice, soaring and crooning, flirting with both tenor and falsetto in the space of a few notes.

Now, only six feet separated Trixel from Leith. *How does she do that – especially in those shoes?* The fixie merely stood, hands clasped, as if contemplating the orbit of fireflies. She wore an expression that softened the flinty lines of her face.

'You need not worry about me,' said the sylph. 'I'll return shortly – I need to do my rounds.'

'Not yet, you don't. You need to claim your prize ... I owe you.'

Leith swallowed. Her face burned; she wondered if Trixel could see her ferocious blush in the darkness.

Of course, she can. Best tracker in the land ... her eyesight is second to none.

'Truly, it isn't necessary.'

'On my honour, it is,' said the fixie. 'You see, I spent a long time trying to figure this out. It's a long walk back from Hiraeth – no wings to carry me. Plenty of thinking time. You caught me off guard – for that, I congratulate you! – and I was left with only my own reasoning.'

Leith stared at the ground, unable to meet Trixel's gaze.

The fixie continued. 'I wear my solitude like a cloak, Leith. More than that: a shield. A whole damned suit of armour, if you like. I have to, don't you see? There's nobody else like me. And if I live to make old bones, how many loves will have come and gone, in those years? How many goodbyes?'

Leith's lip quivered. Never had she heard such candid words from Trixel. The fixie was not known for lies or subterfuge, but this raw honesty came from a place that seldom found utterance.

'How many goodbyes have there already been?'

Trixel stared out to sea. 'A few. None … none for a long time now.'

'Your armour has served you well, then?' murmured Leith, still studying the ground. Have you borne them well? All those long years, spent without risking your heart?'

Leith heard, rather than saw, the fixie shrug. 'I've survived. It's what I do. I survive … nothing more.'

Now the sylph did raise her head, and found Trixel standing right before her. A full foot separated them in height; Leith found herself looking down at Trixel's glistening, violet irises. The bushel of hair, only a hint of green in the dim light, lay clasped in her ornate headpiece. Her hair smelled of sandalwood and pine. Her gown, the black of midnight, wrapped her slip of a form. Straps, featuring a series of decorative fasteners, held it together.

'All my life – all thirty-eight years, mind – I've followed orders,' said Leith. 'Directives from above. A regimented existence. No need to contemplate my choices; often enough, I had none. In a way, it always felt like a safe place.

'The one choice I did make was to spend my life amongst humans. Perhaps that served as my cloak. My armour. Destined never to fraternise, restrained by the decree of Vrendari law. But now...'

Leith paused. She felt the full force of Trixel's attention.

'Now...?' whispered the fixie.

'Now ... here we are, living in a new world.'

The sway of a languid waltz drifted on the night air. This change of pace from Mustapha and the band drew almost every guest inside from the terrace; the moonlight illumined a near-deserted space. Trixel stood with both arms held in front of her, palms upwards ... supplicant.

'What do you say, Leith? Huntress, Conqueror of Qilin? Just you and me, Anato, and about five million stars.'

'Just one dance?'

'Just one dance.'

Leith Lourden grinned, and stepped forward. 'I'll lead.'

Tentative first steps brought the sylph and the fixie together. Leith wondered if Trixel could feel the hammering of her heart, as their bodies made contact. Hand clasped hand; Leith's entire body tingled as Trixel slipped an arm around her waist.

The sylph gave a nervous giggle, and kicked off her heeled boots. Barefoot, she held only a few inches over her dance partner. 'That might make it easier.'

Stilted, uncertain and awkward, their dance began. Neither brought the slinking grace of a hunter, or the practised rhythm of a warrior, to the exchange. Trixel stumbled and lurched, in a desperate attempt to avoid trampling Leith's toes. After a time, they settled into a gentle *one-two-three, one-two-three*-step; Leith sensed tension leaving the fixie's rigid frame.

At last, each surrendered to their yearning.

Perhaps, the music played only in their hearts and minds. Perhaps the King of Rhye found the words, the melody, just for them. In the aura of a stolen moment, it mattered not at all.

I once made a vow
I put my heart in a box
That I might be a better fighter
And think about no other
All my life.

I once lived alone
I put my heart in a cage
That I might pass the years in silence
And learn to need no other
All my life.

Just one dance
I ask for just this chance
I didn't think I'd feel this – ever
But if not now, then never
Just once dance.

The lanterns are lit
Merry laughter fills the night air
I watch your face by firefly glow
This moment I want you to know
I want you to…

The grand embrace of the music carried away all cares. Myriad stars twinkled down from above; will-o'-the-wisps threaded tracer lines of gold between them.

With every lilting refrain, every melodic undulation, the rest of the world receded. For Leith, transient moments of sensation informed her whole existence. Honeysuckle blended with an enchanting woodland spice. Cool flagstones beneath the soles of her feet. Joyful singing in the heady darkness.

Faces pale beneath the moon, scant inches apart, sharing a mystified stare.

A quivering breath.

The meeting of lips.

As Trixel kissed her, a ripple of bliss pulsed through Leith's body, from head to toe. At once enchanting and intoxicating, the sensation of fire flared upon her lips, soon spreading through her chest and belly.

Their faces came apart. Leith released a contented sigh. She stared, uncomprehending, into the eyes of the fixie – too often aloof, guarded, impenetrable.

Trixel stared back. A wide-eyed look of bewilderment, coupled with—

'Trixel? Are you okay? There's no need to be afraid.'

For the first time in her long life, the fixie stammered. 'I-I'm sorry, Leith. I don't know what ... I mean ... I don't know why I did that. I'm not afraid ... I j-just ... that was unexpected!'

'Yes! Unexpectedly good!' said Leith, with a warm smile.

Trixel stepped away, wringing her hands. 'I don't want to confuse you, Leith. This isn't "me", you know? I got carried away.'

Leith bit her lip. *I got carried away too, and I loved it.* 'But ... it *could* be you, couldn't it? Underneath the armour ... are we truly so different?'

'You're nothing like me,' muttered the fixie, downcast.

Leith raced against Trixel's mounting defences. 'Of course, I am!

Isn't it obvious? We have both sealed ourselves off, for far too long. Must we go on this way, alone forever?'

'Alone is all I know how to be, Lourden.'

Leith began to shrivel inside. The music played on, though she no longer heard it.

'This might be our chance, Trixel,' she said, in a low mumble. 'To stop overthinking. To throw reasoning to the winds and let down our guards. To try being happy.'

The fixie continued to stare. Eventually, her head drooped — perhaps in acquiescence. She looked up once more, mouth open, on the verge of a new comment—

'Minister Lourden!' A male voice split the tranquil air. Vital, urgent.

In an instant, the fragile moment fell, dashed upon the flagstones.

Both women spun to face the speaker. The figure of Archimage Timbrad swept across the terrace towards them. He came accompanied by a pair of Violet-clad Warlocks, their bestial faces enshrouded by upturned cowls. All of the Adept wore their signature robes to the Ball; Leith remained uncertain as to whether they owned any other attire.

'I am here,' she said, immediately cringing at the redundance of her words.

'I thought you may have been on your rounds. I regret it has taken some time to find you.' He regarded Trixel Tate, with a glance. 'I offer my apologies, for intruding on your ... moment. I bring tidings of some magnitude.'

The sylph studied Timbrad. The youngest Archimage in centuries, stepping into the monumental shoes left behind by Benjulius. Altogether too polite and gracious. At ease, even in perilous situations. Now, even the dim ambient light could not conceal the angst engraved upon his face.

'Speak of it,' invited the sylph, smoothing the front of her gown, 'and for the hundredth time: please call me Leith.' Trixel remained by her side. Silent. Listening. Her presence left Leith unbalanced. In her flustered state, the sylph struggled to focus her thoughts.

'I keep my story brief,' said Timbrad. 'I took an opportunity to dance, knowing that, at some time, I would encounter the good Lady Mercy. If even for a few moments – in a room so occupied – it might give me a brief window to her personage.'

'You learned something.'

'I did indeed. I discovered more than the Lady's aptitude for the waltz. Throughout our turn, she seemed on the verge of trying to tell me things. Each time, she faltered.

'In the end, she shared with me just two words ... words that compel me to action. It is my advice that we reconsider our security targets, and strategise to protect the welfare of our guests.'

'What did she say to you?'

Timbrad paused, for a single breath. His features grew hard. 'She said, "Save me".'

Leith grimaced. 'Then it is as we feared.' Beyond her shoulder, there came a disconsolate rustling of skirts. Leith had told Trixel little of her discussion with Mustapha and Timbrad, regarding the apparent disposition of Lady Mercy.

Trixel will be stewing to hear more about this.

'She said nothing more?'

'Not a chance, Minister ... Leith. A moment later, she had moved on. She has stayed clear of me since then. I dared not compromise her with pursuant questions.'

Leith's practical mind stirred, sluggish in the aftermath of a romantic interlude. Somewhere in her mind, defensive strategies lumbered into position, as she attempted to relegate Trixel to a lesser priority, for now. The fixie presented a troubling distraction, but a distraction, nonetheless.

'Where is Lady Mercy now?'

'She remains with her Acolytes.'

'Do we think this is safe?'

'I have spent a moment with other members of the Order. Sister Delores. Brother John. They do not unnerve me; not in the same way as Brothers Michael or Aaron do. I may advise that Lady Mercy best retire to her quarters. She does appear pale, after all.' A pointed look gleamed in the eye of the Adept.

Leith nodded. 'This is our plan, then. Delores and John are to escort Lady Mercy to her quarters. We should not separate her from her Acolytes, lest suspicion be aroused. These Warlocks can accompany them.'

The Wearers of Violet gave a synchronised bow. 'As you request,' said one.

The sylph continued, battling the mental fog. She pointed, through the door, to the ballroom. 'Somewhere, in there, is Lance Sevenson. Together, he and I will reassign the upper-level sentries. Senior Officers posted at each exit from the ballroom. A shadow to monitor each Acolyte. None are to know they are being watched.' Red flags fluttered meekly in her brain. Perhaps she miscalculated personnel. Maybe something remained unaccounted for. She could not reconcile the nameless concern that wheedled inside, but to delay wasted precious time. She tried to sound decisive.

'Each Officer shall bear a charm of stealth,' said Timbrad. 'Make your sentries known to a Sorcerer, and it will be done.'

Further plans were then interrupted, by the tinkle of shattering crystal, a loud *thump*, and the swirl of a collective gasp. Only then did Leith realise that the music had stopped.

What now? She wondered, though none wasted time or breath

on words. All five figures whirled in the direction of the doorway, racing in a flutter of robes and gowns for the ballroom. A burble of consternation broke over the room, as they entered.

In one corner, a space opened up; a clearing hemmed in by crowding guests. Within it, Khashoggi, Salacia and Mustapha all kneeled by a fallen figure. An Apothecary, cloaked in Green, crouched to join them. They looked up, as Leith poked her way into the space.

'He may have drunk too much,' declared Khashoggi, wearing a look of dismay.

Leith stared down at the unconscious form of Ackley Fahrenheit.

CHAPTER EIGHT

THE GOLDEN GATE

On the surface, Sammy the butterfly's fortunes had scarcely improved.

Still, he followed directions with a crisp 'Yes, sir!' or 'Yes, ma'am!'

Still, he found himself conducting menial tasks, relegated once again to the bottom of a tall, hierarchical ladder.

Still, he spent the hours in tedium – standing here, marching there, watching this or that.

But oh, what an upgrade!

Many a silent prayer to Oska had he offered, grateful for the turn of events that saw him don the technicolour livery of Babel. Perhaps it was Meadow, more than the God of Fortune, to whom he owed his thanks; yet the change of circumstance seemed more akin to divine intervention, than anything a winsome pixie might have contrived.

No doubt, Meadow's influence did tend towards legendary status. True to the pixie's word, within days of Sammy's first encounter with him, the Emerald Bar began to falter in the eyes of its chic clientele. In her bewilderment, Fanny watched her patronage dwindle. The first night nobody attended the Emerald Bar, she thought it an elaborate prank. The second night she raged, hurling elegant barstools to splinter against the walls. The third night, she sank to her ponderous haunches and sobbed, wallowing in the grit of an unswept floor.

Inspired by Sammy's lead, many departing patrons found their way to the Tower of Babel, where opportunity and a sense of purpose proved abundant. Amongst them stood past heroes – veterans of Rhye; those who had spent much of the past decade avoiding the limelight, and now found a new productivity to fill their days.

Sammy's chest swelled. To be patrolling the upper galleries of Babel ... a life inconceivable only short weeks ago.

His mind boggled at the understated refinement of the Residential Parlour. The honey-glow of lamplight gave a soft warmth to the entire floor, while clever geometry drew the visitor from one stylish room to the next. The butterfly had to pinch himself: with a trusting smile, the Minister for Security herself had allocated this post to him.

Truly, Meadow had put in a good word.

With dutiful rigour, Sammy paced the hallway, linking a honeycombing nest of suites. At their centre, a shaft plunged deep through the core of the Tower, housing a wonder of new technology: a hydromagnetic elevator. The innovation had resulted from the combined efforts of the Mer-Folk (masters of hydraulics) and Khashoggi, who had already pioneered electromagnetics with his ship, the *Khonsu*. The elevator cage could zoom right from the very ground level up to the Residential Parlour; from here, a stair ascended to the King's own Pavilion. Beyond heavy oak doors lay a lavish apartment, along with the fabled Windows that enabled Mustapha to rule his subjects with near-prescient vision.

A pair of sentries stood by the door to each separate suite. Sammy wondered at the apparent excess of these postings — not another living soul walked this floor during the Ball. Seldom were guests admitted on any other occasion, either.

The butterfly paced, mapping a hexagonal path through the main hall. The halberd he bore served an ornamental purpose, given that he had no idea how to wield it effectively. Still, it gave a satisfying *clink* with each rhythmic tap of its iron heel upon the floor. He gave what he perceived to be a salutational nod to each pair of sentries, as he passed them.

Some fresh recruits returned an encouraging smile, as if to say, "Look at us now!" Those more accustomed to a regimented life continued to stare forward, but offered a curt tip of the head. Only the staunch pairing of humans, barring entry to a forbidding set of double doors — the largest on the floor, and second only to the portal to the King's Pavilion — responded with stony glares.

Behind these doors, Sammy knew, lay the Main Gallery, in which a bounty of treasures from across Rhye had been stored. Gracious guests, bearing trinkets and trophies, produce, potions and perfumery, had been directed in and out of this room for the past several days. A parade of precious objects, large and small, had made a one-way trip beyond that portal. Perhaps the most noteworthy had been a tremendous, flat crate, borne by a group of odd monastic types, all dressed in white.

Another lap, and then another. Interminable hours passed, as the revelry carried on, far below. The *clink, clink, clink* of his weapon marked time, unaccompanied by any other sound.

Until, with a flurry and a bustle, more sound did reach his ears. Voices, and purposeful bootsteps, heralded the appearance of clustered figures, unexpected at this hour. With a lurch, Sammy straightened himself, presenting his halberd in a way he deemed official … but not threatening.

Not *too* threatening.

He hoped.

A knot of five robed figures rounded a corner, from the direction of the elevator. Two were Wearers of Violet, their clothes declaring them to be Warlocks. The other three all wore white – the garb of the Order, the same strange newcomers who had brought with them the mysterious and ungainly offering. Two Warlocks, and two Acolytes, appeared to be shepherding the fifth figure, a woman. She bore an expression of wariness on her pale face. Sammy could not tell if she felt protected or cornered by her escorts.

'Stand down, sentry. King's business!' barked one of the Adept, as the party of five barrelled straight towards Sammy. He barely fluttered out of the way, halberd dropped with an unceremonious *clang*, before they charged by him.

He turned to watch them, craning his stubby neck as they continued along the hall. The five stopped at a specific, arched portal, opened the door, and disappeared within.

That room was allocated to Lady Mercy. Could that be the Lady herself? What is the matter? She looked a little shaken. I'd feel that way too if a couple of those gruff Warlocks bustled me off to my room in the midst of a Ball.

For a time, nobody re-emerged from the room. As Sammy bent to regain his halberd, a new racket arose from the direction of the elevator.

Sammy barely had time to register two sturdy automatons, bearing down on him at a brisk pace. 'Please clear a path,' said one, in a voice like an iron hammer. With a waddling gait, they shouldered past the astonished butterfly, who this time found himself knocked to the ground.

He had a moment to observe the mechanical figures as they passed. They moved in single file, carrying between them a third: a human, limp as a sack of yams.

Mr Fahrenheit? The man appeared unconscious, with no sign of injury. *Drunk, perhaps.* His room lay further around the hexagon; sure enough, the automatons trundled in that direction.

Lady Mercy's door opened. Still sprawled on the parquet floor, Sammy observed two Acolytes and two Warlocks step back into the hallway, minus their charge. Outside the closed door, they began an intense four-way exchange.

The voices ranged too low for many beings to hear from Sammy's distance. As with all butterflies, however, he possessed hearing beyond the capacity of most. Curiosity overcame him; he attuned his aural sensors to the most sensitive vibrations.

'Sammy! What are you doing on the floor?'

The unexpected voice boomed, a detonation that lifted the butterfly bodily off the ground. With a shriek, he leapt almost to the ceiling, before fluttering to his feet.

Before him stood a pixie, bedecked in the ceremonial attire of Babel's Officers: smart, leather plating over chest and apron, with a multi-coloured tunic and cloak.

By the Gods! Not just any pixie, but the one named Halliwell. Officer of the Guard. A former Commander of the Fae Army.

Glaring at him, with one eyebrow raised.

'Yes, sir! Sorry, sir! I mean, I wasn't napping on the job, sir! Some automatons passed this way, and they weren't very polite.' Sammy scrabbled for words, as he once again fumbled for his dropped weapon. In a daze, he calibrated his hearing back down to sensible levels.

Halliwell screened him, with a dubious eye. Sammy withered beneath the pixie's ever-increasing frown; for a long minute, the pixie uttered no words.

'This is rather against my better judgement,' he murmured at last.

'Sir?'

Halliwell sighed, fixing Sammy with a stare. 'There is no time for idle chat. I have my orders, and they involve you.'

'They do?'

'Hold on to your questions. Save them for never. Now: I'm to clear out this floor. Sentries reassigned, as per Minister Lourden. It seems you're a favourite of hers, am I right? Don't answer. You, and one other, will remain. I can't say I agree with her on this one – she seemed distracted. But I'm not paid to agree, am I? I'm paid to obey. As are you.'

'Yes, sir.' Sammy knew better than to probe further.

Halliwell's lip curled, a doubtful grimace. 'There's more. Apparently, your station is over there. You won't be roaming; you'll be fixed. Rooted to the spot.' With one hand, he reached behind his breastplate. With the other, he pointed.

Sammy followed the pixie's outthrust finger. Already, he knew the place it indicated.

The Main Gallery.

'As you command, sir!' Duty and trepidation filled the butterfly. Somebody, somewhere, had deemed him worthy of a task that carried no small responsibility. *Either that, or nobody expects any excitement up here.*

Sammy snapped back to attention. Halliwell now brandished a large, brassy key. The butterfly knew, without instruction, that it would fit the lock for the imposing Main Gallery doors.

'This is worth more than your life,' said Halliwell. 'Those humans over there weren't at all happy to relinquish it ... and I'm not at all sure I'm happy yet, either. Do not use it, lose it, or snooze on it.' With a jerk of his head, he ordered Sammy to his new post.

As Sammy turned, he noted that the Acolytes and Warlocks had all disappeared. Giving a mental shrug, he made his way around to the Main Gallery doors. There, the two humans offered him only haughty stares, which slid down their noses at him. He offered a sharp salute in the name of camaraderie, receiving barely perceptible nods in return. The humans sauntered away from their post, with a frosty reluctance.

Moments later, Halliwell tramped back down the corridor, followed by the two humans and a dozen other liveried guards. None gave him a second look, as he settled in for the night.

In a tomblike silence, time passed with glacial slowness.

Just stand on guard. Got it.

No ticking of a clock. No drifting sounds of music; too many floors separated the ballroom from the Residential Suite.

Not even the clink of another sentry on patrol — whoever had been left behind must also have been given a stationary post, somewhere out of sight around the hexagon.

Tedium gnawed.

The urge to whistle or hum twitched inside him. Out of sheer dutifulness he quashed it, though it made him glum to do so.

It's a good job, Sammy, he told himself. *You're on the King's retinue, now. No more Fanny owning every second of your miserable life. You're free! Who knows ... if you do well, you might even get to do something interesting next.* He imagined himself as a Royal Retainer. Perhaps even an Advisor. Maybe even important enough to have his own quarters, high up here in the Tower. He puffed out his chest — The Most Important Butterfly in All the Land.

Winged One.

Sammy started. Eyes darted, left and right. His back straightened, pincers gripping the haft of his weapon. *Did somebody speak? Did I imagine that?* When nothing more came, he drifted back to his reverie.

Winged One.

Again? 'Who g-goes, there?' he stammered, trying to muster a whit of authority. 'Show yourself!'

The hallway lay deserted. No nooks or furnishings nearby could serve as hiding places for a slinking intruder.

Winged One.

'Who are you? What do you want?'

Sammy's auditory sensors told no lies. He noticed, now, the sound tugged at him, beckoning. His heart raced. The voice came not from the hallway, but...

Behind me. With nerves jangling, he turned around.

The Gallery Door loomed behind him. Closed. Locked.

Winged One.

Sammy knew his actions to be foolish. Insubordinate. With every thought he reasoned; with every sinew he strove against it. But that voice ... *such a mesmeric quality* ... he could no more prevent his own actions, than he could best a forest troll in hand-to-hand combat.

He produced the key, and reached for the great, brass lock.

Winged One.

How easily it turned; how smooth the mechanism. The polished handle responded with the barest effort ... though inside, he shouted. Pleaded.

No! Think of what you're doing! Do you want to be thrown out of Babel? After all the good fortune you've had?

Winged One.

He slipped inside the Gallery, leaving the door ajar.

137

A huge panel of windows, assuming almost the entire eastern wall at this level, enabled the rays of Adatar to flood into the Gallery during the day. In turn, that gracious light charged dozens of scrallin stones, within the august space. As a result, when Sammy entered the Main Gallery that evening, the interior glowed as if lit by a constellation of stars.

Around the walls, shelves, niches and cabinetry housed all manner of objects. The rarest of finds were those artefacts brought from Old Rhye; aside from a precious selection of books, earthenware and weaponry, much of that old land had simply vanished, with the breaking of New Dawn. Instead, the King of Rhye collected new things: stores written by bards in the Age of Harmony, as well as art and furniture. Perhaps the most peculiar item in the collection, to date, was an exquisite bathtub. The room served not only as storage, but as a very exclusive place to appreciate new and old, juxtaposed.

For this occasion, much of the artisan furniture had been shifted from the centre of the Gallery – by some indignity, the bathtub now rested against a wall! – to create floor space. Here had accumulated a new wealth of offerings, brought by guests from across the land. A veritable hoard of goods – statues in basswood, carved and polished to a fine degree; shimmering crystalware; ornate receptacles of oil and spice; lush textiles, folded and draped over everything else – now formed a small mountain, directly beneath a chandelier.

Sammy ignored most of the lavish treasure trove. Placed against the far wall, dominating the other chattels clustered all around it, stood the object that held Sammy's wide-eyed gaze in a vice.

With a slack jaw and tentative steps, he approached it.

As tall as a golem and several human paces wide, a giant, golden frame shone in the warm, ambient light. Figures of beasts and men, engraved all the way around, looked ready to spring to life at any moment. Within the frame, a pair of gold-painted panels met at a doorjamb in the centre. Each panel featured a sturdy handle, shaped like a scroll. To Sammy, the object appeared partway between a work of art and an immense portal.

Winged One!

The butterfly twitched. There could be no mistake, now: he did not imagine the voice. It came from within the Gallery ... he would stake his honour on it coming from behind this very door.

He edged nearer, too captivated to even look back, over his shoulder. The golden frame loomed over him. Snarling faces and vicious eyes glared down, locked in some tumultuous moment.

Nearer. He picked amongst boxes and chests, to stand arms' distance in front of the door.

Winged One!

Sammy frowned. *Behind...?* Careful to touch nothing, he tiptoed amidst the hoard, until he could peek around the side of the glinting frame, into the space where it leant against the wall.

Nothing. Of course. Shadows fell on a bare wall. The backing also appeared featureless, obscured in gloom. He returned to the imposing front side.

Winged One!

I couldn't be so brainless.

Sammy reached out and touched the stout wooden door, with its silky, golden sheen. Even this basic contact sent an aura of invitation through him.

This is ridiculous! I shouldn't even be here!

The solid handles felt snug in his grasp.

If I'm caught here, I'm done for. I can't possibly go crawling back to Fanny. I'll be ruined!

Despite the doors' massive size, he knew that they would glide open for him, with the least effort.

Perhaps, just one quick look. Then closed.

Horrified, Sammy watched himself draw open the doors, one leaf at a time. Such exquisite engineering — they hinged open without the slightest creak.

Speechless, the butterfly beheld the mysterious, golden gate. His eyes boggled.

Beyond the frame — skirting, door posts and lintel — he did not see the rear wall of the Gallery. Instead, his eyes met a vision of wooded landscape. On a gentle slope, a dense thicket of larch stood proud, some shedding their yellowed needles in a natural carpet. Vermillion afternoon sunlight pierced the maze of trunks and branches, casting ominous shadows on the knotted forest floor. Scant moments of the day remained, before dusk. A light gust moaned between the trees; a speckled thrush darted amongst the foliage, alighting on a nearby branch—

Sammy gasped in wonder.

That's ... not a painting.

He crept closer still, marvelling at the vitality of the scene, not for a moment expecting to find another whole place beyond the door.

'Winged One — there you are!'

The butterfly blinked, eyes like saucers. No longer did the words come to him as some ethereal message; now somebody called, from a short distance. The speaker strove to gain his attention with a loud whisper, as one might who called from hiding.

'Hello?' replied Sammy, peering into the forest.

'Over here — oh my, it really is you!'

Here and there, dense clumps of highbush blueberry grouped beneath the taller trees. As the butterfly stared, he saw it — a cramped figure, folded amongst the laden greenery.

With deliberate care, the figure teased a way out of hiding. Not completely free of the bush, but enough to be seen, from Sammy's vantage.

A man's face shone white, from his place of concealment, clenched in shadow. A face bright with intelligence, yet pinched; drawn by either hunger or worry, or both. Sammy could not guess at his age – he seemed young, yet imbued with the gentle wisdom of elder years. Cropped hair, like burnished copper, burst from his crown. Somewhere, near his hairline, he bore a laceration. The butterfly could see that blood had run freely down one side of the man's face.

The man jostled about in the bushes, adjusting spidery limbs. Sammy saw him now for a tall man, slim to the point of ascetism. His clothes – Cloak? Breeches? Tunic? It was too hard to tell – were a dirty white, and clad him like a second skin.

'Who are you?' called Sammy.

'Wait,' replied the stranger, in an urgent hush. His pale face darted about, as if worried by a nearby sound. Sammy decided there was something strange about the man's eyes, though he could not quite figure it out. Appeased for the moment, the man looked back across the short expanse of forest. 'We must hurry,' he said. Then: 'My name is Tom.'

'I'm Sammy.' A grin and a nervous bow followed.

'You look like a butterfly, Sammy.'

'Indeed I am.'

Tom chuckled. His voice had a rich friendliness to it. 'Another day, another surprise.' He may have been talking to himself. 'Never second guess the words of a Seer.

'Sammy – I must be brief. There are those who might kill me, if they find me here. But we are in trouble, and we need your help.'

The butterfly peered into the scene, staring about the forest. 'But … where is this? Where are you?'

Tom shrugged. 'I don't rightly know. That, my friend, is part of the problem. We've lost our way, and I'm led to believe the Winged One can help get us back on track. You don't know how lucky I feel to find you.' With another brisk survey of his surroundings, Tom parted the bush in front of him; he looked set to clamber from his hiding place, perhaps dash for the open gate.

'Who is there? Who do you mean by "we"?' said Sammy, baffled. He knew not how he could help a stranger, or several strangers, in an unknown place.

Crashing in the underbrush, and a volley of shouts from the middle distance, cut through the exchange. Tom dived from view, back amidst the foliage.

Sammy knew, then, the danger that thrummed behind the veneer of tranquil forest. Suddenly, threats lurked in every mottled shade. The deep red of sunset seemed to carry a warning of bloodshed. A wisp of smoke, rising far beyond the wooded knoll, might not be a homely residence ... but evidence of destruction.

The butterfly's knees quaked; his eyes glued to the scene.

More shouts. The voices of men. The odd echoes of the forest made it impossible to know how many there were. Once or twice, Sammy felt sure he saw the threshing of undergrowth, and the passage of dark figures. Heavy ... perhaps armoured.

The sounds of disturbance drew no closer. After long moments, the brusque calls seemed further away

Tom risked exposure, appearing from the blueberry once again. 'Please, you must come!' he cried. Self-assuredness had deserted him; desperation clenched his bloodied mien.

'Please! Follow me. You're our best hope!' In a rustle of leaves, he disappeared.

Sammy baulked, frozen by uncertainty. *He wants me to ... go in there? This is preposterous!*

Now he did tear his eyes away, looking back behind him. The Gallery remained silent, empty. The architecture, resplendent and real, embraced him; he, Sammy, already lifted from the shell of a bleak existence to the lofty echelons of the King.

He heard the words of Meadow the pixie in his mind. *He needs a good nudge or those wings will never take him anywhere.*

Sammy chewed his lip, turning a furrowed brow back towards the scene beyond the golden gate.

I want my time to count. To matter.

I want to make an impression.

A butterfly who is remembered shall live much longer than his kin.

'Is this my adventure?' he wondered.

He took a shaking step, through the great, glistening frame. On the far side, solid earth met his feet.

Once through, he felt the crisp, alpine air all around him. Tasted its freshness. Smelled the hint of woodsmoke. Hearing attuned, he knew there to be some kind of settlement, not too far away.

A final glance back the way he had come. There he saw the Gallery, beneath winking scrallin light. Perhaps it promised to wait for him—

There came the ringing of gruff cries and the trampling of many feet. Nearer now.

Sammy yelped. He dashed towards the undergrowth, plunging into the bushes where he had last seen Tom's face. In a blink, he was gone.

The doors of the Golden Gate eased silently closed.

CHAPTER NINE

A TRICKY SITUATION

In the stark light of day, the King of Rhye felt the delicate cracks in his vision grow wide. The ideal of a perfect new land, threatened by traces of damage, now shattered utterly … perhaps fractured beyond repair.

He resisted the urge to cradle his fragile head in his hands. A headache yammered between his ears, along with a bilious malaise in his gut — the aftermath of green spirits and recklessness. He strove to fix a serene look to his face, but knew with woeful certainty that he had meandered from a dignified course.

It meant next to nothing, now. A dose of morning-after sheepishness and a hangover from the Gods themselves (*help me, Phydeas!*) paled into insignificance alongside the news of the world this morning.

Three heralds of tragedy and despair stood before him. No matter how he blinked the grit from his eyes, they remained.

Tangible and terrible.

Mustapha had chosen his most subdued audience room to

receive the slew of dire updates. Low settees furnished the meeting space, while ornate rugs embroidered with fine geometric patterns spread across the floor. Simple lanterns, in prisms of pearlescent white, cast a soft glow. The lack of ostentation or embellishment helped him to focus, to anchor his whirling brain to the words of his advisors. Upon a small dais, he gripped the arms of his high-backed seat as if it were trying to hurl him onto the plush burgundy runner, a few steps below him.

First came the ever-graceful Leith Lourden. The sylph stood with head bowed, perhaps tallying her own failures. Her bright features, somehow dimmed by a lingering shadow, still faced the King with an apologetic resolve. At her shoulder, half a step behind, Halliwell made no mystery of it: he hunched in shame.

The news of Lady Mercy's death fell like a winter chill over the room. A sepulchral silence lay heavy on the small assembly, as the appalling revelation took shape.

'How?' said Mustapha. He may have been speaking to himself, such was the diminutive note of his voice. A plaintive desire to understand.

'My orders would have kept two sentries on guard across the Residential Suite,' replied Leith. An unnamed horror blanched her face, mixed with dire embarrassment, as though she grappled with the realisation of some terrible mistake. She continued, offering explanation as recompense. 'Anticipating any offence, at least one of the two ought to have been able to raise an alarm. As fate would have it—'

'One sentry just ... vanished.'

'Into thin air,' said the sylph, in response to Mustapha's conjecture. 'Our only clue is that the Main Gallery doors were unlocked and ajar.'

The King's face blanched. 'You know what is in there.'

'I do, Sire.'

'Is it possible?'

'Entirely ... he had the key in his possession. Though I don't know where that possibility might lead.'

The others absorbed this cryptic exchange without comment.

Mustapha flapped his hand, dismissing sinister implications. 'Set it aside. That left a lone sentry, guarding the door to Lady Mercy's bedchamber.' *One easily overpowered sentry.*

Emboldened, Halliwell picked up the thread. 'Some of the newer recruits are less adequately trained, Your Majesty,' he said. 'But ... but none—

'—But none of them are trained or equipped to face down a *gun*.' This last word filled the room with an ominous rumble. Furtive glances ricocheted around the chamber.

Mustapha grappled with a garish montage of horrifying mental images. The crumpled form of a human – once a soldier of Via – lying slumped in a doorway. The neat, round entry wounds upon her upper chest and temple. The melange of blood and other ghastly, unthinkable material, sprayed on the door and forming a congealed pool around her form. The door itself, left open in brazen carelessness.

Then, Lady Mercy herself.

Alone. Serene. Laid upon the bed, as if in peaceful repose. Her eyes, staring towards the panelled ceiling, but not seeing it. A single round hole in her forehead.

He had ordered all of her bedclothes to be burned.

Mustapha's grip threatened to pulverise the elegant craftwork of his armrests. *Save me.* She had all but spelled it out for him. Likely condemned herself in the attempt ... while he, the preening peacock, wallowed in debauchery.

Several around the room quailed, perhaps praying to shrink

from the brewing storm in his gaze. He fought to quench the fire within. *The fault is mine. I endorsed Leith's new recruits. I discouraged the Warlocks from conducting a search of the guests. But ... how to foresee such mutiny from the Acolytes? What of Fahrenheit?* The otherworlder remained in his chamber, either deeply asleep or unconscious. *What of Khashoggi? The man knows something ... I will have it out of him. But did he know it all? Did he know about ... the guns?*

There will be justice for the Lady's death. Lhestra...?

The Goddess of Justice did not reply.

As the seraph reeled, struggling to assimilate the tragic news, a second blow came. Another sylph; a male, Reynard Volaire. He wore a makeshift sling, hastily tied. He also wore the denial of death like a mask. A face of bland fealty, frozen over like a lake in winter.

The Order's escape caught all of Babel off-guard. That the Acolytes had left one of their own — a mechanic — to attend the airship perplexed nobody. As a consequence, no Babylonian sentry stood within clear visual range of the entire contrivance. While Leith and Trixel danced upon the terrace, most of the lines anchoring the ship to the Balcony had been quietly stowed.

In the dim hours, as clouds scudded across the moon, the last stuporous revellers made their way to bed. The sentries' attention lulled. By the time anyone saw a cluster of shadowed figures steal towards the airship, a sluggish response came far too late. The Order of the Unhomed left atrocity in their wake, along with a maelstrom of bleary-eyed confusion.

Volaire had been stationed along the Corniche. 'The first I knew of any trouble, Sire, the craft had already taken to the air,' said the sylph. Bitter helplessness edged his voice — the sting of self-reproach.

'Your station held the airship in full view, but at too great a distance to observe suspect activity,' said Mustapha.

'Indeed, Sire. My station served to monitor traffic on the Corniche itself – none expected at that time of night. It was the golem who alerted us first – good thing he doesn't sleep. He spoke to my mind – spoke to all of us. We had a brace of sylphs airborne within moments of that. Every one of us, stationed along the coastal cliffs.'

'Twelve of you took flight in pursuit.' Mustapha pinched the bridge of his nose, eyes closed.

Reynard Volaire had returned alone.

'We pursued it in formation, Sire.' The sylph's voice grated. His raw recollection carried all the warmth of a barren tundra. 'To run down the ship gave little challenge – we had superior airspeed. Something powered it – a kind of mechanical propulsion, like spinning fins in the air – but a thing so ponderous ... no, we caught it easily enough.

'We fanned out, preparing to flank it. The sides of the passenger carriage bore large windows, and were away from the spinning blades that gave the thing momentum. We needed to find a way inside it.

'Little did we know it bore weapons. Ranged weapons, like those we left behind in the old world. The roar of them, Sire ... so many projectiles, I could not count. They tore through the air, and through wing and through flesh...' Volaire dropped his head for a moment. When he raised it again, the face he turned towards the King bore deep lines carved by duty and despair.

'I should have fallen, too. When I felt the cold fire bite me ...' – he glanced at a heavily wrapped shoulder – '... I imagined Death would come for me as well. And yet ... one of us had to bring the story back to you, Sire. For the memory of those eleven souls, lost to the waves below.'

Silence reigned. For several breaths, only the discomfited shuffling of gathered bodies filled the void.

Despondency howled inside the seraph. *Father! Where is your strength now? Under your command, this would not have happened. Do I fail my first true test so miserably?* Another blast of gunfire rang in his mind, and he shuddered. He looked towards Leith – her usual vivacity stayed mired in thick sorrow. She returned his gaze with a certain gameness, though something inside her had broken. *This is not her fault. She cannot be charged with the fate of Lady Mercy and chasing down a band of miscreants. The threads unravel, and we rush to tie them back up. Could the great General Prime Bastian Sinotar have achieved it? Oh, Father!*

Mustapha steeled himself, trying to suppress his headache. The unholy trinity of news still had one item to deliver. He knew it could well be the most devastating of all.

On the plush carpeting alongside Leith, Halliwell and Reynard Volaire, stood the quivering form of a kobold. Mustapha regarded the creature with dismay: of all the Wilden Folk – retrieved from a realm of murk and depravity – the kobolds had proven most surprising. With fervour and enterprise, they had begun to thrive in the world of their King's creation. Like strange hirsute dragons, no taller than a pixie, they burrowed and toiled with earnestness. Least of all did they deserve this grim lot that befell them.

Now, this kobold – Godgifu, recent hero of Below – brought news of exactly what their burrowings had found. Having spent mere days in convalescence in Babel, Godgifu had insisted on returning to aid the excavation crew. In return, the doughty kobold had been granted the task of delivering an update of dubious virtue to the King.

In a barking, grunting voice, Godgifu delivered the words Mustapha had been dreading.

'Your Majesty, it is my honour to bring tidings from the Caverns of Below.' She did not appear honoured; she appeared terrified. 'In the early hours of yesterday morning, before lockdown for the Ball, the delves managed to secure safe access to the Oddity.' She looked to Mustapha with limpid green eyes, claws fidgeting with the thick mane that fell about her body.

Mustapha leaned forward. Chills ran up his spine, icing his headache in a moment. 'Tell us more, Godgifu.'

The kobold drew strength from being called by name. 'It sits in a deep well, Your Majesty. The stair you found winds downward a way, to places deeper than we, or even the delves, knew. At the bottom of a dark pit it sits, a great hulk entombed in stone.'

'What is it?' murmured the seraph.

'It is not like anything I've seen before, Your Majesty. That's for certain. Not until this past week, anyway ... it looks to be an enormous machine of some sort. A bit like that flying machine. The one that ... well...' Godgifu shot an awkward glance towards Volaire, then fell silent.

Mustapha chewed his lip, thoughts churning. *A flying machine under the earth?*

Leith ventured a question. 'Is it safe to be inspected, Godgifu?'

'Yes, Minister,' said the kobold with a nod. 'Torr Yosef sent me with that very advice. He examines the Oddity as we speak.'

'Why could he not advise us himself?' said Mustapha. 'He has called to me across greater distances.'

Godgifu gave a deferential shrug. 'I am uncertain, Your Majesty. It may be that his voice is muffled, so far underground. Or perhaps the Oddity somehow interferes with telepathy. The thing ... it hums. The bedrock seems to quiver around it. Maybe it has a voice of its own...' The kobold shrivelled from her own speculation.

Mustapha stood and gave his wings a brisk ruffle. At this cue, all in the room stood to attention. 'Then there is no question about it: we must go into the Caverns, and see the Oddity for ourselves.' The decision gave him a small shred of confidence, as if he now lurched forth from a quagmire of inaction. 'Volaire – take your leave and attend an Apothecary. I am thankful for your efforts and your valour ... your squadron will be remembered.' The injured sylph gave a low bow, and walked from the room. 'Leith, Godgifu – you both will accompany me. Halliwell – go to Lance Sevenson. Between the two of you, I want you to track down Khashoggi.'

'You wish him to attend, Your Majesty?'

'Yes. He can consider this a summons.'

The populace of Babylon saw nothing extraordinary in the movements of a regal entourage through the streets. It came unheralded, though the storied seraph often appeared at events and occurrences throughout the vast city.

Still, both Leith and Godgifu sent runners out ahead of them. This ensured that they progressed through every corner and byway without hindrance. They did meet clusters and small crowds of onlookers, devotees, rubberneckers ... and folk trying a little too hard to feign being busy about their day.

Mustapha chose to walk. Not all of his party owned wings, or the capacity to fly; he also intended a less ostentatious traversal of Babylon's cobbled avenues. Perhaps the urgency in his step piqued the interest of some – murmurings arose from huddled citizens as the King of Rhye and his entourage swept past.

Tidy market squares and businesses of all shapes and sizes gave way to leafy terraces lined with townhouses, standing in straight rows like suburban soldiers on parade. On they marched, arriving at last at a yawning gateway of sandstone, marking the throat of Below. This same gateway Mustapha himself had swooped through only weeks before, following a desperate call from Godgifu herself. Somewhere far below, in the roots of the land, lay a mysterious craft ... far from where it belonged.

On the landing beside the door stood the spry figure of Khashoggi, accompanied by Halliwell and Lance Sevenson. Khashoggi wore his shirtsleeves and an unbuttoned vest thrown about his shoulders – an altogether dishevelled look for the typically debonair Prophet. The old man twirled his fingers and threw himself into a deep bow, as the King's retinue arrived.

'Your call is my command, Sire,' he declared.

Mustapha eyed him. Khashoggi's cheeks showed an uncharacteristic chalkiness. 'I can still out-flourish you, my dear. We have need of one who has lived the past, and perhaps can glimpse the future. Follow.' The seraph beckoned with an elegant finger and strode down the stairs.

The maze of Below bustled with activity to rival the surface world. Prior to his ascendancy, Mustapha had little appreciation for the incessant, scuttling industry of life underground. These creatures who lived in near-perpetual darkness – kobolds, goblins, brownies and some delves – divided their time differently, without the daily influence of Adatar. As such, there were always active kinfolk in this sunless realm.

Descending galleries of hovels, burrows and nooks wound in a spiral into the earth. Occasional plunging elevation shafts made navigation more efficient, for those heading deeper. Guided by kobolds wielding their ever-present candles, Mustapha and his entourage boarded the polished iron cage of an elevator, and clattered into the depths.

The seraph noted that their entire descent had been signposted with wall-mounted torches of ensorcelled flame. The fires, free from smoke, flickered a vibrant purple – the work of delvish

Warlocks, many of whom spent their lives underground.

Soon, the royal party arrived at the familiar gallery where a collapsed stanchion had triggered a perilous cave-in. Now, rather than a catastrophe of rubble, a tidy throughway joined the established cavern with the forbidding space beyond.

Paired Wearers of Violet stood guard, each side of a makeshift stone archway. The Warlocks' bestial faces appeared ever more menacing in the guttering purple torchlight. In truth, the delves – an ancient race, at home in the dark places beneath the earth – had a reputation for kindly wisdom. In the Age of Sovereigns, many of them had assumed the Violet mantle, learning the arcane Discipline of magic warfare from the Adept. The dark-coloured garb conferred a threatening air, at odds with the delves' innate congeniality.

The portal beyond marked the place where collapsing rock had claimed the lives of many Wilden, and trapped many more. Where Mustapha had whiled away the harrowing hours, when maimed and entombed creatures waited and prayed for rescue.

Mustapha baulked.

Ding ... ding ... ding-dang...

There. The sound he had come to fear; if only because he knew not what it meant, though it chimed in his brain like a harbinger of some wrongness. The bell struck a glancing blow. Tolling in a way that sent shards of ice dancing down his spine. It came to him when he first entered this space. *Does it ring from the Oddity itself?*

The Warlocks offered a formal, synchronous bow. Eyes glittering, they regarded him with respect and curiosity in equal measure.

They can tell I'm uneasy.

Mustapha straightened himself. At his back, his company waited on patient feet for his next move. He clenched his fists and strode through the portal, between the two Warlocks.

And haltered, teetering, at the top of a dizzying stair.

A gaping cavern plunged from the landing, one hundred paces deep in the gutrock, and half as far across. Violet fire flared from dozens of torches, which the Warlocks had set about the circular walls of the pit, in anticipation of the King's arrival.

The accumulative glow of torches turned the cavernous void into an immense cauldron of mystic, flickering light. The descending stair spiralled around the outer wall of the cauldron, marked at intervals by pillars of monumental girth. Each pillar reached from the pit right up to the vertiginous ceiling, where deep shadows danced about the roots of ancient stalactites.

On the nearest pillar, the words of an unfamiliar tongue made their stark proclamation.

FUGIT INREPARABILE TEMPUS

Within the cauldron loomed a titanic shape. An elongated barrel, tapered to a point; not unlike the airship's vast envelope, but turned to the vertical, with a skin of some dull metal.

From the landing, Mustapha could see a familiar figure, standing in the rough-hewn floor of the pit. The recognisable form of a golem, dwarfed alongside the monstrous construct it studied.

'Torr Yosef!' he called. The golem looked up at the party – even offered a muted half-wave – but gave no other response.

Lance Sevenson frowned. 'I hear nothing. Does he speak to you, Sire?'

'No. We should get down there.'

Again, the seraph eschewed the power of flight. Something within him desired to touch this aberrant piece of history. To feel the stone – this ancient staircase, which shouldn't exist – beneath his boots. He started down the tottering stair. The others followed, Mages forgoing teleportation, to go in the wake of their King. Leith kept her wings folded. Halliwell clung close behind her; Khashoggi skulked alone, at the very end.

A strange hum emanated from the craft, like a warning. It came to Mustapha not as a sound, or physical vibration, but an odd theurgy, beyond his understanding. Like a malevolent throb it invaded him, a manifestation of his headache.

Few features marked the exterior of the craft. The uppermost portion, a capsule of sorts, featured a human-sized door and several portholes, lined with dozens of rivets. The sleek fuselage bore almost no adornments, save for the remnants of some etching along one side. It may once have been legible, if not worn away by time.

Mustapha marvelled. No tarnish marred the sickly purple-green hue of the craft's shell. Still, he knew it to be old, much older than the land itself: towards the base, where giant stabiliser fins held the craft upright, tumbled stone and spearing stalagmites clenched the foot of it in a tight embrace.

Torr Yosef stood in a clearing of smooth stone. He craned his gaze towards the machine that towered over him, lambent eyes casting a bright beam upon it.

Mustapha reached him, and wasted no time. 'What do you make of it?' he asked the golem.

The reply, slow and faltering, came after a long delay. *<We ... should not ... be here.>*

The seraph's lips became a tense line. 'I'm getting a grim feeling from this thing. What do you know of it?'

<It ... does ... not belong.> Each telepathic sentence sounded like the grinding of recalcitrant gears. *<We ... should not ... be here.>*

'The delves have cleared the way for us to analyse the machine, Yosef. Do you think it is dangerous—'

<It is magnificent, a true testament to its creator.>

Mustapha paused. 'What?'

Silence.

'What did you say?'

Yosef said nothing more. He turned his massive head to regard the seraph for a moment, his eyes two pools of unfathomable light. Then he turned and lurched for the staircase, staggering up each step with a supreme effort.

The dumbstruck group watched his tortured ascent in the flickering gloom. His clanking footfalls echoed around the cavern.

'Sire ... I know. I know what this is.'

Mustapha spun around, as Khashoggi ambled forward from the huddle. He offered another deep bow, this time steeped in humility ... and perhaps a private anguish. In the winking firelight, his eyes remained in shadow, beneath a furrowed brow.

Mustapha skewered him with a glare. 'I had my suspicions, dear Prophet. What can you tell us? Who made this thing? How did it get here? Why is it in the land that I created?'

Khashoggi winced, as if the seraph's questions were a barrage of physical blows. 'Sire, to answer everything will require deep contemplation. I do not hold all of the answers you seek ... though I do know who built this contrivance.'

'Well?'

'I did.'

A soft cry escaped Leith Lourden's lips. Other surprised utterances may have come from Halliwell, or even one of the Mages. Somewhere above and beyond, the stumping ascent of Torr Yosef continued.

Mustapha merely raised a brow. 'When?'

'The *when* is difficult, Sire. I built this – this *spacecraft* – another world ago. In the world where I first met you: the planet Earth. I built it fifty Earth-years before our paths finally crossed. As time passes in Rhye, that would have been significantly longer.'

The seraph leaned forward, peering into the dark recesses over Khashoggi's eyes. 'What do you mean by ... *"spacecraft"*?'

The Prophet's shoulders sagged. All hubris fled from him. He appeared, all of a sudden, to be a tired, old man.

'Just as a sailing ship crosses the sea, Sire, or an aircraft rules the skies ... a spacecraft is designed to explore the heavens above. 'Twenty humans left Earth aboard this machine. Long before you were born.'

Chills prickled the back of Mustapha's neck. Truths and impossibilities wrestled one another in his crowded mind. 'What became of them?'

'They were ... lost, Sire. They blasted their way to the stars, never to return.'

Only the crackle of Warlock fire punctuated the stillness. Yosef's steps could no longer be heard.

Mustapha stared: first at Khashoggi. Then at the great, brooding machine, suddenly a harbinger of dreadful happenings. Then, back at Khashoggi. In his mind, a cacophony of unwelcome thoughts, ideas and sounds clattered towards an unsavoury crescendo.

The insidious tolling of the bell, warning now of some forsaken peril.

The malevolent thrum of the ancient spacecraft, from a place beyond time.

The golem's inaccessible strangeness.

The chilling, inexorable beat of drums.

The iniquitous Order of the Unhomed, materialised from the fringes of reality.

Then menacing gift of the Golden Gate, and disappearance of the butterfly sentry.

The proof of a land outside his creation, a mockery of his covenant with the Pantheon.

The pale, serene face of Lady Mercy; betrayed, with a bullet through her brain.

The roar of gunfire, swelling to a conflagration of noise, threatening to drown out all else.

NO!

With an immense effort, Mustapha, King of Rhye, stilled himself.

Only after he opened his eyes, did he realise they had been crammed shut. Every face looked upon him, flinching from a great exclamation; he must have screamed aloud. Particles of crumbled rock trickled from overhead. Bitter tracks stung his cheeks – the runnels of hot tears.

Several jostled forward, intending to offer him aid in some way. He waved them off, and brushed dry his face with a trembling hand.

After catching his breath, he spoke. 'Friends: we reach a crisis.' The words brought a bilious taste to his mouth. 'The world can be a strange and wondrous place. I can accept that. Adatar knows, I don't understand everything. But I do know this: If our world is a theatre, and by the grace of Marnis I built this stage ... then why don't I know what is happening, behind the curtain? I fear we are puppets in our own pantomime.'

Khashoggi slouched in the shadows, cowed. Leith's eyes stared questions at him. One of the Mages stepped forward. 'What will we do, Sire?'

With hands on hips, Mustapha cast a defiant eye at the Oddity. 'We do what was ours to do since the New Dawn. We seek answers to the mysteries. We go behind the curtain.

'Khashoggi here will ready the *Khonsu* for a voyage. Those who would journey with us must prepare. The Western Way beckons.

'We're going across the sea.'

CHAPTER TEN

ACROSS THE SEA

'**N**o way,' said Will, with the finality of a vault clanking shut. He paced back and forth on the parquetry, gesticulating with a passion. 'Not for all the silk in Ardendale. Not if the beast of Valendyne himself were at my throat. Not even if—'

'All right, all right.' Mustapha rolled his eyes and cut through his lover's bold declaration with a flick of the wrist. 'I hear your message. You dearly want to go on a death-defying journey into the unknown, and you won't take "no" for an answer.' The seraph sat on the edge of the bed, cradling a small camphor laurel box. He smoothed his hand over the fragrant, honey-coloured timber, trying not to think too hard about what lay inside.

Will sighed, moving to sit beside the seraph. 'It isn't the danger I want, Mustapha. I simply want to be where *you* are. Don't you understand? The last time you disappeared over a sea into oblivion, I had to assume you were gone forever. I almost lost all hope after that – dying at the Pillar of Rhye seemed like a fitting end. What more to live for? Now, you're doing it again … and you want me to stay behind, again?'

'It isn't that, Will darling...'

'Then what is it?'

Mustapha levelled his intense brown eyes at the handsome, square-jawed human. 'You know, some days I don't know which of us is more melodramatic.' He grinned, teeth flashing beneath a well-groomed upper lip. 'I just don't want you coming to harm, that's all.'

Will folded his arms. 'Answer me this then, O King of Rhye: do *you* need to go on this journey? We could both stay behind. You have a populace to rule ... a populace who adore you. Another thing: you have no heir. You are, truly now, the last of the Giltenan dynasty. What if ... what if you...'

'What if I don't survive? What happens if I die out there?'

'Yes.' Will stared at his boots.

'All valid arguments, my dear,' said the seraph, grasping Will's hand. 'But how potent is a king, if only of use to his people while sitting on a throne? If lodged forever within a tower, tucked safely away beyond reach of trouble? One day I will die, whether I voyage the Western Way or not. The question of a succeeding ruler will remain. Besides – I cannot cower in Babel from these omens that taunt me, Will. These bells that ring ... they drive me crazy. I pray for answers and the Pantheon gives no reply. Resolution lies in a place beyond my reach ... but I must reach for it. I must!'

Will gave a solemn nod. Despite the golden light of a summer's day spilling into the bedroom through a row of petal-shaped windows, the pair huddled together. Neither of them spoke; at that moment, no words were necessary. Their palatial Pavilion at the peak of Babel suddenly felt vast and otherworldly. The only sound – a near-inaudible drone – came from dozens of revolving Windows, on perpetual rotation in the room across the hall.

Mustapha had never invested too much energy in wondering where the Windows had materialised from. He had not manifested them himself. He assumed them to be a gift from Marnis – an offertory of godly power, to inaugurate the birth of New Rhye. This may have been true, but if so—

What is it costing me?

A soft but insistent knock at the door dispelled the pensive quiet. Only a handful of friends and trusted Advisors had direct access to the King's Pavilion. Will opened the door to the gentle but harried face of Lance Sevenson.

For more than forty years, Sevenson had served as a rock in the foundations of the Giltenan legacy. First, as a mentor for the young Lady Maybeth; then, as diplomat and Councillor for Lord Rogar. In the last weeks of Old Rhye, he led multitudes of Sonteneans to safety, to bunkers that ultimately saved their lives. For Mustapha, these past ten years, he remained steadfast. Expecting nothing, pledging ongoing service even as his grey hair thinned and the weather of his skin bore the dignity of age. He had sworn to serve Babel 'until the day it comes tumbling down'.

Mustapha set the box aside and ushered the human in.

Sevenson acknowledged Will with a neat tilt of his head and stepped into the room. 'Your Majesty, if it please, I would confirm the identities of those who would join you on this voyage.'

'Is the *Khonsu* made ready then, dear?'

'It shall be ready by the morrow, Sire. Mer Folk work in shifts to secure her seaworthiness, while the automatons require no sleep in their efforts to stow all necessary goods and chattels.'

'On the subject of passengers, there is somebody who would have a word.' The human half-glanced over his shoulder.

Will and Mustapha both leapt as a second visitor burst into the room. Though much shorter than Sevenson, the green-haired form of Trixel Tate brought presence enough to fill the spacious suite.

'Sire,' she intoned, with a brisk bow. The King's honorifics always sounded strange coming from the fixie's mouth; she meant Mustapha every debt of respect, though she had known him since his childhood. To her, a part of him remained the vagabond stripling he had once been. Besides — she had been regent of her own Realm, for a short but pivotal time.

'Relax, Lady Tate,' offered Mustapha. 'You've arrived at a good time. We were just discussing the party to board Khashoggi's ship.'

Trixel's posture softened, though austerity still pinched her face. 'I wish to go with you,' she said.

The seraph peered at her. He noted a redness to her eyes, and a minute tremble to her jaw, as she clamped down on some unspoken emotion. 'Your body says more than your mouth does,' he replied. 'What's the matter?'

Trixel shrugged, keeping her gaze locked on the seraph's. 'There's nothing left for ... I mean, I need this journey. My soul needs it. The waves and the salt air will do me good. Give me a better perspective on life in Babylon.'

'What of your work here?' asked Will gently.

'Conservation? The kingdom can conserve itself well enough while I am gone.'

Mustapha blinked at the flippant response. *Not like Trixel, at all.* 'You do know the dangers of this journey? None of us truly know what we are headed for.'

'I do know the dangers, and I accept them,' the fixie almost snapped. 'A question, Sire: who else will be aboard the *Khonsu*?'

Mustapha saw the flash in Trixel's stare. *Does she know what I did? What I had to do?* 'I shall be going. This is my journey to make.' The fixie said nothing at the concept of a vacated throne. 'Will here has just volunteered his services ... let's call him First Mate.

Khashoggi as Captain, of course. Then there's Harold, Meadow and Dique. Harold and Meadow were on board the moment I spoke to them. Dique is eager not to be left behind, but he has Roni and the sextuplets to consider. I'm not convinced he'll make it; Roni sure knows how to be persuasive.

'As far as deckhands and crew are concerned, we shall have Mer Folk as engineers, one Apothecary to attend to health matters, and automatons to perform any menials. That should take care of it.'

Trixel withered a little, at the pronouncement that the mechanical beings would serve as crew. Yet she continued staring at him, as if waiting for him to say something more. When he did not, she spoke.

'Another question then Sire, *if I may.*'

Mustapha's eyes narrowed. 'Of course.'

'Where is Ackley Fahrenheit?'

She does know what I did. 'He is still quite off-colour, after his indulgence at the Ball. He is attended by an Apothecary as we speak.'

The fixie's face glowered. 'Respectfully, Sire, I ask not who is with him. I ask *where he is.*'

Even Will and Lance Sevenson fidgeted at Trixel's brash questioning. Mustapha returned a cool gaze, striving to appear unruffled.

'He is on board the *Khonsu.*'

A nine-month pregnant pause followed. Trixel's eyes widened a fraction and her cheeks flushed; her mouth worked with the fragments of unspoken thoughts. One last thought she did enunciate.

'Do you know what you're doing?'

Lance Sevenson, eyes darting back and forth between the pair, made to interject. Mustapha held up a hand, palm outwards, to placate him. 'Fahrenheit is essential to our success,' said the seraph.

'He is a broken man!' countered Trixel.

'I am certain we can unbreak him.'

'He isn't even awake, to agree to this.'

'He will come around. When he does, we shall explain it to him. *I* shall see to it personally.'

'How can you do this?'

'I can, and I will!' thundered Mustapha. The room darkened, despite the flood of mid-morning sunlight. 'We cannot push beyond the boundaries of Rhye without Ackley Fahrenheit. Lands exist outside our awareness. We know that now. He is the catalyst to our exploration. Marnis himself has said it: both Fahrenheit's spirit and mine are required to throw back the frontiers of Rhye. If we are to pursue the Order — and find the answers we seek — we must make the attempt.'

Trixel's tone softened. 'What if you are hurting him?'

Mustapha nodded, acceding the point. 'I do not choose to be callous. I have shared that very same concern. I don't fully understand what is happening here ... but I intend to. I also fear that great trouble befalls the entire land, if we go without him, or if we do not succeed. We will palliate Ackley Fahrenheit in any way that we can ... but my word is final. He must come with us.'

A long, wordless moment ensued. Will and Sevenson wore grim expressions, neither man certain where to look. In the adjacent room, Windows whirred on an invisible carousel.

The fixie straightened herself, smoothing down her faultless attire. 'Then I must go too, Sire. I have tended to the human more than anyone else for the past five years, or more.'

Again, Mustapha nodded. 'The *Khonsu* departs tomorrow, midmorning.'

Trixel bowed, the gesture deferential but unapologetic. Without another word, she left the room.

The day of the *Khonsu's* departure shone like a polished jewel, brilliant and clear and full of promise. Adatar beamed his blessings upon the glittering Bay of Marnis. Dozens of small craft bobbed and skittered on the water, each one brimming with curious sightseers. In only three days, the atmosphere in Babylon had transformed from maudlin to effervescent.

Prevailing buzz in the market squares, inns and alehouses upheld the intentions of the King as righteous and just. Most had lived under progressive Sovereigns back in Old Rhye; Mustapha's plan to venture forth in the name of the land garnered approval in districts both Above and Below.

The Marina, busy on any ordinary day, thrilled with expectation. Multitudes crowded the extensive dock, hugging the cliffs below the Corniche as far back as the mouth of Little Wandering. In the shadows of The Works, the cram became almost impenetrable; Babylonians of all shapes and sizes clambered to see the famous *Khonsu* depart, along with her illustrious list of voyagers.

Leith Lourden wore a wistful frown, standing at the head of a column of Warlocks. The Adept once again formed a theurgic cordon, keeping bystanders clear of a runway connecting The Works to the gargantuan vessel behind her. With idle agitation, she adjusted the strange headpiece given to her by Khashoggi for the eleventh time. Impatience broiled, as she awaited word from Yosef that the dignitaries were on their way.

'Mind yourself! Watch what you're doing with that!' shouted the sylph. A nearby automaton staggered under the burden of a large crate, hefting it towards the gaping doorway of the *Khonsu's* cargo hold. A chain of robotic servants scuttled back and forth, loading final supplies; if this one fell, it threatened to domino the queue of automatons in front of it.

A few corrective calculations and the errant machine righted its load. Leith sighed her relief as the work continued undisrupted.

For the first time in the sylph's life, a strange emptiness gnawed at her. A sense of being cut adrift from purpose or direction. A youth spent seeing action in military campaigns and tactical manoeuvres, now replaced by life without war. Then, to learn something of love; to taste the liberation of opening herself up to another, only to have a dream of tomorrow snatched away on the salty ocean breeze.

Why do you act this way, Trixel Tate? Why do you run? It's plain to see, you don't want to leave. Did my foolish heart frighten you away? I'm sorry I confused you so. I wanted only to hold you ... strange, passionate, wistful creature.

Her silent appeal seemed fruitless.

Go, then ... take this voyage. Take my heart with you, for courage and for blessed companionship. Then come back to me, triumphant, to my love's embrace.

Ophynea, hear my prayer.

The sylph looked to the heavens where kestrels hovered, until a familiar voice invaded her mind.

<Leith Lourden. The Royal Family are mobile.>

Yosef seemed to have reclaimed a degree of himself since returning to the surface. Leith questioned the golem on the subject, only to find Yosef unable to shed much light on his strange turn by the foot of the Oddity. *Something unusual inside,* was all he could say.

Leith glanced at the *Khonsu.* All preparation had ceased, all automatons scuttled from sight. Almost all: two remained alongside a mechanical gantry, designed to elevate the voyagers from the dockside to the gigantic ship's entry hatch, high above.

'All is in readiness,' she murmured into the conducting earpiece.

On cue, a resonant fanfare rang out across the Marina. Kestrels and gulls squawked, darting in all directions. As one, the throng of citizens spun about, for the sonorous noise had come from behind them. At the near end of the runway, a tremendous iron door, overwrought with pulleys, wheels and handles, slid open with a ground-shaking rumble. Beyond it lay the industrious belly of The Works.

From the vault of the cliffside complex emerged the vanguard of a royal parade.

An undulating drumroll, crests and troughs of thunderous percussion, heralded the first to march. The crowd swelled in rapturous cries as a column of Mer Folk appeared at the mouth of The Works, setting a stately pace along fifty yards of runway to the glistening hull of the *Khonsu*.

Leith watched the vigorous forms of Mer men and women as they passed. Every one of them lithe and muscular, honed and evolved through millennia living with Cornavrian's cruellest mistress: the sea. Each came clad in robust articles of hemp and woven reeds, every colour of the ocean. Bare feet strode the runway, ankles encircled with rattling cockleshells. All wore their hair long, matted and curled by salt rime, tied back from their faces by leather thongs. Kohl and crushed pearls adorned their faces, shadowing ultramarine eyes. Those at the fore raised conch trumpets to their lips, while those behind pounded a rhythm on the bleached skulls of great sea beasts.

A chorus arose from the throats of many, as the Mer Folk offered their blessing to the voyage.

> *Ghost of Neptune, hear our prayer*
> *Tailwind strong and weather fair*
> *Rest your soul in heaven's sea,*
> *Bless this voyage, mercy be.*

Ho, hey! Salt and spray
Hoist the anchor, cast away
Ho, hey! Salt and spray
Off to sea this blessed day.

God of Nature, hear our plea
With these words we honour thee
Turn upon us now your face
Guide us through your cold embrace.

Ho, heap! Trenches deep
Ancient monsters long shall sleep
Ho, heap! Trenches deep
Safe your souls the Gods shall keep.

Wrathful waters, hear our song
Fear no evil, do no wrong
Time and tide, beneath the Moon
Bear our brethren homeward soon.

Hey, ho! Waves and foam
Upon the sea our ships will roam
Hey, ho! Waves and foam
Prayer shall bring you safely home.

Leith blinked the mist from her eyes. *Cursed sea spray.* As the Mer Folk reached the gigantic slab of the *Khonsu's* side, they split into two groups, forming a corridor of bodies either side of the gantry.

Following the Mer came a company of warriors; sylphs, humans and Fae clad in ornamental armour. Except for the youngest of children, onlookers recognised their gleaming attire as the accoutrements of war – battle raiment from a not-so-distant past. *Not even true Fae Knights or Vrendari,* mused Leith, glum-faced. She knew that most genuine veterans of Rhye would probably shun an honour such as this.

Next came a rectangular cordon of Mages, their robes fluttering like scarlet fire in the light breeze. Within their formation, bold and purposeful, walked the first of the voyagers.

The crowd threw a resounding cheer into the summer sky. Hands waved with wild excitement and parents hoisted children to their shoulders, to witness the passage of history.

Khashoggi took the lead, as draftsman and Captain of the *Khonsu.* Outwardly, his dashing finery and silvered coiffure endowed him with a theatrical confidence. Yet there in his eyes Leith saw it: a shade of something dark, uncertain. The Prophet fretted.

Leith caught her breath. An instant later the look had vanished, replaced by a sanguine twinkle. The sylph shifted her gaze along the procession … and her stomach fell.

Trixel.

The fixie, met by shouted blessings, acknowledged the crowd with a grim wave. As if glad to leave the decadence of ballgowns behind, she wore her hunting gear; tunic and leggings of dark beast hide with sturdy, flat-soled boots. Her one concession to luxury: a glamorous green cloak of ethereal substance, crafted of fern and mist. Again, Leith started – the ceremonial cloak once worn by Lord Oberon, the Fairy King. She had only seen Trixel wear it once. In her verdant hair sat the swept-back headpiece she had worn to the Ball.

Leith no longer tried to contain herself. A flood of tears washed her face, her vision of the fixie blurred to distortion. She wiped them away, relieved in the knowledge that no eyes would be on her.

Come back to me ... please, come back to me.

As Trixel made her way to the gantry, Leith tore her eyes away. The crowd unleashed a roar.

Harold, Meadow and Dique walked side-by-side, each equipped with his fabled instrument and saluting the crowd with jovial smiles. The Horn of Agonies in particular drew many an *ooooh* or a murmured remark from the crowd — once the weapon of destruction for Anuvin, God of War; now beholden to a wise and peaceful wielder. With her hand in Dique's came Roni, face wet with tears of her own. Ahead of them gambolled six pixie youths — the sextuplets, lapping up the spectacle as if the world revolved around them. Dique's family had come to join him on this one last walk. When they reached the waiting *Khonsu*, Roni squeezed Dique hard enough to crush him, or so it seemed; he dropped his Zither to the dock with a clatter.

Leith's face burned. She averted her gaze, lest the conflagration consume her insides, too.

The final spectacle provided ample distraction.

Four sturdy automatons bore the King of Rhye upon a circular stage, hefting him on their shoulders so that the gathered masses could see him. By his side, trying as ever to evade the intense scrutiny all around him, Will offered polite gestures to the throng as they passed.

The seraph stood proud in full regal vestiture: a flowing scarlet robe, trimmed in white and black, which fell to pool around his boots. On his back, an ornate coat of arms, consisting of all the cyphers of Old Rhye brought together. The robe lay between the cleft of his wings which he spread wide, catching the light of the sun in a dazzling display. Upon his head he bore a crown of gold with scarlet silk — elegant without bombast. Leith knew of the crown's existence, though she had never seen the seraph wearing it.

Within the honour guard of Mages, the mechanical figures bore the King forward in a slow procession. Atop the stage, Mustapha held an enormous armful of roses; as he moved forward, he tossed them with vigour into the sea of upraised arms at each side of the runaway. Catchers cried with delight, not least because every last thorn had been plucked from the stems. With his roving gaze, he seemed to strive for the far reaches of the crowd, as if he could include every last creature in this singular moment.

Leith watched him with pursed lips. *He may always have been an imperfect creature, but he is certainly the People's King.*

The citizens of Babylon rallied for another deafening cheer, as the last of the procession reached the *Khonsu*. The Mages stepped aside, arraying themselves amongst the bordering rows of Mer Folk. The automatons took a knee and lowered the stage, allowing Mustapha and Will to take a short step down to the dock. Mustapha, Will, Meadow, Dique, Harold, Trixel and Khashoggi then climbed aboard the mechanical gantry.

One of the lumbering machines moved to grasp a winch at the side of the gantry, and with a *clink-clink-clink* the group began to ascend. Up they rose, dwarfed by the side of the mighty ship. To the sylph, they suddenly appeared very small and vulnerable. Trixel grew smaller by the moment, with her stern, beautiful face and her brain full of unknowable thoughts.

'Halt!'

Mustapha's call rang out, loud and clear; recognisable in an instant. He intended the order for the automaton below, who ceased winching and left the gantry extended halfway to its goal.

Leith frowned, puzzled by the unscripted pause, until she realised that the seraph could now be seen from one end of the Marina to the other, and as far away as the Corniche, against the pearlescent sheen of the *Khonsu*. From this vantage, Mustapha could command the crowd. He spoke, and his words carried as if magnified. A voice fit for the Pantheon.

'Dear people!' he cried, arms aloft. 'Whether you be man, woman, neither or both; beast or insect, creature of daylight or of night – you are, one and all, children of Rhye.' The multitudes roared, sound washing back and forth along the Marina, echoing out across the Bay of Marnis.

'I face you now as your King, by the grace of Ophynea.' Jumbled shouts of 'Praised be Ophynea!' filled the air. 'But that is not the deepest truth of it: I face you as one of your number, a child too of this great and ever-changing land. Born of human and sylph, raised by a fairy, forged anew in the heart of the Wilden Realm. I share with you now this moment, wherein I recognise my destiny – to go forth to challenge the mysteries, to win back the life of harmony that we all deserve.'

The cheering rose to a tumult. Mustapha lifted a single hand, enough to quell the raucous sound to a dull rumble.

'At my side are some of the finest, bravest souls in the history of the land. Fear not! I shall bring them back to you whole, and triumphant! While I am gone, the word of Archimage Timbrad, Lance Sevenson and Minister Leith Lourden is as my own.

'Live in harmony and watch for our return along the Western Way. I love you all!'

A rousing cheer rose once more. Amidst the fray, voices joined in a stentorian chant:

With joyous hearts we will sing along
Long live the King! Long live the King!
We praise your name with our voices strong
Long live the King! We say long live the King!

The clanking ascent of the gantry resumed. The intrepid company rose towards the lofty gunwale, where a small door stood open to accept them. One by one, they entered.

Leith wept. All about her, citizens cried jubilant tears; the perfect foil for her own rampant emotions. The sun shone bright over the Bay and stirring voices rose above the crowd as Mustapha disappeared, engulfed by the *Khonsu*.

END OF PART ONE

PART TWO

THE WESTERN WAY

CHAPTER ELEVEN

NO PLEASURE CRUISE

In the weeks and months following the New Dawn, the land of
Rhye blossomed quickly — an explosion of ideas, manifesting a
world of beauty to rival the old world, scarred by Valendyne's wrath.

Mustapha had only to pronounce his desires and they became
tangible before him. 'Here shall be a lake!' he would cry. 'A reservoir
of glacial water, so clear that I can peer into its depths ... but
unfathomably deep. Deep beyond imagining! May it thrive with carp
and trout and salmon, and draw fishermen like moths to a flame.'
In this way, the Bottomless Lake came into being. Through similar
incantations he brought to life the towering forests of Eleuthervale
and Arboria, the fertile food bowl of the Highlands and even the
monstrous spires of rock, rising above the waves of the Milky Sea.

For his part, Ackley Fahrenheit stood proud beside the anointed
King. He moved through the world, experiencing each and every
new green shoot and rushing stream as if through the eyes of
a child. The frontiers rolled back, revealing a masterwork of
creation. Each place received a name and was thus consecrated;

the returning souls of Old Rhye were able to settle the cities, towns and wilderness, and call these places home.

Mustapha paid little heed when Fahrenheit first spoke of avoiding the places where once he had been in awe. They stood together, high in the Pemblax Mountains, at the very font that gave birth to both Little Wandering and the vital Serpentine. The human lamented that the dark subterranean places troubled him. That the forests threw shadows, which threatened unnameable dangers. At length, he announced that the sprawling city of Babylon, teeming with creatures of every race, could no longer soothe his exhausted soul.

The alliance crumbled. Fahrenheit retreated, his shoulders hunched with a growing list of fears. Beyond the fringes of the world they wrought, a lifeless canvas lay in wait behind a thick veil of mist and unawareness.

To the north, east and south, beyond the King of Rhye's dreaming, there lay a barren waste: the Nameless Plains. Into those places nothing entered, for nothing could survive or flourish.

To the west, the Milky Sea stretched beyond the horizon. Sailors spoke of a place where the mist closed in and navigation become impossible; where fear drove them to turn about and seek familiar waters or risk their lives.

The route to this place of fear became known as the Western Way.

Word came of an island settlement, looming within the mist. None had returned with an account of the place. Sailors and Mer Folk fostered their own myths.

The last stronghold of dragons.

The new Obelis, a heaven on earth.

Not an island, but a slumbering behemoth, to one day wake and swallow the world.

'I told Roni I'd be back for dinner,' said Dique. 'Too ambitious?'

Mustapha glanced sidelong at his friend. A glint in the pixie's eye gave away his jest. 'I know you weren't terribly keen for another adventure, Dique ... but I'm glad to have you with me. Everyone speaks of an adoring populace in Babylon, but life still feels emptier somehow. Lonelier. Will and I often reminisce. We wonder what might have been, if I had never stolen the cinnabar.'

'We'd be dead, that's what. Things are done and can't be changed, and I for one am grateful we can't change that.'

'Perhaps. Anyway, there's a lot to be grateful for in the here and now. You've got a fair maiden, waiting for your gallant return.'

Mustapha watched the flush of rose bloom in Dique's face. He wore the coy smile he kept for moments of true contentment.

The pixie spoke. 'You know how the saying goes. *"May my absence let the heart grow fonder, while this ship sallies over yonder".'*

'I've never heard that saying in my life,' said the seraph. They both laughed.

The pair stood at the fore of the Observation Deck, letting the breeze ruffle their hair as the *Khonsu* lumbered towards open water. Beneath their feet, at the Bridge, Khashoggi took the helm of the immense ship for the first time in many months. The Sorcerers' new fuel source fed ominous power through her engines, bringing a rumble that thrilled her superstructure from stern to bow.

Entering the Western Way provided challenge enough to the captain of a great ship. Upon threading through the massive breakwaters to gain the strait, the route called for a near-immediate ninety-degree turn to port, to navigate beyond the brooding mass of the Leviathan. Despite the *Khonsu's* size, Khashoggi handled the manoeuvre with deft skill.

Her gleaming bow sliced through a treacherous swell in Neptune's Gate. Here, waves thrashed against slab-like cliffs on either side. Rolling water sloshed back and forth, threatening to capsize smaller vessels. The *Khonsu* forged a path through crest and trough, fighting free of Levi's broad shadow.

'Oh, I've never seen the far side of Levi before!' said Dique. He bounded across to the starboard railing and peered through the bars, being too short to see clearly over the top. 'Oh, my,' he gaped in astonishment, for the Leviathan's western face bore features unheralded on the landward side. Immense flying buttresses of stone soared from the upper reaches of the crag; stanchions pounded by the open ocean below. Beneath their great spans, myriad nooks and wide-mouthed caves pockmarked the huge bluff. Dique expected to see a nest-filled rookery of sea birds ... but then peered closer.

'The cathedral of undines,' said Mustapha over his shoulder.

Even as the seraph spoke, Dique saw them: dozens – no, hundreds – of undines. Many waved or offered prayerful gestures from within carven colonnades of stone. Others played and dived between the mighty pillars, each with the girth of a bell tower. Still more frolicked and darted through the waves, racing the *Khonsu*, staying abreast of her prow. The undines followed for a time, then vanished in the depths.

'I've heard it said that sailors offer undines enticements to grant fair conditions on a sea voyage,' said Dique.

'Perhaps so,' replied Mustapha. 'The days of sail are numbered. 'With Khashoggi's hydro-electric-whatsits, we might be less reliant on the whimsical mercy of water spirits, in times to come. Besides,' he added with a smirk, 'I suspect the old sage has found it beneficial to petition the most powerful undine of all ... personally.'

Ahead, across a league of open water, one final island emerged from the expanse of blue. Much smaller than the Leviathan – but every part as fundamental to the lives of undines and Mer Folk

– the Tear rose from the waves as a stark knurl of bare rock. Upon it stood a bold monument – a shrine and mausoleum, the final resting place of the revered Lord Neptune. A stone stairway, its lower reaches encrusted with barnacles and algae, led from the crashing sea all the way to the edifice above. There, ocean-bound pilgrims could pay last respects to Old Rhye's Sovereign of the Seven Seas. Mustapha had shaped the isle as a symbol of sacred bereavement; a drop of saltwater realised in stone, girt all around by the sea itself.

Khashoggi gave the Tear a respectful berth on the starboard side. As they passed by, Mustapha and Dique spotted the tiny figure of Salacia, high up by the mausoleum's portico. She held her hand aloft.

At last, then the *Khonsu* faced only the wild blue yonder ... and the mysteries over the last horizon.

Mustapha felt a new surge of power beneath his boots, as Khashoggi coaxed a new level of thrust from his engines. 'I imagine the crew will hope to cover as much distance as they can before late afternoon,' remarked the seraph, glancing overhead. 'As Adatar dips low, we'll be cruising with the glare – I mean, his godly light – in our eyes. Khashoggi will need to hand over navigation to the automatons ... and I'm not sure just how much he trusts them yet.'

'Any idea what lies ahead?' asked Dique.

'Out there? A lot of water. A few atolls we'll need to swerve around. On here?' The seraph jerked a thumb over his shoulder, indicating all on board the *Khonsu*. 'On here, what lies ahead is a thorny puzzle of its own, my dear. Something tells me this trip will be no pleasure cruise.' He gave the pixie's shoulder an affectionate squeeze, and turned from the railing. 'I'm going to pay a visit to Mr Fahrenheit.'

From his first time aboard the ship, Mustapha recalled the crisp white bulkheads, the skirtings of varnished oak and fittings of brass that adorned the passageways and cabins aboard the *Khonsu*. The handsome interior complemented the bold flair of the ship's Captain; a quirky array of barometers, thermometers and gasometers seemed poised to measure every breath the voyagers took.

The seraph had seldom been aboard the *Khonsu* since her fabled voyage across the Seventh Sea. *Was that truly ten years ago? Where has the time gone? What time is it, anyway?* He noted, with a perturbed crease of his brow that there were no chronometers to be seen.

As he traversed several decks to the passenger quarters, Mustapha encountered signs of industry at every well-appointed turn. No vast, empty chambers or vacant corridors. Automatons chittered about on an endless roster of tasks — measuring this, polishing that, monitoring something else. Each addressed him with a sunny but respectful salutation programmed by either Khashoggi or Torr Yosef. He could not tell which, though the clipped language seemed more typical of the golem.

On the passenger deck, towards the fore of the vessel, Mustapha found the cabin in which Ackley Fahrenheit had been ensconced. Following the relay of warbling machines bringing all manner of blankets, poultices and other medicaments made the search simple enough. Harold's insectile figure leaned against the bulkhead by the door.

'I'm no Apothecary, but this is definitely not a hangover,' said the dragonfly, by way of greeting.

'A good thing we brought an Apothecary then, isn't it?' replied Mustapha with a grim smile. 'Does Gwenamber have any better ideas?'

Harold shrugged. 'I can't be sure. She's been thumbing through a bunch of old books, which isn't overly reassuring.' The cabin door stood open, and he jerked his head towards it. 'You should take a look for yourself.'

Mustapha appreciated the way in which his friends sidestepped the pomp and ceremony that others saw as befitting a King. No false deference, only forthrightness. *Friends will be friends.* He nodded and stepped into the cabin.

The pungent aroma of medicinal herbs assaulted his nose. Something else, as well: not the mustiness of infection, but the sour tang of damp towels and sweat-soaked clothes. The dim flicker of oil lamps danced about the modest space. Mustapha let his eyes adjust.

Trixel Tate slouched in an overstuffed chair by one side of the bed. Her eyes flicked across to him as he entered, then back towards the figure in the bed, for whom she kept a straight-lipped vigil.

Fahrenheit perched in the bed like a catatonic vulture. A feverish light glistened in his aimless gaze; his wire-rimmed spectacles sat on a low table beside him. Lank grey hair lay plastered across his shining forehead.

The Wearer of Green leaned towards him from her stool by the bed, armed with a wooden bowl and spoon. A small tower of leather-bound volumes formed an untidy stack behind her. A pile of utensils festooned the table – a mortar and pestle, weighing scales and thermometer – along with a cluster of labelled bottles and jars. A murky broth, the product of Gwenamber's labour, half-filled the bowl in her hand; at intervals, she raised a spoonful to the otherworlder's lips.

The plump Apothecary looked up from her work as Mustapha entered, her face ruddy in the orange light. She twitched, unable to gracefully unload the concoction in her hands to acknowledge the King.

Mustapha waved away her vexation. 'Please continue. On this ship, I am as any other passenger.'

'Thank you, Sire.' Gwenamber returned from a half-standing position to her stool, giving her attention back to Ackley Fahrenheit. On the other side of the bed, Trixel Tate had made no effort to stand.

Wisps of steam curled from the broth, and from the loaded spoon. As Gwenamber brought it close to Fahrenheit, he opened his mouth to accept it. He did not look at the spoon — he may well have been staring straight through the bulkhead in front of him.

'He responds, then?' asked Mustapha.

The Apothecary nodded. A lock of reddish fringe fell in front of her face; she huffed it out of the way. 'He allows me to feed him. Give him medicine. He offers no reaction ... nor does he answer to voice, or acknowledge us in any other way.'

Mustapha leaned nearer. 'What are you feeding him?'

'A strained broth of gingko, valerian, rhyewort and finely ground shimmershell. Not the most pleasant smell — or taste — but it does aid one to tap into a closed mind.' Fahrenheit continued to accept the spoon, unresponsive to all else. 'I am not sure what has become of him ... but the dreams of a restful sleep may yield some answers. This mixture could help unravel the knots within.' She tapped her own temple with the empty spoon.

'You're breaking into the wrong mind.' The fixie's acerbic words emerged from her shadowed corner.

Gwenamber paused, eyes questioning. 'But—'

'Lady Tate is referring to me,' said Mustapha.

Trixel leaned forward, addressing the seraph. 'I know it's linked to you. It has to be. I haven't quite figured out, but that thing you do ... it's causing him harm.'

Mustapha chewed his lip, watching Ackley Fahrenheit. The human blinked. Something about the fleeting movement flagged in the seraph's brain. *He still responds to needs. And instincts.* 'Will he sleep?'

The Adept's face brightened. 'Yes! He will. This much I have learned, tending to him here these past two nights: he sleeps as if in a trance.'

'Hmm.' Implications jabbed at the seraph's brain like thorny briars. He tried to push through to reach for the answer, only to have his thoughts become more entangled.

The answer doesn't lie ahead. It lies behind. He considered the land of Rhye, frozen on the cusp of unlimited expansion. His time spent with the human, watching the vast, pale mists rolling outwards ... *No, contracting inwards...?* To a singularity. A focus of white light, containing a covenant. A promise the Pantheon had made him ... and a promise he had made in return.

He reached a decision.

'Tonight, when he sleeps ... it's my turn to keep vigil.'

'Do you think we should find the airship in only seven days?' asked Dique. 'The homeland of the Order? It seems improbable.' He dipped a hunk of cornbread into his bowl of steaming goulash and stuffed it into his mouth. Optimism laced his tone, though his eyes were full of calculations.

The *Khonsu* featured two dining spaces. The principal mess — adjacent to the galley kitchen — saw most traffic from Mer engineers, coming on and off shift. Khashoggi kept a separate dining room for private use, near to his stateroom. The voyagers repaired to this parlour of oak furniture, silken wall hangings and thick woven rugs for the evening meal. Service machines beetled in and out, delivering dishes and replenishing wine from crystal decanters.

Khashoggi chuckled. 'Alas my friend, it would be optimistic to expect a journey as swift as the one Brother Aaron described.'

'We all hope to return home soon, Dique,' said Will, tearing his own bread into pieces. 'Most of us have never been to sea before ... but I imagine that flying ship's airspeed is more than even the *Khonsu* can replicate, out on the open water.'

The Prophet nodded, tipping his glass to acknowledge Will's comment. 'There certainly is that to consider. There is also the small matter of a vast maze of atolls, through which we must weave. No luxury of travelling as the albatross flies!'

Harold chimed in, elbows on the table and pincers steepled, in a contemplative pose. 'At least we have a solid bearing. Thanks to Volaire's mission report, we know the direction the airship took. At night, we can use the stars to find our way.'

'Right again,' said Khashoggi. He leaned aside, to allow an automaton to clear his plate. Another followed behind it, delivering a new course of cold cuts, cheese and fruit. 'By day, we travel due west, more or less by dead reckoning. Under the light of Anato, stars will help us correct the meanderings of the day. But while only navibots attend the Bridge, I dare not raise our speed any higher than Half Ahead. That may well cost us time, but at least we won't heave-to on an uncharted reef in the middle of the night.'

Meadow and Dique proceeded to ask Khashoggi all manner of questions. *How big are the engines?* (Meadow). *How fast can the* Khonsu *go?* (also Meadow). *How does the MHD generator overcome the insufficiency of low electrical conductivity of seawater?* (Dique). Mustapha tuned out, dangling a small bunch of grapes and plucking them off, one by one, with his teeth. All the while, he studied the Prophet.

The consternation of recent days appeared to have fled

Khashoggi's face. Confidence and alacrity again governed him, as if the despair of events had been a fleeting thunderstorm.

Mustapha frowned. *The sight of the spacecraft definitely spooked him ... and why wouldn't it?* The seraph had himself been perplexed at how the craft had arrived, not only from a different reality, but across the vastness of time ... to appear in the roots of the earth, directly below Babylon. For a moment, Mustapha dismissed that part of the quandary. Something more had troubled the Prophet. Something existential. *What about the twenty souls on board the spacecraft? What became of them? In a fashion, Khashoggi sent them on their journey. Did he realise they would arrive in Rhye, or didn't he? So many questions.*

Clearly, the Prophet felt once again in his element, out upon the open sea. Or perhaps just being aboard the *Khonsu* succoured him. Either way, he appeared to be pushing the horrors of death and sinister mystery aside, as if it were happening to someone else.

Mustapha plucked one last grape, resolving to interject with a question of his own—

'Qilin!'

The exclamation jolted Mustapha out of his thoughts. Indeed, all around the table flinched; Meadow managed to spill his drowseberry wine.

Trixel Tate sat upright, her glass empty but her plate of food barely touched. She had fired her first word of the evening in the direction of Mustapha.

'Qilin?'

'Qilin,' she repeated, with greater certainty.

'Yes ... beautiful creatures. Are you all right, Trixel?'

'I am,' nodded the fixie. All eyes were now on her. 'I think I've worked it out – what happened to Ackley.'

Mustapha shifted in his seat, thoughts of questioning Khashoggi shelved for the moment. 'You have? Then, please, we must hear it.'

'Yes, please share!' agreed Harold.

Trixel Tate glanced at Mustapha. Her elfin face still held something of the umbrage she showed the seraph back in Babel. She appeared to school her features, preparing to explain herself.

'Ackley Fahrenheit harbours great fear,' she began. 'He cultivates it, like a farmer tends his crops. But his fear is unnatural. He did not come to Rhye an inherently fearful man. Something has made him this way – something that changed who he is.'

Again, several automatons buzzed about the table in wordless formation. Filling crystal, clearing plates. As they left the room, Will spoke. 'Do you have ideas, Lady Tate?'

The fixie nodded again. 'Ideas, yes. For several years, I have watched the human shrinking away. I wondered what was causing it. Somehow, his connection to our fair ruler here' – she gestured with an open palm towards the seraph – 'created a taint in him. I couldn't quite figure out how.

'Before the birth of the first qilin in Eleuthervale, Ackley loved the forest. I think the streams, the glades and the wildlife reminded him fondly of his home world ... perhaps more than any other part of Rhye. Once qilin roamed the forest, for a time he remained enamoured by it. But then, in a matter of weeks, he withdrew. He all but stopped going there. He would ask me if there were qilin about ... spoke of them in fretful tones. I asked him about it. First, he tried to explain, and couldn't. Then, he wouldn't.

'Mustapha ... you created them using him as a conduit. In some way, that birthed his fear.'

Mustapha sat with fingers interlaced, chin on hands. 'I see what you're saying,' he replied, 'but that is just one particular example. How do you explain the fact that he's afraid of *everything*?'

'The theory holds,' said Trixel. As she closed in on her point, the energy fairly crackled from her. 'You created the Tower of Babel; Ackley Fahrenheit developed a fear of heights. You said it yourself: when he first arrived, he wanted little else but to see the Pillar of Rhye. To scale it. To see our world from a lofty perspective. Now, he must live in a single-storey cottage.'

'Reasonable,' said the seraph. Heads nodded in dawning enlightenment around the table.

'You brought the people of Rhye together in one great city,' continued Trixel. 'Ackley became fearful of crowds. Worse — he now loathes socialising, as if to see people will bring him some contagion.

'Do you see how he must live now, on the very fringe of Hiraeth, where the Swamp meets the Nameless Plains? Even the lands you created together are distressing to him.'

'I see it,' said Mustapha, 'but I don't understand it.'

'I might be able to help you.'

The Prophet sat stroking his beard, in the aftermath of his interjection. Whether he paused to gather his thoughts or simply for theatrical effect, Mustapha could not be sure; but his words drew six pairs of eyes towards him.

'Nothing like a bit of wisdom to settle a meal,' said Meadow with a crooked grin.

'You have the floor, Khashoggi,' said Mustapha.

The Prophet gave an incline of his silvered head. 'I believe *innovation* is the key here.

'You see, in order to create truly original things — be they creatures of flesh and blood, or a mechanical contrivance, or even a unique environment — one must harness the power of innovation. This is the responsibility with which Marnis both blessed and burdened you ... though he may not have shared the entire story.'

This much Mustapha understood without question. The joy of

the Creator's blessing he had felt almost instantly, like lightning in his veins. Each time the land flourished and expanded in a new way, the pleasure of it all quenched the needs of his soul. Then, as time passed, the magnitude of ruling his creation weighed more heavily upon him. 'Go on,' he said.

Khashoggi continued his lecture. 'There are two by-products of innovation. Two consequences that may not be readily apparent at first. One of those is awe: that tingling of the spine – the hairs at the base of your skull, which seem to stand on end – at the realisation of a monumental breakthrough. Anyone who has ever had the fortune to invent something has experienced the awe; I have been fortunate to feel it myself a multitude of times.

'As there is light, there is also shade. The other consequence of innovation is fear.'

Harold leaned back in his seat. The dragonfly said nothing, but the pensive lowering of his eyelids gave away his understanding.

Mustapha continued to drill Khashoggi with his gaze. The Prophet still appeared disconnected from the controversy that swirled around them all. Mustapha felt now, more than ever, that a skein of some diabolical truth connected the fate of Ackley Fahrenheit to that of twenty otherworlders from a long-distant time.

'Give me an example,' said the seraph.

Khashoggi blinked, but proceeded without faltering. 'Consider the airship you have just seen,' he said. 'The harnessing of technology – not too far beyond our grasp – which has allowed our outworld friends to conquer the skies. In all of Rhye, only the sylphs, the dragonflies and the butterflies may ascend to the clouds and commune with Adatar. Oh, and yourself, of course, Sire.

'Consider then, the reaction of the crowd upon the Corniche, and the Balcony, on the day that airship alighted. Many were the gasps of awe, the restless wonder of those born without wings, who immediately dreamed of a life in which flight is possible.

'Listen deeper, and you would have heard the ruminations on concern for safety, or the dread of falling from the sky, to dash upon rocks or ocean waves. The grave affirmations that civilisation evolves too fast; that we are trying to run before we can walk. Those are the murmurings of fear.'

Mustapha flattened his palms on the table, allowing the solid oak to steady him. He glared across the table. 'You know how all of this ends, do you not? The airship may be an innovation beyond *our* grasp, but it isn't beyond *you*, is it? What of the spacecraft resting below Babylon? What of those doomed souls who climbed aboard?' Mustapha's voice rose to a shout. 'You, who call yourself Seer – what happens next?'

The seraph's outburst brought a flare of passion to Khashoggi's ice-blue eyes. Just as quickly it dimmed; the Prophet showed his hands.

'Alas, I have not borne witness to the fate of that crew,' he said. 'Until recent days, I thought them relegated to oblivion long ago. I would suggest the answer lies with the human who now travels with us.'

None had a response to this. Mustapha massaged his temples, eyes closed. Other eyes remained downcast, uncertain where else to look.

At length, Mustapha spoke. 'Then it is as I have said. Tonight, I take my turn at vigil over Ackley Fahrenheit.'

'That will not be required,' grated the voice of Ackley Fahrenheit.

All leapt to attention. Two figures stood at the entrance to the dining room. Gwenamber, the Wearer of Green, wore a mask of exhaustion. Beside her, the once-scholarly form of Fahrenheit loomed in spectral shadow. Beneath a darkened brow, his eyes burned like proclamations of doom.

CHAPTER TWELVE

'YESTERDAY' MOMENTS

When Archimage Timbrad offered Leith a few days' leave of absence, she saw the warmth of concern in his autumnal brown eyes. She could not guess at the Wearer of White's age – if he were human, she might place him in his mid-forties; as such, he appeared little older than she – yet his demeanour towards her remained every inch as fatherly as her true father had been.

For his part, Timbrad indicated that he would survey the state of industry at The Works, in place of Khashoggi. The sylph understood this to mean that he would check in on Torr Yosef, a responsibility with which she had tasked herself. The golem's stewardship of all things mechanical had seen him once again express interest in venturing to the buried spacecraft – a compulsion that resonated strangely in his telepathic voice.

Leith knew why the Archimage suggested she step away from Babel. 'Take some fresh air,' he had said. Timbrad sensed her distraction, a scrambled aura uncharacteristic for the sylph. He may not fathom the root of her turmoil, but Leith felt disinclined to confide private matters to the astute Adept.

Two days after the departure of the *Khonsu*, she strode from Babel, headed for the verdant vastness of Eleuthervale. She wore a dark cloak that gathered between her wings and fell all the way to the ground, and a satchel of provisions slung by a sash across her breast. Choosing to avoid the broad eastern verge and the fire trail beyond, she threaded through the maze of Babylonian streets with a voluminous hood shadowing her face. If the sentries at the Merchant Quarter Gate recognised the Minister for Security, they gave no sign. Without a word she loped past them, eyes fixed on the lofty aegis of the forest.

The paved road soon became a gravel path, then a rutted track. Travellers by this route were quickly swallowed by the trees, forced to choose from a maze of wooded trails amidst the towering sentinels of the vale.

Cool, fragrant air welcomed Leith, bringing the fresh scent of pine and the shrill twittering of birdlife. Even in summer, the perpetual dappled shade caused her to settle her wings about her shoulders, and draw in her cloak. In a sentimental way, it reminded her of the foothills of the Vultan Range. She felt the cold, but it felt like her old home.

On any other occasion, the sylph would have flown high above the canopy. Her destination lay scant hours away, should she take to the air; to soar on a summer breeze provided a tempting alternative to hiking. But she needed time. Time to think. To allow rationality to supplant the churning emotions. With great irony for a sylph, she found that solid earth beneath her boots helped her to focus on the more tangible conundrums, affecting the world beyond her own skin. It had always been that way.

Sammy the butterfly had disappeared. Had he been killed? If so, the perpetrator had removed the body; this made little sense, given the carnage so carelessly left behind. Though he showed diligence, nothing singled out the creature as worthy of a focussed assault.

The alternative — that he had voluntarily strayed from his post — seemed improbable. No other sentry had reported seeing Sammy. The sentry on duty with him had been slain.

Sammy didn't get very far.

Leith knew what lay inside the Main Gallery. She had personally catalogued each and every gift brought for the King and stored therein; Warlocks had assessed each item for any sign of ensorcellment. The Order's gift — the Golden Gate, as it had become known — drew immediate attention. Imbued not with magic, so the Warlocks told, but with a power more fundamental. Perhaps even divine.

So, the High Priestess and her Acolytes brought us a door, transcending any potential known in Rhye. Either the otherworlders possessed even greater technology than we understand, or else the Golden Gate was somehow constructed by the Pantheon.

Leith grimaced at the notion that Sammy might have opened the massive door. Stepped through it. *But why? And to where?*

Whatever had happened, he might be lost forever ... nothing left to be done about it.

The sylph strode onwards. Squirrels darted across her path, seeking refuge in the knotted boles of hickory trees. Her grim countenance registered little of the beauty around her as her thoughts ventured deeper.

The Order of the Unhomed.

The High Priestess, Lady Mercy, explained that the Order had been founded one thousand years earlier. That meant the Age of Sovereigns, with the year falling in the late 1730s After Godsryche. Their ministry began with the discovery of twenty refugees. *Wanderers. From a place far away; perhaps even another world. How was all of this hidden, lost to history? Did nobody stumble upon this Order, with its peaceful mission – right in the depths of Nurtenan – and decide to write it down? Surely somebody knows!*

Head down, embroiled in a storm of thoughts, Leith almost collided with a tree. She pulled up short with a start.

Somebody does know.

Khashoggi knows.

She walked on with renewed vigour. Perhaps the Prophet had already shared his insights with those aboard the *Khonsu*, or perhaps not. Either way, the sylph drew closer to the one place where she might find an answer. She only hoped it might still come in time to aid those voyaging the Western Way.

Shadows deepened. Dappled sunlight began to fade as the hour grew late. Leith headed southeast through the wild, leaning into all of her senses through the encroaching darkness. Close at hand, she knew she would find a hut built of stone. An overnight shelter, provided by forest-born labourers under the governing hand of a certain green-haired Minister for Conservation.

At last, with stone walls around her and a fire in the hearth, Leith felt able to put aside her ruminations for the night.

In a sunlit glade, nestled between Dragonfly Hollow and the ever-vibrant Papilion, the Repositree reached for the heavens. The archive of all things written, preserved for the future of the land.

Early the following morning Leith arrived at the Repositree, while birdsong still marked the coming of day and dew glistened in the grass. She never failed to marvel at the sight of the tremendous elm, its branches spanning almost the entire glade and ballooning towards the sky like an emerald fortress of leaves.

Even at this hour, the glade thrummed with activity. Most visitors were dragonflies and Adept – innate scholars, questing for enrichment of the mind. Plenty of humans, sylphs and Fae creatures also sought wisdom and entertainment amidst the countless leaves. Leith had been surprised to find, on occasion, goblins and kobolds upon the Repositree's boughs. The Wilden races still preferred the shadowed corners of New Rhye, and generally stayed away from this shared place of learning.

A dirt path ran down the short slope from where the sylph stood at the glade's verge. It ended at the steps to a huge timber stage, built around the foot of the great tree. From this platform, dragonfly librarians aided visitors to find the appropriate bough of the Repositree, directing one way or another towards elevators and rope ladders rising into the canopy above.

Leith's journey on foot had not been spent in vain. By the time she gained the platform — the 'foyer' of the Repositree — she knew exactly where she needed to go.

A dragonfly met her under the elm's gigantic eaves. 'How may I direct you, m'Lady?' the creature droned.

Leith offered a polite wave. 'Non-fiction: Reference. After Godsryche ... Northern Realms, please.'

The dragonfly gestured with an outstretched pincer. 'Second elevator on your right, m'Lady. First bough on your right, stepping off.'

'Thank you, ah—'

'Herb.'

'Herb?'

'Yes, m'Lady,' said the dragonfly, puffing out his carapace. 'Short for "Herbacio P. Botany".'

'I see ... thank you, Herb!' She sidled past the insect, who gave a tidy bow.

Dragonflies, given no names at hatching, often adopted appellations derived from their personal interests. Evidently, Herb enjoyed researching plants, just as Harold – known as *Herald*, once upon a time – chose to recognise his beloved trumpet.

Leith crossed the platform to the place where several large wicker elevators rose and fell beside the Repositree's extraordinary trunk. Beside the proffered elevator stood a sign marked '*HISTREE*', with an 'up' arrow. She boarded with a handful of others, the last of whom closed a small wicker gate behind them; with a slight jolt, the elevator began its ascent into the vast library of leaves.

Several Adept shared the ride – a Gold-clad Elemental and two Astrologers in Deep Blue; the trio huddled to converse amongst themselves. To Leith's delight, a pair of sylphs also stepped aboard: a woman held the hand of a young boy, who threw Leith a gap-toothed smile and fluttered his wings. Under his spare arm were stuffed a bundle of paper scrolls, while a writing stylus lay at a rakish angle behind one ear.

'Good morning, Minister Lourden,' said the female sylph with a blush.

'Please, it's Leith.' *I didn't anticipate being recognised ... but better a pair than a crowd, I suppose.* 'And what do you have there?' she said to the child.

'School assignment things!' cried the boy. 'Due today.' His beaming face grew glum.

'Good luck!' said Leith with an encouraging grin.

The elevator creaked upwards. She peered through the wicker bars into the network of enormous boughs and branches all around. Despite the early hour, dozens of creatures wandered the boughs, each searching for a lush blade to read.

Leith focussed instead on the elevator mechanism. She knew the car to be hoisted and lowered on dense vines as thick as a manuban's trunk, though she had never caught sight of the Repositree's renowned hamadryad. As the elevator rose, she studied the great core of the elm, until …

There she is!

At the main bifurcation, where several boughs sprouted from the trunk, dwelled Ulma. The famed hamadryad lived as an extension of the tree itself, as with all of her kindred spirits throughout the forests of Rhye. Ulma's daunting size and statuesque appearance were not her only notable features: she also bore ten tremendous arms, with which she operated the suspended elevator cars. Ulma had no voice with which to speak, but performed her monotonous task in perpetual silence.

A moment later, Leith alighted from the elevator and made her way along the bough designated *HISTREE*. Large amber leaves indicated subcategories, to be found along smaller branches: 'Ancient Histree (Pre-Godsryche)', 'Sylphic Histree', 'Sontenean Histree' and many others. Leith chose a branch that led into the Age of Sovereigns – the final era of Old Rhye. The sylph had lived through the end of that Age, marked by the anointment of the King of Rhye and the rise of Adatar at the New Dawn. But much lay concealed in a dim and war-torn past, reaching back over two and a half millennia to the Godsryche itself.

Intuition had brought her this far; only a degree of luck would help her locate the leaves she sought from here. Leith murmured a brief plea to Oska.

She eased herself down onto a branch, letting her legs dangle over the edge. The dizzying height gave her heart no cause to thrill; a youth spent soaring amidst the spires of the Vultan Range had left her inured to any fear of altitude.

A branch heavy with leaves hung well within her reach. She leaned forward and plucked the nearest one from its stem – a broad green blade the size of her two palms, with fine serrations along its edges. A neat, printed label identified it: *Brixton Wolds. Age of*

Sovereigns, Year 1700AG. Rolling the leaf into a tube, Leith held it to her ear.

The lightest breeze whispered through the vast canopy around her, rustling leaves near and far. Though it came as nought but forest sounds to the unadorned ear, the placement of a Repositree leaf funnelled new sounds to the reader – the words with which a particular leaf had been imbedded.

On an enchanted susurrus, a passage came to her from the distant past.

"... transport of food and merchant wares through the northern lands by caravan at this time became especially hazardous. Many contemporary reports agree that spriggan migration contributed greatly to this issue [25-31]. Galleo's response to the matter was to increase the size of eastbound caravans and introduce armour plating to his manubani [31,32]. This enabled trade to continue during the winter of 1700AG, though caravans slowed. Transit time increased to sixteen days, and dispersal of goods into the northern reaches of the Brixton Wolds ceased altogether until the following spring ..."

Leith removed the leaf-tube from her ear and cast it away. It danced, spinning in dizzy circles as it fell, before igniting and disintegrating with a *whumph* in a tiny cloud of smoke. It disappeared long before it reached the forest floor.

An identical leaf would re-grow from the stem in only a few moments. In the meantime, Leith rubbed a finger along the side of her slender nose.

If I'm looking for evidence of twenty lost otherworlders, I won't find it along established trade routes, or everybody would know about it. Best to search off the well-worn path. Who would be moving through unpopulated frontiers?

The military.

The Vrendari.

She reached further along the branch, pulling free another leaf. *Vrendari Campaigns in Nurtenan: Age of Sovereigns, Years 1500-1800AG.*

"... the platoon spent that October in the foothills below the Eyrie. There they found the remains of Vrendar's Rest in a state of disrepair, and immediately set about affecting renovations. This not being a time of conflict, the soldiers anticipated uninterrupted work. They did disturb a rookery of harpies, which prompted a frantic skirmish. Each of the creatures purportedly bore 'scythe-like talons' and 'an obnoxious cry that came howling from a similarly odious breast' [5,8].

Lieutenant Gwydir does not record any casualties from this encounter; most of his writings document the work undertaken to restore Vrendar's Rest. Interestingly, a quarter-league to the west of the Rest, a cache of skeletal harpy remains has been excavated. In the same place was identified a shallow grave, unmarked and not containing Vrendari accoutrements."

Well, that's interesting.

A faint smile touched Leith's lips. The second reading shed no further light on the mystery of marooned travellers, but it did whet her appetite for long-lost Vrendari lore. Moreso, it brought a mention of fabled General Prime Arnaut Vrendar — a sylph who had risen to legendary status an entire Age before even this historic account.

Leith chided herself. *Must stay on track.* Instinct told her the trail was now warm; she would focus on this specific branch, where events in the depths of Nurtenan, one thousand years ago, held eerie promise.

She grabbed another leaf.

"Skirmishes in the Northern Wolds at this time were frequent but small scale [17,18]. Gwydir and his contemporaries describe uprisings of gypsy clans, none of whom were sufficiently equipped or organised to provide significant challenge to a squad of Vrendari ..."

And another...

"... the two factions: one intent on repairing it, the other on rigging it for destruction. Reports suggest that the Winged One was active in Nurtenan during that period, and turned the course of events through acts of divine wonder. Such reports are not substantiated and are classified here as anecdotal [citation needed]. There is debate about the relevance of these events amongst the Astrologers' Guild ..."

... and another.

"... columns of locally-quarried granite, to the height of three stories and engraved with the General Prime's most renowned exploits [1,2]. The remains of Vrendar himself were laid at double the standard depth below the ground, directly beneath the altar. The altar-stone was carved from a single slab, atop which they chiselled the encircled, seven-pointed star known as the Sigil of Marnis ..."

She crushed this last leaf in her fist before tossing it away.

Leith sighed, rubbing her eyes with the heels of her hands. *So many leaves to read!* Her mind swirled with history more recent; tales of yesterday that felt tender, like a bruise. Patrolling Ardendale with Trixel and a brace of dryads, clearing the forest of orcs and redcaps. Countless hours spent in conference at the Ministry, sharing bored eyerolls and smirks with the fixie cross the table. Running down qilin in Eleuthervale only a few weeks ago. She shook her head free of maudlin thoughts.

Wait.

Leith looked down between her dangling legs, watching the falling leaves spiralling, vanishing in puffs of smoke. *Whumph. Whumph.*

I don't recall learning about that *in History class.*

She drummed her fingers, waiting for the leaves to re-grow, from freshly denuded stems dripping with sap. The moment a leaf had sprouted anew, she snatched it once more, rolled it and jammed it against her ear.

"*In his chronicle of the year 1739AG, Foucault provides an account of a ruined landship, and the band of gypsies who claimed to have travelled within it. Strangely dressed they were, and displayed strange customs; perhaps hailing from lands to the east of Fenmarck Haunte. Other outlandish claims they made, including that their vehicle had been designed to travel in the air, and from places far beyond the frontiers of Rhye.*

A network of rural folk from Brixton Wolds reportedly formed to aid these addled voyagers [1-3], who displayed quite clear signs of deranged faculties. Severe, divisive bickering ensued, centred around the fate of the ruined hulk that had borne them. Differing motivations drove the two factions: one intent on repairing it, the other on rigging it for destruction. Reports suggest that the Winged One was active in Nurtenan during that period, and turned the course of events through acts of divine wonder. Such reports are not substantiated and are classified here as anecdotal [citation needed].

There is debate about the relevance of these events amongst the Astrologers' Guild, though reports of such a contrivance were so prevalent that, by the early 1800s, extensive surveys of the region were undertaken [4-8]. As of the recording of this document, no substantive evidence of the contrivance, nor outworld gypsies, nor of the performing of miracles by the Winged One, has been confirmed."

Leith Lourden stared into space, as if she could look back across the aeons.

She did not watch the leaf fall from her numbed fingers, dancing in the air on its way to disintegration. Indescribable dread knotted her stomach; nausea that caused her to squirm, as threads of uneasiness entwined themselves within her.

With her first rational thought, Leith wondered if Torr Yosef had power enough to project his telepathy to the voyagers on board the *Khonsu*.

CHAPTER THIRTEEN

GUILT IN THE TIDE

The Milky Sea became the world itself. A blue demesne stretched beyond sight in every direction, both inexorable and inevitable, a glittering azure fact of life.

At times, the serene undulations welcomed the voyagers — tempted them, like a languid seductress. Just as often, the sea turned tormentor; rolling banks of thunderheads formed in the blandest sky as if conjured by Cornavrian himself, whipping the waters into vengeful whitecaps that lashed the *Khonsu*.

As sure as day followed night, calm seas followed torrid. Crystalline skies replaced the violent grey-green of Nature's wrath. Each time the fairer weather returned, so did the undines. The lithe aquatic spirits dashed beside the ship, sunlight glinting on ultramarine scales along their supple flanks. Once or twice, Meadow claimed he saw a much larger shape as well, looming in the cavernous depths below the ship. When he told his friends of it, they gave him a dubious eye; Harold began monitoring the casks of drowseberry wine in the galley and the hold.

Upon the illimitable sea, even an imposing vessel like the *Khonsu* became as a tiny life raft, a vital capsule on which the voyagers depended to survive. The sea may have become their world, though it remained capricious and uninhabitable, while drawing them ever westward to a fate unknown.

A week passed.

Khashoggi spent most of his daylight hours at the ship's Bridge, dialling up 'Full Ahead' whenever conditions were favourable. He spent most of the nights there as well, leading the others to speculate as to when exactly he slept, or took his meals. Mack and Mandel, the paired automatons, bumbled in aimless circles around him. He ignored their offerings of food, fresh clothing and even, on one occasion, an unsolicited tub full of steaming, sudsy water. The Prophet gave them looks fit to seize their gears, but said nothing.

The seraph knew better than to probe Khashoggi further. Dinner on that first evening had proved incendiary enough; Mustapha's challenge left Khashoggi exposed, bereft of a reply. Whatever the Prophet knew of the entombed spacecraft, he had buried within one of the most introspective moods he had ever displayed.

Instead, Mustapha dismissed Gwenamber and spent hour after thankless hour in the company of Ackley Fahrenheit. The human had deigned to grant Mustapha an audience in his cabin, a dynamic with which the King of Rhye had become wholly unfamiliar. They sat together in the dim confines, the passing hours outnumbering words spoken.

'It's a strange feeling, being so far from anywhere,' said Mustapha, seated beside the bed.

Fahrenheit offered no reply. Not with words. He sat in a second high-backed chair, at a modest writing desk. Aside from the bed, a nightstand and a basic wardrobe, these were the only furnishings in the room. The austerity of the space seemed to suit the human.

Gleaming, red-rimmed eyes gave a vacant stare, but slid across to Mustapha as he spoke.

Finding himself uninterrupted, the seraph continued. 'Considering the abundance of life out here — just think of it: we must surely be surrounded, all the creatures of the sea below and around us — it's still so awfully peaceful out there, on a fine day. The skies, though ... the skies are a different matter. I expected to find them empty. They very nearly are, except for the blasted kestrels. Where are they coming from? We've been at sea for a week, and there's no sign of landfall. I've checked all over the ship. I can't find where they're nesting. Anyway, perhaps it's good to have them around. An empty sky might be a little too serene.'

Nothing.

Mustapha drew a deep breath and slowly let it out. 'This voyage is more important than you can imagine,' he said. 'You don't know the half of it, but there are a lot of innocent people who are depending on us to succeed.'

'You've said the same thing to me every morning for the past five days,' said Fahrenheit, his parched voice like dust in a wasteland. 'I am yet to hear any evidence of value.'

'That's because I could never be sure you had heard me,' returned Mustapha, filling a cup with water from a jug on the nightstand. Fahrenheit accepted it, quaffing it in one long draught. 'Now I know that you do ... I want to apologise. I've been a little rough with you.'

'A little rough? Pah! You threshed me into a coma with your overblown theatrics, and dragged me on board this tub without my knowledge. "Rough" be damned!'

'I have no excuse for that, it's true. But given our plight, it was really the only choice I could make.'

The human continued to glare. *'Our plight,* you say. Enlighten me.'

'Some sort of outworlder cult attended the Ball,' Mustapha explained. Fahrenheit registered vague recognition, but said nothing. 'The Order of the Unhomed, they called themselves. I welcomed them as distinguished guests, but the night evolved into absolute chaos. They slew over two dozen people, though it seems the main target was their own High Priestess. Most peculiar. Aside from that, they left behind a strange object. A gift, they said. It's a kind of mystic gateway, though even the Adept aren't entirely sure how it works, or where it goes.'

'An assassination and a case of lost property,' said Fahrenheit. His ire had dulled, only to be replaced by suspicion. 'None of this explains why I am on a boat with you, headed for the boundaries of the known world.'

Mustapha stroked his moustache, finding his words. 'Before she was killed, the High Priestess told us of the Order's vocation: to provide guardianship for the displaced denizens of Rhye. Those left wandering by the trauma and destruction of war. Apparently, there are many people still left without a home, after the creation of New Rhye — our job has been left unfinished. It's up to me to find them refuge. A new beginning. I'm not sure if Lady Mercy was killed for telling me that, but that's how it appears. She also seemed to think I could prevent the Unhomed from needing me in the first place. I've no idea how, but I have to track down the Order and find out. They fled into the west—'

'No.'

'I ... I beg your pardon?'

'I said no. I'm not helping you.' Ackley Fahrenheit crossed his arms.

Mustapha gaped. Though he had anticipated Fahrenheit's

refusal, the vehemence of it caught him off-guard. Once again, life in the court of Babel had seen him grow accustomed to deferential subjects. Even sycophants, at times ... whether he sought them or not.

'I need you,' he pleaded. 'The Order comes from a place beyond the Western Way.'

'Then we are at a literal and figurative impasse.'

'What will it take? How can I help you see...?'

Fahrenheit laughed. A harsh laugh, without humour. 'Take a look around, *Your Majesty*. We are surrounded by ocean. A boundless expanse that waits to be our doom. We are stuck here on this ship. There is nothing you could possibly offer me. Better had I never left Hiraeth ... better still, had I never left Brighton-Upon-Sea.'

Mustapha felt himself trembling. Competing passions wrenched his gut. He began to understand Fahrenheit's predicament; guilt flowed in the seraph's veins, reminding him of toxic cinnabar. In ten years, the human had never referred to the earthbound place where he had once been. Where the world he knew had left him behind.

On the other hand, he considered the plight of an untold number of souls. Refugees, if not from war-torn Rhye, from another time and place. The crushing weight of responsibility pressed down on him.

Nobody asks for this. Father! What would you do? He pictured the leonine head of the unflappable General Prime. A sylph who had stepped up to the needs of the populace every single day.

He knew what Bastian Sinotar would do. *Serve the greater good.*

'I need you,' he repeated. Not a plea this time.

Fahrenheit's eyes grew wide, as did his wretched grin. 'No,' he mouthed.

'I saved your life!' Mustapha rose from his chair, fists balled at his sides.

'... And then you ruined it! You have drawn me from world to world; from the earth where I belonged, to the Old Rhye I came to love, to this new world I cannot bear. I tire of it. The place I remember from my youth is a fading memory. There is no way back home for me. The only place I feel safe has retracted – shrunk to the size of a ship's cabin. I have little else, but I still have this choice.'

'Don't you get it?' shouted Mustapha. 'Neither of us have a choice! The Order have left behind a thing of God-power. I don't know what it is, but given their proclivity for wanton violence, it can't be good. I can't ask the Pantheon about it because they don't seem to be listening. As I see it, the only way forward is to seek out the Order. Perhaps, to accomplish the task they have set – to find the Unhomed.

'I cannot do that without you. We're two halves of a whole. Or, King and loyal subject ... whichever way makes it clearer for you. So: we're in this together, whether you like it or not!'

Mustapha's blood boiled. Unsure if Bastian Sinotar would have handled things this way, he careened on regardless. *I am King, am I not? Perhaps I should not be "just as any other passenger". Perhaps I need to remain King on board this ship, just as back in Babylon.*

Fahrenheit returned a stony glare. 'You overstep, Sire.'

'Blast it! To refuse me is treason. You must do as I command, for the sake of Rhye!'

The moment overwhelmed the seraph. He fumed at the grimacing wretch sat before him. Fahrenheit's eyes moved towards the door. Mustapha followed them, to see the tousled hair and horrified face of Will, standing there for an unknown length of time; his blanched face and slack jaw suggesting he had heard the worst of it.

Will shrank back from the opening, disappearing down the corridor. Mustapha, torn between chasing him and resolving the matter with Fahrenheit, ground his teeth and yowled in fury.

More than anyone else, the pixies embraced the spirit of adventure aboard the *Khonsu*. Within the first two days, Meadow and Dique had managed to poke, squeeze and ferret their way into every corner of the ship from bow to stern, no matter whether or not two pixies had any place being there. They quickly grew bored of investigating the unoccupied staterooms and cabins, and instead found their way to the crew quarters.

Sparse but still of generous proportion, the crew quarters were divided into customary rooms for the Mer Folk, and a more utilitarian space in which automatons could draw on the ship's power source to recharge. Meadow soon declared the automatons to be 'boring buckets of bolts', so the pair decided to infiltrate the on-board domain of the Mer. Hitching a ride in the dumb waiter – taking the ladders seemed altogether too mundane – the pixies found themselves in the expansive galley.

A haven of polished steel, wooden bench seats and long tables bustled at every hour of day and night. The *clang* of pots and *clink* of pewter kitchenware accompanied scrumptious aromas, welcoming the *Khonsu's* crew to a parlour to satisfy their appetites. Mer and servibots shared the task of food preparation; a near-continual feast of stews, soups and the inevitable fish dishes appeared by the vatload.

'I may have misjudged you,' said Meadow, eyeing the pearlescent shell as it disappeared once more under a pewter cup. He and Dique sat elbow-to-elbow at a long table with a rambunctious crowd of Mer Folk, fresh from their labours and angling to slake well-earned thirsts.

Men and women alike wore simple clothing; sleeveless shirts or bare chests, vests of leathery kelp, and trousers hitched to the knee. Bare feet lacked the webbed toes of their undine counterparts, though the Mer also sported gills for long periods underwater. Sparse jewellery included bone spines or coral fragments, piercing an ear or hanging about the neck. Women one and all bore a wild beauty, with oval-shaped eyes and Grecian noses forming a comely aesthetic. The men, firm of jaw and broad of face, showed a spark in their eye like sunlight on the ocean.

'Do you misjudge me, or my entire race?' Cyreus, the swarthy engineer to Meadow's left, began moving the trio of inverted cups about on the tabletop. A hint of mirth coloured his baritone.

'Your entire race, if I'm being honest.' Meadow found the looping course of the cups to be strangely hypnotic. Cyreus's deft hands worked the sleight with baffling speed. Then they stopped; several Mer tossed their kinsman a silver coin, each indicating a cup. 'I always thought the Mer were a little … proper, if you know what I mean.'

The comment drew hearty laughs from those who heard it. Cyreus grinned wide. 'We know how to do pomp and ceremony, Master Meadow.' He raised the cups to a barrage of howls and cheering, while more coins changed hands. 'By good fortune, we also know how to surprise.'

Reka, a woman with salt-swept, grey-blue hair, gave a disarming smile and slid a coin across the table for the next round. 'You two seem to have found your sea legs pretty quickly.'

'We can stagger with the best of them,' said Dique, casting a buy-in of his own.

Meadow nodded. 'Being on board the *Khonsu* is just like a week-long night at Smokies'.'

The game continued. While the stakes were low, the playing kept morale high. Word had passed around of Khashoggi's introspection, Fahrenheit's nihilism and Mustapha's outburst. The Mer intended to keep to their treasured engines, boisterous sea shanties and games of Shell Cups.

'I could think of worse vessels to take on such a momentous outing,' said Reka. 'The Prophet has crafted a thing of wonder here. We Mer are in awe of the work he has done, bringing three energies together with such synergy. With this technology, Artesia could have been the most advanced Realm in Old Rhye.' The domain of the Mer Folk, an underground basin outfitted with labyrinthine chambers, hydraulic lifts and turbines powered by the sea, already represented a masterwork of the bygone Ages.

'The Works is the place that Artesia could have been,' replied Meadow. 'I do agree, though: this ship is the machine of a dream. You ought to take me down to the Engine Room for an inspection, some time.'

'With pleasure,' said Reka, blushing.

Dique rolled his eyes. A burly Mer-man interrupted the courtship by delivering a squat cauldron of hot broth to the table. He set it down, setting coins, cups and shell bouncing in all directions.

Cyreus peered over the rim. 'Oi, Tertis! Where has the rest of it gotten to?'

The muscular chef, who had begun to turn away, paused. 'Rations for everyone, from today,' he explained. 'This trip is looking longer than the one we provisioned for. Besides — some of you look like you could use smaller helpings.' Tertis roared with laughter as he returned to the kitchen, ducking a flying spoon as he went.

Pixies and Mer Folk inhaled their broth; nobody spoke during the ritual slurping and spoon-scraping. Afterwards, the gathering began to disperse. As bodies thinned out, Meadow and Dique spied a lone figure sitting at an adjacent bench – a fixie, hunched over a bowl with steam curling about her emerald fringe.

'Not one for a game of Shell Cups, Lady Tate?' inquired Dique, as they slipped onto the bench beside her.

'I don't gamble.'

'We're only playing for small change, really. Who knows if coins are even useful, wherever it is we're going?'

'It isn't the money,' said Trixel. 'I don't like the feeling of losing control.' She pushed her bowl away.

Meadow twiddled his thumbs. 'I think this is one of those situations where we aren't supposed to ask awkward questions.'

'I believe it is,' agreed Dique.

Trixel studied the table top.

Dique pursed his lips. 'So ... why do you look like you've been crying?'

'I haven't been crying. I'm tired.'

Meadow shuffled nearer and looped his arm through hers. Trixel's body tightened, though she made no effort to extricate herself.

'Come on. You can tell Uncle Meadow all about it.'

Glassy, violet eyes swivelled to look at him. 'Be mindful: I was once your Regent.'

'Ah – a glorious month it was, too,' said Meadow. 'Apologies, my Lady. But we are all now in a new predicament. I sense that you are the one needing our guidance, this time.'

Trixel bit her lip, seeming to mull over the pixie's words. 'How do you do it?' she said at last, barely a whisper.

'Do what?'

'How do you' – she swallowed – 'how do you show your heart without having it crushed?'

The pixies looked at each other. Dique shrugged. 'I've been a tinkerer, an apprentice cheese merchant and even a Fae Knight ... but I've never been a relationship expert.'

'Look at what you have!' Trixel cried. 'You meet an incredible woman, raise a houseful of kids with her and sail away, knowing your bond will withstand the greatest of tests. And you' — she looked to Meadow — 'you change women like you change your breeches, and never come away burned. How is it done? How do I survive the perfect woman?'

A deep *'Aaah'* moment settled over Meadow and Dique. While the fixie bowed her head, Meadow mouthed a silent question to his friend.

Erinfleur? The Elemental?

Dique shook his head.

Witherwind? The fairy from the Treasury?

Another head-shake.

Then who?

Must be Leith. I saw them kissing at the Ball.

Ah.

'You don't survive the perfect woman,' Dique said to Trixel. 'You surrender yourself to the journey, knowing that you'll be utterly undone.'

Meadow raised an eyebrow. Trixel threw her head back, a tear silvering her cheek. 'I've made a terrible mistake.'

'How?' he asked.

'I got on this damned ship because I was afraid. Afraid because a door opened and I didn't want to step through it. I didn't want to get hurt ... so I hurt her instead. Now I'm here ... and we're further apart every day.' She shivered.

The pixies had never seen Trixel Tate so vulnerable. To them, she had always been a warrior; a fearless tracker and hunter, and for a short time, wearer of the Antlered Crown. 'It's rotten luck,' said Meadow, 'but I suppose there isn't an awful lot you can do about it.'

'I've prayed to Ophynea every day since we left home,' said the fixie. 'For guidance. For a sign that one day we'll be back together. So that I can tell her how much I adore her. If only ... if only she could live as long as I.'

'And let me guess ... you're not getting any sign that Ophynea has heard you.'

'That's the strange part: there's some kind of stirring. I hear whispers. If it is Ophynea, I wouldn't know. The voice sounds far away, and it fades quickly. I think about Leith, and I pray for her by name ... and I get visions. Of us being back together somehow. At times the scenes are quite vivid ... but there's always something wrong. I don't know what to make of it.'

'I hope you do make it back to Leith,' said Dique, sympathy softening his face. 'For your own sake.'

Harold fretted.

Standing on the Observation Deck, he riffled through the pile of charts and tables once more, triple-checking his calculations. Then he turned back to the odd-looking star-tube, adjusting one of its many dials. Just two clicks. He placed his eye to the viewing window, frowning against the eyepiece.

This can't be right.

Despite the season, a chill air drifted in from the west. The morning sky had been blood red these last two days. *Could a storm be coming?* He turned his naked gaze to the heavens; the dome above winked with a million stars, from one horizon to the other.

Not a single puff of cloud.

Khashoggi had called the strange tubular device a 'telescope'. Said he had learned about them during his years building the

Khonsu, and managed to construct his own. Harold developed immediate interest, spending time every night staring skywards … noticing, little by little, a worrying truth.

Leaving the telescope, he bundled the charts under one arm and scurried for the spiral stair.

Khashoggi sat on the floor, legs crossed, head bowed so that his straggling beard splayed across his chest. Several automatons moved about him, monitoring readouts, feathering levers; undertaking precalculated instructions. They circled around the Prophet as if he were another piece of nautical equipment. The engine order telegraph showed 'Half Ahead'.

Harold crouched beside him. Khashoggi had worn the same yellowed shirt for three days or more, open at the neck and sour with sweat. The dragonfly wrinkled his nose.

'Khashoggi … there's something you need to know.'

The Prophet muttered into his whiskers. At first, Harold could not tell if the old man spoke to himself. Lank hair fell across Khashoggi's face, concealing his gaze; he peered out between the strands like a man trapped behind bars.

'I followed your word … fulfilled your designs for me. Oh, how I have been rewarded! The glory and the wisdom … the years and the memories. Oh, wine, women and song! Those were the days … all gone now. You, with your awe and your wonder … do you have it all, even now? Was I enough? Have I done enough?' As if only noticing the dragonfly for the first time, he raised his head.

'What have I done?'

Harold absorbed the diatribe in silence. How abruptly the Prophet had fallen; at one time — not so long ago — a storied Seer, teller of the land's fortunes and an exalted visionary. But now…

'I know what you haven't done. You haven't had a bath.'

Khashoggi laughed. 'What a thought! If only one could truly

wash away sin … cleanse the blood from ignoble hands.'

'What are you talking about?'

'Do you still wonder, Harold? Do you look about this world in awe, yearning to understand, to conceptualise, to create?'

Why can't you answer anything directly? 'Well yes, but—'

'Then rein in your impulses or witness the ending of the world.'

The dragonfly shook his head. *Again? We already did the ending of the world.* Khashoggi's rantings made little sense to him, yet the Prophet did not appear insane. Not quite. His words unsettled the dragonfly, as would a malign portent.

A prophecy.

'I understand,' said Harold. 'I mean, I don't understand at all … but I'll try. In the meantime: there really is something you need to know.'

'Mm. What might that be?'

'I've studied the sky. With my own eyes, and through your telescope. I've checked the charts, several times. Despite our speed in the last few days, it would appear we have not gained a single league. Somehow, we're sitting in the same spot.'

Khashoggi laughed. 'You don't say!'

'Another thing: I think there's a storm coming.'

The laugh grew wilder. Perhaps the Prophet had begun to lose his mind, after all.

CHAPTER FOURTEEN

WATER IN MY BRAIN

Despite Mustapha's best efforts to explain his treatment of Ackley Fahrenheit, Will remained unconvinced. A troubled frown stayed pinned to the human's face throughout a turbulent late-night analysis. Will went as far as to suggest he move to a vacant stateroom. Certainly, the spark in his eye reserved for Mustapha seemed to have extinguished.

'I think you should give Fahrenheit some space, too,' said Will. 'Gwenamber can keep an eye on him. I'm not surprised he's overwhelmed.'

'Oh, Will. What a dreadful situation. For some reason, ruling a kingdom proved easier than keeping order on a blasted boat. What to do?'

'Don't sulk about it. There are better ways to direct that energy.'

'Perhaps … but you're acting like I have some kind of hex. Or disease, or something.'

Will had already begun to walk away. 'Take a good look in the mirror, Mustapha. You need time to figure it all out. I'm sure you can. Don't fret ... I still love you.'

Despite Will's offhand assurance, Mustapha felt he had died a little inside.

He retreated to his room in contemplation. He dismissed thoughts of prayer; it seemed futile. Instead, he delved to the bottom of a large travel trunk by the bed, retrieving two objects that now shaped his meditations.

He found cautious solace in cradling the camphor laurel box, running his fingertips over the smooth, tooled wood. Fine carvings on the lid of the box shouted a warning to him: a veritable armoury of weapons, in symbolic arrangement around the image of a great tree, warped and twisted. Mustapha derived a sense of security from holding the artefact, though he would never open it; the two tiny grains of sand within were perhaps the two most devastating specks of matter in all of Rhye.

The only remains of Anuvin, God of War, and Valendyne, God of the Inevitable End. They would be with Mustapha at all times, travelling with him wherever he went.

Right until the ends of the earth.

The second item, a weathered leather document envelope, contained something equally important and of much greater sentiment to the seraph. Reaching inside the envelope, he withdrew its contents with great tenderness – a single sheet of parchment, stained, bloodied and folded.

Mustapha carefully opened the document. So worn were the creases that small tears had begun to form at the edges of the page. A single word had been written on the parchment in a strong but elegant hand: the hand of Bastian Sinotar.

Bismillah

In the name of God.

A word from the other world. To invoke it had placed him in the presence of Ophynea. The Goddess had come to him in recognition of his greatest latent gift — the gift to channel Love and to create harmony with it. His death and rebirth had followed. The King of Rhye, risen from a coronation pyre. Wreathed in flames, just as his mother had been at her own transformative death.

Mustapha scoffed to himself. *What a farce. I can't even keep harmony with my own lover.*

This jaunt is cursed, and it's barely been more than a week. We should be focussed on the future of the land. Instead we're all starting to lose our minds.

The soft sounds of music filtered into Mustapha's consciousness. It took him a moment to realise the melodic strumming was real, not imagined. There were voices too and the clatter of pots and pans. The tune carried a whimsical jangle, reminding him of bygone days in the forests of Petrichor, roaming from one Fae village to the next in search of inconsequential adventure.

Muffled as they were by the ship's bulkheads and the constant low rumble of engines, Mustapha could not fully appreciate the tune. No matter: he did not feel whimsical in any way. He replaced his belongings and perched on the edge of his bed.

Thinking.

Harold tapped his foot and hummed along, though it irritated him to do so. He didn't want to be enjoying the song. Not really.

He stood at the railing of the Observation Deck, staring out to sea. He wore his helm with the visor down, as a cool bluster had been whipping his eyes. To keep his pincers busy, he polished his treasured Horn. The instrument, imbued with the Breath of Cornavrian, had helped him turn the tide in the Battle of Two-Way Mirror Mountain.

But Harold did not dwell on the past. He stared forward into the hazy distance, at a looming shadow on the horizon that drew no nearer.

Into this ruminative moment had burst the pixies, with their blasted earworm of a song. Where did they find their verve? Were they oblivious to the decay of rationality all around them? Or did they respond to it with this rhyming jingle?

Dique gave his Zither a hearty pluck, while Meadow beat a clangour on borrowed items from the galley. Together they sang, unbridled and without a care:

> *We're a mighty long way from home*
> *And in case you didn't hear*
> *We'll be stuck on this tub forever more*
> *So, let's have a little cheer.*

> *We're a mighty long way from home*
> *And in case you couldn't tell*
> *Everyone's going slightly mad*
> *And we're cracking up as well.*

> *If we don't find some land soon*
> *There's going to be a brawl*
> *We're running out of food*
> *And it's bringing down the mood*
> *'Til there ain't no mood at all!*
> *Hey!*

> *We're a mighty long way from home*
> *And it's getting pretty grim*
> *If there's going to be catastrophe*
> *We'll be headed for a swim!*

On it went, an interminable ditty to disaster. For all Harold knew, it would continue for another seventeen verses. Still, he did not have the desire to crush the pixies' spirit. Nor did he need to join in ... he continued polishing the Horn.

Footsteps rang on the iron of the spiral stair. Mustapha emerged on the deck, bare chested, clad in white breeches fit tight to his lower body. Lightning slashes, black as midnight, ran down each leg to his sturdy white boots. A storm gathered at his brow, reflecting the ominous bank of darkness on the western horizon. The pixies' song dissolved mid-lyric; the seraph gave it no acknowledgement.

'Flight uniform, Mustapha?' asked Harold.

'Something's out there,' Mustapha replied, staring straight ahead, far beyond the *Khonsu's* bow. 'Past the storm ... or perhaps within it. A strange force is keeping the ship in stasis, but maybe I can make it through.'

'You've gone completely bonkers,' said Meadow.

'Water in your brain,' agreed Dique.

'That may be true,' said the seraph, 'but I also have the Pantheon's fire in my veins. I cannot be denied.'

Without another word, he rose into the air. Two vast wings spread wide, catching the rays of Adatar; beneath them, two smaller pairs unfurled. Six wings in total, beating with a *whoomph-whoomph-whoomph* that almost forced his companions to the deck. He spiralled upward until well clear of the *Khonsu*. A moment later, the seraph blasted into the west. Only the fragmented sound of choral voices, drifting on the breeze, marked his passage.

Harold and the pixies watched Mustapha vanish in the distance. A hollow *boom* rang in the air as he breached the speed of sound.

'He'd fly even faster without those rocks in his head,' said Meadow.

'I'd better make sure we're keeping a similar bearing,' replied

Harold, taking the stair.

To his great surprise, he found the Prophet standing straight as a signal beacon against the instrument panel. With a brimstone gaze he stared in the direction taken by Mustapha.

'Are you coherent today?' inquired the dragonfly.

'The seraph blazes a trail into the west,' said Khashoggi, by way of response. 'I think not to his doom, though he shall return with ill tidings.'

Harold moved to the Prophet's side. The recent crowd of automatons at the bridge had thinned, leaving only Mack and Mandel in his presence. Harold wondered if the two kettle-shaped machines had any capacity for detecting how unhinged the man had become. *Or maybe it's me they're watching?* He eyed them with suspicion. They each bleeped a casual greeting to the dragonfly, otherwise proceeding with undeclared directives.

Harold did not ask what the 'ill tidings' were — they would all find out soon enough, and he could happily defer new disappointment. 'The Pantheon seems to have left you with the power of prophecy,' he said, 'if even just for the coming few hours. Though if I'm being honest, I could have predicted more bad news myself.'

'Blast the Pantheon!' cried the Prophet. Harold's eyebrows jumped. 'Where are they, to watch and guide us in our hour of need? Where was Lhestra during the slaughter of innocents in Babel? Where was Augustine as Wilden Folk lay dying, their homes falling down around them? Where was Marnis, when I—' he broke down in a fit of coughing, the spittle of rage forming at the corners of his lips and flying from him in droplets.

Harold retreated, but did not quail from the embittered Seer. 'A valid point, if a heavy-handed one,' he said. He would not go so far as to agree with Khashoggi — not while an iota of faith remained to him.

223

Faith.

'You believe us alone, then,' said the dragonfly. 'Do you yet have faith in yourself? What of the *Khonsu*, your own creation? Can it get this task done?'

Khashoggi rumbled, a sound from deep within his chest. A vein pulsed at his temple as his eyes darted about. Assessing. Evaluating. 'It closes in on me. Cloying, like a vault. A casket. Out there' − he pointed out to sea − 'that is the true creation. Limitless in its strength and wonder ... and malice.'

Harold shivered. *Casket.* 'What do you mean?'

The Prophet rounded on him. 'Hear me and mark my words, dragonfly. This is a one-way trip. For you, for me, for everyone on board. There is no coming back. The Western Way shall remain unnavigable.'

'What a hopeless attitude!' Harold exclaimed. 'You came rather late to the show, when many of us were clinging to dear life at the Pillar of Rhye ... but things have been a *lot* worse than this. I literally stared Valendyne in the face! To hear his voice is to know evil. I don't know how you can possibly think ...'

Harold's rebuke trailed off, choked to silence by the lambent strangeness in Khashoggi's eyes. The Prophet loomed, cloaked in theurgy that spoke of storm clouds crossing in front of the sun. His voice echoed with a borrowed power.

'Do not misattribute evil. Consider that shades of the soul exist. There is *no* God of Evil. The divine beings are capable of both darkness and light, in their own way. So are you and I. Does evil come from the hearts and minds of sentient beings then, or is it put within our souls to test us? To know this is to know the will of the Pantheon.

'You seek prophecy, dragonfly? Then I will give it. From this journey, we do not return. The only one who could have saved us from our fate lived and died so long ago. It matters no more.

'History shall not remember this moment ... for at the root of the land resides the bane of all.'

'Wait. But who—' Harold scrambled for a clear thought. 'Didn't Mustapha—?'

'The coming of the King of Rhye was foretold,' intoned Khashoggi. 'So too is foretold his ultimate failure.'

Harold's heart sank to his stomach. 'That's not possible!' he cried, though the words tasted insipid in his mouth. He clutched himself to keep from shaking. Before his eyes the Prophet seemed to wither, shrinking back from his own pronouncement, to slump against the instrument panel. Fatigue greyed his face, his once-dapper clothes stained from exertion.

'I don't know where all of that came from,' said Harold, 'but I sure hope you're wrong.'

Khashoggi stared out to sea, some clarity returning to his gaze, though the futility of his dire forecast still clung to him. 'The impossible and the improbable are two entirely different things, Harold ... but I hope so, too.' He extended a finger out over the rolling waves. 'Look, the seraph returns.'

A winged shape hurtled towards the *Khonsu*, taking on the form of Mustapha as it approached. He raced against a backdrop of malevolent slate-grey and green; an undeniable storm stretched over one hundred leagues from north to south. A tottering column of cloud reached to the heavens, flickering from bolts of lightning within.

Mustapha extended his wings to billow behind him. He slowed a short distance off the *Khonsu's* prow, his great wingspan backlit by a distant flare. Those at the bridge lost sight of him then as he descended over the Observation Deck. A clatter sounded on the stair and the door to the Bridge flew open. Mustapha entered, with the two pixies at his heels.

'There will be … no escaping … the storm,' panted the seraph without preamble, slamming the door behind them. His skin glistened, slick with rain or dense mist; his chest heaved, words forced out between ragged breaths. Myriad droplets beaded on his feathered wings, dripping to the floor by his boots. 'Even were we to engage Full Reverse … it closes in too quickly.'

Khashoggi nodded, as if to say Full Reverse had never been his plan. He reached for the engine order telegraph, settling for Slow. 'I shall bring us to a stop presently,' he said. 'To overwork the engines at this stage is pointless.' He turned to Mandel. 'Advise the Mer to prepare for an extreme weather event. Ensure the bilge pumps are in Standby mode. Do it now.'

Harold frowned. Khashoggi had found lucidity after the melodrama of his prophecy. *Is he trying to save us now?* Could the discharge of manic passion have returned him to a place of sanity? He wondered what to tell Mustapha of the Prophet's fluctuating mental state.

'There's something more,' continued Mustapha. 'A landmass. I can't tell how big. It could be an island or a whole continent. But there is definitely land beyond the storm.'

'How will we ever reach it if we are trapped in place here?' asked Dique.

Khashoggi's grim visage answered the question without the need for words.

A charcoal sky hung low over the Bay of Marnis, bringing with it an oppressive weight. Humidity ushered in a general disdain for manual labour – or indeed outdoor pursuits of any kind. Fewer seacraft skimmed across the Bay than usual. Those who used the Corniche or the Marina did so with occasional glances above, as if expecting the heavens to open.

Impervious to complaints of sweat or drowsiness, automatons continued to buzz about the foyer to The Works. By far the most hospitable space in the entire facility, visitors could enter the foyer for information about active construction projects, tours of the scientific laboratories or for quotes on the commissioning of servitors – those automatons issued for mechanised labour throughout the city. Beyond the foyer, The Works soon became a rambling maze, honeycombing the southerly headland – nobody had yet been reported lost within the technologic sprawl, though that seemed more due to good fortune than good management.

Seven Adept were accepted beyond the foyer without question. They carried authority sufficient to override all but the King himself. The offer for a chaperone to enter the deeper facility was met by a curt declination.

With grim faces, the Adept proceeded, combing the Works with fastidious caution. The deeper they ventured, the less activity they encountered. At length, they trod the gloomy, grated gangways alone.

There, in the recesses, did they find their quarry.

'Tell me again: How many souls did you carry from Old Rhye?' asked Archimage Timbrad into the darkness.

The Wearer of White flexed his fingers. An instinctive twitch, readying defences. He felt no fear, only a grim sense of duty. The six Warlocks at his back were a precaution.

Or so he told himself.

A combination of sun-powered scrallin and the latest electronic filament in blown glass – an innovation of Khashoggi's – illuminated the gargantuan network of passageways and laboratories – the vast hive of mechanised industry where invention and production thrived together. Here, in this dingy corridor buried deep, the light struggled to penetrate. Only twinned lamps shone out of the shadows, a short way ahead of Timbrad.

The lamps glowed a dull red.

A telepathic response came to the Archimage's mind without hesitation. A mechanical sound, like marching pistons and greasy cogs.

<Five million, seventy-eight thousand, six hundred and seventy-two.>

Timbrad had clenched his jaw. He had already asked the golem for the population of Babylon and surrounding regions. Had already established the figure fell short, by just more than one million souls. Those poor beings lived still; stranded somehow beyond the King's percipience, at a place outside the frontiers of Rhye.

He had a new question. 'Now tell me: How many souls did you deliver — how many departed your exoskeleton — at the arrival of New Dawn?'

A slight hesitation this time. Only momentary. A cold, mathematical calculation.

<Five million, seventy-eight thousand, six hundred and seventy ... one.>

Timbrad felt the tensing of Warlocks behind him. Beneath those Violet cowls were delves, creatures of cavernous places. The industrialised bowels of The Works resonated with them, a place much like — and yet so very different from — the skyless realms of their history. It had been little challenge for them, seeking out this refuge of the rogue golem.

'We are one soul short, Torr Yosef. Do you know who the final soul belongs to?'

Metal whined and clanked as the mechanical giant shifted. A glint of dull alloy showed in the dismal light.

<Yes.>

Timbrad waited five heartbeats. 'Who?'

<*It is m ... mine.*>

'*Yours, Yosef?*'

<*Yes ... mine. A small price only. Just ... one task.*> The red lamp eyes gleamed.

'You were given a soul, in exchange for performing one task? What task was that?'

The golem repositioned again. There came a violent *CLANG*, the sound reverberating in the corridor's confines. Timbrad and the Warlocks flinched, leaping back. Two Wearers of Violet drew blades of theurgic fire; the Archimage waved them down. 'No naked flames in this place!' he warned.

The flare had revealed the massive golem in a moment of violet light. He crouched in one far corner of a sparse storage chamber at the corridor's end. He did not move to engage the Adept.

A loud *CLANG* came once more.

Torr Yosef struck himself.

<*No. I must not ... you need to go.*>

'I want to understand, Yosef,' said Timbrad, clenching and unclenching his fists. He eased forward, to the door between corridor and storage chamber. The twin lamps followed him. Timbrad searched the depths of his own mind, as his eyes pierced the shadowed space. The golem had long since demonstrated a capacity to think, to consider, to revere. A soul afforded little further opportunity, except ...

'What is happening to you?'

<*A battle. A gift. A task. Conflict.*> Yosef's voice sounded like the juddering of tortured mechanics. <*The spacecraft. I have to go there ... I cannot go there.*>

'Why, Yosef? Tell us your task!'

CLANG. <*I cannot.*>

Timbrad ground his teeth, mind racing. Something manipulated Yosef; he fought for control. Control of self ... whatever that meant, to a golem.

'What will happen if you tell us of your task? Will you be destroyed?'

Now Yosef did stand. He lurched to his feet, a towering shadow, head almost brushing the metal panels of the storage chamber ceiling. Twin crimson beams shone down on the Adept. Timbrad held his ground.

<*No. You will be destroyed.*>

In an instant, with mere thought, the Wearer of White cast a protective aura about himself. The Warlocks did likewise. They knew not if an attack would come, but the halo of white-gold could deflect a hurricane of physical blows.

'We are not here to do battle, Yosef. We must find a way to help you. Fight against this thing that compels you! We will rid you of it.'

<*You cannot. Strength ... too great. I will fight from here. You need to go.*>

CLANG. To watch the golem hammer his own stellite shell brought shivers to the Adept.

Maintaining his protective aura, Timbrad turned away from Yosef. The six Warlocks had assumed a defensive array in the corridor. 'You heard him. We go back. I must speak to Leith. Babylon must ready itself for imminent danger. Protect the Oddity. Secure all the districts of Below.'

CLANG.

Warily, the Adept filed out the way they had come. A three-dimensional maze of elevated walkways, hydraulic lifts and gigantic machines now seemed like a cage, hemming them in. Every hiss of steam and crackle of electricity had a sinister edge. All the while, the fraught sound echoed after them.

CLANG. CLANG. CLANG.

As Timbrad led the way towards the yawning entry portal, the golem's voice came to him once more.

<We are coming.>

CHAPTER FIFTEEN

NO WAY BACK HOME

The first rainfall spattered against the outside of Ackley Fahrenheit's modest porthole. Within minutes the world outside blurred, obscured by blotches that became streaks as wind drove the downpour against the glass.

'There was only more water to be seen out there anyway,' said the otherworlder with a shrug, turning away from the porthole. He smoothed non-existent creases from his wool jacket, finely spun by Fae hands.

Trixel sat by the writing desk, fidgeting with a stylus. Beside her, the Apothecary Gwenamber gave her sheaf of case notes a redundant shuffle. Both women watched Fahrenheit with an appraising eye. Trixel gave the Adept a sidelong nod.

'That's right – I'm fine,' said Fahrenheit, running a hand through long grey hair. 'I thank you for your concern, but I no longer need to be fussed over by a medicine woman. Besides, if I understand our situation correctly – and I believe I do – there will be little point in continuing to write things down about me.'

Gwenamber flushed, eyes flicking down to her notes. 'I am glad for your recovery, Mr Fahrenheit. Do stretch your legs on board the ship.'

'I will move about as I see fit. Thank you,' he concluded in a firm tone, as Gwenamber collected her effects and departed his cabin. The door closed behind her with a soft *clink*.

The fixie wasted no time on awkward silences. 'I'm sorry, Ackley,' she said, setting the stylus down.

Fahrenheit studied her with the same critical gaze he had just received. 'What do you apologise for? For bringing back the pestle-pusher just now, or for dragging me to the godforsaken Ball in the first place?'

Trixel exhaled. The human continued to stand, which made her uncomfortable. 'Both. But more so the second one. You have to understand: Mustapha and I agreed there were reasons for you to attend Babel—'

'The time for explanations has come and gone,' said Fahrenheit, cutting her off with a wave of his hand. He bared his teeth in a smile, though it came nowhere near his eyes. 'We are all on board this ship, for triumph or disaster. There is no going back to change that. You should be pleased to learn, however, that you now know just as much as I do about that contraption buried below the city.'

'It's Khashoggi's.' Trixel stared at her lap.

'Yes, it is. I once lived in the township from which he launched it. How it arrived here, I have no idea; nor why someone felt it necessary to carve a comment about the passing of time on a stone column.'

'You understand the inscription?'

'I do. I understood from the minute you first told me. I tried to tell Leith Lourden about it. It is Latin, an ancient language of my world, and the origin of many others. "It escapes, irretrievable time." Awfully apt in our current circumstance, I'm afraid, though it proves nothing apart from the writer understanding the language. Put simply — one of the voyagers from the spacecraft carved it.'

Trixel nodded. Both were silent for a time. Beneath their feet, the *Khonsu* gave a ponderous lurch; the Milky Sea grew rough. The rising wind could now be heard as a low howl on the other side of the window. The turbulence caused Fahrenheit to lower himself into a chair, at least.

'You must feel cheated,' he said in an absent tone, staring at the porthole.

'I beg your pardon?'

The human turned to her, removing his spectacles. A faint smile now curved his lips, giving his face a wistful air. 'To live centuries in one world, then barely ten years in the next. Was New Rhye worthy of the price of admission?'

Trixel Tate frowned, then tilted her head in contemplation. '*Was*? You believe we are doomed, as well? You're no better than Khashoggi!'

An ember of intensity flashed in Fahrenheit's eye. He shook his head. 'That man opened a window in my awareness. Pulled me through the doorway into a new reality. A new understanding, as to what *living* truly is. I think of standing with him, looking over the ruins of Fenmarck Haunte to the Pillar of Rhye, and I feel the moment in my soul. But there, our shared experience finishes.

'To Khashoggi, the *Khonsu* is a means to an end. A conduit to exploration, to discovery. Me? His conduit has become my whole world. Wretched fear! Fear of tight spaces. Fear of crowds. Fear of—' lightning flickered outside, followed after only a few beats by the rumbling *boom* of thunder; he flinched '—fear of storms. Very soon, perhaps, fear of the sea itself. That shall be my downfall. Fear, and the ruin of best intentions: the legacy of New Rhye. Long

Live the Age of Harmony.' He gave a mirthless chuckle.

The *Khonsu* rolled. In the belly of the ship, her engines still throbbed, in a vain attempt to hold position against a tumultuous sea. Both human and fixie braced themselves. Trixel halted the oil lamp as it threatened to slide off the desk. She clenched it tight. *I'm a creature of the forest. What, in the name of Cornavrian, am I doing out here? Leith – I'm sorry!*

She tried to distract them both. 'What do you remember of your home world, then?'

'Khashoggi convinced me that much of my life was a lie I'd told myself in grief,' replied Fahrenheit. 'So, I can trust relatively few of my memories. Jenny, though … I can trust Jenny. No matter how my reality changes, that true love remains constant. It is as if her spirit follows me in an attempt to keep me sane.'

Trixel swallowed. Gall swilled in her stomach, and not wholly due to the restless dance of the *Khonsu*.

'Would you go back, if you could?'

'To be with her once more? Of course. I would do all of that again and not change a thing. No, that's not quite right – I would take back some of Gwenamber's medicaments. Try to save Jenny's life.' Now, a warmth did show in Fahrenheit's hazel eyes; there for a precious moment, then gone again. 'That world was my world. Then Rhye became my world. Now this. Ever onward … life is relentless, is it not? Perhaps I should let go and embrace madness. Alas, I am forced to compromise for the sake of my beloved's memory. For her, I clutch sanity, despite all this world would bring me. I will learn to survive until the day we are reunited.'

Tears streamed down the fixie's cheeks. She made to brush them away, abashed and angry with herself—

The *Khonsu* rolled again.

In the pitch and heave, both Trixel and Fahrenheit were thrown from their seats. With well-honed reflexes, the fixie managed to twist, hitting the deck with a shoulder. As she went to ground, she watched the oil lamp tumbling, as if in slow motion. She snatched for it, arresting it before it could smash.

Fahrenheit struck the deck head-first. He gave a sharp grunt and lay still. 'Ackley!' Trixel doused the lamp, set it aside and skittered across to the prone figure. *Still breathing. Just unconscious.* Blood ran from a small laceration at his brow to pool on the polished deck.

Trixel swayed to her feet, dragging a sheet from the bed. Tearing a strip, she knelt by Fahrenheit and tied a hasty bandanna. Then, against the tilt of the ship, she clambered into the corridor, shouting 'Gwenamber!' as she went.

Perilous trench followed towering crest, as the storm riled the sea and engulfed the *Khonsu*. The day vanished behind a boundless veil of dark cloud. Sheet lightning cast garish silhouettes within the veil, chased by violent peals of thunder. Rain slashed at an obtuse angle, driven by a frigid bluster.

Will chose to visit the engine rooms and offer a hand – all Mer were now on duty, with no rest for anyone during the peak of the storm. For a change of scene, the pixies went with him. Cyreus found them all something to do, and it aided morale in the belly of the ship to have voyagers pitching in.

Mustapha opted to remain at the Bridge. Harold had confided his concerns for Khashoggi, leaving them both uncertain as to how far they could rely on the Prophet to remain steadfast. Already he had adopted an intermittent torpor – the phrase 'what's the point?' could be heard amongst his limpid ramblings. Regardless, he continued to stare out over the churning Milky Sea, wizened fingers hovering over the instruments.

An occasional wave rose high enough to crash over the ship's prow. In those moments, it seemed even the mighty *Khonsu* might be nothing more than another toy in the maw of unbridled Nature. Her nose dipped low, but surged upwards again each time with a tremendous spray of foam.

In between bouts of pacing back and forth, Mustapha glared forward into the tempestuous west. 'Look! Look, look, look!' He cried to Harold, jabbing a finger out through sheets of rain. Despite terrible visibility and a see-sawing horizon, the dragonfly had to agree: something quite substantial lurked beyond the storm.

'*Landmass confirmed,*' warbled Mack by Khashoggi's side. '*Distance zero-point-five nautical leagues. Topography consists of low to moderate elevation, with a central mountain range. Vegetation cannot be assessed in these conditions. Signs of civilisation: affirmative.*'

'Signs of life!' exclaimed Harold.

'Little good it does, when our forward speed is nil,' mumbled Khashoggi.

'Time to destination, Mack?' asked Mustapha.

'*Time to destination, given current bearing and travel speed: Infinite.*'

Mustapha stifled a moan. Harold's wings drooped.

The seraph began pacing again. 'Mack, estimated time remaining on current food rations?'

'*Three days. Maximum duration of food supply, given minimal rations for survival of all carbon-based life forms: Six days.*'

'After that, we're on a liquid diet,' remarked Harold. 'If we survive the storm.'

'What good is starving on a diet of water, if we're not moving forward?' Hands on hips, Mustapha paced. An answer coalesced in his mind. Audacious — reckless, even — but perhaps the one answer left to them.

'It is as I said,' declared the Prophet, without a whit of arrogance or pride.

'Not yet it isn't,' said Mustapha. His heart clamoured in his chest. 'It can't be, it can't!'

Harold and Khashoggi offered him looks of doubtful sympathy. Mack and Mandel would have raised their eyebrows, if they had any. 'What would you do?' asked the dragonfly.

Mustapha did not answer. If he heard himself explain his plan out loud, he thought he might just abort it. Instead, with a growl and a fierce eye, he said: 'Wish me luck. I'm going outside.' He doffed his jacket and flung it to the deck.

He heard only garbled shouts of wonder from those behind him, as he opened the door and was greeted immediately by the roar of the rain.

The full throes of a maelstrom met the seraph on the Observation Deck. Water sluiced back and forth as the *Khonsu* rocked in the waves, runoff being constantly replaced by the wash of downpour. A gale whipped his body, his face, his wings; he struggled to keep them folded against his back. He had to hold on tight to the rail, lest he lost his footing. Rain struck him like a hail of tiny bullets.

No time to waste.

Standing at the very fore of the deck, feet planted wide, hands white-knuckling the rail, he screamed into the wind.

'BISMILLAH!'

A prodigious shockwave burst from him, in all directions. The superstructure of the *Khonsu* rattled beneath his feet; somewhere, a porthole shattered. The wind and rain turned into wild eddies, driven off-course by sheer seraphic power. His searing voice, multiplied one-hundredfold, blasted into the tempest all around him.

For a moment — just an eerie moment — a stillness ruled the Milky Sea. The winds regressed. The rain eased. The tempest encountered another force of nature and was brought low.

But only for a moment.

As Mustapha stood, arms wide as if to embrace the ether, dozens of lightning bolts flared in an instant that turned gloom to brilliance. Several bolts struck the *Khonsu*, lacing over the cigar-shaped hull with a crackle. Mustapha threw himself to the deck, clapping hands over ears to block an eardrum-bursting thunderclap.

The aftermath rumbled, a drumroll from the heavens. The winds howled anew and rain hammered down on rampant waves. Mustapha righted himself from the sodden deck.

Then he heard it.

The echoing rumble became a thing of ire. Of spoiled mirth. A bellowing shout from the sky, in an ethereal voice distorted by the storm.

Shock and anger ignited the seraph. 'Who laughs? Who ... laughs ... at ... me?' he shouted, with a fist to the sky. The thunder cackled as it faded, mocking him.

'Mustapha!' An earthly shout, straining to be heard above the tumult. 'Don't be a fool! What are you doing?'

The seraph spun around, fists balled tight, face clenched with rage. Slick rain steamed from him. At the top of the spiral stair, soaked and worried, stood Will.

Mustapha almost ran to him. Every muscle fibre twitched. *How simple it would be, to run to those arms and stay there ... leave all of this aside. Drown or starve, we'd be together.* Instead, he anchored his boots to the deck. *Let his embrace be my reward, for getting us out of this.*

'I've got to keep us alive, Will.' *Got to set things to right.*

Another jagged flash of lightning. Another thunderclap, courtesy of the wrathful heavens.

Mustapha crouched, unfurled his wings and blasted straight up into the sky.

Within the granite thunderheads, the seraph felt the frigid winds might strip the flesh from his bones. Flecks of ice swirled about, lancing his bare torso like tiny blades.

With passion, he hardened himself to the cold and the screaming currents of air. With his eardrums throbbing and face benumbed, he flew directly into peril, intent on ending the torment. The subterfuge.

Must get above it all.

In the belly of the storm, lightning walked in deadly arcs between the clouds. The rumble and groan of thunder followed. Another sound came to him: a shrieking, bleating cry, as if the tempest spoke with the voice of a tortured beast.

No – how could it be? There truly is a beast.

A shadow loomed, a way off in the billowing cavern of cloud. As Mustapha streaked upwards, another flash came, illuminating the scene.

He saw the creature there.

Thrashing, roaring; issuing peals of anguish that rang through the storm. A great beast, ensnared by tendrils of air. With a titanic body covered in hair and the great, shaggy head of a bison, the beast seemed potent enough to drive the very storms of an apocalypse. Yet it could not break free of its restraints. Through its wild protestations, the tempest raged on.

Byorndrazil...?

Mustapha knew him. Had seen his image, etched with skill on the walls of a long-forgotten cave. Had seen him, along with his twenty-three Ogre brethren, burst from the ancient root of Two-Way Mirror Mountain to destroy the army of Anuvin.

He who can summon lightning.

The seraph swallowed a shout of dismay. He could not emancipate the bound creature; to do so would sway him from his goal, expend his reserves, perhaps cost him his life. He burned ever skyward, streaking towards the stratosphere.

Exploding through the upper layer of cloud brought him to a place of sudden calm. Above the storm's havoc, he shot through air of tranquil stillness. The air thinned ever so slightly, though it also grew warmer. Beneath him, the vast cloud blanket glowed white. Occasional flares of lightning only hinted at the cataclysmic weather below.

Mustapha opened his wings, basking for a moment in the splendour of the sunshine.

Adatar.

Only now did the seraph baulk at the audacity of his own plan. Yet, to cower from it now …

It must be done.

Squinting, he faced the familiar light. Felt it caress his cheeks. Held his arms aloft, palms outward in reverence.

'Gracious Adatar!' he cried. 'Hear my prayer. I seek your eternal wisdom and light, in the name of the Pantheon.

'God of the blessed Day, do you hear my prayer?' Suspended between hope and sheepishness he trembled, holding his breath.

Silence.

At this altitude, no birdlife broke the monumental quiet. Only an untraceable hum – perhaps the vibration of the very earth – sent the slightest ripple through the atmosphere.

He tried again. 'Adatar, I beseech you! As the grace of Ophynea runs through my veins! A creature of Cornavrian is enslaved and must be set free! Will you grant me the strength?'

Nought but the infinite sky. The storm below and the cosmos above.

'Adatar? The people of Rhye name me King, yet I fail them. I seek restitution for blights of the past and preservation of our future.

My mission is sacrosanct, yet it is threatened ... and only the Sun, in its glory, can help us now.'

Mustapha would never learn whether this appeal carried indulgence enough for the egotistical Adatar or if his earlier attempts simply had not been heard. But on this third occasion, the air began to shimmer as if in a heat haze, despite the persisting chill. The hum of the earth seemed to coalesce, forming words as resonant as an earthquake.

'I hear you, seraph.'

Mustapha gasped. 'Merciful Sun! I thank you for granting me this audience. I face a dilemma that touches on the very fate of the land and—'

'Quiet your pandering tongue, seraph.'

At least I got your attention, Adatar. He hovered, biting his tongue.

The vast resonance continued. 'I have seen you. Your ship sits dormant on the sea. An ill aura cloaks your voyage.'

'We see land ahead of us, Lord Sun ... but we cannot reach it.'

'Ah, yes. You will be lowering your anchor there.'

'Indeed, Lord. We will need to gather supplies.' *Perhaps Adatar can see beyond the frontiers of Rhye. He might tell me if ...*

A deep laugh rumbled through the atmosphere. 'You will lower your anchor there because I have a task for you.'

'Yes ... Lord. In the name of the Sun.' *What am I getting into now?*

'In the name of the Sun!' bellowed Adatar. Mustapha felt the air around him warming. A gentle warmth, a balm on his skin. 'The land you see – the people there have lost their way. They have wandered from the path of the Pantheon. Their city is filled with debauchery and sloth. You will go there and meet with them. Tell them of our discourse. Bring those people back to the light. Let them see my face, so that they may worship the Sun once again.'

Mustapha's eyes grew wide. *Lost their way? Wandered from the path? Are these people the Unhomed?* 'Yes, Lord. I will do it. I will go there and speak to them of our meeting. I will name their home the City of the Sun!'

'Then it is good.'

In his excitement, the seraph almost forgot the questions that brewed within him. With a start, he leapt at the opportunity for divine insight.

'Great Adatar. There is a mighty creature, the Ogre Byorndrazil, trapped within the storm. How did he get there? Why is he so ensnared?'

The air cooled. The vibrations rang not with laughter, but with a stiff ambivalence. 'The ways of the Pantheon are convolute. I concern myself not with the twisted choices of my children.'

Mustapha frowned to himself. *Not helpful.* He tried a different question. 'I pray to the Gods and Goddesses, O Adatar, and receive no reply. Has the Pantheon forsaken us?'

The atmosphere rumbled. 'It is as I have said. I do not intervene in the schemes of my children. They decide their own alliances and live their own consequences. Death broke the unity of the Pantheon, and it remains fractured.'

The seraph shuddered. The Sun spoke of a long-held feud with Valendyne. *Adatar has borne a grudge since the Age of Obelis. I guess when you're divine, petty infighting really can last for millennia.* With such evasive answers, Mustapha began to wonder if Adatar even knew the whereabouts of his other offspring. Either way, he seemed disinclined to indulge a lowly mortal.

'Divine Adatar. I thank you for your mercy and wisdom. You will help us, then, to reach the land on our horizon? The City of the Sun?'

'I shall,' answered the luminant God, with a warning tone like a solar flare. 'Though it shall cost you.'

Cost me? Didn't I agree to—? Mustapha sniffed. 'Lord Sun, I am ever in your debt ... but did we not already negotiate this?'

Adatar blazed. 'You will meet my price, or you and your subjects will drown at sea. Which do you choose?'

No mercy. No quarter. No alternative, then.

'Please, Lord Sun. Name your price.'

The voice of the Sun glowered, relishing his pronouncement. 'You must relinquish all of the powers bestowed upon you by Ophynea.'

What?

Mustapha caught his breath. *Ophynea – no!* His head swam, memories swirling within. The coronation of scarlet fire. His old life dismantled in flame; his soul repainted with the wings of holy butterflies. With Ophynea's blessing, he had vanquished the foes of Rhye and risen to the King's throne. The realisation of prophecy. Everything he had become would now be reduced to ash.

Other considerations fought for dominance.

My friends are going to die.

Others have already given their lives. Fae. Sylphs.

Lady Mercy.

My destiny rests with the Unhomed.

'I accept your price, Lord Sun.'

The air shimmered once again. The golden orb, too bright to lay eyes upon, swelled in the sky. 'You breathe rarefied air, seraph. None but the divine may bask in my aura. Yours is not to seek an audience with me, yet I have countenanced you. Now be gone, and know that your price is paid.'

Mustapha's wings burst into flame.

In shock, he shrieked. Feathers burned, fluttering from him in palls of white smoke. He sank in the air, flapping with frantic energy; falling, falling ... wind whistling through seared and blackening tissues. Reason shouted somewhere in the recesses of his brain: *You fool! Ophynea gave you wings, as well!*

He plummeted towards the blanket of cloud.

Trixel left Fahrenheit once again in the capable hands of Gwenamber, assured in the knowledge that the human suffered only a mild concussion. The Apothecary had tucked him in bed, lest he roll and be injured further in the storm.

The fixie slewed her way in a drunken slalom down the main corridor towards the Bridge. Ornate lanterns flickered as she passed, throwing strange shadows from the bustling automatons as she veered around them. With every dip of the ship's prow, she felt the need to clutch her stomach. Yet she stumbled onwards, eager to confirm the welfare of her friends.

By the time she arrived at the Bridge, it surprised her to find a tense knot of voyagers already there. Khashoggi stood ever glued to the forward instrument panel, while Harold and the pixies huddled around a soaked and bedraggled Will, cloak thrown around his shoulders. All had pallor and shades of green about their faces. The pixies were also black with grease, from fingertips to elbows.

'What happened to you two?' she asked, unable to keep a certain motherly concern from her voice.

'We've taken on some water, and the circuitry to the bilge pump shorted,' explained Dique. 'We've been working them the old-fashioned way.'

'Harold rang down to us, to say that Mustapha had gone and done something crazy. Again,' added Meadow. 'Otherwise, we'd still be down there – the Mer could use the extra hands.'

There it was. No quip, no snide remark; just the report of an exhausted pixie. Trixel envisioned dozens of Mer, sweat soaked and heaving, exerting themselves to keep the majestic *Khonsu* afloat.

'Where is Mustapha?'

Drawing the cloak tighter about him, a shivering Will pointed upwards. 'He flew into the storm,' he explained in a flat voice.

'No...' Trixel staggered to the control panel, where she proceeded to expel a quantity of bilious vomit. Beside her, Khashoggi appeared not to notice. Wiping her face with a sleeve, she stared out the pilot's window into the wild squall beyond.

'Could he have anything to do with that?'

'Do with what?' asked Meadow. The pixies and Harold crowded beside the fixie at the broad pane of glass, to gawk at whatever had caught her attention.

From deep in the darkling cloud, a chasm of brilliance formed. The thunderheads yawned wide as if opening a window to the heavens; rays of golden light poured from within, casting a great beam of light that reached down to dance upon the Milky Sea.

'What in the name of Adatar...' muttered Dique.

'Adatar indeed,' said Harold, who had once seen the fields of heaven alongside a team of sacred winged horses.

'Take heed!' exclaimed Khashoggi. The others jumped, for he had emerged from gloomy lassitude to issue the warning. 'I sense peril is near at hand. One of our number faces appalling danger.'

'Just one of us?' said Meadow.

'Wait, look!' cried Harold, pointing. 'Something is falling from the cloud!' A tiny shadow fell, spiralling, trailing a plume of smoke that bloomed yellow in the transcendent light. 'What do you make of that, Trixel?'

No reply.

'Trixel?' The dragonfly looked around.

Howling winds battered the open door to the spiral stair, bringing rain in torrents onto the Bridge.

Echoes of memory stirred in the mind of Trixel Tate. She stood upon a gleaming parapet, in another Age — another land — when armoured heroes swooped and dodged blasts of deadly dragon-fire. The blare of a Horn and the blast of miraculous white light rent the air. How she had feared for their lives, watching from that hallowed Pillar ... feared for that one particular life. How she had embraced the sylph, hoping her tear of joy would not be seen.

Now, Trixel stood atop the *Khonsu*, staring into a sulphurous sky. The ship rocked beneath her feet; towering waves crashed, whitecaps rising as high as the deck on which she braced herself. The violent sea could not prevent her from watching Mustapha fall.

His wings aflame, the seraph tumbled from within the clouds. Lightning crackled all around him. Sure enough, he fell so very near the ship ... she could almost reach out and grab him, before the raging sea swallowed him up.

Rain pelted her face as she stared. The wretched shape of him, in a gut-churning fall.

I can catch him.

In her memory, she stood atop the Pillar, watching the winged warriors grow nearer, her heart in her throat. Willing them home.

Voices cried out behind her. Trixel could not hear them, focussed as she was on stepping onto the railing. Stepping onto the parapet. Near enough to reach.

Mustapha fell. *So close.*

'Noooo!' Harold's raw scream seemed out of place. Trixel frowned, hearing the dragonfly's voice. *You're not here. You're out there. Fighting Valendyne.* She heard the whir of insect wings; the swoop of a dark shape over her shoulder. *Get out of my way, insect!*

Harold flashed into the sky, as the ship lurched and Mustapha fell adrift of it. Their bodies collided mid-air, above her.

In a bone-crunching moment of brine and agony, the giant wave smashed onto the Observation Deck, sweeping Trixel over the side. Dazed, she knew only a floating sensation. The wall of seawater carried her into the void.

Falling. Enveloped by the icy cold, numb in her fingers and toes. Her head throbbed, though she felt an odd calm, as if she had long awaited this moment.

To live centuries in one world, and barely ten years in the next. Fahrenheit had said that. How astute.

She entered the sea's embrace amidst a churning swirl of salinity. Pounding forces sought to tear her apart, thrusting her every which way. She let herself be pulled deeper; below the tumult, where the current flowed around her like a gelid shroud. A turbulent trail of bubbles left her lips.

At this depth, shadows darted about her in the grey-green murk. Fleeting shapes — hallucinations? — undulated at the edge of her vision. She flicked her eyes, too sluggish to track the dark shapes with her head. *Undines, come to carry me to my watery bed. How very kind.*

Finally, she sank so deep that she drifted into a cave. A dark, dank place where the sea could only be heard as a hollow roar. Surprisingly warm, and surprisingly dry, though the floor of the cave felt damp and soft.

Trixel curled up inside the cave, water swilling all around her, and let her world fade to nothing.

I failed.

CHAPTER SIXTEEN

REST YOUR WEARY HEAD

Mustapha watched the storm remnants scud away to the east from his place on the sandy shore. Grey-green waves rolled up to the beach and crashed in a roil of froth. Warm sunlight fell upon his bare shoulders; despite its golden embrace and the azure dome overhead, the seraph knew only the bitter taste of Adatar's bargain.

Am I even a seraph anymore?

His whole body ached. His deep sinews burned where once great wings had sprouted. The immolation of those wings had left no mark upon him.

No physical mark, at least.

He did not truly watch the diminishing cloud bank. His despair ruled him, while the peaceful beach in a sheltered cove may well have been the substance of a dream.

Sandy footsteps announced the arrival of Will by his side. The human draped a light cloak around Mustapha. The damp material cooled him. Soothed his burning shoulder blades. Will sat beside him, facing the rippling wash that scurried up the shore and back again.

'What cost a life?' said Mustapha.

Will replied in his usual gentle tone. 'We don't know that she is lost, yet. Harold still searches.'

'Oh, come on, dear. You're saying she survived the whole night in a raging sea.'

'It was only half a league from shore ...'

'That's an awfully long way, when you're drowning.'

Will sighed. 'At least I'm trying, Mustapha. You may choose to be pessimistic, but I'm not ready to relinquish hope yet. Look at you! You almost died. Again. But you made it, thanks to Harold. Is it not fair enough to live in hope for Trixel as well?'

'Choose to be pessimistic? You make it seem so simple, to *choose*. Recently, every choice I make leads to suffering. People have died.' Mustapha's moustache drooped, the light dim in his eyes. 'The choices of a king must benefit the whole, though they may disadvantage the few. I get that, but I can't stand it. Perhaps it is well that I no longer feel like a king. All of that is stripped away. I am only me. A strangeling.'

Will made to protest, but faltered. Perhaps choosing between measured argument and consolation, he chose the latter. As the pair sat together, he took Mustapha's hand in his own. 'You are unlike any other creature in existence,' he offered. 'You are you, and the word *only* has no place in that sentence.' Mustapha relaxed against him. Together they watched Mandel potter up and down the shore, collecting sand. Rocks. Water samples. Analysing them. Overhead, sea birds circled above the coast – gulls, cormorants and kestrels. They soared in wide arcs over the waves, returning to a rookery in the craggy hillside behind the beach.

'The last time I felt we were being watched by a bird,' said Will, 'we were being watched by a bird.'

The observation successfully distracted Mustapha from his bitterness. He nodded. 'The raven, right? You said it guided you in Banwah Haunte. I saw it again, in Nevermore. That was Augustine. Now, these blasted kestrels. I can't help but think that someone is treating this like one big joke. I was laughed at, do you know? During the storm.'

'Well, we've gotten this far. One step closer to figuring it all out,' said Will.

A few hundred yards off shore sat the *Khonsu*, where Khashoggi had dropped anchor. He remained on board with the Mer and automaton mechanics, who had a task ahead of them, repairing damage to the superstructure and malfunctioning circuitry. With few words, the Prophet ushered the companions on board his high-powered nautiloid launch, bringing them within wading distance of the beach before returning himself to the ship. He left them Mandel, to assist with mapping and learning about their new environs. Will added that they should all make use of daylight to orient themselves. Meadow and Dique volunteered to 'use their stealth' to explore the land beyond the rocky coast, while Harold flew off immediately to perform an airborne search grid for Trixel Tate.

The dragonfly alone showed little of the exhaustion they all felt. Curiosity drove him, along with a bravado borne from his miraculous mid-air rescue of Mustapha. Foolhardy though it may have been, the five of them were alive, together and had dry land beneath their feet.

As Adatar had decreed, the storm dissipated within an hour of Mustapha's fall. The voyagers found they had survived another night, emerging into early morning.

In the light of a fine day, it became clear they had arrived at a large island. Mustapha opined that it lay at the fringe of known Rhye, given that neither he nor Ackley Fahrenheit had played a role in conjuring it from the sea. A desolate slab of rock escarpments, gleaming red-gold beneath the sun, met cascading dunes that tumbled down to the beach. In the distance, a spine of mountains rose like jagged vertebrae towards the sky. The vegetation that Mack had struggled to detect consisted of paltry shrubs and grasses at the crest of the dune, and a stand of spindly palm trees beckoning to a pass between the nearest escarpments. In this direction had the pixies determined to conduct their reconnaissance.

'I see Harold,' announced Will. He stood straight, hand shielding his eyes from the sun, voice tinged with optimism. An enlarging speck approached in the eastern sky, resolving to the shape of a lone dragonfly.

Harold alighted; the despondent look he wore negated the need for words. He stripped off his helm and dashed it to the sand. He threw himself to the ground beside it, sweat and tears streaking his greasy face.

'Don't fret, Harold. You did the best you could,' said Will. 'Besides, you did rescue Mustapha. That took great courage.'

'I guess we could have lost you both,' said Harold. 'Oh, poor Trixel!'

'Mark my words,' Will replied. 'That lady lives a charmed life. I doubt we've heard the last of her.' His words faltered, voice cracking.

Mustapha gave a weary, lopsided grin. 'She had it in for me when we first met, so she did. Always looked at me like some kind of interloper. First time she showed any sign of appreciating me was the night she saved my life. She and Yosef dragged me out of the Charnel House of Giltenan. I owed her for a very long time after that.'

Solemn nods all around gave way to a silent reverie. A light breeze whispered over the dunes, a rustling moan like a lament for the dead. Beyond the breakers, the *Khonsu* bobbed in the gentle swell, the great white testament to the perils of their voyage.

Mandel pootled past, then circled back to sit beside them, as if to share in the communal mourning.

'I hear squeaky footsteps,' said Harold. In a heartbeat, they all spun around to face the dunes, the stand of palms and the looming rocky bluff.

Meadow and Dique stumbled down the sandy slope. Their vigour suggested that they bore good news; the others climbed to their feet in hopeful anticipation. They didn't need to wait long.

'There's an oasis!' cried Meadow.

'There's a city!' shouted Dique, in the same instant.

'There's an oasis city,' explained Meadow as the pair drew closer. He spied the downcast faces of his friends. 'No luck finding Trixel, I gather,' he added, all joviality gone from his voice.

'None,' answered Harold. 'I flew a sixteen square league grid over our position during the storm, and ... nothing.'

The pixies bowed their heads. After a moment, Meadow's shot up again. 'Couldn't the Mer help us conduct a better ocean search?'

'What a wondrous idea, Meadow,' said Mustapha, a glimmer returning to his brown-eyed gaze. 'Assuming some of the crew can be spared from the repair effort.'

'I'm sure I can arrange it,' offered Harold. 'Meadow and Dique, why don't you tell us all about your magical oasis city. If we're off to investigate, I can fly over to the *Khonsu* first, then catch you up.'

Thus, the companions had a plan. The pull of intention helped shake off their weariness, though one and all still dreamed of refreshment and a place for vital rest.

Meadow and Dique had not been as stealthy as perhaps they thought. As they had made their way across the beachside dunes, along a ridge lined with an avenue of palms and through a pass overlooking the wadi beyond, keen eyes charted their progress.

In the shade of a natural arch, formed by the meeting of tumbled red monoliths, Harold rejoined them from his detour to the *Khonsu*. In a positive development, damage to the ship would be reparable, but this would take most of a day. In the meantime, Cyreus detailed a small search crew to scour the sea.

As Harold relayed this news to his friends, two figures emerged as if growing from the stone and sand. They floated to the ground on whirring wings, dusk-coloured hoods and cloaks billowing about them. From hidden shelves in the rock escarpment they came, like desert spectres. The pair — two women with butterfly wings — brandished halberds with sharpened blades; they kept the weapons ready, but did not aim them at the companions. With bright searching eyes, they surveyed the odd group, seeming to assess and judge them at the same time.

Two pixies, weary and well outside their comfort zone.

An artificial creature, like a golem only much smaller. Possibly valuable.

A human, competent and broad-shouldered, but worn thin by some external pressure.

A strangeling, with the ears of a Fae creature, but wearing a human moustache and a defeated look.

A dragonfly with a noble, inquisitive face. An insectoid who had seen and done much.

In one swift movement both women knelt, their noses bare inches from the ground, halberds laid by their sides. One of them spoke in a taut, formal voice.

'Your Majesty! It is as the tales have foretold. The King walks among us, delivered by heaven's wrath upon a great white ship! Welcome, then, to Phydeantum. You and your party shall be guests at Grandville Palace, if it pleases you.'

Mustapha blinked. *They anticipated us?*

Harold spoke first. 'Ah ... perhaps you should stand.' He gave it the inflection of a query. *Fairies?* he mouthed to the strangeling, as the women rose to their booted feet.

'I am Honeywind,' declared one.

'I am Glimmervane,' announced the other. 'We shall escort you to Grandville Palace, where resides Lady Antoinette, Potentate-Elect.'

Mustapha and Harold exchanged a bepuzzled glance. Indeed, the women bore the usual vacuous names of fairies, yet these two seemed hardened, ready to survive a sandstorm. Perhaps years on a desert isle had shaped them.

Mustapha addressed the fairies. 'The two of you live in a city nearby, then? My friends here spoke to us of a settlement by an oasis. It might be best if you took us there ... to your...' He faltered, caught in the gaze of the two fairies. They stared at him with quizzical frowns.

Honeywind spoke. 'Your Majesty, do you deign to allow the half-breed help to speak in your place? Your patience and grace are extraordinary. To show such levity, even to one of the misborn, befits none as highly as you. Will you follow us, Lord?'

Honeywind's golden eyes and sun-swept face were turned towards Harold.

Mustapha reeled. *Half-breed? Misborn? What in all of Rhye...?* Stunned to silence, he found himself without the energy even for reproach. He took a moment to collect his thoughts. In that moment, he determined to use this turn of events to learn something of their new hosts. *These fairies think that Harold is the King!*

Harold had also baulked. Mustapha faced him, in such a way that Will and the pixies could also see him. Mandel stood at the rear, oblivious to the exchange.

'Forgive the transgression of your servant, my Lord,' said

Mustapha, offering the dragonfly a deep bow of obeisance. From the nadir of the bow, he glared up at Harold with a look that shouted: *Just go along with it!*

Harold gave a fractional nod. 'Yes, er ... strangeling,' he boomed, with more than customary pomp. 'You have my mercy this time. We shall deal with this ... transgression ... later.' The fairies peered at him, working hard to cover their dubious expressions with due respect.

'The heat of the day will soon be upon us, Lord,' said Honeywind. 'We humbly suggest you come to partake in the palace shade, where refreshments to sate your every appetite are in plenty.'

The companions needed little time to weigh the invitation. Within moments, Honeywind and Glimmervane led them onwards through a pass littered with scree and parched shrubbery. The fairies walked with Harold between; Mustapha scrambled along after them, like the servant he had become. Will and the pixies followed at a short distance, in a knot of whispers. Mandel trundled along behind them all.

The City of the Sun — a place the fairies had named *Phydeantum* — hugged an oasis of vibrant ultramarine. Here the palm trees thrived, lush and tall, though they were dwarfed by soaring domes of silver and a forest of pale minarets. Hundreds of squat buildings, gold as the desert sand and decorated with ornate motifs in every colour, crouched in concentric rows, fanning out from the foliage at the water's edge. Dotted throughout the city were squares covered by broad, angular shade sails.

At one end of the settlement, a tremendous stone edifice could only have been the Palace. Ringed by elegant spires and capped with a burnished dome, its inward face featured level upon level of terraced balconies, framed by archways with slender columns.

From either side of the palatial construct ran a high-topped stone wall, surrounding the inner buildings like a desert citadel. Beyond the crenelated wall, ramshackle huts and drab tents clustered in their thousands; a city dwelled outside the city. Smoke rose in lazy wisps from one hundred campfires, while the clatter of a great population could be heard even at the far end of a broad wadi. From the fringe of the city, sand rose in majestic dunes, rolling away to distant escarpments and the mountains beyond.

Mustapha stared at it all in wonder. Searching his brain, he had no recollection of imagining this sprawling marvel of a city into being. *Then how? Or perhaps ... who? Marnis?*

The companions followed Honeywind and Glimmervane in loose file down a winding trail towards the oasis. Crusted dirt crumbled under their boot soles and heat radiated from the baked earth. Away from the beach and the cove, Adatar seemed to hang lower in the sky, trying to scorch the land from existence. The fairies moved with efficient strides, navigating the uneven path without having to watch the placement of their feet. Mustapha picked a path close behind Harold, desperate to exchange thoughts with his friends, but eager to maintain the silent air of the subservient.

His pointed ears picked up fragments of hushed discussion from the two behind him, who shared his bewilderment.

'... for some reason, they think it's Harold.' Meadow's voice.

Dique: 'It's his wings, I think. They singled him out straight away.'

Meadow: 'Perhaps. Whoever is on this island, they know at least that the King of Rhye has wings. But if they've been living out here since the New Dawn, they probably don't know what he looks like.'

Dique: 'That makes sense ... which is surprising, for you.'

Will: 'You're probably right, Meadow. I'm more concerned about how they decided Mustapha's station. He's the only one of mixed race amongst us. I'm a touch apprehensive about what we might find here ...'

The discussion continued, but Mustapha tuned out. Instead, he pondered the desert-wise fairies. Creatures who would normally wilt at the very notion of an arid climate. These had faced adversity. Adapted to an unforgiving environment. He wondered if ...

Could they be ...? The thought remained incomplete.

At the edge of Phydeantum, clumps of shabby grey dwellings hugged the trail. The packed earth formed a serviceable road. The companions shared it with minimum foot traffic, with most oasis-dwellers seeking shelter as noon approached. Faces peered forth from behind tent flaps and curtained doors, concealed further by shawls in earthen colours. Mustapha studied the curious faces, though none of the sunken cheeks and wary eyes revealed their race of origin.

Until the children appeared.

A hubbub erupted ahead on the road, drawing Mustapha's eye away from the grimy tent city. From left and right rambunctious figures burst out of the warren, crowding the path to a towering gateway beyond.

Youths one and all, they appeared clothed in the same roomy, flowing garments of other desert folk. The revelation came within, for amongst the children there were none of pure race: impish pixie faces paired with the platinum tresses of sylphdom. Feathered wings sprouted from the backs of freckle-cheeked humans. In some, the blend showed only in subtle traits, though in others, intermingling features produced a striking beauty, impossible to ignore.

'Great Lord!' cried the children, throwing themselves in the grit before Harold and the fairies. 'A piece of gold? A scrap of cloth? A token? Share with us your glory, Lord! We who have nothing, cast out in the fearsome desert.'

Mustapha wanted to cry out. *These are my people! Not as subjects to a king, but as brethren – children of mixed birth! I know it now, sure and certain.* They are stranded in this place since the Battle of Two-Way Mirror Mountain, born of one million innocent souls. Why do they endure? Why do they live like this? He reached for the courage to face down the armed fairies; only to find a fire inside him had quelled, his powers gone.

Impotent.

He stood in mute shock, along with his friends, as the fairies responded.

'Clear the way, halflings! Be gone, back to your homes, before we punish you and your families as well!' Honeywind snarled, sweeping the butt end of her halberd across the road. Children scattered left and right, wailing as they sought the safety of their hovels. None had caught the blunt heel of the weapon, though many a story would be shared of a narrow escape.

Will made to step forward. Meadow twitched with restless anger at his back. As they reached Mustapha, the strangeling held up a surreptitious hand. With bewildered glares, the pair stood down from confrontation.

Mustapha drew a deep breath. *It will serve no purpose to ignite conflict here in a strange land, with us weakened and still outside the city gates.* He yearned for his friends to understand.

Honeywind and Glimmervane ushered the companions onward with an apologetic demeanour. Mustapha surmised their apology came prompted by the beggars' intrusion, rather than by their own behaviour.

The road brought them to a massive sandstone wall. Huts of the outer dwellers stood right up against it; battlements ran the length of the wall until it curved out of sight. A great gate, beneath an ogee arch, stood open. Paired sentries adopted a casual stance, anticipating little traffic in or out of the citadel; they snapped to attention, eyes boggling as the ragged group trudged towards them.

The sentries bore all the hallmarks of the sylphic race, clad though they were in voluminous cloaks of royal purple with golden trim. Their hands rested on the pommels of menacing broad swords, points sitting on the ground.

An involuntary shiver enveloped Mustapha. He recalled standing at the gates of Wintergard with Harold, convincing the sylphic guards there to let them in from the cold. *To see my father.* He shot a glance at Harold, though the dragonfly looked set to engage the fairies as they stopped beneath the arch.

'A wondrous place,' declared Harold, capturing the streetscape ahead with a sweeping gesture. Still, he struggled to keep a nervous quiver from his voice. Silently, Mustapha bid him strength.

'We live upon the grace of Providence, my Lord,' replied Honeywind. 'Though the sands of this isle are harsh, the meeting of two dissipated rivers formed this valley, and through the mercy of Phydeas, water sprang from the desert floor.'

'We owe him our lives in this world, as we did in the last,' added Glimmervane. 'To worship him is to live in his embrace.'

Mustapha could only frown. These people showed no recognition of their land being created by the King of Rhye. He himself could have questioned it, in that moment.

Within its imposing gate, Phydeantum sprang to life, just as the thriving date palms, fig and peach trees growing at its centre. The air grew cooler, courtesy of vibrant sails that covered passages, roadways and market squares. The road of packed earth became an avenue of gleaming shale. On either side, running in curved rows around the precious body of water, the homes and business places of the wealthy stood, each one a declaration of status.

Everywhere, the city hummed with life. Merchants hawked

wares from overflowing shopfronts. Citizens bustled from one brightly curtained doorway to another, hauling baskets of goods, carrying important parchments or chasing the last shaded spot outside a coffee parlour, ready for the noonday meal. Even a hulking manuban lowed and snorted as a trader hitched his rickety wagon to its yoke.

'It's incredible,' marvelled Dique. 'And I can just smell the fresh scent of the oasis from here, can't you?'

'I must admit, all I smell are the cooking spices,' replied Will, creases wrinkling his nose. 'Unless that's manuban dung.'

Mustapha stayed silent. He preferred to conserve his energy for placing one foot in front of the other, though his furtive gaze noticed things. People. Fashion. Here inside the city – *the City of the Sun, ha!* – the flowing, heat-friendly style remained. Shawls and hoods were common, even veils drawn across faces. But here, the materials burst with colour. They also became finer, more delicate. Daring, almost, showing flashes of bronze skin beneath diaphanous fabric.

He also noticed the wide-eyed surprise of those who spied the group, with the dragonfly flanked by fairies at its fore. Many stooped low in bows or took a knee, showing the tops of their heads as the companions passed them. Murmured exclamations followed Mandel, as well: no other automatons graced the streets of Phydeantum.

All of the onlookers were sylphs. Or humans, or Fae races. No halflings.

Meadow craned his neck, watching a winsome fairy sashay down a side street, disappearing towards the lush waterfront. 'Can we visit the oasis?' he called to their escorts.

'Certainly, in time,' answered Glimmervane. 'It would be remiss of us not to first make introductions with Lady Antoinette, at the Palace.'

'How much further is it? My feet are tired. And I'm more than a little bit thirsty.'

'Your patience is rewarded, master pixie,' said Honeywind. 'At the next right turn, we have arrived.'

They reached a tiny square with an olive tree growing in the centre, and the fairy's promise proved true. At the end of an avenue of blue awnings, the glorious façade loomed over them: a spectacle of archways glinted bright beneath Adatar's rays. Towering minarets speared towards the heavens, capped with spires of crimson tile. The domed roof, with its pointed centre, could scarcely be seen from this vantage.

'Bit much, isn't it?' remarked Meadow.

'You prefer Babel?' grunted Dique.

'Right now, I do.'

Cafes lined the final approach to Grandville Palace. Outdoor seating faced the street, with slouching citizens filling a number of broad-backed easy chairs. One and all, they smoked: if not cigarillos, then from curved, wide-bowled pipes; if not from pipes, from ornate hookahs sitting on the ground in front of them. Purplish smoke arose in wisps and wreaths, dissipating in the languid air. The plumes smelled of rich spice, fragrant and alluring, reminiscent of mulled wine and oud.

'People do like a smoke around here,' observed Dique redundantly.

'Pass-time of the privileged and affluent,' replied Honeywind, 'and their guests. A miraculous plantation of riddle-reed grows at one end of the oasis. It is cultivated for its ... recreational effects, and it never falls to short supply.'

'A gift from Phydeas,' said Glimmervane.

These folk don't seem terribly recreational, thought Mustapha, swiping at a drifting cloud as they passed the smokers. The fragrant tendrils caught his nose; at once he knew a modicum of calm.

My friends have lifted a weight from my shoulders.
Somehow, this will all end the way it is supposed to.

Just as the whiff of riddle-reed took hold, the entourage arrived at Grandville Palace.

Lady Antoinette, Potentate-Elect of Phydeantum, wallowed in a low curtsy. Countless yards of vibrant damask, woven with intricate patterns, wrapped her curvaceous form and flowed in rippling trains all about her. Her chins quivered in hungry delight as she absorbed the vision of her unexpected regal guests. In one hand she clutched a slender cigarette holder of carved and polished ivory; the stub within it wafted streaks of purple as she waved it in effusive gestures.

'My Lord, King of all Rhye! What an absolute pleasure and surprise. Had I known of your arrival, Sire, I would have better prepared to receive you!'

Antoinette took her audience in an airy chamber, which occupied much of the topmost floor of the Palace. Sunlight flooded in through an elegant colonnade that ran along three of the room's four sides, giving the high ceiling a sense of weightlessness. Overhead arced the interior of the dome, decorated with a gaudy relief of the Pantheon.

An abundance of lounges and soft furnishings gave the space the feel of a private sitting room or boudoir. Lavish throws and rugs in burgundy and orange-gold bespoke luxury of an exclusive nature. Scattered low tables featured brass bowls filled with dates, figs and plums, alongside jugs of water or wine. Sprigs of honeysuckle bequeathed the air a light perfume, subtle and enticing.

Others mingled throughout the room – 'pure breeds', of course. Antoinette introduced them as her viziers and ladies-in-waiting; upon the voyagers' arrival, they sprang from their respite and presented themselves, faces flushed with indulgence. Men and women alike wore the most sheer material yet, with billows and cascades of finest organza, voile and muslin concealing little. Heads bore circlets of gold, while feet were bare.

The group absorbed the scene in astonishment. Harold, now the inadvertent figurehead, seemed to collect himself with admirable speed.

'Mine is a holy mission,' replied the dragonfly. 'It is through the grace of Adatar himself that my voyage brings me to your shores. In his name, I bestow upon Phydeantum a new epithet: City of the Sun. May you grow and prosper ever more in his worship.'

Over Harold's shoulder, Mustapha nodded to himself. Back on the beach, he had taken a moment to explain to his closest friends the discourse he had shared with Adatar. He could not have known how useful that precious moment would become, mere hours later.

Claps and titters of delight rose from the courtiers of Antoinette. 'How wonderful!' and 'City of the Sun!' came as murmured pleasure from the lips of many. Some of the sylphs even made prayer signs with their hands.

Lady Antoinette held her meaty, bejewelled hands aloft and the burbling ceased. 'Your Majesty. You have undertaken a long and perilous journey to reach us here, so close to the edge of the world. No doubt you are weary and seek rest. I pray our humble home is a welcoming shelter for you, and the pure-born of your kingdom. It would honour me greatly to serve as your host, offering you every luxury that Phydeantum can provide.'

'It would please me to partake of your hospitality,' said Harold, settling into his self-importance. 'I would learn of your great city; its people, its customs, and its struggles at the mercy of this desert isle.' His eyes slid towards the colonnade and the city outside, out over the sea of hovels crammed against the sandstone wall.

'Then it is decided!' cried Antoinette, clasping her hands. Further coos of excitement arose from the beauteous creatures around the room. 'It is well that you have already met Honeywind and Glimmervane – they make excellent scouts and attendants. They will show you and your company to our most sumptuous quarters … just name your desire. Tonight, we feast and speak of our wondrous lands!'

The two fairies materialised from their places of discreet concealment. As Honeywind made to lead the group away, she looked askance at Mustapha.

'And the halfling, my Lady?' she asked. 'To await his masters, at the fringe of the city?'

'Yes, yes,' answered Antoinette, affecting a disinterested wave; then, 'Hold!' She wobbled across to where Mustapha stood, containing a silent rage of which she had no knowledge. She peered at him from beneath lids heavy with kohl and gold dust. 'You … you look familiar.'

Mustapha remained wordless, watching her.

'You may speak, halfling.'

'Forgive me, my Lady. I have travelled much, but I do not know you.' The words tumbled over a thickened tongue, whispered from parched and cracked lips; the first he had spoken since meeting the two fairies.

The Potentate's eyes narrowed. 'Were you not once a servant in the court of Lord Rogar Giltenan?'

Mustapha stiffened, though he tried to conceal his surprise. 'Yes, my Lady. Indeed, I was.' He knew not if he should divulge his connection to the Sovereign of Humankind, so he chose to omit it.

Antoinette's pudgy face split wide with a grin. Her eyes sparkled. 'I knew it! The manservant of Lady Belladonna, no? I was once of that court, as well! You might disguise yourself, halfling, with your

cropped hair and that ridiculous little moustache, but I see you!'
she shrieked, jubilant in her own cleverness.

Mustapha said nothing. *Does this woman not know what Lady
Belladonna became? Is she crazy?* She seemed pleased to know him
by association. It made the hairs on his neck stand on end. She
executed a rotund pirouette, purple smoke orbiting from the stub
in her ivory holder. The haze wafted past Mustapha's face and
again he knew a bleary-eyed bliss, blunting the edges of his alarm,
awakening his more primal needs.

What strange, beautiful people.

What a gorgeous place to rest.

But first – we dine!

Beside him, Honeywind wore a deflated expression. She jabbed
him with a finger. 'My Lady? Your instructions?'

'He stays,' replied Antoinette, through a languorous smile. 'Do
not toss him out, like a pauper with a crust of bread. Tonight—'
she brandished a finger – 'tonight, he eats cake.'

CHAPTER SEVENTEEN

PLEASURE DOME

Mustapha might have regained a degree of status in the eyes of Lady Antoinette, though to the fairies he remained a second-rate creature. Once they were dismissed from the Potentate-Elect's chamber, Honeywind disavowed all responsibility for him, leaving him with her subordinate. Glimmervane struggled to find lodgings in the Palace austere enough to suit a mere halfling; she compromised by dragging a palette into Harold's room and dumping it at the foot of the dragonfly's enormous bed.

'It's okay, Mustapha,' said Harold, eyeing off the massive four-poster draped in silk. 'You can share this bed. It's big enough for fifteen dragonflies to have a party in it.'

'How do you know they haven't?' countered the strangeling, making Harold grimace. 'Thanks for the offer, but I will take the palette. Sleeping there will keep me angry.'

The grimace became a frown. 'Why would you want to stay angry?'

'It might be the one thing keeping me from losing my mind. I was already going slightly mad in there, weren't you? These hideous people seemed beautiful. Their ghastly notions palatable. I should be angry! Why didn't I argue? Or fight?'

'You didn't want to be clapped in irons and carted away?' shrugged Harold.

'In my own kingdom? I'm telling you Harold, there was something amiss in that place. This whole Palace does funny things to one's head.' He marched across the majestic suite to a handbasin and wrought-bronze faucet. Guzzling, splashing sounds ensued, as he began slaking his thirst without ceremony.

Beside the bed, tall shrines to Phydeas and Floe stood frozen in marble. Around the other walls, wardrobes and sideboards appeared immaculate but empty. Huge curtained windows overlooked Phydeantum, facing the way back towards the cove where the *Khonsu* lay anchored, beyond sight.

Upon the bed were laid fine garments, befitting dinner guests at Antoinette's court. Mustapha curled his lip at them, then flopped down on the palette. 'You did an incredible job back there, Harold,' he said, staring at the ceiling. 'Thanks to your diplomacy, we're here as guests of honour. Perhaps I should abdicate, once we get back home.'

'Don't be silly,' said Harold.

'Silly about what? Abdicating, or getting back home?'

Harold had no answer.

'Wake me when it's time for dinner, please,' said Mustapha, closing heavy eyelids.

With the fall of evening, light of a rosy hue shone upon a large round dais, directly beneath the dome. Strategically placed scrallin lanterns caught filtered rays of sunlight during the day, to illuminate the stage by night.

The fresco Pantheon stared down at a troupe of a dozen dancers, as they glided about to a graceful but unmarked rhythm. Mostly sylphs, accompanied by the odd lithe-limbed human, they pranced and swayed through delicate forms, creating gauzy spirals with their scant clothing as they turned. Palm-to-palm they converged, couples squaring up with smouldering gazes, before separating and pairing anew with the next performer in the circle.

As they danced, the troupe raised their voices in song. A sensuous chorale rang around the dome and caressed the ears of Lady Antoinette's guests. A welcome – or perhaps an invitation – to the King of Rhye and his travelling companions.

A spark becomes flame
In the dark, the barest whisper
You hear me call your name
Come a little closer – feel your way
Leave the world behind
Forget it for today

Let the beat invade
Let the sights and sounds persuade you
Take the time
To unwind
And you will find
It's fine to ... surrender

Leave the desert heat
In the cool and languid air
You can rest your tired feet
Put your mind at ease – let yourself go
Here you know you will
Find that sweet release

Hurled through space
Breaks your soul, you feel displaced
Take it slow
Breathe it in, you've nowhere else to go
Feel my touch
We've waited long – wanted this so much
All is well
Don't resist – don't break the spell

Let the beat invade
Let the sights and sounds persuade you
Take the time
To unwind
And you will find
It's fine to … surrender.

Meadow and Dique observed the sultry performance with benign smiles, though their eyes held stony glares. They each looked ridiculous: their hosts had found them jaunty suits of black and silver, with leggings and skirts and lace at the sleeve. Meadow had a great white ruff for a collar, with which he fidgeted as though it choked him. They stood out like sore thumbs, amongst the silken veils of Antoinette's court.

'Perhaps these clothes were left over from a children's dress-up party,' reasoned Dique with an uncomfortable squirm.

'Are you kidding? They were left over from some other century,' retorted Meadow. Harold – not far from the pair – had fared better, provided the rich robes of a truly distinguished visitor. The dragonfly wore an awkward expression; whether due to the clothes or the implication of them, the pixies could not tell. Only Mandel had been spared any kind of indignity, stood in a corner wearing only his usual burnished shell. It became apparent that the Phydeantines considered the automaton to be closer to furniture than to a living guest. 'How a wardrobe like this survived the New Dawn, I have no idea,' he continued. 'If it's any consolation though, at least we don't look like Mustapha.'

When it came to costuming the strangeling for the night, the last laugh had gone to Glimmervane. Mustapha looked like nothing if not a gigantic prawn. Far from leaving him the featureless garb of a servant or 'misborn,' the fairy had laid out a bright red one-piece, a full-bodied tunic like a vermillion shout from head to toe. Red ribands and peacock feathers adorned the whole article, leaving one to assume that Mustapha might indeed be a court trickster. To his credit, the strangeling had accepted the snide gesture with implacable calm, carrying off the stupendous costume with aplomb. He divided his attention between Will, who looked every part the handsome desert prince in much more orthodox attire, and Harold, who carried the unenviable task of playing King for the evening.

Guests and courtiers alike perched or sprawled on comfortable divans, while servants in loose-flowing beige threaded through the chamber, delivering platters laden with food. The pixies' eyes widened at the parade of fine delicacies: giant baked grouper dusted with cumin and paprika, finished with dill and glistening olive oil; fresh, plump figs heaped alongside honeycomb and walnut; stewed stone fruit and loaves of crusty rhyebread. Pitchers of wine and goblets aplenty appeared on every low table. Then the servants left the chamber, with solemn and tight-lipped bows.

The servants were halflings and interracial creatures ... every last one.

'Praise be to Phydeas!' cried Antoinette with a flourish of her cigarette, a rousing incantation that inspired a delighted squeal from assembled courtiers. Without further ado, the feast began with much slurping, lip-smacking and other sounds of enjoyment.

Mustapha picked at a sparse plate. His brief nap had been little more than a tease, a momentary respite from the avalanche of fatigue that threatened to lay him flat. The rich food, fine wine and luxuriant furnishings seemed likely to finish the task, though he fought to keep his wits, eager to learn the truth of these Phydeantines.

To leave a mark upon them somehow.

He sat at the right hand of Harold, who naturally had the ear of Lady Antoinette, lounging like an exotic walrus on the divan alongside him. The dragonfly wasted no time: as Mustapha listened, his friend needled the Potentate-Elect for insights as to the origins of the strange desert settlement.

'A miracle occurred at the crumbled foot of Two-Way Mirror Mountain,' explained Antoinette, sucking the remnants of honeycomb from her fingers. 'Where in one moment there lay a vast field of fallen warriors, in the next it had become a great outdoor feast – as fine as this one we lay before you tonight, but large enough to spread across the battlefield. Bounteous enough to provide a morsel of sustenance for every hungry mouth among us.'

'You and your people must have felt as if you had stared Death in the face and survived,' said Harold.

'Our prayers were answered – Praise be to Phydeas! And to Floe, for watching over our children – though the ordeal was far from over. Bloody arguments broke out, as people fought over food and supplies. They fought! Even as the tide began to turn. Even as that harrowing, month-long night drew near an end; even as you stood aloft that brilliant tower and welcomed the New Dawn, greed drove survivors to madness and violence. Many died. So many! Then, as the sun split the horizon, there spoke a voice that delivered a promise. The voice of Providence no doubt, with a covenant that we would live on, in a place where his bounty would sustain us forever.'

Harold gave a thoughtful nod. 'That explains much. I looked upon your citadel as we arrived earlier today and I saw a settlement of far fewer than one million people.'

'Ah, yes,' said Antoinette, averting her face to push a plume of smoke sideways from the corner of her mouth. 'Perhaps only half of us remain now, huddled around the precious gifts of this oasis.'

The dragonfly waved a pincer at the decadent banquet all around. 'Such a wealth of provision you have here, Potentate-Elect. Yet I see no place for livestock farming, no large-scale agriculture, here on this desert island. Are half a million souls supported here by little other than their faith in the divine?'

'But of course, Your Majesty. Was it not your own faith that saw you rise to vanquish our oppressors? It is the same for us here. We pay our debt of honour to Phydeas; in turn, he keeps the oasis welling up, full and free of taint, the providores' parlours bursting with fresh fruit and game, and the riddle-reed lush by the water's edge.'

Beside Harold, Mustapha pursed his lips. Though she addressed the dragonfly in error she made a fair point. *Ophynea? Where are you now? Does any part of your blessing remain, or have you forsaken us, too? How is it that Phydeas continues to bless these survivors of Two-Way Mirror Mountain, when so many of you have fallen silent? Lhestra – is this the face of Justice?*

Caught up in his musings, Mustapha did not anticipate the dragonfly's next question of Antoinette.

'What of those outside your city's walls? Are they faithless? Your servants – those of mixed race, who are near-transparent to the courtiers they serve – do they not hold fervour for the God Phydeas? Have they renounced him, or somehow fallen short of his mercy?

They seem not to share in the surplus of this thriving city. This city now blessed also by Adatar, who shines down upon us all with equal grace. The City of the Sun.'

Several conversations in the vicinity fell silent. Sylphs and humans alike cast surreptitious glances towards Lady Antoinette; not so much offering her support, as hoping the Potentate-Elect had an answer to their royal guest's prickly question. Mustapha held his breath.

Antoinette's eyebrows rose; she flushed from her jowls to the roots of her coiffed hair, but she recovered in a moment.

'We are upholders of tradition, Your Majesty,' she replied. 'Respectfully, I say: since the time of Montreux Giltenan, the bloodlines of human and sylph have been kept pure, never to cross. We seek only to maintain those bloodlines. To preserve the rich cultures of Old Rhye—'

'Cultures evolve,' interrupted Harold. 'Entire nations evolve, and their people with them. Take a look around you, Lady Antoinette. The land upon which you make your home has changed, irrevocably. Already – in just ten short years – your people have had to adapt, to survive. Your fairy foot-soldiers no longer wear the frivolous attire their culture became known for. They are desert-savvy, ready to scour the dunes for any resource your inner circle needs, to stay fat and happy.'

Antoinette's smug countenance had begun to wither under Harold's barrage; after this last statement, she affected a silent shriek. But the dragonfly had not finished.

Not by a long way.

'Do you believe that the sylphs of today are the same, in body and mind, as those who fought under the battle standard of Arnaut Vrendar? That the Fae are unchanged to those who first held court with Lord Oberon, before the Godsryche? You are mistaken.

Societies move forward, and our thinking must move too, or else history leaves us behind.

'You speak of Phydeas, and the grace he bestows upon you. You speak of Floe, who protects your children, as she did when armies clashed at the foot of the Mountain. Yet beyond these city walls, the multitudes cast out by your leadership survive in squalor — adults and children alike — presumably shielded from the love of Phydeas and Floe by that very wall.'

Aghast, Lady Antoinette could only mouth soundless words, cigarette hanging in limp fingers by her side as Harold closed in for the final blow.

'There is one last thing you must know,' he said, no sign of a self-conscious tremor in his voice. 'The King is indeed among us tonight ... though it is not I. Nor is it one of these pure-blood pixies, nor this perfect specimen of a human. Lady Antoinette, I stand before you as a mere herald, for you are in the presence of Mustapha, King of Rhye: part human, part sylph; crowned in fire by the very Pantheon you claim to worship so dearly.'

Strangled murmurs broke in a susurrus around the room. Courtiers fidgeted, faces unable to conceal confusion. The dragonfly had spoken, yet had declared himself not to be King. Should a commoner be heeded then, if even a purebred one? He had announced that the King sat among them, though he came from mixed blood. *A misborn King!*

Dark anger crowded Antoinette's features, beneath a thin veneer of civility and a thicker veneer of rouge. With a physical gulp, she attempted to swallow the flare of emotion that suffused her face. After all, one of the creatures in her presence lay claim to the throne of Rhye.

Inner turmoil flooded Mustapha, as well. First the embarrassment, rippling through him as a wave of pinpricks and

275

dimpled skin. Then the warm glow of pride; love for his friend, who spoke without fear against unchecked bigotry.

Then came the burn from deep within. The quiet heat of unquelled embers.

Duty.

With deliberate slowness, Mustapha rose to his feet.

From a nearby chaise, Will stood in solidarity. So too the pixies, who looked set to fight their way out of the room – out of the palace, off the island – if required.

Into the precarious moment, Lady Antoinette spoke first. Honeywind and Glimmervane had appeared beside her, their ire cloaked as thinly as their sinewed bodies.

'Your Majesty,' said the Potentate-Elect, now facing Mustapha, 'I am disgraced in my own home. Yet tonight I invited you to eat cake, and eat cake you shall. Such a wondrous place is Rhye ... that the manservant of a Lady can rise to rule the land, anointed by prophecy and the favour of the Pantheon.'

A cautious cheer arose from the assembled, a disjointed chorus of salutation.

Her eyes flashed as she continued. 'I beg pardon to withdraw from this chamber, to save face. I pray you and your noble consorts will lavish yourselves upon this abundant feast, and the engaging acquaintance of those who share it with you.'

Mustapha felt the gaze of uncertainty upon him, from all about the palatial space. But in the eyes of servants, poised with trays and amphorae in their hands, he saw something more: the fleeting light of hope. Of anticipation.

They're just like me, and they know it.

'You may withdraw with grace, Lady Antoinette. Know that you welcomed me into your home, despite my heritage. Know also that Harold, Dragon Bane and Horn Wielder, speaks the words that are in my heart. From the occasion of this feast and onwards, halflings shall stand on equal footing in this desert province. Cast your gates wide to the underprivileged and undernourished beyond your city walls, so that all who bask in Adatar's light may also take the bounty of Phydeas in common.'

Antoinette gave another of her wallowing bows, teeth bared in a taut smile. 'As it please you, Majesty. A parting indulgence if I may, before the servants divest themselves of their responsibilities to this house: I bid them throw open the humidor, that our royal guests might enjoy the finest riddle-reed to be found in any corner of this vast land!'

Now, genuine enthusiasm spurred an outpouring of celebration from the men and women of Antoinette's court. Halfling servants shared enraptured glances, while cries of 'Hail, King of Rhye!' were enjoined by *clinks* of raised crystal.

With a sweep of bright damask, Lady Antoinette retreated from the room. Honeywind and Glimmervane stalked after her, making little effort to conceal their disdain. They offered stiff bows before departing. Several other faces still shared the fairies' dour expressions, though there could be no doubt: a festive spirit prevailed.

Mustapha schooled his face to neutrality as he watched the women leave. He did not believe for a moment that the day had been won. A sinister malevolence welled within the corpulent human, a hunger for control that would not be extinguished so readily. He knew not what more the night would bring, but he lowered himself back to the divan surrounded by the adoration of friends and Phydeantines alike.

'We did well,' exclaimed Harold, clapping him on the back.

'You did well. I'm still struggling to catch up.'

The banquet resumed. Upon the stage, the performing troupe once again danced and sang, a melange of sound and vision to allure the appetites of revellers. A parade of servants emerged from the depths of the Palace, bearing cartons of cigarillos, a selection of fine pipes, and hookahs of blown glass.

The last of the bitter atmosphere soon disappeared, in a fragrant billow of smoke.

'A question then, for any who can answer it: how far are we from the edge of the Milky Sea?'

Mustapha posed the question to the sprawl of courtiers crowding his divan, now eager to give him an audience. Will sat beside him, popping a last portion of delectable fig into his mouth. Both had abstained from partaking in riddle-reed, conscious of the need for a clear head ... though the wafting clouds still induced a certain giddiness.

A handsome satyr responded; bare of torso, with dark eyes and a smile of even white teeth. 'Four to five days' sail under a fair wind, Your Majesty. But the last voyage in that direction was almost lost in a sudden and dense bank of fog, amidst which lies the Nameless Ocean. Now, none venture there. It is forbidden – every last Phydeantine ship was destroyed by decree of the Potentate-Elect, some years ago.'

'Then you are effectively cut off from the world,' replied Mustapha. *Four days' sail would be no more than two days, aboard the* Khonsu.

'That is true, Sire,' said a young woman, a human with auburn hair and a dusting of freckles across her nose. She fluttered her eyelids as she spoke. 'But it is not to say we have been without contact from the outside.'

'I had wondered as much. Pray tell, have you encountered any outsiders in recent weeks?'

The satyr nodded. 'Certainly. Not only in recent weeks, but

periodically these past ten years. It would seem we have neighbours on this vast sea, somehow arriving from beyond the impenetrable curtain. Humans, arriving by sea or air from the hidden west. The first visit came within months of the New Dawn, when Phydeantum existed as a mere child of its current glory. In fact, they aided us in the construction of Grandville Palace, demonstrating great skill in engineering.'

Will sat forward, wine goblet in hand. 'Humans,' he echoed. 'Did they hail previously from Sontenan? From the sovereign lands of the Giltenan clan?'

The satyr turned his exquisite face to Will, one manicured eyebrow cocked. 'Not if their claims are to be believed, my Lord. If what they say is true, then they have been stranded a lot longer, and much farther from home than have we.'

The glance Will shared with Mustapha required no elaboration.

'They came to us in Babylon, not two weeks ago,' said Mustapha, 'arriving in an airship, the likes of which we have never seen before.'

Similar looks of recognition passed between the lounging courtiers, who sat up or drew even nearer at the airship's mention. 'We saw it also. Lady Antoinette took audience with a group of penitents, who described a bizarre mission from their ruler. A mission to seek out the Winged One.' The satyr shrugged, as if the very notion were preposterous.

Mustapha's brow furrowed. He squinted at the handsome vizier, aware of his own lapsing concentration. *Pull yourself together, strangeling. This is the important part. I could probably be more focussed, if only his rich voice wasn't so distracting. Stop it! What would Will think? This blasted smoke is driving me crazy ...*

'Who sent them? Who is their ruler?' he managed at last, face flushed. Sneaking a glimpse at Will, he found that the human's gaze also wandered.

The satyr lay close to them now, the woody scent of him intermingled with the aroma of toasted riddle-reed all around them. His words sounded like chocolate. 'A man who names himself Mephistopheles. The penitent travellers — the Order of the Unhomed, they called themselves — claimed to be under his direct jurisdiction, though that is doubtful. Antoinette sought an account of him from several among their number, only to find no two stories the same.

'One thing seems beyond refute: he is a man of great power and influence. The Order described for us the city from which they came. If reports are reliable, their civilisation boasts a population in the millions.

'Surely enough, Your Majesty, we should put these subjects to rest? We while the night away with inconsequential musings. Could we not interest you in a freshly packed pipe, to celebrate your momentous visit? I am yet to see you unwind, after a journey so arduous.'

Something in Mustapha's mind flagged the conversation as anything other than *inconsequential*, though he chose to ignore it.

Put your mind at ease — let yourself go —

The sylph arrived from nowhere. Yet there she stood, alongside reclining viziers and ladies, smiling a sweet smile down at him, as he perched on the edge of the divan. Her arms were laden with paraphernalia; a basket of pipes and dried riddle-reed on one side, and hookahs on the other. For several moments, he failed to notice that she wore only a translucent sarong of voile, slung about her hips. Lustrous platinum hair spilled in thick tresses over her shoulders and torso, which were otherwise unclothed.

'No thank you, no,' said Mustapha, uncertain if he convinced even himself. Questions still nagged in a receding part of his brain. *These people are so lovely. Surely, they can help me just a little more.* 'The

Winged One,' he mumbled.

'I beg pardon, Your Majesty?' asked the satyr.

'I said, why is the Winged One so important?'

A crease of mild irritation marked the satyr's forehead. He gave a shrug. 'That part made no sense, Your Majesty. The Winged One turned the tide of war in a bygone Age. He has been dead for a thousand years or more.' He nodded up at the sylph, who delivered a coquettish curtsy and placed a hookah beside him. Within moments the satyr had the bowl packed and warming. He wielded the mouthpiece with a savouring gleam in his eye, as if he had left the conversation behind.

Mustapha fought to connect the disparate snippets in his head. *The Winged One is long dead.* He blinked, in slow motion. *Mephistopheles rules a city of satyrs … no, an oasis of humans … all of them beautiful.*

'Will?' A pulsing rhythm pounded in Mustapha's head. He tried to push it away but it returned, like a headache.

Let the beat invade —

Let the sights and sounds persuade you —

'Will, I don't think we should be … Will?' He looked around. His lover had shifted to a nearby lounge, where he chatted with merry abandon to a lithe, female fairy. *Or are they a man?* The effeminate creature seemed to straddle the divide, an androgynous mix of fine jaw, high cheekbones and full lips. Will clenched a long-stemmed pipe between his teeth.

Mustapha spun left and right, scanning the chamber. Meadow lay with his head in a pixie's lap, while another massaged his feet. A cigarillo dangled from one hand. Dique cavorted on stage, waving a golden chalice above his head. All about him swirled the telltale purple haze. Harold sat close to the stage, egging Dique on with a dizzy grin. Mandel alone stood unmoved, just visible against the wall in the dimming scrallin light.

Take the time

To unwind —

The sylph had not moved. She smiled at him still, waiting for something.

What could it hurt? He gave her a sluggish nod. With smooth efficiency, she set a tall, glass hookah between his knees. In moments, charcoal glowed upon the plate, and the intoxicating scent of riddle-reed drifted towards his nose. The sylph bent towards him, holding the hose. Offering him the mouthpiece.

The first inhalation flooded his senses with a potent rush. There followed an overwhelming calm. The world, with all its danger and complexities may well have ceased to exist. The crowd of bodies, the sinuous tangle of flesh, grasping hands, brushing lips and silken materials consumed him.

And you will find

It's fine to … surrender.

A curtain of violet cloud concealed all. It carried the now-familiar heady aroma; the scent of enticement, an invitation to explore.

Mustapha held his hand before his face and flexed his fingers. *Feels real enough.* He reached out, testing the smoke, which wafted in delicate tendrils as he probed.

Something beyond the veil of smoke cast a warm glow. Light shimmered, glancing off tiny particles, turning the miasma shades of gold and rose pink.

The sounds of a tryst reached his ears. A rhythmic knocking, accompanied by moans that suggested pleasure, not pain. Mustapha cast the veil aside, stepping through the smoke.

In the centre of a luxurious apartment, dimly lit by rose-coloured light, stood an enormous bed. The other furnishings bespoke a noble residence; perhaps even that of sovereignty. To the right, a door of panelled glass opened on a generous balcony.

Covering the parquetry floor all around the bed lay a carpet of naked figures – entangled, writhing in their ecstasy. Knots of glistening, indiscriminate passion surrounded the bed, like fervent pilgrims praying at an altar of lust.

Upon the bed, a woman sat astride her lover. She had her back to Mustapha. Glossy hair the colour of midnight flowed down to her waist. With every thrust of her hips, the great carved bedhead knocked against the wall.

Mustapha took a tentative step through the orgiastic crowd.

No, not an orgy ... these people are dead.

Now to his eyes, the figures appeared lifeless. A sea of corpses.

With a switch of her ebony hair, the seductress turned to look at him over her shoulder. The surprise of discovery mingled with sinister glee on her face.

'Belladonna!' he exclaimed. Though he spoke the maligned name, no sound came from his mouth.

Her smile grew to an unnatural width; a forked tongue flicked from between her teeth. A dragon's maw. Around her bed, the blanket of corpses had skeletonised, becoming an entrapment of pale bones. Moving once again. Rattling back to a borrowed life. The bodies of the damned clattered to their feet, turning to face him.

'No! Not now, not ever!'

The cry of another woman broke the trancelike moment. A resonant voice filled with power and urgency, coming from outside. The bold whickering of a horse followed.

A horse ... or a pterippus?

The glorious winged creature, the yellow-white of starlight, touched down on the balcony. A woman sat armed and armoured upon the beast, her aura strong, like one favoured by the Pantheon.

She unsheathed her sword. Held it aloft. To Mustapha she turned her countenance, fierce and bright. 'You must come, quickly!' she called, nodding to a place on the steed's back behind her.

Mustapha bounded towards the warrior woman. The air slowed him, like running through molasses. Over his shoulder, the seductress hissed, a reptilian sound of vexation.

The scene changed.

He sat astride the pterippus, clinging to the midriff of its rider. She spared no breath for conversation — with all of her focus she spurred the flying creature onward through a bleak sky. Forked lightning bolts jabbed down from a dark blanket of cloud.

An endless sea raged green below them, waves tipped with crests of luminescent white. With each jagged burst of light, Mustapha could see beneath the surface, into the unfathomable deep … and his heart quailed.

Countless bodies thrashed below the waves, kicking and stroking, but not quite breaking through for air. Even as they drowned, they groped for each other; hands reaching, questing for a touch, a caress of doomed flesh.

The pterippus whinnied. Mustapha clung tight to his saviour. The winged horse baulked in mid-air. A towering wave formed below them — a giant peak of green and white, growing skyward. The wall of seawater began to funnel, becoming a mighty column reaching up into the night.

Right in front of them.

The column became a titanic figure, with torso, arms and head rising out of the frenzied sea. If not a god, then a being of prodigious power, imbued with all the colossal anger of a storm-torn ocean.

A face took shape upon the figure.

The face of Trixel Tate.

Wild and tormented, the giant spectre of the fixie lashed out at them. The pterippus weaved a zigzag course through the air, straining to dodge a limb of water that would surely crush them.

The sudden jerk unseated Mustapha. With a wordless shout, he slipped from behind the armoured woman's back.

The scene changed.

He did not fall towards the violent sea. He fell towards the opening of an enormous box made of camphor laurel. The shadowed interior gaped wide, a rectangular trap that he could not evade. As he plummeted down, a chorus of voices rang out from within it. Celestial voices. A cacophony of holy distress. One voice he could isolate, rising above the clamour with a one-word cry of pure sorrow: 'Trapped!'

Ophynea?

The scene changed.

With a great *whump* he landed on the rocky earth. No walls of a giant wooden box surrounded him; instead, he lay upon rugged and sloping ground, open to the night sky. A sulphurous pall of cloud drifted high above, behind which the atmosphere glowed a dull red.

His body lay twisted, an impossible mess of warped limbs. By rights, he should have been in agony, though he felt nothing. He lay immobile, shallow breaths coming to him, while the sound of far-off violence reached his ears. From the heavens, gentle raindrops fell. They pattered on his face; cool, soothing, like a kind of redemption.

Mustapha craned his neck – he found this movement remained to him – to observe his surroundings. A shallow hillside, covered in fragments of rock, stretched away into a wide marshland below, clenched in darkness. A thin mist clung near the ground, through which he could see numerous spot fires burning.

A dark shape watched him from within the mist. Perhaps a man, though an indistinct blur marred the borders of the figure. It stood, waiting. Or perhaps contemplating.

'Mustapha!'

His benumbed body jolted at the sound of a gruff male shout, coming from much closer by. The figure in mist came no nearer. In a moment, with a scrabble of loose stones underfoot, another stood over him.

Tears streamed down Mustapha's face. Never could he fail to recognise the lordly bearing, the competent stance and the flinty gaze of the sylph by his side, clad in ornamental metal, like an armadillo.

'Father!' he whispered, through a tightening throat.

Blood spattered the armour of the sylphic General Prime, though he appeared uninjured. *The blood of others, then.* He said nothing for a moment, regarding Mustapha with an indecipherable stare, somewhere between reverence and nonchalance.

'Father? Father ... did we win?'

Sinotar spoke with a steely growl. 'Aye, we won. But you! You're not supposed to be here.'

Mustapha tasted blood through his lopsided grin. 'Are you able to get me out of here?'

'That's not what I mean.' The stare grew stone cold. 'You shouldn't be here. In this battle. In this Age. You're meant to be dead already.'

Mustapha felt his blood turn to ice. His cheeks grew taut with horror. From somewhere within his sky-blue mantle, Bastian Sinotar drew an ornate pistol. Without ceremony he raised it, the barrel a gleaming finger of accusation and death, pointed at the strangeling's head.

The report of the gun shattered the dream, the hillside, the entire world.

CHAPTER EIGHTEEN

WHISPER ONCE MORE

Salacia had endured debilitating nausea for several days. She reeled from bedchamber to basin, then onto the balcony for fresh air, and back again. In between bouts of swooning and vomiting, she rallied the constitution to describe to Leith what she felt.

'A potent ill ... sullies the ocean,' she said, more green than usual around her gills. 'A desecration beyond mere pollution ... or geologic upheaval.' She leaned, retching, against a porcelain washstand.

Leith could spare little time to visit the ailing undine, but she did so out of sympathy ... and because Salacia's explanation perturbed her. She wanted to know more.

'Where does this "ill" come from ... can you tell?' she asked, seated on a velvet lounge in Khashoggi's apartment in Babel.

'A long way off,' replied Salacia. 'A place beyond my percipience. But it draws nearer ... a foul entity, manipulating sea life. Making brutes from placid creatures' — she paused for a moment, on the brink of purging her stomach, then recovered – 'and it draws nearer to the coast of mainland Rhye.'

Persistent gloom now clung to Leith's mien. *I know I shouldn't worry about things I cannot control … but that seems like an inadequate excuse, now.*

She had gleaned that nugget of philosophy from Torr Yosef. Renewed thoughts of the golem only multiplied the knitted lines on her forehead.

Following a report from Archimage Timbrad, she had made the heart-wrenching decision to evacuate and lock down some deeper sections of The Works. Somewhere in the stygian maze, Yosef battled with a force that harboured malevolent intent. *Has he been possessed? If so, by what?* Leith knew that nothing would torment the golem – with his strange intelligence and quiet pride – more than the curse that had plagued his now-extinct race.

No! Not extinct. Not quite.

A great population of Mer Folk held lodgings within The Works, given their unimpeachable work ethic and the familiarity it shared with their historic home, Artesia. As such, the streets of Babylon now teemed with an overflow of displaced Mer, who would have otherwise spent their time between the cliffside industrial complex and the vast ocean itself.

Now, they added their number to the multitudes who, in their uncertainty, mulled in alcoves and alleyways, courtyards and thoroughfares, waiting for the oppressive air to break.

Leith felt very ounce of their pressure as her own private hell.

The race of undines faired almost as poorly as their esteemed Salacia. They came crawling out of the Milky Sea, keening, describing some heinous assault on their senses. Fearful at the prospect of returning to their grottoes and cathedrals, they too milled in the streets, as figurative fish out of water.

Owners of public bath houses threw their doors wide, now finding themselves with a new vocation as innkeepers. More robust undines made other choices; many made a pilgrimage up Little Wandering to the pristine haven of the Bottomless Lake.

The day the tension broke, Leith strode the gangways of The Works, visiting a small security force posted close to the storeroom of Torr Yosef's annexation. The guards' strained faces brightened at the sight of her. The sylph knew her visits were as much about moral support as about obtaining a situation update.

'Sometimes he speaks to us,' murmured one man. An older human, wearing a haunted expression.

'Or at least he shares his monologue with us,' added another, idle hand grasping at where the hilt of a sword might have been.

Leith pursed her lips. 'What does he say?'

The first answered, his face unfocussed in recollection. 'It is a one-sided argument. *"I am me,"* he says. *"My shell is dominion." "No-one can wrest me away."* Over and over. Then, there is the other side. A different voice. *"You cannot deny me." "One soul for one task." "Turn it on."* It makes the skin crawl, my Lady.'

'Two voices?' Leith winced. *Possession.*

The *clang* of urgent bootsteps on the grate behind her prevented any further rumination. She turned to find the breathless figure of Erinfleur, the Elemental. Trailing behind the Wearer of Gold came a young Mer woman, barely beyond her adolescent years, with a pale face and round eyes.

'Minister Lourden!' panted Erinfleur, her mass of flame-coloured curls bobbing. Known for her serene nature, her red cheeks and heaving chest were a concerning sign.

'What's the matter?'

'You must come … the beach … quickly. It's the Ogre. It's Mher. He's—'

'Take a minute, Erinfleur. Slow it down, catch your breath. What is this about Mher?'

'He's dead.'

'What?'

'On the beach, my Lady. This young Mer lady found him, not half an hour ago. A fair crowd will be starting to gather, I'd say.' Erinfleur mopped her brow with a kerchief, breath slowing. Still, her words tumbled into each other. 'But there's more, I'm afraid. Another body. I didn't get a close look. I don't know how long they've been there—'

'It looks like Lady Tate!' blurted the Mer woman, shaken.

Leith's heart froze in her chest. Both women continued to talk at her, but she heard none of it. For a full minute, she fought to control a maelstrom of thoughts.

Over the top of it all, laughter thundered in her mind. The voice of a man — no, a male of implacable age. A wicked yet somehow playful tone, as if a dangerous game had been played ... and won. The voice carried some of the characteristic mechanical warp of Yosef's, yet it sounded twisted. Spoken not by him, but through him.

Leith started. By the time she had registered the awful mirth, it had passed. Neither the guards nor the women appeared to have heard anything.

'Which beach?' she asked, just above a whisper.

'To the southwest, my Lady,' replied Erinfleur. 'Beyond the heads of the Serpentine. A narrow strip of sand at the foot of the cliff, below the ... below the Ogreshrine.' Erinfleur clamped her lips tight, eyes downcast, realising an irony for the first time.

'You ... you didn't run all this way...?' Leith's jaw dropped open, dumbfounded.

'Not at all. We begged some sylphs to airlift us here. Officers of

Babel, they were – knew you would be visiting The Works today. Anyway, they offered to return to the beach and keep a perimeter. You know ... around the bodies.'

'I see. Thank you. Thank you, Erinfleur,' Leith mumbled. She threw a perfunctory sylphic salute – hands interlocked to form wings, palms inward across her breasts – to the men standing watch over Yosef. Then she started back along the gangway at a trot. 'I'm going alone,' she called over her shoulder.

Despite an insulating blanket of grey cloud, chill gusts whipped the coastline. Leith thought little of the cold itself, being born and raised amidst snow-capped mountains, though it registered in her mind as an unseasonal change.

From above, the growing clump of spectators were as colourful pebbles on the long, narrow strip of white sand. They formed a crescent around two shapes, the smaller of which had been ringed by several pebbles of a very distinct colour. *Thank the Gods – perhaps they did manage to enforce a perimeter, after all.*

Leith flew nearer, heart hammering against her ribs. It gave her a crumb of solace to consider the relative remoteness of this beach – were it closer to Babylon, the tragic scene might have drawn great herds of unbidden passers-by.

Some dignity, at least.

There, atop the stark bluff high over the beach, the Ogreshrine faced out to sea. Constructed by the delves – who had shared their underground realm with the Ogres for two and a half millennia – it represented a true passion project, with the frieze of hulking figures hewn from the cliff itself. Three tiered rows of monstrous demigods looked set to leap from the clifftop into Nature's embrace; fitting, for they were the foster children of Cornavrian, having been forsaken by Marnis, the Creator.

Take comfort in my sorrow, Cornavrian, for today we have both lost someone.

Leith winged her way over the bluff's edge, buffeted by a brisk updraft. Few hiking trails led from the southern highway, through the wilderness to the Ogreshrine. Fewer still wound their way down to the beach from that high place. The lack of settlement leant the place an untameable beauty.

Yet there were people: mostly Mer, undines and sylphs, Leith observed. Those who could access the remote beach with the least difficulty.

As she alighted on the sand, wings high and wide like the billowing sails of a caravel, she saw that Adept were among the small crowd. Not only Elementals like Erinfleur, who tended the surrounding forest and acted alongside the delves as custodians of the Ogreshrine, but Wearers of Green, too. Having seen the illustrious Minister for Security arrive, the circle of onlookers parted to let her in.

Dominating the scene, a large mass lay slumped at the shoreline. Tiny waves lapped at the shape of Mher, the size of a cottage, lain on his side. Leith had never before seen Mher in the flesh, though she had heard much of him from Mustapha, and from the delves who carved his striking visage in the cliffs above, amidst his brethren. To see him now filled her with a potent blend of awe and sorrow.

Glassy eyes turned towards the sea, but would never again view it. A blackened tongue lolled from between wide, rubbery lips, while a torrent of spume dribbled down the side of his face to the sand. His features, like that of a giant frog or a newt, were convulsed in the Ogre's final throes of agony.

The state of his hide caught the breath in Leith's chest.

Mher's bloated torso, his dark grey-green skin laid bare, revealed countless wounds. Needle-thin scratches and lacerations marked almost every square inch of him, while deep gashes trickled blue blood, ragged edges foaming, ripped as if by teeth ...

'Has he been ... *chewed*?' she asked of nobody, swallowing rising bile.

A nearby sylph answered. Perhaps one of those who had borne Erinfleur and the Mer woman. 'It seems that way, Minister Lourden. Though the soul may quail to consider it, it appears the Lord of the Ocean has been savaged by creatures of his own domain.'

Leith shivered. With quick fingers, she weaved a prayerful sign. To by-standing Mer Folk, she said: 'He ought to be buried at sea. Not condemned to the depths, where he sustained these mortal injuries. Create a barge. Bring him by ship to calm waters ... and let the barge be his funeral pyre.' Nods and confirmatory mumbles assured that her will would be done.

Her eyes stinging now with acrid tears, Leith stumbled through the sand around the fallen Ogre, to where the second figure lay beneath a huddle of vibrant robes.

A Mage and two Apothecaries crouched over the much smaller form. 'Please, stand clear!' urged one of them, with a gesture to the encroaching spectators. Spotting Leith, he moved aside to make room for her in the huddle.

Steeling herself, Leith knelt in the sand alongside the Apothecary.

'We found her face down, limbs arranged like she had been crawling,' he explained. 'Crawling ... away from his mouth.'

Leith wiped her face, but said nothing. She only watched as the Adept fussed over the wretched figure.

Trixel Tate now lay on her back. Pale and drenched to the bone, darkened fronds of hair plastered across her brow, she could readily have passed for an undine. The Mage had lain his Scarlet cloak across her body, and uttered an enchantment with which to bring an enhanced warmth to it. Despite his efforts, her teeth chattered between tight blue lips, her sunken cheeks pulled inward by every rattling breath.

Her teeth chatter. She breathes …

'She lives!' Leith exclaimed, startling the Apothecary by her side.

'She does,' said the Mage, his face grave. 'Though we have little time. She is uninjured, but appallingly weak, with fluid on her lungs. These Apothecaries have done what they can, but Lady Tate must be conveyed to the Healers' Guild.'

To know that Trixel clung to a spark of existence galvanised Leith. 'We must alert Babel.'

'Already done, my Lady,' said the Mage, with a firm nod.

'Are you able to translocate with her?'

'That will be hazardous,' the Mage frowned. 'To do so is simple enough, but the enactment draws life energy from any who are conveyed by such a means. I fear it may sap what remains of Lady Tate's strength. We wait only for these sylphs to catch their breath – they have only now returned here from Babel – that they might make the trip once more, bearing her with them.'

'I will take her,' declared Leith. 'A debt of gratitude to you both,' she added, turning to the pair of sylphs in the crowd. 'You have already done so much.'

The Mage eyed her with a sober expression, seeking to confirm her own fitness for the task.

'I will take her,' repeated Leith, in a voice clad with an iron will. Her certainty speared the Mage, who could only blink and stand aside.

Hoisting the limp figure from the sand reminded the sylph that she had carried the fixie in flight once before. Years ago, on the banks of the river Granventide. *How could I have known the next time would be for your life?* The Fae creature drooped in her arms. The Mage spoke the truth: time could not be wasted.

She launched into the air, offering a silent prayer of thanks to poor, dead Mher as she went.

Agonising tension burned for the following twenty-four hours. Within the Healers' Guild, a small host of Apothecaries worked the depths of their powers, concocting unguents, potions and poultices, drawing fluid from Trixel's lungs and restoring strength to her spent muscles. Leith paced the halls of Babel for half a day, until the Wearers of Green announced that Lady Tate would survive; though yet to wake, the tenuous thread of her vitality would hold firm.

She needed precious time to convalesce. Leith relinquished her own apartment for the fixie, taking one nearby for herself – the room in which Lady Mercy had been murdered. The re-allocation proved redundant: the sylph spent every available moment by Trixel's bedside.

The next morning, a young Neophyte crept into the room, bearing a tray on which sat a breakfast pastry and a steaming mug of blackroot tea. He cast a dubious glance at Leith as he sat the entire tray down on a carved hickory table beside her. Leith had folded herself into an awkward position on a small sofa, long legs hanging over one end. Her tousled hair looked as crumpled as the blanket of manuban wool that lay on the floor.

'I took the liberty of boosting the tea with a little extra mana,' he explained, with a waggle of his fingers that suggested an incantation.

'I appreciate it,' replied Leith through a yawn, stretching and ruffling her wings. 'But I will do better to get outside. The mornings have been cool … cooler than usual, for this time of year. A brisk flight will invigorate me.'

'Great. I'll have it, if she's not drinking it,' mumbled Trixel Tate with a thick tongue.

Leith jumped. Moments before, the fixie lay motionless, somewhere between sleep and coma. Now, through dreamy eyes she stared at the food on the tray. Her gaze drifted sideways to Leith, bringing a wan smile to her lips. 'This could be heaven,' she said.

'What?'

'What? I asked you if you could fluff up my pillows.'

The blushing Neophyte sidled out of the room. Leith stifled a grin as she rose to attend to the fixie. Trixel's complexion still matched the bedsheets, violet eyes sunken in the caverns of her face. Leith moved about her as she would a porcelain doll, propping her up, smoothing fever-stained sheets. She dragged the table nearer, bringing the tray within Trixel's reach.

'Trixel, I ... don't know what to say.' She dropped herself back on the sofa.

'Then say nothing. Not yet. I'm hungry.' Trixel grabbed the pastry and began tearing it apart. She devoured it piece by piece with ravenous enthusiasm, then turned to the mug to wash it down.

Leith watched the display with an ardour she did not care to conceal. Eventually, the fixie sank back onto the pillow. The very effort of eating had sapped her vigour.

The sylph looked at her with chin in hands. She dared not blink, lest the remarkable creature vanish. 'How ...?' she breathed, misty-eyed. The single word encapsulated so many questions.

Trixel managed a smile. Soon it faded. she stared towards the window, perhaps contemplating her strange fate. 'You know as much as I do. Mher must have swallowed me. Can you believe it?'

'I can. I saw the proof. I see it right now.'

The fixie sighed. 'I'll never know why.'

'All the creatures of the ocean must have turned on him,' said

Leith, hanging her head. 'Oska may have helped bring you back, but Cornavrian has abandoned his charge.'

Trixel screwed up her elfin features. 'My luck is my own. Oska ... Cornavrian ... the whole lot of them have abandoned their posts. It's a wonder Adatar and Anato remain in the sky.'

Leith twitched. The blasphemy caught her off-guard. *Something happened on board the* Khonsu. *Something important.* Trixel's miraculous survival presented a singular opportunity: the chance to learn something of the Western Way; to know if the voyagers fared well, or if misfortune had visited them. *We will talk, in time. Not yet.* Even as the sylph watched, Trixel's face softened, the bitterness melting, giving way to sorrow. She turned her pallid face to Leith, eyes brimming.

'I'm so sorry,' she said.

'What for?'

'For getting on that ship. For running away ... for rewarding your bravery with my cowardice.' A wracking sob turned into a cough; a wet sound, coming from lungs not yet fully recovered.

'You really don't need to—'

'I'm apologising here, Leith.'

'Okay, I accept it. But while we are being forthright, I must insist that you get some more rest.'

'You missed your calling as an Apothecary,' said Trixel, closing her eyes.

A light laugh escaped the sylph. 'Oh no. I was born a fighter, not a Healer.'

'That's not what my body said when you kissed me.'

Leith's mouth hung open. Unsure how to respond, she sat in silence, her cheeks burning. *Trixel is here. She is going to live.* The joy welling inside her, she could only stare at the fragile creature in the bed. In that moment, Leith struggled to conceive that the same woman had been a champion of the Fae Folk; holding, albeit briefly, the Antlered Crown. In her current state, a staunch wind might snap the fixie in two.

She is going to recover. She must. I have so much to say.

As Trixel drifted towards sleep, her outstretched palm lay close to Leith. The sylph reached for it, interlocking fingers with the other woman. On contact, a ripple of electricity enveloped her, from head to toes.

CHAPTER NINETEEN

THIS NIGHT AND EVERMORE

R espite proved fleeting.

Salacia and the ocean-born races soon recovered from their malaise. She reasoned that the same malign force that turned sea creatures against Mher must have upset the constitutions of those water-spirits upon land. The answer did little to succour her, for the wielder of such a force could only be divine.

Despite a prompt recovery, a discomfiting atmosphere remained. Unseasonable cold descended on Babylon over a few short days. Civic workers lined the streets with braziers for the benefit of a swollen populace caught out in the strange inclemency. Sorcerers enhanced the fires to provide a perpetual, permeating warmth. Alleys became shelters, housing clusters of Mer and Wilden Folk who milled with nervous energy.

The borrowed cosiness did little to stave off the unsettling chill in Leith's bones. She remembered well the unnatural thunderstorms heralding the end of the previous Age. The close of another epoch seemed improbable after only ten years, yet with the midsummer cold came the disquiet of dread.

Astrologers only fuelled anxious speculation. With much steepling of fingers, they advised the Archimage of a troubling portent. The difficulty lay, they said, in the reading of stars; those twinkling signposts most often foretold the passage of souls. The night sky told of a threat most dire, with an uncertain prospect of major loss of life. Shoulders were shrugged, and fretful hands wrung.

In the late evening, one day after Trixel woke, the assault began.

Automatons across the breadth of Babylon abandoned tasks and stations, as if uncoupled from the very edicts that drove them. No sound or vocalisation marked the moment their shackles broke. Servitors focused on an errand in one instant simply ceased to comply, turning on the spot in response to some new objective.

Torr Yosef, hunkered down in the dank enclosure of The Works, did not move.

Within the Tower of Babel, one goal appeared to unite all machines. Whether keeping house or handling goods in the storerooms or attending to the maintenance of lifts and scrallin lanterns, the automatons made a beeline for the Barracks and offices of the Fighting Adept.

Astute staffers noted the aberrant behaviour within moments. Lines of communication buzzed through the Tower, even as the machines marched in eerie unison, polite but unstoppable.

'It is advisable for you to evacuate the facility.'

'Please make your way to the nearest exit.'

'Do not detour via the Barracks. It is now in lockdown.'

Attempts to re-route the rogue automatons were met not with outright violence, but with a chilling lack of regard for their regular programming. A hapless pixie soon learned that the pacifism had a limit. Upon trying to force a servitor to follow historic commands, he found himself hurled bodily out of the way, striking a wall with the *pop* of a dislocated shoulder.

Other Fae and sylphs now swarmed the corridors of Babel, monitoring the march of the machines with incredulous stares. 'Stand back!' cried one. 'Regroup! Nobody is to engage. Send word to Minister Lourden, immediately!' The *clang* of metal echoed up from lower floors, followed by a raw scream.

Deep within The Works, Torr Yosef still did not move.

Leith stood poring over a table covered with loose sheets of parchment, comprising the notes she made from her readings at the Repositree. As a means of keeping herself from crowding Trixel, she had buried herself in ruminations of the Winged One's ancient miracles. Outside, the wind howled and rattled the panes of her broad window, adding to the foreboding menace of the night.

Her thoughts lay deep in the history of the land when a Warlock appeared at her open door. It stood with Violet cowl thrown back from its bestial face; its elongated snout and pointed ears like those of a jackal, identifying it as one of the delvish races.

'I bring word of a present and imminent threat, Minister Lourden,' said the creature. A harsh sound, tempered by the diction of intelligence.

'What kind of threat?'

'Automatons are malfunctioning, my Lady. They attempt to commandeer the Barracks chambers. All but eight of my coven are within. They also move to line the streets, directing foot traffic to some uncertain purpose.'

Leith's head jerked up from the jumble of pages, the bells of warning pealing in her brain. *It's happening.* The land's history vanished from her mind. She strode for the door, scattered parchment fluttering in her wake.

The Warlock swept along after her, up the last grand staircase to the King's Pavilion. Leith fought to ignore the eerie emptiness left by the departure of Mustapha and Will, driven by frenzied determination into the adjoining room. The pinnacle of the Tower. Dozens of Windows clapped open, a discordant noise of shutters, hinged panes and wooden screens; a malevolent applause of ensorcelled casements. Leith stared at the revolving carousel, alarm growing like a chancre in her gut.

Through every portal a similar image came, in various guises. Whether it showed the avenue of gingko trees, or the Corniche, or the downtown market squares, or the leafy neighbourhood by the gate to Below, the scene through every Window revealed the same unnerving sight. Hundreds of automatons – no; thousands, even tens of thousands – responding to some unspoken directive. Clanking, with that jerky waddling gait, in mass formation to accomplish an unprogrammed goal. They lined footpaths, two or three deep, as if waiting for a parade through the city.

Leith turned to the Warlock, teeth clenched in urgency. 'Timbrad?' she asked.

For a moment, the creature's large, fathomless eyes seemed to gaze inwards. Then it replied, 'The Archimage has already reached the Barracks, as per the protocol, my Lady.'

'How many are with him? Can you see?'

'Only a few. Fewer than we had planned – many Adept are barricaded inside. Presently there are no available exits by which they may escape.' The Warlock spoke with calm detachment.

Leith expelled a huff. *We must keep to the plan for Babylon's defence.* The protocol saw the Archimage co-ordinating a response to any offensive movement on Babel, while Leith would focus on defending the Oddity.

'You can come with me,' she said to the Wearer of Violet. 'When we get back to the room where Lady Tate rests, you are to stand guard at that door … and do not move.' For a second, she considered the hefty price of one Warlock in a situation of possible conflict; then she banished the thought from her mind.

'As you command, my Lady.'

Leith needed one last visit to her borrowed apartment, where she had not been idle in making her own personal preparations. Her battle armour lay, oiled and polished, waiting for her. Turning for the door leading back through Mustapha's Pavilion, she scoured the Windows one final time.

There, amidst the clattering portals, she saw it. The thing Timbrad had warned her to anticipate.

The thing she dreaded most.

In a shadowed vault, lit only by twin scarlet lamplight eyes, Torr Yosef began to move.

A lambent red glow panned around featureless metallic walls and over nondescript piles of junk, as stellite hips and knees engaged.

With the first movements of the golem, wavering shouts left the throats of the guards on duty. Frantic calls of 'Golem on the move!' rang through the labyrinth, one pair of sentries to the next, at last reaching the ears of the 'runner' — a young and competent sylph, ready at any instant to convey the alarm to Babel.

The sentries could not have known that their call to arms came too late, for the city already lay in the grip of turmoil.

No longer hunkered down in his dismal corner, Torr Yosef moved with astonishing speed. The humans watching over him released strangled cries as he loomed towards them, crushing them against the corridor walls on his way out of the makeshift dungeon in which he had crouched.

He met few obstacles within The Works. With giant strides he cleared the evacuated floors, moving without hesitation towards more arterial conduits, leading to the world outside.

Within him a strange resonance echoed, like the tolling of a bell struck at a funeral march. A baleful chime that spoke of a new presence dwelling in the void of his being; new, yet somehow stirring for some years. An abhorrent worm growing inside an apple.

The resonance directed him. Cajoled him. Jeered at him. He could no sooner cast it out, than a puppet could lose its strings and still function. In between the chiding and condescension, the resonance promised him peace – if only he completed his task.

A task that could destroy Babylon.

Still, amidst those miasmic chimes – between the pistons and cables and metal innards that threatened to corrupt – his own driving force persisted. The Yosef who knew how to make a stern fixie smile, or impart counsel to a gloomy strangeling. And so, the internal war raged on, even while his titanic shell stormed out into the night.

Upon the Marina, beyond the wide portal of The Works, stood a brace of humans and Fae: Officers of Babel. They held a loose formation, unpractised in the discipline of combat. Weapons rattled in their timorous hands; blades and shields that had not seen conflict since the Pillar of Rhye glinted beneath pale moonlight.

'Stand down!' bleated a pixie, sword aloft. 'Whatever compels you, lay it low! We need not fight.'

<No! I beg of you, stand aside! Or you will doubtless be hurt.> Yosef shouted into their minds. Despite his own warning, his limbs conveyed him forwards.

The defenders did not heed him.

Swords were swung with little commitment, wielders knowing even as they glanced off Yosef's exoskeleton that the attack would be futile. Thick arms swiped at them with pulverising force, sweeping the knot of fighters left and right. Giant fists bashed and crushed. Feet stomped against the stone of the Marina, mashing bone and flesh beneath them.

Within moments, humans and Fae alike lay unmoving in growing pools of blood.

Yosef stepped through the carnage. Inside, he wailed in despair. His head refused to turn, to allow him contemplation of the horror he had wrought. With unnatural speed, he strode towards the city.

In the root of Babel, Archimage Timbrad studied the vault-like door of the Barracks with a face of granite.

Too few high-ranking, combat-ready Adept remained to him. With a begrudging heart, he had divided the precious coven of Mages between the streets of Babylon and the defence of Below. Only two were still by his side, along with four Warlocks. *Only four!* Four more he had directed to the Oddity.

In an unanticipated manoeuvre, a host of automatons had positioned themselves in front of the Barracks doors, effectively trapping most Wearers of Violet inside.

Timbrad glared down a broad staircase, which funnelled towards an elegant landing at the Barracks entry. Flooding the foyer were hundreds of mechanical creations, from rangy maintenance bots to the typical kettle-shaped servitors; they formed ranks several deep that arced across the landing, arms held out as if to embrace the Adept.

Though they held the high ground, he vastly outnumbered Adept were in no position to take the Barracks doors by direct frontal assault. Timbrad intended to break through the robotic barricade with an array of weaponised magic.

'*Spears of Cornavrian!*' ordered the Archimage.

From the outstretched arms of the Adept, blinding theurgy crackled as lightning across a distance of twenty yards towards the automaton barricade. Bolts of ice-blue power leapt from one machine to its neighbours, enveloping them all in a chain reaction that Timbrad hoped would short circuit the robotic army. Within moments, skeins of electricity fizzled from the last of them, the effects of the offensive spell nullified.

'Attempts to disengage our systems will be unsuccessful,' spoke one automaton in a polite, synthetic voice.

Timbrad uttered an uncustomary curse. He could have anticipated that Khashoggi and Yosef would insulate their inventions against such power surges.

A rumbling *BOOM* sounded from behind the ranks of automatons, followed by an outward bowing of the massive double doors. Not the first, and likely not the last: a host of Warlocks strove to break free from within, even as Timbrad fought to free them from the outside.

With a militant *clank*, the automatons latched their upper limbs together. The defensive chain held the door closed.

Several of the Adept twitched by Timbrad's side. 'Advance ten paces,' he said, acknowledging their desire to engage. They moved forwards down the stairs, halting at a point just above the landing.

'They may be inured to lightning, but perhaps heat will agitate them out of formation,' he continued. *'Thalalladon's Blight!'*

With the dire, sucking sound of conflagration, gouts of fire spewed across the narrowed divide. An inferno engulfed the central ranks of automatons, licking columns of stone in its path.

In the heart of the blaze, the machines stood. They rattled in the scorching heat. Several rivets popped, zooming to ricochet off walls and ceiling. But the line did not break.

The flames roared higher — the heat more intense. Rather than break formation, those machines at the centre of the blast began to soften, melding together in a molten mass that slumped against the doors behind them.

'Stop!' cried Timbrad, extinguishing his own volatile cast. Sweat ran down his face, grime darkening the neckline of his White cloak. 'We will only further obstruct the door and roast ourselves, if not the Warlocks inside.'

On cue, another titanic *BOOM* echoed from within the Barracks.

'They seem intent on stalling us, my Lord,' said a female Mage to Timbrad's left.

He nodded. 'With this tactic, they divert us from their true purpose,' he replied. 'It serves them to sequester our Fighting Adept. I speculate with dread as to their greater scheme.' *Or what malign entity commands them!*

'We must balance deliberation with urgency,' said the Wearer of Scarlet.

'I agree, though I had hoped to avoid such a display of power at the foundations of Babel.'

As he spoke, the automaton frontline – the foremost rank, flanking those who had melded together – disengaged from their neighbouring machines and began to lurch forward. A steady, tramping march, arms still outstretched, reaching for the Adept.

'Prepare for direct combat,' commanded Timbrad. Then, with a glance at the paltry formation of Adept by his side: 'Has anyone ever armed themselves with the *Blades of Adatar*?'

'We are all of adequate skill,' replied a Warlock, without inflection.

'Then we speak the summoning rite.' There followed a unified chant; archaic words in a tongue seldom used since the horrors of Mage's Pass, many centuries before. Weapons of brilliant argence flared in the hands of the Adept. Imbued with white-hot light they quavered, at times resembling curved swords, at other times the coiling length of a whip. Upon their faces appeared sorcerous shields, dimming the blinding glare in their own eyes.

'*Blades,*' commanded Timbrad. With a phase-shifting hum, all weapons took the shape of the curved sword, shining with a fatal energy.

'Engage.'

The Adept swept down the stairs and across the landing in a line, spearheaded by the Wearer of White. They met the advancing machines with dancing blades and a shower of golden sparks.

From an overhead vantage, Leith surveyed the city with a festering unease. For half an hour she swooped and soared on the chill night air, gathering intelligence on the hivelike movements of automatons in the streets below.

Her pulse quickened as she watched roving machines across the centre of Babylon abandon their evening toils. They migrated single-minded towards broad thoroughfares that bisected interlacing urban streets. An ominous metal cordon lined the snaking passage on both sides, a gargantuan parade stretching from the Marina, right along the populous Corniche, crowded with jaunty townhouses, all the way to ...

Leith's stomach fell, her suspicions confirmed.

She landed upon a flat rooftop terrace, high among the spires of the city skyline. Her eyrie. Sylphic Officers — once proud Commanders of the now-defunct Vrendari — already occupied the rooftop. They directed aerial traffic, as dozens of other sylphs conducted broad, circular sorties over the city. Dark winged shapes dove down to street level and back again; monitoring, observing, conveying directions to a multitude of grounded figures. Down below, Officers of Babel strove to shepherd milling citizens to safety, away from the scrallin-lit streets overrun by automatons. Dexler Roth strode stiff-legged across to her as she landed. He had once been a Commander under the Generalship of Bastian Sinotar. Now a grizzled veteran, Roth carried disgruntlement over Babylon's restructuring, as did many other sylphs. Regardless, his sense of duty and pride in his work prevailed. He offered Leith a Vrendari salute, as if in remembrance of better times. She returned it.

'There is good news,' he reported, without wasting time over official titles. 'The machines mount no offensive. Citizens are being advised to return to their homes, and are allowed to depart without obstruction. The main obstacle remains those who have already evacuated The Works, though many are being offered shelter with those who live in Babylon proper.'

Leith nodded without looking at Roth. *It was my directive that put all those Works-dwellers on the street in the first place.* She served herself a silent admonishment before lifting her chin. 'Thank you for the update. Please continue with current directives.' He gave another curt salute in reply.

Alone, she moved to the edge of the rooftop, overlooking the illumined tapestry of Babylon. Mustapha had created a truly wondrous place, a bold cityscape to dazzle the eye; a sprawling, soaring offertory to the Pantheon that seemed at once progressive and timeless.

As Roth had indicated, the streets were mostly quiet. The majority of citizens had heeded the warning given. *They know nothing of Yosef's threats. Was I right, to give a public directive without explanation? I sought only to avoid widespread panic. What irony … a peril unknown brings the strongest sense of foreboding. People are more afraid because I told them nothing.*

Leith's own foreboding grappled with the electrifying thrill she had felt at touching the hand of Trixel Tate. Trixel, who had left her; Trixel who only came home alive through an Ogre's miraculous act.

Trixel, whom she had held in her heart for every moment in between.

Overhead, Anato shone down with indifference. *Of course. What do you care about Love? Do you contemplate the burden of Time, or Death, or these mere mortals below you? Tonight, I see them as you do – tiny things, inconsequent beings, scrambling for their fragile lives.* She looked down once again, along the glorious Corniche, curving away around the Bay of Marnis.

And saw him.

Yosef –

The giant golem stalked along the coastal road, as fast as she had ever seen him move. At the same time, his menacing stride seemed stiff, as though he resisted his own terrifying pace. Shining red eyes cast a vivid swathe of light before him, along a Corniche already lined by the lamplight eyes of an automaton host.

A mechanical guard of honour.

'Roth!' she cried, pointing. The old Commander scrambled to her side. In another moment, he had given the order: a golden flare, rocketing up into the star-smattered sky. The sign awaited by winged creatures stationed at the high places of Babylon.

'He was good enough to warn us of his coming, at least,' grunted Dexler Roth.

The elder sylph's gruff words barely registered in Leith's ears. In a daze she had contrived this manoeuvre, hoping it could succeed and fail simultaneously.

The city is in danger. Whatever lies within him must be stopped. He is a noble being. My friend. He is not yet lost. He cannot be lost. His is but one life, in exchange for the lives of many. Does he even live?

She looked down from her eyrie, chest tightening. An airborne host of sylphs and winged Fae fell upon the Corniche, diving from multiple vantage points in a planned counter-strike. Leith saw them as a swarm of fleeting shadows, converging in a dizzying spectacle on the golem's advancing form. As she watched, Dexler Roth appeared beside her, along with several other sylphs.

For several moments, the counter-strike squadron battled with the golem hand-to-hand. He swatted them away without breaking stride, before they regrouped to attempt an attack *en masse*.

Leith chewed her lip. *I should be down there with them. Would I be attacking him or defending him?* Her feet remained planted on the rooftop.

'What's going on?' muttered Roth, peering at the spectacle below. Yosef's exoskeleton began to glow a dull red. Soon it radiated, almost matching the red luminescence of his eyes. The flocking sylphs backed away, unable to approach.

A stone's throw ahead of the golem, a brace of Sorcerers assembled on the road. Following a swift incantation, their rippling Sky-Blue robes became a wall of water, curling into the golem's path. It struck him, erupting in a great plume of steam, though he marched on.

As the dousing waters sluiced away, the true terror began.

Automatons lined up and down the roadside brandished piston barrels and telescoping metal conduits, fashioned into makeshift armaments. The mechanical army fired a fusillade of shrapnel in a deadly hail at the soft flesh of their oppressors.

'They've ... engineered their own firearms,' muttered Leith, staring in abject horror as defenders dodged, scrambled or crumpled in screaming piles on the roadway. Some Sorcerers conjured theurgic shields or armour, intent on continuing the offensive. Others, including Fae and sylphs, were forced to fall back as the unspoken directive to mount arms rippled down the automaton line towards them.

Yosef stamped onwards, heedless of the wounded and fallen at his feet.

Desperation thrummed on the rooftop. Sylphic Officers pointed and threw urgent shouts at circling subordinates, anxious for some direction.

'The golem has himself a lethal escort,' remarked Roth. 'Without a properly armed and armoured Vrendari corps, we cannot take down so many machines. The Sorcerers are too few, and not all of them are battle trained. Minister' — she turned to look at him, having used her title — 'we can only slow him down. He cannot be stopped. Not here.'

'It is costing too many lives already ...' her eyes now returned to the terrible skirmish. The Adept rallied with offensive spells and weapons of arcane magic; with each wave came a counter-strike, machines unleashing a barrage of metal fragments while defences were lowered. The forces of Babel lost steady ground, carnage mounting on the bloody Corniche.

'Fall back. Everyone falls back to safety, immediately!' She mounted a small wall at the rooftop's edge.

'What will you do?' asked Roth.

'I need to get underground ... before Yosef. The Adept will already be there. I have to join them.' *To defend the spacecraft was my objective. To defend it ... from my friend.* She leapt from the wall, unfurling her wings.

Urgency and fear crackled on the night air, weaving from the Corniche right through the knotted avenues of the Urban Quarter. Quivering warnings passed along streets of mottled shadow and silver like flitting wraiths, sending the meek and infirm fleeing for their homes.

The last golem rampaged.

Any who opposed him were swept away, fodder for killer machines.

Urban citizens wealthy enough to own a servitor cowered from it, whimpering, expecting at any moment to have a murderous appliance tear them to shreds. No-one ventured outside, lest the towering shape of a red-eyed golem fall upon them.

In the shadowed corners of Below, kobolds prayed. Satyrs and goblins rediscovered their wavering faith. Still, a rumble of protestation brewed under the earth, for the Wilden Folk and other cavern-dwellers knew that the golem came for the thing sitting directly beneath them.

The yawning well in which the Oddity sat became an anathema of darkness.

Leith descended into the abyss like an armoured spectre, wings outstretched. To save precious time, she ignored the crumbling spiral stair, wrapped around the walls and tucked behind the towering stone columns, a giant cage buried deep in the earth.

Time had become a vital commodity. For halting the possessed golem. For bringing Trixel back to health. For all of Babylon.

It escapes, irretrievable time.

The sight of the hulking spaceship never failed to unnerve her. But not only the sight of it. The thing emitted a resonant hum that gave her gooseflesh. It now became even more menacing, with the inevitable approach of Torr Yosef. Somehow the two were destined − doomed? − to come together.

At the foot of the machine, in a pool of Sorcerers' firelight, a small knot of Mages and Warlocks stood in readiness. They looked up as she approached, faces resolute.

'Yosef is near,' she said, fighting for steadiness in her own voice. The words rang with enormity in the vast chamber.

'We are ready,' answered Samsara, a beautiful raven-haired Mage. With gravity in her tone, she added: 'The golem shall be destroyed.'

Leith shuddered. She knew Samsara spoke the inevitable truth. In this sanctuary – this place in which the golem's task might be realised – there could be no room for a defensive strategy. To simply hold him at bay served no purpose. The golem could wait forever, having no need for sleep or sustenance. The parasitic entity within acted with such premeditated maleficence, it may well have waited for an Age already.

The last golem advanced towards his own destruction.

Samsara handed Leith a pair of smoky-lensed goggles. Leith felt she was being blindfolded for her own execution. 'For when it gets bright in here,' explained the Mage.

In the flickering dark, in the abysmal cellar of the land, they did not need to wait long. Soon, a swelling chorus of distressed howls arose from the caverns above, heralding the ominous *tramp-tramp-tramp* of feet that grew nearer, crushing pebbles to dust beneath them. One and all, Leith and the Adept heard the telepathic voice: Yosef's desperate whine, bastardised by the malignant glee of his tormentor.

<I am here.>

With a final crash of pulverised rock, the golem appeared atop the spiral stair. Red heat still cast a dire glow upon his shell. He threw down an imperious gaze, limned in scarlet light.

'*Blades of Adatar,*' commanded Samsara. Every Adept equipped themselves with an eldritch weapon, casting stark light high against the walls of the pit. Freakish shadows leapt from jagged rock; the golem's own shade rose to tremendous proportion against the recesses of the space behind him.

He gave a clanking laugh and began to descend the stair.

Leith drew her own blade, knowing the futility of it even as she did so. She needed to grasp something in her trembling hands. To steady her mind.

To steady her heart.

Ancient stairs cracked beneath Yosef's feet as he progressed, though they held. He threaded his way around behind high-reaching columns, disappearing for tense moments in the shadow of the gigantic spacecraft. He reappeared, still lower down, on the other side.

Yosef still had some two dozen stairs to descend when Samsara wielded her radiant whip in a vicious coil over her head. Her entire body pivoting, she lashed it with tremendous force, its serpentine length unravelling as the whip struck out for the golem. It wrapped around one mechanical leg, just below the knee.

In an intuitive blink, several other Adept followed suit; whips wrapped themselves like tentacles about his lower limbs. With a burst of enhanced strength they heaved, bringing the unbalanced golem toppling from the stair. A reverberating *crunch* and an explosion of rubble marked his arrival on the floor of the pit.

The Adept did not wait for Yosef to recover from the fall. With his massive form still prone, the Warlocks began hammering him with pulsatile blasts of Violet force. The Mages exchanged whips for blades with a rapid phase-shift, then crept nearer for an opening to sever a limb or decapitate. Leith, paralysed by terrible wonder at the spectacle, backed up to the very foot of the Oddity.

Yosef's tormentor retaliated faster than anyone anticipated.

He wrenched free a stalagmite while rising to tower over his attackers. He cast the tapered rock with appalling speed and accuracy; before anyone could react, the shard speared Samsara through her skull. Her lifeless body collapsed in the grit.

'Shields!' hollered the remaining Mage, though the order proved needless. Rectangular plates of energy materialised in the Warlocks' clawed hands, ready to fend off further projectiles.

Yosef lunged, a mountain of gleaming metal charging at the Adept before they could regroup. Two more were hurled high in the air; one careened off into the darkness, while the other struck the spacecraft's fuselage with a sickening splatter.

'Stand aside!' growled a Warlock to Leith, urging her to clear the volatile arena. She crouched by the foot of the craft, protected from radiating heat and lethal brilliance as the battle raged.

The last of the Adept rallied – one Mage, two Warlocks – for a final effort against their monstrous foe. A barrage of pure theurgy pummelled the golem, driving him back. Enveloping his shell. Furious power scorched him. Yet he advanced, one ponderous step at a time, gaining, with a prodigious display of strength, the vast side of the spacecraft close to Leith.

She saw his eyes flicker then; from red to white, and back to red again. A sputtering signal from within. Yosef still clung to his own sentient spark.

<Leith,> he said, with an inner stillness that belied the violence all around. <Leith.>

'I hear you, Yosef!' cried the sylph, heart pounding. 'What shall I do?'

<*This cannot be stopped. The new alloy of my shell will withstand even this. There is only one end to this encounter.*> Inexorable footsteps carried him forward, against the escalating might of three Adept. A few more paces would bring him to the ancient machine, and the culmination of his task.

<*Leith … it is my desire to end. In rewarding me for this deplorable task, the evil thing within me has also granted me a true will. I have a soul – a soul, Leith! – and with it, an awareness of myself.*>

<I shall not end while this task is yet incomplete; for without me, my possessor faces no true opposition. I have remained if only so that you, and these Adept, may have time to escape. I only fear it could now be too late. I suggest you fly, while you still can.

<Once this thing is done, I am ended. Inside this shell there will be only silence.>

'Yosef, NO!' Leith screamed, hot tears flooding her eyes. Her lenses fogged.

<This is as it must be, dear friend. I cannot exist with the consequences of these actions. These limbs move, and I know them not. I am spent.>

Yosef's eyes flickered red.

Reaching the heart of the theurgic storm, he swung a tremendous blow and swiped the three Adept away. Amidst gurgling wails, they crumpled to the ground. The maelstrom of wild magic ceased. In the aftermath of madness, Leith stripped the goggles from her face.

Unimpeded, the golem stepped to the foot of the giant spacecraft. Looked it up and down, appraising a long-lost treasure. Tendrils of smoke and steam arose from his battered shape, testament to the last efforts of the Adept.

Barely ten feet away, Leith stood her ground; feet planted firm, hands gripping the handle of her sword against the passionate tremor that shook her limbs. She accepted her fate with a deep breath, though the golem came no closer to her. Instead, he studied the panelling on the spacecraft as if she did not even exist.

In a sudden movement, he tore away a lower panel from the shell of the craft with a rending shriek. The sheet of metal clattered on bare rock, discarded.

Horrified fascination riveted Leith's gaze to the craft's exposed innards. Yosef's action revealed a simple instrument panel hidden beneath the shell, in a position clearly designed to be reached by someone standing on the ground. The instruments consisted of a large toggle switch, a six-digit numerical display and a strange conduit that might have been a keyhole.

The static numeric display read:

$$72:00:00$$

Yosef reached for a recess in his exoskeleton, rifling around in the attitude of someone searching their pockets. After several moments he stopped. With a violent outburst, he swung a mighty punch at the side of the craft.

Leith gasped. *Frustrated?*

The golem studied his hand, flexing and extending mechanical fingers. Then, without ceremony, he used his other hand to tear the phalangeal casings from his index finger, exposing the tensile cabling and segmented metal probe within.

Leith jammed a fist in her mouth, suppressing a startled outburst.

With clinical nonchalance, Yosef again studied his vandalised hand ... then slid his denuded index finger into the keyhole. He turned his wrist, full circle. With his intact hand, he threw the switch.

Such a rumble arose that the ground shook, causing Leith to stagger. The mounting whir of machinery sent vibration through the abyss; loose pillars of stone wobbled and fell, and fine trickles of gravel poured from above. After several moments the ominous sound stabilised, at a frequency that caused Leith's insides to churn.

The Oddity — the ancient craft that defied understanding — rumbled to life. Deep within the contrivance, circuitry thrilled with electrical energy, brought back from oblivion by the possessed golem. He stood before it now, finger embedded in the keyhole, watching the numerical display.

Leith watched it too, wordless in her bewilderment.

72 : 00 : 00...

71 : 59 : 59...

71 : 59 : 58...

71 : 59 : 57...

Her knees buckled, legs giving way beneath her. She fell to the dirt, back slumped against the stirring goliath.

Yosef's head turned towards her, lamplights flickering white once more.

<*It is done, and I am undone,*> he said.

'Yosef, please ...' Leith mouthed pointless words. No further sound emerged, but for a mournful sob.

<*Farewell, Leith Lourden.*>

The twin lights dimmed ... and extinguished.

A short while later, when Archimage Timbrad arrived atop the stair with a formation of Mages and Warlocks at his back, he found the sylph sitting on the ground by the spacecraft, hugging her knees.

CHAPTER TWENTY

BLOOD AND SAND

68 : 45 : 21

'**L**ord Mustapha.'

'Mm.'

A blood-red mist swirled all around, the residuum of a blast that had destroyed him.

Destroyed by my own father.

My own father, whom I ... killed?

'Lord Mustapha.'

His chest expanded, drawing in a tremendous gasp. A gasp of terrified awe. A gasp of wonder, of revelation.

His eyes flew open.

'Lord Mustapha. We must move. Danger is imminent.'

At first, he saw nothing. The darkness blinded him. While his eyes adjusted to the gloom, he registered two things: a pounding headache and the mechanised voice, warbling an alarm by his ear.

He turned to face the voice. Beside him, Mandel's metallic visage appeared in the dim light. His head lay turned on its side.

No ... I'm horizontal.

Mustapha swung his body upright on the sofa. He regretted it in an instant as the drumbeat thundered in his brain. He assimilated his surroundings. The dim rose lamplight casting a soft aura upon the stage; the scattered array of tables and decadent seating; the tangled undulations of so many naked forms.

'Danger is imminent—'

'Yes, yes, I heard. Someone, remind me never to touch that horrid stuff again.'

'—I calculate that we must leave this room within thirty-seven seconds, to evade capture.

'I now calculate that we—'

'All right! I heard you. Danger ... what danger?'

'—thirty-three seconds. The guards of Grandville Palace are on their way.'

'Mustapha!' Another voice. A hissed stage-whisper, intended to raise his attention, but no-one else's. Will's voice, coming from a place nearby.

'Come quickly, Mustapha! We've got to get out of here!'

Meadow.

He saw them now, throwing frantic gestures from behind a row of columns, to one side of the stage. Dique and Harold stood with them, barely discernible in the warm but dismal light.

Of course. Mandel. The only one of us not affected by that horrendous riddle-reed. He's had to drag us all out of a stupor. Mustapha lurched from the sofa, now wide awake, eyes accommodating to his surroundings.

Carpeting the floor – and draped on all of the room's furniture – lay the bodies of men, women, sylphs, fairies, satyrs and numerous other races. Not dead, as in his dream, but breathing in the deep, slow rhythm of sleep. Dozens of courtiers who slept where they had fallen, in a knot of unrestrained debauchery.

He tiptoed through the tangled forms, as deft and nimble as the wild-haired strangeling who had once stalked pterippi in the depths of Petrichor. Mandel had a tougher time navigating the slumbering revellers with a stiff waddle. Soon, the companions were reunited beside a delicate colonnade, beyond which a grand stair led to lower floors.

'*I recommend haste,*' said Mandel, his placid tone at odds with the import of his message. '*A squad of armed fairies approach this position and will be—*'

'How did you know?' spluttered Mustapha to the automaton. '*Lord?*'

'How did you know of the danger?'

Mandel paused for the briefest moment, then: '*My sound receptors work even when I stand still in a corner, Lord Mustapha. I overheard some courtiers arranging for your imprisonment, once that toxin caused your circuits to malfunction.*'

'*Ten seconds.*'

'Imprisonment!' cried Mustapha, incredulous.

'Hey, you two!' interrupted Meadow, calling from a double door at the rear of the parlour. 'There's a stair here. It looks deserted. If you don't want to fight your way out of here, let's go!'

'Stay right where you are!' called a shrill voice from the far end of the room. Another wide door — the portal through which they had entered Lady Antoinette's lounge of licentiousness. Through the door poured a flood of fairies and nymphs, dressed not for raunch and riddle-reed, but for an interaction much less cordial. Honeywind led the unlikely squad, gripping the haft of a short spear. She hoisted it to her shoulder, fixing the companions with a fierce glare.

'But why...?' gasped Dique.

'Gotta leave!' cried Harold, pushing the baffled pixie towards their only exit. 'Hurry, hurry, hurry!'

And they fled, with the squadron of armed guards stumbling through the crowded parlour after them.

Certainly, Honeywind had not anticipated finding the companions awake, for they found the rear staircase devoid of life. They blundered on at full speed, conscious only of self-preservation. Only a vague knowledge of Grandville Palace steered their hasty flight. *Down and out*, their instincts screamed, though the Palace boasted many floors and a sprawling layout.

They dived down the imposing stair, bounding two at a time. Mustapha sprang to the lead. Harold zipped ahead on whirring wings, scouting a way. Will and Meadow claimed the rear, keeping Mandel with them. The automaton negotiated stairs as a cauldron might manage a mountain trail.

Meadow threw many an anxious glance behind him. 'My left ear for a weapon right now!' he exclaimed.

'Or a shield!' cried Will, as a spear thudded into the balustrade behind him.

The stair curved past a balcony level before arriving at a sumptuous gallery below. Floors of polished stone reflected the soft glow of crystalline chandeliers overhead. Huge statues shouldered the weight of the balcony; figures of Phydeas looking both portly and grotesque in his exertions.

Ahead, the gallery also lay deserted.

'This way!' buzzed Harold, pointing to a hall that plunged deep into the Palace. His friends needed no convincing. Once on even ground, Mandel lumbered after them without difficulty.

The fairies drew nearer in pursuit, able to forgo the stairs on fluttering wings. They moved with a lethal grace, an alarming adaptation of their usual frippery. A forest of spears chased after the fleeing friends.

Harold's guidance brought them fortune. The hall led to another gallery; this one a grid-like maze of decorative columns.

Places to hide. To evade.

'Fan out,' said Mustapha. 'We'll try to lose them in here. Everyone head for the far end of the room – there must be another way out.'

'I see weapons on the walls,' remarked Meadow. 'Looks like some kind of museum in here.'

Without another word, they slipped amidst the columns. Mustapha scanned ahead; the gallery stretched some thirty yards, the far walls obscured in parts by an array of columns like soldiers on parade. Behind, the rumble-patter of light bootsteps warned of approaching fairies. He zig-zagged deeper into the gallery, losing his friends in a moment to the elegant pillars and the confusing shadows they cast in the spaces between.

As Meadow had seen, the room contained a wealth of objects and artefacts on display. Polished weaponry lined the walls; criss-crossed swords, pikes, halberds and spears, alternating with shields of numerous designs. Interspersed between the columns, mannequins in macabre poses wore Fae and Wilden clothing, as well as the garb of the Mer Folk. None of it spoke of ancient history – indeed, anything on display might have come from the latter years of Old Rhye.

Or a time even more recent, thought Mustapha with a frown, relieving the nearest mannequin of a short staff.

At that moment, the clash of weapons and a cry of surprise rang out from somewhere across the gallery. Mustapha spun about, ears swivelling; soon his feet spurred him through the haunting rows, towards the sounds of vicious melee.

As he approached, a female fairy pounced at him from a pocket of shadow. He swung the staff, deflecting a blow, then parried with a lunge at the creature's midriff. She doubled over with an inelegant howl. Thrusting her out of his way, he hurried on.

Beyond the next column, five fairies cornered their quarry against the wall. Meadow, armed with a short sword and shield, and Will with shield alone, fended off their winged assailants.

Mustapha danced into the fray, disrupting the ambush with a flurry of strikes. His distraction broke the fairy cordon, enabling Will to snatch a curved blade from the wall.

A frenzied skirmish ensued. Blade against spear haft, staff against sword, the clangour drew more fairies to the fight. The trio fell back, edging their way closer to the far end of the room.

Echoes of Psithur Grove awoke within them. In the heart of Petrichor, all bar Mustapha – in the grips of a coma at the time – had been blooded in combat, forging a bond in battle that would see them fight for survival until the end of it all, atop the Pillar of Rhye. By contrast, the fairies – hardened by desert life though they were – knew stealth and hardship, but not the rigour of conflict. One by one the trio dispatched their assailants, until they collided with Harold, Dique and Mandel at the end of the gallery. The pixie and the dragonfly breathed hard, shrugging off their own vital encounter. Mandel could have been standing around at a picnic. For a moment, free of pursuit, they caught their breath.

'How is everybody doing?' asked Will.

'We're all right,' replied Dique. He alone bore a laceration on his cheek. The others, while shaken, carried no injuries. 'But I don't understand. Yesterday we were welcomed as esteemed guests ... now our hosts are trying to kill us?'

'A trap from the start,' said Mustapha, anger darkening his face. 'Their game was to lure us with opulence, weaken us with riddle-reed ... for what, I don't know. But we need to keep moving. Apparently, even a royal party outstays its welcome here.'

'I said we'd be fighting our way, from inside out,' growled Meadow, appraising his bloodied weapon.

Before them, a carven double door stood open. It led to another downward stair ... and the promise of being nearer to freedom.

The drumbeat steps of Grandville's guards drifted up from below, followed by the bounding shapes of a dozen armed satyrs.

'Lot of Phydeantines awake, for this hour of night!' said Meadow.

'They anticipated us,' reasoned Mustapha, as the hooved Fae spotted them, unleashing wild shouts. 'Quick everyone, back into the gallery for a new plan.'

'Leaving here won't be easy,' puffed Harold, 'but I saw another passage, back along the wall. It may be the only way!' He led the group back into the field of columns, even as the satyrs arrived atop the stair.

After a hasty search, the dragonfly located the passage once again: a narrow portal, with a sturdy wooden door. An otherwise plain lintel featured a carved likeness of Oska, God of Fortune, in the centre. The door swung open at the press of a brassy handle.

'Praised be Oska!' cried Harold, peering into the darkness beyond.

'Get in there!' yelled Mustapha stuffing his friends through the doorway. Satyrs wielding pikes and spears charged at them with murderous eyes.

'Not today, darlings!' he said, blowing them a kiss and slamming the door shut behind him with seconds to spare. He wedged his short staff beneath the inside door handle, holding it shut from within. A series of juddering impacts marked the collision of satyrs with the outside of the door.

'It looks like we're taking our chances with this passage,' said

Harold. His voice echoed in the dim space, as if he spoke into a well.

Dique: 'There are more stairs here. They spiral down.'

Meadow: 'Off you go, then! We're right behind you.'

Dique: 'I can't. You're standing on my foot.'

Will: Mandel, can you help?'

Mandel: *'Affirmative.'* With a snap, the automaton's lamplight eyes illumined the circular stairwell encased in stone. Scrallin sconces offered weak assistance, failing to penetrate the full depth of the spiralling descent.

The door still rattled behind them as they wound single file into the foreboding dark; Will helped Mandel down the stairs at the fore, while Mustapha stayed at the rear.

The strangeling felt they were climbing down the very spine of the Palace. At each turn of the dank spiral, a slit of a window granted a fleeting view of the outside world. The vista revealed only desert wilderness, undulating across the island's interior. The pink and purple hue of pre-dawn settled on countless dunes and the distant slopes of slumbering mountains.

After a half-dozen turns, another door appeared in the outer wall of the stairwell, which otherwise continued into the shadows.

'Down, or out?' asked Will.

'Out!' voted the pixies in unison.

'We can't be at ground level yet,' said Mustapha, 'but it wouldn't hurt to see what we have here.'

The door, either seized or locked shut, refused to budge.

'Excuse me,' Mandel intoned, waddling through the group to the door. He held a mechanical hand to the lock. *'Shield your eyes,'* he said. A dazzling jet of bright blue flame roared from an outlet at his wrist, producing a blade of flame that seared hot enough to knife through the metal bolt holding the door closed. He repeated the process with each hinge, and the door

fell cleanly away from the frame.

'I didn't know you could … what exactly is that?' asked Mustapha.

'Oxy-acetylene torch,' explained Dique. 'Another little piece of sorcery that Khashoggi brought back from … well you know the place. That other world.'

'Well, that's one way to open a door,' remarked Harold, with an appreciative nod.

The portal led outside. Crisp desert air, yet to be warmed by a morning sun, caused teeth to chatter. Stars still dotted an indigo sky, which brightened to a rosy pink at the horizon. All lay quiet in the desert and the darkling sky, except for the odd *clank* of irons, somewhere out of sight.

Outside the doorway, a narrow balcony curved around the exterior of the stairwell turret. The companions found themselves still half a dozen storeys above the ground, near to where the tottering city wall of Phydeantum abutted Grandville Palace.

'Did you hear that sound?' Will asked of nobody in particular.

'It sounds … big,' said Dique.

'Big … and in manacles,' added Harold.

'It's coming from over this way,' said Mustapha, leading his friends around the sweeping corner of the balcony. They reached a point where the balcony met the crenelated battlements of the city wall and peered over the edge.

Meadow gasped.

Dique yelped in dismay.

'For the love of Cornavrian,' said Will, under his breath.

The barren desert floor stretched all the way to the foot of the wall. In the distance, sparse tufts of shrubbery and spinifex dotted a serene ocean of sand. In the miserable corner by the edifice of stone, cratering pits pockmarked the landscape, exposing a deeper layer of clay beneath.

In the nearest crater hunched an immense figure, swarthy and muscular, turning its knobbled ridge of a spine towards the stunned companions. A hide of dark brown and purple drew taut over the beast's mammoth shoulders. It dipped a hairless head low, scratching idly at the clay on which it sat. Tremendous chains, each link the size of a human's head, bound the creature by the wrist to a massive pike of burnished metal, speared into the base of the crater beside it.

Then, there were skeletons.

Countless piles of sun-bleached bones lay scattered in and around the pits of clay like a horrific open-air ossuary ... or the exhumed contents of a mass grave. Eyeless skulls stared up at the sky, from amidst a junkyard of brittle vertebrae and spindly ribs. Scraps of clothing lay with the morbid clutter: faded robes of every colour, stout leather jerkins, even pieces of bloodstained armour.

'What in the name of Marnis is that?' exclaimed Meadow.

'You mean *who*,' said Mustapha, in a voice so quiet the pixie almost missed it. '*Who* is that.'

At the sound of voices, the enormous creature swivelled its body, turning a grotesque and mournful face up towards them. One great big eye focussed in their direction. Dark tracks streaked from each corner of the cyclopean orbit, staining the deep creases of its visage.

The strangeling shook with fury, grasping the balcony wall. 'That ... is Goron,' he said.

'Goron's alive?' exploded Meadow, staring.

'If you call that "alive",' said Dique.

A red mist played at the periphery of Mustapha's vision. He knew this noble creature – a living artefact of ancient Rhye – just as he had known Byorndrazil. He well recalled the tale of the Ogres; the secret history recorded for none but the delves and their own race, beneath Two-Way Mirror Mountain. The way those creatures had fulfilled a prophecy and met with their destiny, on the final battlefield of the previous Age.

And now reduced to this... Mustapha barely registered the arrival of Will by his side. The fortifying arm around his shoulder.

'How does he come to be in this place?' asked Harold, in rhetorical fashion.

'The Gods only know how he got here,' whispered Mustapha, as Goron's wary eye drifted back to him. 'But I can see what is happening now ... and as sure as I am the King in this land, it is going to *stop.*'

'I don't understand ...' said Dique. He and Meadow had leaned away from the strangeling, as if he radiated an uncomfortable heat. 'What's going to stop?'

'This whole place – Grandville Palace – is one enormous lie. At least, our hosts are feeding a lie to the people of Phydeantum.' His voice, quiet and clear, matched the stark clarity of the desert morning.

'How do you reason that?' asked Harold.

Mustapha watched Goron with stern pity as he answered. 'Think about it. We were told that the oasis provides limitless bounty. That fresh produce, game and abundant riddle-reed just appear there, as if by magic. The gifts of Phydeas, we are led to believe. But what evidence do we have, that Providence still walks this land, when so many other Gods and Goddesses have abandoned it? Meanwhile, crouched in a filthy pit of clay, shackled to a great pike, is Goron ... an Ogre *who can craft food from clay.*'

A few faces registered the dawning of realisation. Dique, staring down at the foot of the wall, appeared not to hear.

Harold still frowned. 'So ... you think that last night's banquet was Goron's work?'

Mustapha nodded. 'More importantly, Antoinette and her

cronies are weaponising him, and his abilities, to stay in power. To force a divide between the privileged and the rest. Those people living in camps outside the city gates ... I'll wager they have no clue what happens on this side of the wall.'

'What do you propose we do, fearless leader?' asked Meadow.

Dique looked up from his clandestine observations. 'I have an idea. But we'll need an exit strategy to go with it.'

'Delightful!' said the strangeling, rubbing his hands together with vicious glee. 'What do you have?'

As Dique proposed his plan, Mustapha's toothy smile grew wide, for the first time in many days. He felt the warmth of admiration for his pixie friend, the homely Fae who never pursued adventure, but oft had a solution when there seemed to be none.

Will, Harold and Meadow's eyes grew wide with astonishment. Mandel remained expressionless, though he hummed in his own mechanical way.

'Audacious!' cried Mustapha. A heady mix of fury and exultation ignited his spirit. 'Harold: in order for this to work, I need to ask you a teensy-weensy favour.'

The dragonfly gulped. 'Yes ...? I mean no ... what is it?'

'I only need you to pop down there and draw a little pictograph on the wall, so our friend Goron understands the plan. Come dear, don't look at me like that! He can't reach you; he's chained in the pit. Just fetch some clay from the next pit over, and use it to draw on the wall where he can see it. Then you can fly back up. We will wait. Simple! But hurry. There must be overripe fairies flooding the place by now, looking for us.'

Harold expelled a great huff and gave Mustapha a meaningful stare. 'You owe me.' Then he flitted over the wall.

Once the deed was done, the escapees returned to the spiralling shaft and continued their descent. No guards lay in wait for them, though with the coming of true morning, the sounds of activity rang from somewhere beyond the stone-clad stairwell.

After a further six turns, they arrived at a dim basement and another door – unlocked – that opened into the lowest reaches of Grandville Palace.

They emerged in a grim den, a huge oblong space lined with massive grey-green blocks of stone. Thick pillars supported a ceiling twice the height of a tall human. Here again scrallin brought dull illumination; though from a couple of apertures, morning light beamed in at a low angle.

'It's a dungeon,' observed Will.

Mustapha began scouting the vast room, a sense of urgency in his quick strides. 'Not for us, it isn't.' His companions fanned out, exploring the room lined with stone partitions like a stable. No furniture adorned the grimy cellar ... nor did any prisoners.

'It's over here,' called Dique, pointing to a dark hole the size of a crawl space, covered by a rusted iron grid in the rough-hewn floor. 'The grate. I spotted the other end of it on the outside of the wall.'

Mustapha appraised the barred opening with a bleak look. *The kind of grate that would sluice excess water out of here, were this level to flood ... only I can't see this place ever getting inundated with rain. Perhaps ... it's for blood.* He left his musings unspoken.

'Ah!' exclaimed Will, from the opposite side of the room. His voice carried a jubilant note. 'And here is the thing we sorely needed: a door out of here.'

Only a heavy oak door, bound and hinged with iron, stood between the companions and the world beyond. They crowded around and took turns peering through a small window, also barred, revelling in a familiar view: the desert trail that led by a rocky pass back to the beach.

'How convenient,' said Mustapha. 'We leave this way, we don't need to weave our way back through the city streets, or around the oasis.'

'Is it too convenient?' asked Will. 'Do you think Antoinette meant for us to come this way?'

'I've no doubt about it. But she meant to trap us here ... I don't think she counted on us having an automaton with a cutting torch.' He turned to Mandel. 'Can you remove this door, as you did the one upstairs?'

'*Affirmative*.' The automaton bustled to the front of the group and with a burst of blue flame set about the work.

'Excellent. But advantage or not, we must hurry.'

'*Affirmative. The bootsteps of many reach my auditory sensors. Hostiles co-ordinate and move on this position*.'

All fell silent straining to hear, though the thick dungeon walls and the din of Mandel's labour prevented distant sounds from reaching fleshy ears. After a moment more, the door collapsed with a dull *whump* and shower of sandy grit.

Meadow stared at the empty portal, grey-brown hues of early morning spilling in from the western side of the Palace surrounds. A cluster of parched palms beckoned the way towards the distant escarpment ... and the *Khonsu*. 'That's it?' he said. 'A dungeon with one door, leading to the outside world, just like that? And no guards posted? Something seems off.'

'We're in a desert, Meadow,' answered Mustapha. 'A desert on an island, surrounded by vast ocean. Where would an escapee go, running from a civilisation without ships?'

'When you put it that way ... but what about the ships people came here on?'

'Those skeletons outside,' continued the strangeling, pointing over his shoulder with a thumb, 'are the remains of others who have gotten this far. They've realised that this is near to the edge of Rhye, but all too late. Antoinette and her cronies destroy their ships, trap them here, and ... sacrifice them. To Goron.'

'You don't say...' Dique gulped.

'Antoinette is keeping the Phydeantines in her thrall with distraction,' said Mustapha. 'The cultish following of Phydeas. The confounding riddle-reed. And worst of all, the segregation. Which brings us to this.' He knelt by Mandel, who waited in silence after completing his task.

'Mandel, you have served us with true diligence. Perhaps saved our lives. For that, I thank you. I have just one last directive for you. I want you to hear it, record it, and execute it in full. Do you understand?'

'*Affirmative, Lord Mustapha.*'

'Dique found us that grate over there. See the one? The drain itself looks large enough for you to crawl into. I want you to remove the grate and go through. You will be outside with Goron.

'I want you to free him. Those manacles will take some time ... focus on the chains. I'm sure he will understand what you're doing.

'Now. He won't comprehend speech ... but he does know pictograms. Show him the one Harold drew. Then I'd suggest you stand well out of the way.'

'I'm no artist,' admitted Harold, 'but it's hard to mistake a drawing of an Ogre bashing down a palace wall.'

'I don't think Goron will need any more cues after that. Once he is busy gaining retribution, you must go back through the breach. Navigate the Palace, making your way out into the city. Don't worry about guards – they will be too distracted to focus on you.'

Harold interjected, a slight tremor in his voice. 'Quickly, Mustapha. I hear guards approaching.' The pixies drew their blades.

Mustapha pressed on, rushing the last of his directive. 'Keep going until you reach the encampment on the city fringe. Tell everyone there what you have done.

'The time for restitution is now. You will be the hero of all Phydeantines with mixed blood. Do you understand?'

'*Affirmative, Lord Mustapha.*'

'Then go! May the grace of Lhestra go with you ... wherever she is.' And with that, Mandel waddled off towards the drain.

'What becomes of these people, once the Palace is torn down and Goron is no longer providing them with food?' wondered Harold.

'There is bounty enough here for a population to thrive on for some time, if handled wisely,' answered Mustapha. 'In the meanwhile, I have a little theory about my own abilities. If it proves correct, I'll be able to provide these people with the means to start building their own boats again. They can make their way out of here for good—'

'Well, look here!' boomed a voice from the far end of the room. Through a broad archway — the interior entrance to the Palace basement — swanned the Potentate-Elect, flanked by Honeywind and Glimmervane. At their backs followed a small army of guards and courtiers, bristling with weapons. 'Our guests are seeing themselves out! What pitiful hosts are we to neglect their departure? You didn't mean to slip out without a goodbye, did you? O *King of Rhye*.' Mustapha's title came from her as a condescending jeer.

Mustapha stepped forward. Meadow and Dique joined him one to a side, echoing the menace of the twinned fairies. Will and Harold sidled towards Mandel, as if they could shield him against the horde.

'The game is done,' said Mustapha. 'Your tyranny ends today.'

A saucy glare flashed across Antoinette's face. Soon it passed, replaced by the pensive lowering of her eyelids. 'I see there will be no misleading you, halfling. Nor any barter or negotiation; I will not waste my time on it. You are convinced of some guilt of mine; some evil you see as wrongdoing here. Might I remind you that this city has flourished these ten long years ... prospered and grown, with or without your pallid rule.'

Mustapha schooled his face to calmness. He could sense Meadow's fury to his left, matching his own. The pixie itched to fight, though the odds were stacked heavily against them. *Keep her talking. This should be a battle of words, for as long as possible.*

'The outer townsfolk would beg to differ,' he said through clenched teeth.

Antoinette laughed; a sing-song laugh of bitter notes. 'Come now, halfling. You of all people must realise, that with equality of wealth comes the stagnation of society? Not everybody can be rich.'

'There is a difference between having little and being destitute,' replied Mustapha. 'Half of your people are starving, while you and your ilk frolic amidst the trappings of exploitation. You maintain this charade in the name of divine Phydeas, who plays no role in it. Your favoured thrive off the suffering of those with mixed heritage ... and you torture an Ogre to achieve it.

'You are no ruler, *Potentate-Elect* ... you are a despot. A fat sewer rat, decaying in a cesspool of ill-gotten pride.'

A momentary pause gave Lady Antoinette away. Mustapha assumed it due to his revelation about the Ogre, rather than his petty name-calling. *Either way, it's the reaction I needed.* He had unseated her for precious seconds.

She recovered with a sneer. 'These charming accusations will matter naught when you are brought wailing before the mighty creature of the Gods. Did you imagine your ingenious mechanical servant could stand up to a living force of Nature? I see your ploy, sending the creature out through the drain. It will be crushed ...

as will you, shortly after it.'

Mustapha smiled. The gleam in his eye again unsteadied the corpulent woman. She snapped her fingers to the force of armed creatures at her back. 'Take them all,' she squawked. 'Take them alive.'

The Palace guards advanced, blades and spear tips lowered.

'Run,' said Mustapha to his friends, pointing to the open door. He gave no backward glance to them. 'Harold, fly on and alert the *Khonsu*. I am right behind you all.'

The spear-wielding Fae hastened towards them, closing a gap of fifty feet.

One trick remained in Mustapha's arsenal. A revelation; an epiphany that reached him from the blood-red mist of a nightmare. He had no song, but he had a voice ... and with it, a hope.

He blasted nonsense sounds at a devastating pitch. 'AYO!'

The structure rumbled. A great rent tore the ceiling. A huge chunk of stone and plaster fell from above, shattering in front of the startled guards. His friends, sluggish in their escape, dashed wide-eyed for the open doorway.

'AYO!'

More debris tumbled down, along with heavy iron furniture from the floor above. The oncoming forces scattered; some advancing through the debris with faces turned upwards, while others retreated.

Mustapha gave a wicked grin and threw a salute to the mortified Lady Antoinette.

Oh, my dear ... your troubles have just begun. Now you can kiss my ass goodbye.

'AAAAAAAYO!'

An avalanche rained down on the dungeon, as the lower floors collapsed, obstructing the room with an enormous pile of rubble.

Amidst falling fragments of stonework, Mustapha bolted for the door.

As he pursued his fleeing friends, a greater explosion and a tremendous roar marked the moment that Goron breached the Palace, bringing with him an unfathomable rage.

With Harold on his way to the *Khonsu* by air, the four remaining friends dashed for their lives. The sun had now risen; a desiccating heat would set in within the hour. For now, the cool of the night still clung to the low pockets of the wadi.

They picked a trail skirting the outer reaches of the city, taking little time to revel in the views it granted of the lush oasis. All around the city, those within the vast sea of tents and slums would be stirring, preparing for a new day ... a day like no other in recent memory.

Their chosen path afforded scant cover, though Mustapha had bought them a considerable head start. They thought little of hiding, intent on simply covering ground. In the distance, the escarpment beckoned ... the pass that would lead them out of the nightmarish desert.

'Is it too soon to ask how you accomplished that?' asked Will between heavy breaths. Sweat streamed down his face.

'It is,' answered Mustapha. 'I'll explain ... once we're safely on board the ship, with this place far behind us.' He had no breath to waste on words. The rising heat parched his throat with every inhalation.

The escarpment now loomed ahead. As they clawed their way out of the wadi, Will glanced over his shoulder. 'I am guessing Lady Antoinette survived,' he said. 'Here comes the pursuit.'

Far too late, a swarm of armed fairies rose from behind the city walls, a cloud of tiny shapes above the now distant Phydeantum.

'Still, we must hurry,' urged Mustapha, though he felt his own strength waning. 'They will close that distance in no time.'

Their pace had slowed, sapped as they were by the now-monstrous heat of Adatar in the morning sky. Wasting no breath on gripes and complaints, they ambled as best they could into the craggy pass, where shade and a drop in temperature proved fortifying.

The fairies of Grandville were within earshot by the time the companions stumbled onto the beach. Rabid cries like harpy-song echoed through the pass behind them, accompanied by the ominous whir of many wings.

With glad eyes and grateful hearts, they tumbled into the shallows, where Cyreus, Reka and a crew of burly Mer Folk stood ready for them. Strong, capable arms hoisted them from the water, helping them aboard the nautiloid craft, which idled, rocking in the gentle swell.

Exhaustion threatened to snatch Mustapha from consciousness. Moments of awareness came to him.

The frustrated screams of pursuing fairies, beaten down even as they flocked overhead.

Buoyant arms, raising him to still other arms, receiving him gently on board the *Khonsu*.

The bearded face of Khashoggi, standing at the rail — calm, confident, serene.

CHAPTER TWENTY-ONE

SHIVER DEEP INSIDE

59 : 58 : 01

Despite her protesting instincts, Leith Lourden abided by the Archimage's stern recommendations that she lay down and rest. In her presence, he worried aloud that she appeared haggard — not just of body and face, but of spirit. Incomplete somehow, as if her exertions in recent days had rent her in two.

She needed replenishment.

Through half-hearted grumblings, she acceded. Timbrad diffused her frantic remarks of the doomsday clock beneath the city, by pointing out that all manner of engineers, Sorcerers and authorities in subterranean geology now grappled with the problem. A procession of Babylon's finest toiled by the buried spacecraft, in six-hour shifts that ran all through the day and all through the night. What more could a lone sylph do? Especially an exhausted one, now wound so tight she might unravel and shatter her own fragile self-control.

With reluctance, she kicked off her boots and threw herself onto the bed in the guest apartment. Part of her feared to fall asleep, lest an excessive slumber tear away the precious hours. Another part of her willed to black out and escape the waking nightmare.

She stared at the ceiling. The elegant lines and geometric leaf motifs formed a beautiful grid-like pattern. *Not as beautiful as gazing at the stars, though.* The Astrologers' hand-wringing had become worrisome; they still claimed obscure readings from the cosmos offered few answers. She assumed them to be lying, for the sake of preventing panic.

Sleep stole her away from fitful thoughts without warning. In one moment, she fretted about what might happen when the dreaded clock counted down to zero; in the next, she hurtled through an abyss of fragmented imagery. A torrent of vignettes reeled through her subconscious mind. She could no sooner choose them as hold onto them as they passed by.

The shape of Torr Yosef towered over her in the dark. Only the flickering light of flame limned his shell and the dull purple-green fuselage beside which he stood. His countenance, ever an immobile mask, now carried something of implacable sorrow.

In a new instant, a younger Leith wore the raiment of a Vrendari Brigadier, once again walking the halls of her beloved Wintergard. Beside her strode the leonine figure of Bastian Sinotar. His lips moved. Though she could not hear him, she knew what he said. She stood poised to succeed him, the first female General Prime in many lifetimes. But cataclysm loomed; she may never see the mantle, even if she were to survive.

Next, an adolescent Leith hurried through vaulted corridors, late for class. So very unlike her. She clutched the history books tight to her budding breast. If she took the long route, she thought she might avoid the bullies — those who cajoled her, chastised her for the way she looked at that other girl. Yet there they were, waiting to dash the books from her arms. Call her hurtful things. Kick her to the ground, like some kind of outcast. As she limped to class, wiping the blood from her cut lip with a sleeve, she contemplated the warrior's life. To fight ... to become self-reliant. To have a reason to tuck her heart away, out of sight.

The girl had saved the seat beside her in class. Gave her a sweet smile, etched with sympathy. That cheeky, elfin face. That wild green hair—

Trixel?

Leith's eyes flicked open. She looked up at the ceiling. *Just a few minutes ... no harm done.* But the light in the room had changed. Hues of amber and gold, in bold overhead streaks, suggested that afternoon had arrived. She caught her breath.

Wait. What's that smell?

The sweet aromatics of a bouquet reached her nose. As she sat upright and swung her legs over the side of the bed, the vibrant mass of delicate, curved petals and lush green stems came into view, laid upon the vanity.

A dozen red roses.

Rising, she walked barefoot across the room to appraise the fragrant gift. A small card lay tucked between the stems, which Leith noted had been denuded of thorns. The elegance of the cursive script surprised the sylph.

> *This is thanks for looking after me.*
> *I felt better enough to go for a walk –*
> *As far as Mustapha's Garden, at least.*
> *I don't think he will miss these.*

> *T x*

PS: You drool when you sleep.
But because you cared for me, I wiped your cheek.

Beneath the text, a cartoon face with a wave of spiked hair poked its tongue out.

An embarrassed guffaw burst from Leith. She clamped a hand over her mouth and glanced at her pillow, where a telltale dark patch marked the spot where her head rested when she passed out.

She donned her boots, intent on going in search of the fixie. The fleeting vignettes of sleep still turned over in her mind. She pushed the tribulations of youth into her mental recesses. For now, troublesome nostalgia seemed like a waste of time. Only two things mattered to Leith in that moment: the implications of a ticking clock and the suggestive flurry of butterflies inside her.

In her own apartment nearby, Leith found the bed empty. Various personal effects lay strewn across the room, while the tattered clothes in which Trixel had been found lay slung over the back of a chair. On the nightstand, Leith found a second small card.

ROAR ... I'm a qilin!
Are you hunting me?
Try the kitchen ...

The sudden pang in Leith's innards, followed by an insistent rumble, supported the notion of finding food. She struggled to remember when she had last eaten a substantial meal.

The Upper Kitchen, which serviced the King's Pavilion, the Residential Parlour and a host of other higher-level suites, lay several floors below. Leith took the lift, a gleaming cage of polished brass. She encountered not a single soul on her journey, until she arrived at her destination floor.

There, a hive of activity greeted her. Babel staffers — most of them human or pixie — busied about, restoring order and normality to the seat of power in the aftermath of the automaton mutiny. *Well … the illusion of order. The façade of normality.*

Leith had issued a broadcast message to Babylonians. An alarm blasted far and wide, carried by heralds and news-runners to all districts. She struggled with the decision, knowing that it might cause widespread panic. *A strange weapon lies beneath our feet.* In the end, no real choice remained to her. At street level, citizens were urged to consider their movements around Babel and within the depths of Below. Some immediately took the initiative to evacuate for less populous areas, though most had no such luxury.

These staffers, loyal to the end with heir diligent care of the King's domain, would probably stay even if presented with the alluring alternative.

Few Officers milled about in the generous, open-plan kitchen. Those who dined at lunch had already come and gone, while the dinner crowd were yet some hours away. Leith enjoyed a blooming moment of pride — the dedicated staffers adhered to a well-honed sense of order, even amidst such fearful chaos.

Order requires a satisfied hunger. Visions of a towering sandwich, stacked with smoked game, aged cheese, a hint of greenery and a dollop of chutney danced in her head. She blamed the awoken rumbles of appetite on the suggestive powers of the fixie.

As she pulled open the coldsafe door, a weary voice called over her shoulder.

'Minister Lourden — a fortunate thing, to find you here. I made it my next task to find you … though as it transpires, all paths lead, in time, to the kitchen.'

Astrologer Mayhampton. The wizened Wearer of Deep Blue

spoke with his typical worldly eloquence, now tinctured with worrisome resignation.

Leith took a moment to acknowledge him. Inside the coldsafe, a giant sandwich fought for her attention. Atop the multi-layered construction sat a folded note, drawing her eyes like a magnet.

Duty beckoned, a prickle that ran up her spine to tingle in her brain. She hoped Mayhampton brought an encouraging update from the dark tomb of the spacecraft. At the same time her belly rumbled, her mouth salivating for a bite of succulent game – *and pickles!* – on rhyebread. Then came the cramp in her chest – Trixel's note called to her, triggering a curious spark that ignited a chain reaction, running down, down to the deep places below her gut.

My heart, my head and my stomach are at war. This is not the battle I needed right now. With a grimace, Leith snatched the note, shut the door on the sandwich and turned to face the Astrologer.

Mayhampton sat at one of numerous long dining benches with Fistral, the Chief Mer Engineer. The weathered grey hue of Fistral's usually handsome face shocked the sylph. Long locks clung like damp seaweed to his pate as he nursed a mug of brine. Mayhampton fared little better: his wild white curls appeared frizzled and frayed, a halo of frustration around his kindly face. Leith sat on the bench across from them.

'I don't need you to tell me,' she said. 'It's on your faces.'

'We've got our backs against the wall,' conceded the Adept with a nod. Though his eyes twinkled, sadness pinched at his deep crow's feet.

Fistral scowled. 'The more we learn of the craft, the more dire the news becomes. That numerical display? That's a countdown clock, all right. It's wired to a nasty-looking box within the hull, and ne'er the two shall be parted.' He slurped his brine, heedless of the trickles that ran into his dreadlocked beard.

'Can the whole unit be separated from the craft?' asked Leith.

'Pah! There'd be a whole range of traps and snares entangling the device. We can't be certain of teasing them out, without sending us on a one-way trip to eternity.'

'Huh ... eternity,' mused Mayhampton, aiming a wistful gaze at nothing.

'It is an explosive device then,' confirmed Leith.

'Aye, it is.'

She persisted. 'I assume we can't just stop the clock somehow? Or slow it to buy us some time?'

Fistral threw up his hands, raving at the ceiling. 'For the love of Onik! I'm afraid not, my Lady ... we cannot stop it, any more than we can stop time itself.'

The sylph knitted her brow. She tapped the folded note on the table with an absent-minded rhythm. 'Mustapha would have an answer to this. Maybe he already does and is on his way home right now. We can only hope ... can't we? So long as they haven't all been lost at sea, like so many others!'

'They're not lost,' asserted Fistral with a curt tone. 'Not with Cyreus and his crew on board the *Khonsu*. That Mer could drive any tub to the ends of the ocean.'

'You are both correct,' said Mayhampton. The ague twinkle in his gaze had resolved into focus. 'They are not lost. Hope is not lost, either. Mercury has just entered Virgo.'

'I beg your pardon?' said Leith.

'Make plain your nonsense,' scoffed Fistral. 'The stars are for finding his way home, not pontificating about hope.'

The Astrologer steepled his fingers, ignoring the engineer's affront. 'There may be chaos here, but our good King has reached a place of calm. A place where his mind can open. He may not realise it, but he is at precisely the right point ... in the stars, I read that a great truth will soon come to him.'

Fistral curled his lip. 'With the Mer and the Prophet guiding him, I could almost believe you. But is it the right point for us ... or for him?'

Mayhampton wore a serene smile. 'For him.'

'Then what more can we do here?' asked Leith.

'Little more,' answered the Astrologer. 'Work continues on the spacecraft. That is enough. Do what is in your heart, Minister Lourden. The time is coming for us all to be at peace with our lives.'

'You can't honestly mean that!' cried Leith. Fistral pushed his empty mug away in disgust. Heat bloomed in the sylph's face, and a knot of dismay settled amidst the melting pot of sensations already churning inside her. Mayhampton only continued to smile, crinkling those sad crow's feet.

Leith scrunched the note in her hand. She rose from the table, her head a storm cloud. A thunderous rumble gave her a start, until she realised her stomach once again vied for her attention. She left the men to their mope and gloom, and returned to the coldsafe.

The first few bites of sandwich revitalised her, like mana from Aerglo. She sat alone in a corner, contemplating the Astrologer's words.

They are not lost. Hope is not lost.

She yearned for the possibility, however faint; how Mayhampton knew this from a planet crossing a constellation, she could never guess. *I'm not the Astrologer here.* But through hundreds of skirmishes, battles and combat situations, she had known the pull of desperate hope all too many times. In her memory, she flew once more over the Pillar, dodging Death and dragon-fire, with the Horn of Agonies resonant in her ear. A slavering, undead host seethed on the dark plain below; the last flame of hope guttered in her bosom as she alighted on the besieged Pillar.

Into the arms of Trixel Tate.

Do what is in your heart.

Leith shoved the last morsel of sandwich in her mouth and wolfed it down. Then she retrieved the crushed piece of parchment, smoothing it out on the tabletop.

Well done!
Only liars hunt on an empty stomach.
Now fly – fly! – and find me where first we danced.

PS: If you are not Leith Lourden, do not eat this sandwich
Or I will gut you in your sleep.

Leith smirked, flicking a self-conscious glance at the handful of maudlin diners with whom she shared the Upper Kitchen. Fistral and Mayhampton had disappeared. Nobody else paid her any attention.

Is it right, to indulge in this game while Babylon trembles in fear?

What good remains, if one cannot seek joy in their darkest hour? The crease in her brow dissolved, the storm cloud lifted.

Limited routes joined the Upper Kitchen to the terrace overlooking the avenue of gingko trees. Most staffers would need to take the gilded lift cage, or the agonising descent by the stairwell.

One balcony opened from an otherwise unbroken profile of shimmering bronze buttresses, arrow-straight lines and fanning motifs in marble and glass. Leith dashed back to the lift, cranking the handle for 'Up'.

The leap from Mustapha's outlook thrilled in every nerve and sinew of Leith's body. When she had last dived from on high, the cold march of automatons put the chill of fear in her heart. Now, golden shafts of afternoon sunlight washed over a cityscape of eerie stillness. Even now, a mechanical cordon lined the street; silent as metal bollards, motionless as tombstones. They remained as a scar on Babylon, a reminder of recent horror.

Yet a buoyancy held the sylph's spirit aloft. She soared in a wide arc, circling Babel, marvelling at the glittering play of sunbeams on its beguiling splendour. Below, the Balcony, the xanthous columns of gingko and the overlooking terrace beckoned. She swooped and landed on agile feet.

It took only moments to find the loose chunk of granite weighing down the next piece of parchment atop the stone wall. Leith's lips tingled, as she stood in the very place where the fixie had kissed her.

She read the neat cursive script.

Soon, the sun will set.
I thought you might like to watch it from here.
Will you linger then, though your quarry escapes?
Find me in the Garden of Remembrance,
Where willows weep and falling water shall wash away our fears.
The King won't mind ... perhaps he'll never know.

Ophynea curse you, Trixel Tate.

Leith's wry grin belied the lone tear that welled in her eye, tracing a delicate curve down her cheek. She watched Adatar sink in the western sky, falling towards the horizon over which she had farewelled her friends. Golden rays beamed through a low bank of cloud, marking the passage of their travel. Now, of her companions only Trixel remained. Rather than emptiness at their departure, the thought filled her with an amorous warmth. The heart-hammering wave of longing ...

The insistent burn of a different hunger.

Stop running from me.

As the sun dipped into the glittering sea, Leith sprang from the terrace. Through the Tower grounds she sprinted, pumping legs aided by the occasional flutter of wings, driving her even faster. Dutiful sentries watched her flash past their posts with worried faces; throwing them a sheepish smile, she shouted 'Everything's fine!' over her shoulder. *Don't lose your head Lourden,* she told herself. *Get the girl, but remember: there are frayed nerves all around.*

With this feeling of guilty pleasure, Leith burst into the private aegis Mustapha shared only with Will. For a brief moment, a sense of intrusion froze her in her tracks.

Entering the Garden of Remembrance felt akin to stepping into another world. A place where the Rhye beyond – with all its worry and disarray – could be left behind. The cold shroud of self-consciousness fell away from Leith, replaced by awe at the sight of giant statues, arranged throughout the lush environs in a poignant memorial. The sculpted visages of past Sovereigns peered from amidst an explosion of vibrant flora, nestled among a calming verdant backdrop. From a far corner, the rush and burble of falling water undercut the chirrup of evening cicada song.

Leith walked through the Garden. As she passed an elegant willow, realisation settled upon her: *This is where Mustapha came to escape. To be somewhere else. To be someone else, perhaps.*

In this Garden, the world outside doesn't matter.

She made a beeline for the waterfall.

In a grove at the back pocket of the Garden, a semi-circular pool lay at the bottom of a tumbling drop, some fifteen feet high. The shimmering curtain fell from the upper reaches of a gully that entered Babel's grounds from the north. The turbulent rush of water and billowing mist filled the air in perpetuity.

Leith stood by a knee-high stone wall, bordering the pool. *Falling water shall wash away our fears.* With a shrug, she stepped out of her boots and into the rippling semicircle.

Frigid eddies swirled around her feet, rising just above her ankles. Brazen, splashy strides took her across the pool, until she stood cloaked in mist, an arm's length in front of the waterfall. She craned her neck, watching water tumble towards her from above. Overhead, the pink of dusk peeked through a fringe of nearby trees.

Amidst the laughter of water bubbled the mirth of a true voice. The sound of cheeky merriment.

Leith stared at the waterfall. The constant, glossy veil so close she could reach out and touch it ...

When the giggle sounded again, Leith dived through the water. The moment of icy shock cleansed her mind, heightened her senses. She crushed herself against the body of Trixel Tate, leaning against a wall of smooth stone behind the waterfall. She pinned the grinning fixie in place and stared down into those violet eyes.

'No more notes?'

'No more notes.'

'How long have you waited for me?'

'Long enough and far too long, as it turns out.'

'What if I didn't show up?'

'Stop asking questions, Lourden.' Then she giggled again – the sweetest sound the sylph had ever heard from her.

An urgent meeting of lips cut the laughter short. Leith pressed herself against Trixel, kissing her hard and holding her as if the spry creature might try to escape again.

She need not have worried, for Trixel returned the kiss with abandon. Leith revelled in the taste of her companion, an enticing blend of ripe forest fruits and sweet wildflowers. The fixie drew her in, an invitation to enchantment, pulling on her lower lip with gentle teeth.

The need for air — for clarity — hauled Leith out of the kiss at last. From a distance of inches, she gazed with intent at the other woman; appraising her, as a gift bequeathed by Ophynea.

She saw then, the fragility that withered the fixie's slender frame. Fatigue still hollowed her cheeks and enhanced the stark ridge of her collarbones. The slip of a dress she wore — *a dress! The second one she has ever worn!* — clung to her like a pale, sodden sheet, revealing the taut lines of her sinews beneath. She trembled, despite a bold light in her eyes that both begged and challenged the sylph to continue.

'You're shivering,' said Leith, clutching the fixie tight. 'Now that I have bested you, my qilin, I shall grace you with the honour you deserve ... somewhere warm and dry.'

Trixel offered no resistance. She sagged against Leith's athletic figure, as the sylph eased her back through the cleansing curtain.

The warm candescence of scrallin lamps made a welcoming haven of Leith's apartment. The room remained as it had been during the fixie's convalescence; no housekeeper had touched the homely tangle of sheets and thick woven throws covering the bed. The bookshelf and desk scattered with papers completed a studious atmosphere, contrasted with the ornamental armour displayed in one corner.

Leith guided the quivering Trixel through her apartment to the stone-tiled recess in which she showered. A flick of the lever brought torrents of steaming water into the space. Without apology, she stripped the soaking dress from her companion. Trixel stood unabashed in her nakedness, holding herself as erect as her weakened state allowed. Gooseflesh pebbled every inch of her, until Leith grasped her shoulders and stepped her back beneath the hot shower.

The fixie stared at her from beneath a dripping green fringe. 'Do you plan to stand and watch?' she asked, the hint of a smile tweaking her mouth.

Leith blinked. She had been gawping at Trixel's slender musculature, the smooth skin marred by a multitude of fine white scars. The physique of a being who rarely indulged, living a life dictated by the whim of the wild for centuries.

'No. I ... ah, no,' mumbled Leith, her face burning. 'I'll just go and ...' she pointed to the bedroom and stumbled out.

Leith opened a small hutch, retrieving several towels. She left them in a pile for Trixel, before retreating to sit on her own bed.

Her brain rang with so many dizzying thoughts. She hung her head, trying to make sense of the tumult; trying to order the knot of words.

Trixel.

Thief of my heart.

You steal the very breath from me.

Every time you move ... every word you say –

It destroys me. Shatters my mind. That well-ordered place I go to, in order to find myself, has forever changed because of you.

I love you, Trixel Tate.

Leith scrunched her face. 'Don't say that, fool of a sylph. You will ruin everything.'

'What did you say?'

The sylph jerked her head up. Trixel stood before her wrapped in a generous towel; her arms, legs and feet bare, tiny tendrils of steam still rising from her glistening skin.

'Oh! Nothing.'

'Good ... because there are things *I* need to say.'

Leith swallowed. 'Mhm?'

'Leith ... we're both being stupid.'

The sylph's heart iced over. *Oh, no. I knew it.* She hung her head again, so Trixel would not see the hot film of her rising tears.

'We've carried on like a pair of twits for far too long,' the fixie continued. 'Now, we're facing a truth we can no longer deny.

'Time is running out. If what the Mer and Adept say is true, we may have only days left before some great disaster strikes. I, for one, have no intention of running from it.

'There no longer exists any reason for us to lie to ourselves.'

Leith raised her head, staring with red-rimmed eyes at the fixie. She could not find her tongue.

Trixel pressed on, an uncommon emotion sweeping her words along. 'Leith ... I don't want to die without you knowing the truth of my heart. I no longer fear the slow, agonising death of a lifetime spent without you. These days with you are all I want ... all I need.

'I love you, Leith Lourden.'

The words fired a shooting star through Leith's heart. Now she did cry: tears of wonder, of fervent longing ... and of joy.

Trixel dropped her towel. 'Will you stay with me tonight?'

In the evening, a storm erupted.

Not outside the window, where the silver light of Anato joined the glitter of ten thousand stars in a cloudless sky.

In the cosy confines of the sylph's apartment the maelstrom raged, fit to rival the passion of Gods and Goddesses.

It began as a tender exploration – a tease, a caress, a sigh. In the sultry warmth a blissful dance ensued. An entanglement of arms and legs; writhing, striving to bring naked bodies together. With every stroke and pinch came a delighted squeal, a giggle, dissolving into wordless groans as lips met, again and again.

A rhythm built. Slowly, at first. A delicious friction that promised so much, while yearning to be sustained for the longest time. Warmth became fire, a molten heat arising from deep within a place of primal need.

The rhythm grew. *Faster. Harder. More.* Pounding hearts and needful breaths urged the desperate tryst towards crescendo.

Then, with unrestrained cries, the storm broke; the frisson of pleasure triggered cascading waves of ecstasy that rippled through the aching bodies of sylph and fixie.

At the last, when the maelstrom subsided, an aura like soft magic settled over the two expended women.

Countless leagues away, standing aboard the *Khonsu*, Mustapha gripped two sheets of parchment. He wore an incredulous look, having just read the words scribed upon them.

No matter how great his surprise, nothing could prepare him for the electrifying wave that suddenly thrilled along every nerve, shooting the bolt on his mind.

Throwing it wide open.

A declaration rang inside him. Words spoken with strident ardour, by a voice he knew. The voice of a Goddess.

She who had come to him with a luminous swarm of butterflies, bringing a coronation of fire.

She who had been closed to him, by the bargain with Adatar.

Ophynea, Goddess of Love, spoke with a force that rattled Mustapha from inside out. She spoke with a haste ill-befitting one of demure grace.

'FROM THIS PLACE OF MY ENTRAPMENT, O KING OF RHYE,
HEAR ME SAY:
DEATH IS NOT THE ENEMY.

FIND YOUR OWN PATH; TRUST NOT THE—'

Then the voice of Ophynea spoke no more, snuffed like a candle in the darkness.

CHAPTER TWENTY-TWO

AT THE RAINBOW'S END

44 : 27 : 50

On the morning after the companions fled Phydeantum, Khashoggi woke in his bed in the captain's stateroom aboard the *Khonsu*. At Harold's urging, they had travelled Full Ahead all through the previous day and night. The dragonfly explained that their destination lay only a couple of days' travel to the west, and the dwindling supply of rations would allow for little more time. Besides, none of the bedraggled group seemed interested in staying on the desert isle any longer.

If any further encouragement was needed, an attack from the barbarous fairies had been incentive enough to push off with all haste.

The Prophet arose and drew a hot bath, luxuriating in water that lapped at his frosty white beard. He revelled in the modicum of buoyancy, easing the weight of his limbs, as the water bore a part of the burden.

He stepped from the bath, eyes lingering on the swilling water.

Dried himself from head to foot. Next would come the clothes, the ritual that had brought him so much clarity for thousands of years.

First, he pulled on undergarments of cotton — so breathable! — then a fresh white linen shirt. Sturdy pantaloons he fastened with a leather belt about his waist, followed by a firm-fitting vest in a dapper charcoal stripe. For the occasion he chose a silken neckerchief, azure as the bejewelled Milky Sea outside his window. Thick woollen socks and his trusty Balmoral boots he pulled onto his feet. A brocade jacket in navy and gold completed the look.

'Good morning, Captain. Are you seeking breakfast in your stateroom today?'

Khashoggi turned to find Mack, the automaton, in the entry to his quarters. These past couple of days, Mack had doubled down his efficiency and attentiveness, in the absence of Mandel. The Prophet had become fond of the machine's competence and hard-wired sense of charm.

'Breakfast?' he replied, spending a moment in thought. 'I don't quite know what to choose. Perhaps it's best to skip it. You may walk with me though — I have other instructions for you.'

Khashoggi did not impart his orders right away. Instead, he moved about the stateroom, making the space presentable with a meticulous eye. Another ritual; one that Mack had become accustomed to. Every wrinkle straightened, every crease smoothed, every object in alignment with its neighbours. Upon his desk, he tidied away a sheaf of papers, with the exception of two pages he left with his brass pocket watch to weigh them down. The watch had been the only timepiece on board the ship. Khashoggi mused that it had stopped working more than a decade before.

'This way,' he said to Mack, with a beckoning finger.

Were the automaton capable of surprise, he did not show it. In the past two weeks, Khashoggi had displayed such a spectrum of behaviour that now nothing registered as extraordinary. The old man led Mack through his suite to a stylish double door, opening onto a small balconette at the rear of the ship.

Below, beyond a decorative rail, the stern of the *Khonsu* fell away with a sweeping profile. Huge turbines drove rotating blades beneath the surface, churning the sea to opalescent foam and propelling the ship ever westward. Beyond the muffled roar of wash, tranquillity reigned. Scant puffs of cloud floated on lazy paths across the blue yonder. The diamond-studded sea danced under the sun. A lone seabird glided high in the southern sky; Khashoggi pondered the implication of landfall nearby ... nearby, yet beyond charted reaches.

The Prophet spoke in measured tones to Mack, by his side on the balconette. He took comfort in the automaton's limitless capacity to listen. To hear his musings on a lifetime bound to the ponderous weight of his gift. The gift of seeing, of knowing, that drained away the mysteries of the world.

The vast sea danced before his eyes, perhaps the last great mystery.

The ultramarine frontier had beckoned him and he had answered. In return, he had received an answer of his own. A destiny made plain.

He whispered now, as if to himself. 'Forgive me, Salacia. In this way, I stay forever in your embrace.'

In a deft movement, he swung his legs over the rail. Leaving Mack behind, he stepped off the *Khonsu*, plunging into the Milky Sea.

Mustapha needed little more than a solid sleep to recover from the ordeal at Phydeantum and the escape across the barren sandscape. Indeed, the vitality in his veins confirmed a ruminant theory that he planned to share with his companions when next they came together. He shrugged off the diligent ministrations of Gwenamber, who otherwise dedicated herself to supporting Ackley Fahrenheit.

The strangeling studied himself in the mirror, pinching his cheeks, restoring a flush of colour. He regarded his unkempt moustache with a disapproving frown. His careful, preened appearance had grown rugged for lack of self-care. Almost immediately, he berated himself. The instinct had come from a place of vanity — a laughable, indulgent vanity, in light of recent events.

He felt a squeeze around his torso and Will's face appeared over his shoulder in the reflection. The human seemed to read his mind. 'What good is a beautiful face in a world where everything important lies unseen?'

Mustapha turned thoughtful brown eyes towards his lover's reflection in the mirror. He took a moment to process the esoteric remark. 'Thanks for trying to keep me on track, darling. If my perceptions — and the advice of the satyr — are right, soon we will come to it. What lies beyond the Western frontier is daunting enough. I've no intention of tackling it looking — or feeling — like I've been trampled by a manuban.'

'Are you certain you can do what is needed?'

'Absolutely not. I'm not even sure I know what is needed. But after everything it has come to this, Will. I must do this.'

Will's warm smile spoke of admiration. 'Those are the words of leaders and champions, my man. Not so long ago you wanted little more than to build a shiny city and be loved for what you had done. Now, far from adoring subjects, you push for some kind of victory? Have you considered that your achievement might never be celebrated?'

'Are you testing me?' Mustapha found a knowing grin. 'I don't need a parade or a trophy, dear. Whatever would I do with those? No, no, no! I just need to fulfil my little role in history. So many generations of Sinotars and Giltenans, watching from beyond Obelis … waiting for me to play my part. What else is there to do?'

Still smiling, Will gave Mustapha a light kiss on the cheek. 'I had started to believe I had lost you. Corrupted by power, the way power is wont to corrupt. Without your seraphic powers I am seeing *you* once again. The *you* that I have missed.'

Mustapha allowed himself another brief smile. 'Then … you'll let me in your heart again?'

Will ruffled the strangeling's dark hair. Despite his own affable smile, a guardedness remained in his eyes. 'The only way we are getting through this is together.'

Mustapha appraised his strapping blond companion and gave a mental shrug. 'I've had some thoughts on the matter of "together" and "getting through",' he said, ducking out of Will's attempt at another kiss with a wily grin. 'Let's go and find the others.'

Meadow and Dique, having spent the previous day purging themselves of the torrid after-effects of riddle-reed, found their focus by tuning their neglected instruments in the ship's hold. Dique had never seen a drum being tuned before — especially not Meadow's Drum, originally intended for war. Meadow held a certain pride in showing him the different tones he could achieve with a slight tweak here or there. The exercise seemed fruitless, but it kept their idle minds busy.

When Mustapha arrived in the hold, pulling Will along behind him by the hand, he found the pixies in the throes of a musical interlude. A bottom-heavy thunder of pounding drumbeat and impossible rumbling Zither notes washed over him.

The strangeling shuddered. The relentless rhythm conjured in him a jarring memory, a dissociative feeling as if he were in the presence of an opposing force.

'What are you two up to?' he cried over the din.

'Isn't it great?' said Dique, as the relentless sound clattered to a halt. 'Meadow tuned his Drum you see and I found some low notes on the Zither. Had a tricky time of it. Usually, it's missing half its bottom octave. But a little fiddling with the wires, and ... well, what do you think?'

'It's a racket,' replied Mustapha.

'A glorious racket,' said Will, giving the strangeling a nudge.

'I guess.' The galloping beat had stirred something within Mustapha – something that writhed, made his pulse quicken. He found his head as it subsided. 'Listen, I've been meaning to talk to you. I've a theory about my voice, and why it—'

Harold burst into the hold, all waving limbs and quivering wings. Cyreus strode in his wake, grey features as bleak as a bitter sea. Poised to comment on their good timing, Mustapha baulked at the taut expression on the dragonfly's face.

'Has anyone seen Khashoggi?' asked Harold. The room responded with frowns and contemplative shakes of the head.

'The automatons and the ship's systems are all issuing the same signal,' explained the Mer man. 'An obstruction lies ahead, no more than a couple of hours at our present travelling speed. Beyond it, nought is navigable.'

Mustapha's frown deepened. 'This is it, then: we're coming to the edge.'

Harold nodded. 'We wanted to alert Khashoggi. We all know he's been erratic of late, but yesterday he seemed something of his old self. He's not in any of his usual haunts ...'

'Haven't seen Mack either, come to think of it,' said Dique.

'Best check his stateroom, then?' remarked Meadow. 'Seems the obvious place to look.'

'It would be an awfully long lie-in for the Prophet,' said Mustapha, 'but you're right.'

Cyreus returned to the Bridge while the companions headed aft, to the old man's sanctum.

The immaculate stateroom relinquished all of its secrets without obfuscation. After a preliminary knock and call, the group threw open the door.

A serene but hollow breeze drifted through from the rear double door. There upon the balconette they found Mack — still as the lifeless metal from which he had been built. He was unresponsive to any command.

Mustapha found the letter first, in plain sight upon the stately desk. He lifted the pages, taking in the Prophet's elegant hand.

As he read, a creeping chill numbed his fingers.

Dear Friends.

I deactivated Mack, lest he report to you regarding my early morning walk. Or worse ... forestall it.

You see, it must surely take no divine ability to appreciate a basic truth: I cannot complete this journey.

I cannot go beyond the veil, to that place where the Unhomed, in their untold masses, await in perpetual angst.

Why?

The answer is simple: Because I put them there.

Because they will know I am to blame for their generations of restless suffering, the moment I set foot amongst them.

Because I am thus a coward.

That is not entirely fair, not to me; but it is the simplest way to summarise thousands of years of cow-hearted self-preservation. I have worked, tirelessly — recklessly, at times — to ensure my ongoing place in the annals of Time. Now, Time has caught up to me.

I hope you will indulge me as I explain.

I am a Seer. As of the present Age of Rhye, I am one of only three Seers to have ever walked this land. I am also the last, for the other two have already passed into the hallowed grounds of Obelis, or Heaven, whichever we should choose to call that paradise beyond the maw of Death.

No! Do not lament the fading of so rare a lineage as the Seers. I do not gnash my teeth at the prospect of ending such a line. For we, the Children of Lhestra, have endured lives that are cursed as much as they are blessed.

This is something that you, our beloved King, will understand. Rhye has, does and always will nourish and sustain itself on a vital diet of the AWE and WONDER of those who view it, in all its splendour. You have seen this for yourself, in the enraptured gaze of Mr Ackley Fahrenheit, through which a New Rhye was born.

Such has been the case in every Age of the land. But from where do these visitors come? And who is responsible for their carriage? That, my illustrious companions, is the duty of a Seer.

Our gift is to see beyond the present; a gift given form by the all-knowing spirit of Onik. Our burden — the cost of this gift — is that we are tasked with travelling. We move through the space between places, bringing new and innovative minds into the land, to nourish it forever more. This cost was sanctified by none other than Marnis, the Creator.

It is worth a mention that, of the three of us, only Lily resisted the holy call to travel for all her long days ... though for her stubbornness, she paid a wholly different price.

I digress. I sought not only to meet the challenge Marnis set, but to transcend it, in fervent honour of his decree. My good friends, I am abashed to admit now that I bit off more than I could chew. For while the land of Rhye may be sustained by one new and fertile mind for every Age of existence, I conspired to bring as many as twenty all at once.

And so, one thousand and ten years ago — or a little more than fifty years ago, on that other plane — I did construct a spacecraft, with which to lure not just one, but a wealth of awe-inspired minds into our midst. Lo, it worked — oh how it worked! Yet as you shall see, it also failed in spectacular fashion. Far from basking in the love of Marnis for what I had done, I knew misery.

Why?

To create requires the fuel of INNOVATION.

But — as we once discussed on board this very ship; as Lady Tate so keenly deduced — the byproducts of innovation include not only WONDER, but also FEAR.

You have seen it, in the timid and spectral light that haunts Mr Fahrenheit's eyes. Where once he wondered, he now shrinks away. His entire world has become his cabin, for the world around it has become a terrifying and abhorrent thing.

Now imagine the same, on the scale of a civilisation! No doubt you will soon encounter the damning result of my folly. I fret that beyond the frontier lies the monstrous lovechild of both innovation and abject fear. All the gloried prospects of invention, with all the fallout of ghastly terror. Tread carefully, for there lies an energy all-consuming.

I admit, I knew all of this from the moment I first heard about the Oddity. It stilled my heart to lay eyes upon the machine, buried below Babylon. How it got there I will never know, though it raises existential questions. What was done with the machine will also

remain a mystery to me, for I remained on Earth through all the
years of the travellers' ordeals, and well beyond.

Despite my own trepidation, it has been an esteemed honour
to Captain the Khonsu on this, her final (yet perhaps) most
momentous voyage.

So, I reiterate: I cannot complete this journey. I commend
my soul to the one true wonder that remains to me – the azure
mysteries of the sea. There, may my beloved Salacia know and
remember me forever. Good journey, one and all – the fate of Rhye
once again rests upon your valorous shoulders.

Yours, from the space between places,
Khashoggi.

Mustapha stared at the page and then through it. The finely
inked script blurred as he dwelled on the implications of the
Prophet's final words.

Before he had a chance to share the message with his companions,
Mustapha knew another astonishment: the rush of beatific power
took his breath. He gasped, for a moment unable to contemplate
anything beyond Ophynea's desperate words. A discomfiting
strain marred the saccharine tone of her voice.

As the message cut to abrupt silence, Mustapha found several
pairs of eyes boring into him. Faces waited in perturbation, breaths
held, for him to say something. Anything.

'Did anybody else hear that?' he asked.

'I heard a soft sound, like music,' offered Harold.

'Me too. Like a bell chime,' confirmed Dique.

'Ophynea spoke to me,' Mustapha explained. 'Something is
dreadfully wrong.' Fearful theories tumbled like whitewater rapids
in the flows of his mind. The turbulent stream found its way at

last to a still pool, chilling and deep.

The Pantheon haven't forsaken us. They haven't vanished. They're trapped.

But how ...?

Meadow's impish face crinkled. He craned his neck, looking over the strangeling's shoulder. 'What do we do? What does the letter say?'

Mustapha stared out the door to the balconette. Such a beautiful day outside.

'Khashoggi ... Khashoggi's gone. We're in the Mer Folk's hands now to complete the voyage ourselves. He seemed ... confident that we could. That we will, I mean. I'm not sure what happens next, but we must be ready for anything.' He strove to keep his tone optimistic, to protect his friends from Ophynea's fragmented warning. *Death is not the enemy.*

How ...?

'Did Khashoggi ...?' began Dique, with a vague gesture towards the open door. A horrified pallor drained his face.

A sombre lull blanketed the entire room. The presence of Mack's motionless form out on the balconette only made the emptiness — the void left by the Prophet — even more complete.

'Cyreus is at the Bridge,' said Will, harnessing the conversation. 'He has covered for Khashoggi rather a lot of late. He does not know what happened here. We need to tell him.'

'And quickly,' agreed Mustapha.

News of Khashoggi's death rippled through the *Khonsu* like a shockwave. Cyreus, stony-faced, demanded that his crew be informed. For the Mer, death and burial at sea represented a sacred ritual; a return to the fundament of their birth. The Prophet's final act stunned them, a subversion of their natural order.

Despite any sense of urgency for the journey ahead, the Mer Folk insisted on gathering in the hold to offer a brief rite. Reka led a wordless hymn that swelled in sonorous waves around the voluminous space. Cyreus remained at the ship's controls, satisfying himself with a gruff prayer through clenched teeth. The absence of a body to commit to the waves made him and many other Mer uncomfortable.

At the same time, the automaton host on board the *Khonsu* ground to an incremental halt. As if driven by the sheer force of Khashoggi's will, the mechanical beings completed their programmed tasks and simply ceased to function. Dozens of them froze – in corridors, galleys, cabins, the hold; even the engine room and Bridge – and would not respond to new directions.

While Dique scoured the decks examining one robotic statue after another, Harold triple-checked maps at the Bridge with Cyreus. Mustapha and Will climbed the spiral stair to the Observation Deck. A stiff breeze, accented with salt, whipped against them on the brief ascent.

'The wind blows cold,' remarked Will, raising his voice over the howl. 'Are we due a change in weather, do you think?'

They gained the upmost platform. Adatar still climbed in the eastern sky, painting tufts of cumulus cloud a luminous white. In the west, beyond the splicing prow, a vast pile of cloud rose into the upper atmosphere. Beneath it, a dense wall of grey gave the impression of an oncoming shower. The vibrant arc of a rainbow disappeared into the murky wall.

'Rain,' shouted Will, in answer to his own question. 'Do you smell it?'

'I smell something,' replied Mustapha, 'but it isn't rain. Take a closer look.'

They stood side by side at the rail, peering into the west through slitted eyelids as the gust billowed around them. The *Khonsu* speared ever onward, dauntless, as the thick curtain edged nearer.

It stretched to vanishing points in the north and south, far broader than a natural weather front. The wind blew with a strange pulsating turbulence, carrying an odour quite unlike the earthy tang of rain and sea-spray. It made their hearts race.

Mustapha gripped Will's hand where it rested on the rail. 'That's no stormfront, darling. That's it: the veil. The edge. The frontier. Nothing lies beyond it.'

'Are you sure?'

The murk seemed to tug at their consciousness, while promising nought but oblivion. 'I couldn't be surer,' said Mustapha. 'That's the same odour that drifts off the Nameless Plains, the swamps beyond Hiraeth and the fringe of Arboria. I know it now — it's the smell of awe, Will. Awe ... and fear.'

'I am not afraid,' said Will. He set his jaw, though Mustapha could feel the strength of his white-knuckled clamp on the rail.

'Fear travels with us, love.'

The foreboding veil now lay no more than a nautical league distant. Beneath their feet, human and strangeling felt the throb of the *Khonsu*'s engines slowing; evidently, the Mer intended to approach the doom of sailors with all the respect it deserved.

Harold and the pixies emerged atop the stair, joining their companions to observe the colossal grey curtain first hand. Wind buffeted them like the Breath of Cornavrian. The pixies, slight as they were, had to stand fast against the rail.

'What will we do about that?' called Meadow, twisting his head towards the veil. His blond locks whipped in a crazed bouffant atop his head.

'I have a theory,' replied Mustapha. 'Gather round, so I don't have to shout ... not until it's necessary, anyway.' The group huddled together, facing away from the wind. At their backs, the veil emanated a calamitous energy that now seemed to suck the *Khonsu* towards it.

Mustapha could feel the tension in the sinews of his face. *It's only a theory, but it's all I have.* 'Adatar granted us passage through that last storm, beyond the thrall that kept us in place. Saw us safely to landfall. As it turns out the price of a God's favour isn't cheap.' As if on cue, a painful prickle jabbed at his flesh where once his wings had sprouted.

'We ought to be grateful,' growled Meadow, 'but it seems it only got us as far as that crazy island.'

Mustapha granted the remark little more than a withering glance before continuing. 'Adatar withdrew the powers that Ophynea gave me. But he left me with something more powerful. More useful. You see, it wasn't Ophynea who gave me my Voice – it was *Lhestra*, with the aid of my mother. Likewise, it wasn't Ophynea who granted me the task of pushing back the frontiers of Rhye. It was *Marnis*.'

Harold frowned. 'That's all fine and dandy, but aren't we missing something, without Fahrenheit? A conduit, for whatever creative force you have up your sleeve? I have an idea ... maybe this will help.'

Harold reached to his back where, between quivering, pearlescent dragonfly wings, he carried the Horn of Agonies. 'It's worth a try, isn't it? We're near to the edge now. If this wind keeps picking up, it will be fit to rival the Breath of Cornavrian.'

Mustapha gave the Horn a dubious eye. It gleamed with menace and hope, in equal measure. 'I'm not sure Cornavrian has anything to do with this,' he said. Visions of subjugated Ogres flashed in his mind. Binding chains. A web of lightning. 'But we can give it a try. Show us what you've got.'

The dragonfly nodded. He braced himself against the bluster.

One pair of pincers held the rail while the other pair grasped tight to the sacred instrument. The bringer of despair at the Godsryche, wielded by the God of War; then the summoner of salvation, courtesy of Harold himself, upon a crag at the peak of battle.

He lifted the artefact to his lips.

Despite the wind, the sound came strong and clear, a stentorian note that pealed across blue-grey waters and swelled to fill the sky. Harold played a melody that rose and fell like the Milky Sea itself; deep as the fathomless trenches, lofty as the clouds overhead. He blew the Horn as if he had come into the world with it, every run the greatest he had ever played. Will and the pixies stood in silence, their wind-narrowed eyes flicking between their friend and the monstrous veil, coming nearer.

After several moments, Mustapha raised his Voice, joining the haunting melody. He sang mostly a wordless hymn, punctuated at times with a brief ode to Marnis, to the Milky Sea, or to all of New Rhye.

Voice and Horn duelled with the howling wind. The veil quivered, a seething sheet of mist that writhed in response to the wistful paean. And yet …

'It's not working,' said Meadow, his blunt comment heralding the closing strains of music.

'Sorry, folks,' added Will. 'A gallant attempt.'

'It never was going to work. Not without me.'

The group reeled at the shouted declaration. A spectre stood at the top of the stair, or so they thought. The robed and bearded form of Ackley Fahrenheit, the deep lines of his face like the weary stigmata of resignation. Sunlight and sea-spray glinted on his small, round spectacles. Behind the thin glass windows, a burning light shone in his eyes. His ascetic form leaned on the balustrade; trembling, from brisk wind or trepidation, or both.

At his shoulder came Gwenamber, dutifully clad in her Green Apothecarial robes. The look on her oval face pointed at her own hopes and fears.

'Fahrenheit!' called Mustapha, as he and Will crossed the Observation Deck to stand with the human. 'We're honoured you've joined us. Look! Ahead lies the frontier. I trust it doesn't strip the heart from you.'

Fahrenheit stared at the towering curtain, looming near off the ship's prow. Cyreus and his crew had brought the *Khonsu* to a standstill barely a stone's throw from it. 'Awed,' he said, upturned face showing the whites of his eyes. Then: 'Tear it up, my Lord. Tear up the wrathful blanket of mist that conceals the places beyond. May your vision give form to the land, and the people, that Rhye has long forgotten.

'I feel it, as do you: this is not where your world ends. We are deceived. Cast away this veil. Open our minds ... let us step inside.'

Mustapha's heart hammered. With renewed vigour, he resumed his effort. Remembrances of the New Dawn filled him. Pealing bells rang in his mind, as they had done at the rebirth of Rhye.

As before, the straining song rose above the ambient roar of sea and ship's engines. The music soared improbably over the tumult, filtering heavenward.

Fahrenheit snatched the spectacles from his face.

Curlicues of mist hung in the air, as thick vapour tumbled from clouds above. It drenched the companions, exposed on the open deck. Still, they faced it, watching as here and there it thinned, holes rent in the concealing murk. Shadows deep within the veil emerged, ghost-like, becoming more tangible with each passing moment.

Between fragments of wordless song Mustapha spoke, arms thrown to the heavens.

'In the name of Marnis the Creator, I pray! May the western

frontier be revealed to us, no longer hidden by this impenetrable veil.

'Show to us the forsaken land of the Unhomed. The domain of those abandoned souls, for far too long exiles in their own kingdom. I come now as King of Rhye to the seat of Mephistopheles. For here lies a wondrous city: a place of grand design, with spires and monuments and temples. Show us a people not ruled by fear, but by wisdom and courage!' This last phrase he gave with the utmost fervour, the final words of Khashoggi a blight in his heart. *You will be wrong, poor Prophet!* He hoped beyond hope. *At the last, you will be wrong!*

'It is done!' screamed Fahrenheit, lurching, withering against the forward rail. Will stooped to catch him. With a roar the veil of mist disintegrated. The shadows within it solidified, becoming things of the real world. A sprawling silhouette of domes, spires and hulking, boxy shapes, now coming to life.

The shadows dissipated. Colours seeped in, banishing the shade. Sunlight fell upon gleaming white and gold, here and there a sprig of green, a shard of silver. A monstrous shape emerged from the tattered shreds of mist and became known to them.

Less than half a nautical league distant, a magnificent cityscape beckoned. Overhead, the cumulus clouds rolled on, lighter, whiter, as if they no longer bore purpose. Adatar's rays beamed between them, flooding the newly revealed city with shafts of brilliance.

From the *Khonsu's* position, glittering waves rippled towards the foreshore – part beach, part docklands, for the civilisation teetered right to the water's edge. The docks bristled with ships, all of them shining marvels, like enamelled teeth in the jaws of a behemoth. The *Khonsu* would have sat proud amidst that flotilla, for they bore the same mark of a master shipwright.

Above the city skyline, still more wonders hove into view.

Dozens of airships, like full-bellied dragons, drifted north and south between places unknown. With grace they threaded between the tallest of buildings, as lords of the air.

'Mercy,' muttered Ackley Fahrenheit. 'It looks like …' His voice faltered; the thought left unfinished. A silvery tear streamed down each cheek.

Beside him, lined up against the rail, the companions remained speechless. Absorbing the city's majesty – the place of the Unhomed – reduced needless words to ash in their mouths.

Mustapha let his keen eyes flit from one remarkable sight to the next. He nodded in silence to himself. Now, more than ever, the wheels of his mind turned. *So … the Unhomed have a home, after all. Dear Khashoggi … what wonder, what fear lurks amongst those streets? What will of the Pantheon awaits us here?*

The depth of his wondering almost sufficed to drown out the insistent thumping beat, which never ceased its insidious pounding in the back of his mind.

Almost, but not quite.

Without a sidelong glance, he reached across to take a tight grip of Will's hand.

END OF PART TWO

PART THREE

THE FUTURE OF
YOUR WORLD

CHAPTER TWENTY-THREE

THE SOUND OF THE BEAT

40 : 00 : 40

After a long, critical stare through a brass eyeglass, Cyreus had suggested that they avoid making a spectacle of their arrival. Something about that forest of stone and metal, the untold acres of bristling architecture, made his blood run colder than usual, he told them. They should wait until at least dusk, making their approach under the cover of shadow.

Harold wondered out loud if they might in fact have already been seen. The extravagant contours of the *Khonsu's* hull did not blend well into the featureless Milky Sea all around it. If this were true, no curious advance party came to investigate. No boats patrolled the waters beyond the crammed shoreline. Airships continued their north-south drift like bloated cattle in the sky, none deviating from their path.

Mustapha stood upon the Observation Deck for hours in silence, keen brown eyes drinking in every detail of the massive city. The very implications of it had him teetering on the brink of disbelief: the civilisation had existed beyond sight for thousands of years; part of Rhye, and yet altogether separate.

One insidious force prevented his utter immersion in the spectacle that confronted him. Within the confines of his skull, the relentless pounding rhythm throbbed. The same insistent pulse that first accompanied the arrival of Lady Mercy and her Acolytes in Babylon. It haunted him, luring him to some predestined fate while also warning him.

Repulsing him.

His fascination faded into tight-lipped trepidation. He recalled approaching a darkened shore aboard the *Khonsu* ten years earlier, brimming with bravado.

No wings to carry me this time.

Adatar's burning orb settled behind a new horizon that evening, leaving an aura of gold, crimson and violet over the cityscape.

Then came the floodlamps.

Beams of ivory white snapped towards the heavens, illuminating the upper reaches of gilded towers many stories high. From a place at the centre of the city, a cluster of spires like giant candles thrust toward the stars. Perhaps the steepled skyline of a house of healing or worship; the spires glowed as ghosts caught in a moonbeam. Several floodlamps picked out the paths of wandering airships, unperturbed by the failing crepuscular light. The strangeling marvelled at those beams. More potent, more brilliant than scrallin could ever be. *Electricity. Reined lightning.* The Hammer of Cornavrian, harnessed by Humankind; a force so primal, so primitive, woven into the tapestry of the future.

If I could Home the Unhomed ... would it make Rhye as we know it unrecognisable?

'Beautiful, isn't it?' The voice of Ackley Fahrenheit caused him to jump, so absorbed in his wonder that he failed to register the human's approach.

Mustapha replied with a slow nod, taking the opportunity to appraise Fahrenheit with a sidelong look. Questions and comments formed an assembly line in his head. Altercations in the opening leg of the voyage had left him with little opening to explore his questions with the human. He resolved to do so now, lest it be the last chance he got.

'Is this what big cities look like,' asked the strangeling, 'back in your old world?'

Fahrenheit gave a 'Humph,' and a half shrug. His bearded mouth moved in the suggestion of a smile as he stared across the water. 'Spent most of my life in Brighton-Upon-Sea. Khashoggi's creations were by far the most advanced constructions in that old town. Many years before, I visited London, Paris, even Constantinople … they weren't a shade on this. But you have to understand it was a different time. Given another fifty years, they might look like this too … perhaps.' He bobbed his head, as if confirming a vision of those cities, advancing into the present day.

'Does it unnerve you? To see this, now?'

Somehow, the vague smile and wistful gaze remained, though Fahrenheit's pale, slender hands remained clenched at his sides. 'That does not begin to describe it.'

'And yet here you are, staring it all in the face. Why?'

A dry laugh broke from the human's throat. 'What else would I do? The truth be told, I have had a lot of time to think lately. This much I have realised: the only way out for me is through. To turn around now would do nought but present to me the horrors at my back. Not that there is a way to turn around, of course. I have to believe that the answer for me lies in there.' He raised an arm, pointing to the twilit city and the continental mass beyond.

The strangeling considered Fahrenheit's words. Will had said something similar. *The only way we're getting through this is together.* 'It's my fault you're here,' said Mustapha. No woeful swoon. No dramatic gesture. 'I've done nothing but punish you, and I deeply regret it.'

Fahrenheit waved him off with a gentle hand. 'Let go of your regret, Lord. It will bring only misery. You could not go back and change your decision, though you might want to. Were you able to choose differently, we may well not be here now, at the point of breakthrough. I set aside futile animosity some time ago … perhaps that is why I am able to stand with you and behold this city.'

Mustapha stroked his moustache. He noted how talking to Fahrenheit distracted him from the relentless beat. 'To go back … to change a decision. Would you? Could you? You chose to leave the world of your birth behind. No regrets?'

'None. To even contemplate second chances fills me with my greatest fear of all.'

'What is that?'

Fahrenheit smiled. His eyes remained cold. 'The fear to hope, where there is none.'

With nightfall, Cyreus and Reka readied the nautiloid launch. The Mer woman elected to pilot the craft, leaving Cyreus in charge on board the *Khonsu*. The sparse Mer crew would maintain a cautious distance offshore, awaiting any kind of signal from the advance party.

Nobody could know how long that would take, though rations dipped to perilous levels. Mustapha announced that ensuring a safe dock – or at least a supplement to their supplies – would be a priority upon making landfall.

'Bring your instruments,' he ordered Harold and the pixies. He need not have bothered: his Fae friends had no intention of leaving the ship without their fabled belongings. Not after their hostile experience in Phydeantum. Meadow looked the part of a four-limbed mollusc, with the Drum strapped to his back. Will wore sturdy clothes, perhaps more suited to a wilderness hike than a city excursion, equipping himself only with light arms and a flare gun. Fahrenheit seemed satisfied with his Babylonian cloak and a stout cane.

Mustapha dressed himself without ostentation, in plain white trousers and a matching sleeveless tunic. Wanting to present himself as neither monarch nor marauder, a small Mer dagger of whittled and sharpened coral was his one concession to self-defence, tucked into a studded belt. He clutched the camphor laurel chest under a protective arm, ill content to leave it out at sea.

Not this time. *I need to meet with this Mephistopheles. He must learn the importance of what lies in this box.*

Anato cast a soft glow on rippling waters as the companions cast off aboard the launch. Huddled together as they were, it held the seven of them without difficulty. Reka took a wide, bare-footed stance at the controls, opened the throttle and sent it zooming from the ship, her eyes primed on the distant city lights and the interceding body of water.

Mustapha regarded the receding bulk of the *Khonsu* as they sped away from it. The majestic vessel he had first seen moored at the decrepit docks of Brighton-Upon-Sea, in that fever-dream foray to another world. It belonged in that place. It fit in amongst the eccentric designs and technological ambitions of Humankind.

Humans ... always humans. Pioneers of gun warfare. The diabolical machinations of Figaro the Ploughman. Now Khashoggi, harnessing golem technology to fill the streets of New Rhye with automatons. His magnificent ship, capable of pushing beyond the boundaries of this world. It had stirred its fair share of wonder and awe, in a kingdom not altogether ready to embrace the explosion of such unbridled advancement.

Innovation.

Despite himself, Mustapha shuddered. The *Khonsu* receded further, melding into the all-encompassing dark of the eastern sea.

Reka had counselled the group that the harbour — a broad scallop that sheltered the docklands — would afford the best opportunity to make landfall without drawing undesired attention. This advice she had given after a thorough reconnaissance of their options through the eyeglass. The beach, a long strip of golden sand lined by slender palms, seemed to draw a great many people for swimming and recreation, even as the daylight failed. The rugged landscape beyond the city limits, while host to only a smattering of residences marked by twinkling yellow light, would also provide an arduous trek back to the city proper. Mustapha noted with a wry grin that the docks, on the city fringe, lay cloaked in relative shadow and inactivity at this hour. He surmised that the merchants of this city were simply unaccustomed to conducting trade across the water by night. He hoped that the sentries spent the evenings at rest as well, however unlikely this might be. *Why would they be expecting visitors now when they've never had them before?*

Hunkered down in the launch to keep the whipping salt-spray from their faces, his companions bore a variety of expressions. Meadow stared with a beetling brow at the approaching city lights; Dique beside him wore a curious frown. Will chewed his lip while fighting to maintain a noble dignity: perhaps he intended to bolster the strangeling's confidence, despite his own misgivings. Fahrenheit leaned towards frank enthrallment, his mouth slightly open and his features a-glow like the rapture of a child. It looked odd on the man's recently dour face, but Mustapha would not deny him the moment.

As for Harold – the dragonfly's demeanour troubled Mustapha the most. He hugged his knees with one pair of arms, while drawing a grey greatcoat about rounded shoulders with the other. It bunched at the back, where he had tucked his wings inside it. His face, long and pale in the moonlight, stared at the city as if at some imminent calamity.

'What's the matter, Harold?' said Mustapha.

The dragonfly turned wary eyes to him. 'We're going to stand out, you know.'

'Stranger in a strange land,' chimed Fahrenheit, sitting beside him. 'I've been in this boat before – figuratively speaking. Tugs at your gut, doesn't it?'

'I don't mean we're tourists,' returned Harold. 'I mean ... for so many generations, this settlement has been predominantly human. Mr Fahrenheit, you and Will are likely to fit in the most here. As for the rest of us ... well Mustapha, I know you wanted a quiet entrance – see the lie of the land – but we might be a little conspicuous, don't you think?'

Mustapha did think. The problem sat like a belligerent brownie in one corner of his mind – the corner not already crowded by the duty of kingship, tight-lipped wariness and that constant, godsforsaken pounding – but if he meant to give voice to a solution, his attention was snatched away by the down-throttle of the nautiloid's engines to a quiet rumble.

Reka had brought them, via the wide mouth of the harbour, to the docks. All around, the gargantuan shapes of sea vessels loomed over them, limned in silver-blue moonlight, dwarfing their launch. For a time, she cut the engine altogether, letting the small craft drift on currents and eddies that flowed between them. The *plap* of tiny waves against gigantic hulls came as the only nearby sound.

The dock held both commercial freight carriers and leisure craft like floating mansions, denoting both power and luxury. Sleek superstructures sat alongside ornate sea-going pagodas, nestled atop fin-shaped hulls that could knife through the sea. Mustapha wondered just how far afield these ships had travelled. Perhaps as far as the desert isle, he mused, based on the tales told by Phydeantines. To receive visitors by sea and air, seemingly from beyond the end of the earth, must have fuelled rampant superstition.

Yet here they were.

Feathering the throttle, Reka guided them to one of several empty berths, along a great concrete dock that jutted into the harbour. A rusted, barnacled ladder reached down to the lapping water; at the top could be seen the roofs of enormous storehouses, the scene revealed by swathes of yellow lamplight.

Reka tied off the launch, then one by one they ascended the ladder. Reka volunteered to go first and survey the scene, though Mustapha followed close on her heels. In a few moments, they all stood together on the dock.

Landfall at last.

Not a soul greeted them. Pools of light fell upon a barren stage between the nearest ship and an oblong storehouse that stretched into the distance. Huge cargo doors punctuated the facing wall of the storehouse, each almost the size of the entry to The Works.

'Well, here we are, all-conquering nobles of Rhye,' said Meadow. 'I prefer the dignitaries' approach, if I'm being honest. You know — turn up in a fancy vehicle, get a parade, a welcome feast ...?'

'I agree, it would have been nicer,' said Mustapha. 'If we could guarantee it. But remember how the Acolytes responded to their welcome? They killed their own dignitary and slaughtered twenty-seven citizens of Babylon, if you count the Officers of Babel and the sylphic squadron. Khashoggi also warned us … I'm just not sure we can count on a hero's welcome.'

'We've come this far,' Dique said with a shrug. 'No turning back. We need to find out, one way or another.'

Will nodded. 'Dique is right. We came here to make contact. To learn about the predicament of these people—'

'Their *predicament* looks fairly bloody comfortable to me,' mumbled Meadow.

Will cut him off with a wave. 'Surely this — Mephistopheles — will have a palace, or what holds as a seat of power in a city such as this. From our current position,' he added, pointing northward, 'the streets are that way. We only need to find our way out of this dockyard.'

'My task keeps me here,' said Reka, peering into the shadows between shafts of lamplight. 'I expect there will be supplies, perhaps even crates of foodstuffs, inside these buildings. If I can find a way in, I will *borrow* some to take back to the *Khonsu*.'

Determined looks and mutters of 'Oska's fortune' passed between companions. Then the Mer woman stole into darkness, leaving the remaining six to make their way towards the city. Mustapha led in the direction Will had pointed; Harold brought up the rear, blending into stone and concrete in his greatcoat.

Leaving the dockyard proved simple beyond expectation. They encountered not a single soul as they hugged walls and corners, until reaching the main roadway exiting the complex. A pair of sentries clad in strange suits stood at the main double gate, facing out towards the city — human, in keeping with Harold's theory. With a puckered brow, Mustapha noted that each shadowy figure carried some kind of firearm. Evidently, they guarded against unwanted visitors from the outside, with little consideration to who might arrive oceanside through the complex itself.

Avoiding the guarded gate, they crept to the perimeter, marked by a high fence of ornate, interwoven metal. Harold found he could readily sheer through the diamond lattice with his pincers; in a matter of moments, he had fashioned an opening in the fence large enough for all to scramble out one at a time. Soon they stood together, nothing between them and a veritable jungle of concrete and steel. At the heart of it lay the goal of their quest.

Or so they presumed.

'Are you ready for this?' asked Mustapha with a grim smile.

'Oh, I'm hanging on the edge of my seat,' replied Harold, coat clutched about his carapace.

If the city appeared a gleaming bastion of civilisation from the water, it now showed them a perspective altogether different. The companions swept like spectres through an oily, dank underbelly, at odds with the spotlit wonders of the city canopy high above.

Massive concrete stanchions held aloft mighty towers that speared up into the night, but threw the undercutting passages into blackness. Tight alleyways wound between streets like defiles and created gritty spaces devoid of purpose. From iron grates in the pavement, foetid tendrils of fume arose, forming a knee-high soup that skirled around them as they passed.

'You think they have an underground community, like Below?' asked Dique, peering through a grate with a doubtful wrinkle of his nose.

'I hope not,' answered Meadow. 'It smells like something Lord Ponerog cooked up in a vat down there.' A sulphurous stench wafted up from beneath the ground, mingling with a foul mix of odours, reminiscent of burning coal and vomit.

The passageways through which they threaded were not devoid of life. More than once, gravelly shouts of 'Hey, you!' or 'Move on!' rang from dim alleys. Dique stumbled on the outstretched legs of a grimy vagrant seated against a wall, who responded with only a disconsolate grunt. Another man lay face down in a runnel of collected drain water, darkened by blood. He failed to move; judging by the bloat and greying skin, he never would again.

Other voices, other sounds echoed in the near distance. The garbled shouts of a drunkard. Footsteps plunging in puddles, the rhythmic splashing of flight and pursuit. Sinister whispers that made the companions jump at shadows. Beneath it all, the dull rumble of civilisation, reminding them that the glamour of city lights and night-time bustle existed seldom more than two blocks away.

'It could be any of the great European cities,' chanced Fahrenheit, as they passed through a gloomy alley, hemmed in by sandstone walls. 'Newer cities built atop the old. I'd wager there are ruins beneath our feet, dating back to the very first of the Unhomed.'

Mustapha frowned. In his mind, Khashoggi's spacecraft squatted hugely in the bottom of a cavernous pit. A hole in the earth that should not exist.

It escapes, irretrievable time.

The frown still clung to his features when they arrived at a broad arcade, awash with dim blue light from the moon above. A rough quadrangle with a shattered slate floor, lined on one side by the pillared roots of buildings that shone in the illustrious skyline far above. Along the far side of the space ran a crumbling structure; a much older construction of clay brick, consisting of three tiers of soaring arches, running the entire length of the space and beyond.

'It's an aqueduct,' observed Harold, looking up at the ruins. 'It must be … rather old.'

'It would be considered ancient where I am from,' remarked Fahrenheit. 'This kind of water-conveying technology existed on Earth thousands of years before my time.'

Mustapha did not look up in admiration. Instead, he peered at the row of figures – statues, twice the height of Will – one standing beneath each arch, along the whole arcade.

He set out across the deserted quadrangle, dragging his companions with him. The statues, forlorn and neglected, held a fascination for him, staring as they did upon a public space no longer used. He walked slowly, boots grinding gravel to powder beneath his feet, studying each one before moving on. Meadow trundled behind, absently counting them.

'One ... two ... three ...'

At first expecting the Pantheon, Mustapha did not recognise the strange stone faces in their gallery of antiquity. The statue of a man followed that of a woman, then another woman, then two more men; some with long hair, some with short, some with beards, some without; a thickset woman then a tall, thin man. All were human. Neither the years nor the many generations that passed them by had been kind. Erosion wore at once-sharp sculpt-work, perhaps water dripping from the conduit above. Cracks had formed in many; one had sprouted a vinelike weed. Another had lost an arm and its head, crumbled to dust on the ground below.

'Eleven ... twelve ... thirteen ...'

Several, defaced by graffiti, bore the epithets and slurs of recent generations. *Simps of Aaron intoxicate our brains*, read one message, smeared in blood-red paint across the carved figure of a handsome middle-aged man. *Do you feel like suicide, Michaelites?* jeered another in vibrant blue lettering, upon the statue of a slender man with delicate features.

Mustapha's stomach churned at the childish yet sinister tone of the effacing words.

The spiteful words of two tribes at war with one another ... who perhaps feared one another.

'Seventeen ... eighteen ... nineteen ...'

Each sculpture stood on a stone pedestal the height of the pixies. On the front face, engraved letters declared the figure's name. Despite the obliterating effects of erosion, Mustapha did recognise *AARON* and *MICHAEL*. He could also read *DELORES*, *MARIE* and *NEIL*, though many other names were too far gone.

'There are twenty of them,' announced Meadow, his voice booming in the grand, forgotten place. 'No, wait,' he corrected. 'There's another one, tucked at the end here. Twenty-one. He looks a bit diff ... he looks—'

Meadow never finished his sentence. Mustapha turned to him, to find the pixie's face wide-eyed and white with horror.

A masculine growl from the shadows snatched their collective attention. 'You there! Yes, all of you. You'll clear off, if you know what's good for you. This is no place for a bunch of freaks ... and kids.'

As one they flinched, eyes darting about. The terse growl bounced off surrounding walls; its owner remained concealed.

'Who is there?' demanded Mustapha.

The owner of the voice stayed hidden. 'I'm tellin' you: get out! It's about to get hot in here.'

Approaching footsteps spurred them to action. Boots crunched on gravel, unmissable in the eerie quiet. At the far end of the arcade, where the promise of light and the babble of street life streamed down a flight of stairs, a male figure appeared, casting a long column of shadow. Swift and determined strides brought him into the derelict sanctum.

'Hide!' hissed Harold, pointing towards the statues with frantic gestures. Within a moment, they had all ducked for cover.

The man wore outlandish apparel, as far as the denizens of Babylon were concerned. A long coat concealed much of his form. The garment looked not unlike Harold's, only more tailored, with a sash cinched about his waist. Nor could they get a clear look at his face, for he wore a peaked hat with a brim pulled low over his eyes. How he could even see in the dismal light Mustapha could not guess.

The figure moved arrow-straight through the arcade, the rhythmic crunching like a string of tiny detonations in a dank tunnel. Purpose compelled him.

'That's near enough,' called another man's voice – the same man who had warned the companions away. He spoke as if his leathery vocal chords were soaked in Rhye whiskey. He stepped from the darkness, facing the hat-wearing newcomer. With a start, Mustapha realised they had nearly been sandwiched between the two.

'Do I gotta have you searched?' said Leather Voice in a strange dialect that Mustapha thought resembled the pidgin speak of some Wilden Folk.

'Come on, pal,' replied Peaked Hat, patting down his own clothes in pantomime. 'How many times have we done this? I ain't carryin'.'

Leather Voice grunted. 'Get on with it, then. Spill.'

Peaked Hat took a brief look over his shoulder before he spoke. 'Lulu Belle's makin' her move. She's got a bullet or three with Leroy Brown's name on 'em.'

'When?'

'Next Tuesday. Ten o'clock.'

'Where?'

Peaked Hat shuffled on the spot. 'Show me the dollar bills first.'

Leather Voice reached inside his own coat. The other man tensed. Leather Voice grated a laugh, drawing a bound stack of folded papers from within his clothes. He tossed the bills halfway between the two men, where it landed in the dust. 'Where?' he asked again.

Peaked Hat eyed the money. 'The station.'

Leather Voice guffawed. 'She worried Leroy's gonna blow outta town? He's Vice President, for Michael's sake. All he's gotta do is wait for Mephistopheles to roll over and he's kingpin of this place.'

'That'll never happen. They say Mephistopheles can't die. Got some sort of power.'

The second man's mirth continued. 'Rubbish. You can't believe them fairy tales!' Then his ugly grin faded. 'Wait. That's the whole game, ain't it! Lulu the Aaronite takes a pot shot at Leroy … she reckons she can be Big Mama 'round here!'

'No, no!' cried Peaked Hat, supplicant hands held before him. 'That ain't it at all. She don't want him dead. Only … outta the way for a while.'

Leather Voice leered. 'For your sake, I hope so. Take your money and run back to your little safehouse … simpin' Aaronite. Be here same time next week, or I got one or three bullets with *your* name on 'em.'

In his hiding place behind a nearby statue, Mustapha's breath had caught in his chest. He watched Peaked Hat step forward to retrieve the money from the cracked slate at his feet.

'I misspoke,' said Leather Voice, a malicious grin widening on his face. 'I got a few bullets for you anyway.' He brought two fingers to his lips and let off a sharp whistle.

From the dark rectangle of a door recess emerged a third man. In both hands he carried a sinister device, with a cylindrical cannister and a dull metallic muzzle, which he aimed at Peaked Hat.

The weapon flashed and a repeating roar boomed around the arcade. The gun's report came like the stuttering howl of a great beast. Peaked Hat seemed to dance on the spot, holes blasting a line across his chest. Crimson blood sprayed from his wounds even as he crumpled to the ground.

The murder triggered bedlam. Several more figures peeled from the shadows, brandishing snub-nosed black pistols. Mustapha realised they had already been in hiding behind pillars and stanchions, and his blood ran cold. Both sides of the exchange had brought an armed posse, ready to double-cross.

Within moments, a lethal exchange of gunfire erupted, bullets criss-crossing the dim arena. With *zings* and *placks* they tore chips of stone from the surrounding monuments. Soon a bluish haze of powdered stone fragments hung in the air. At intervals, a *thunk* and a gurgled yell marked the demise of one miscreant or other. Whether through accident or design, an early round took the first gunman clean in the temple, sending him to the dirt ... and whatever afterlife he believed in.

Mustapha's heart pounded. *Nobody is getting out of here alive. It's time to go.* He hoped he and his companions could escape in the confusion. Moreover, he hoped they could see and hear him over the chaos of gunfire.

'Friends, with me!' he cried, dashing from his hiding place. He clung to the aqueduct as he bolted for the stairs and the glow of city lights.

His sinews thrilled, blood like lightning in his veins. He felt he could outrun those bullets and he knew then the boon of Maybeth's tear — the gift of Lhestra, transforming the cinnabar to quicksilver inside of him — still retained its eldritch power. Yet he reined it in, glancing over his shoulder to see that the others followed him. They did, five frantic shapes stooped and running through the deathly hail for safety.

For a moment, Mustapha imagined they might somehow escape the skirmish unscathed and unseen. The hollering shout, the staccato *rat-tat-tat* of gunfire and the yelp of pain from behind him proved him wrong on both counts. As he streaked from the frying pan of the arcade to the fire of the illumined street, the strangeling risked snatching another look back into the gauntlet.

The shout had come from one of the armed toughs. He must have seen the cloaked form of Harold, retreating through the bedlam and dust, and mistook him for a rival ... or a witness, at the very least. The dragonfly had half-turned; the first bullet tore through his coat, catching one arm, spinning him like a top. Just as well, perhaps: the second bullet grazed him, and the third ricocheted off nearby brick as he performed his involuntary pirouette. With a *whump* he went down, bashing his helmeted head on stone.

'Harold!' cried Will, the nearest to him. He dashed back to the dragonfly's side, hauling him up from the grit. Harold moaned. Will hefted him easily enough, for the creature was tall but slight. Amidst the clamour of shouts and the crack of wild shots skimming over their heads, the companions raced for the stairs, bursting from the underbelly out into the main street.

At first, they squinted against the brash glare, shielding their eyes as they emerged to a dazzling streetscape that little resembled Babylon.

Sleek towers scraped the sky, their ornate designs thrown into stark relief by beams of light from below. The luminous shafts reflected in the slick black surface of a broad thoroughfare, along which rumbled the strange contrivances of Humankind. Without the need for horses or manubani, carriages of metal rolled along the street, concealing passengers behind panes of glass. Barely a sprig of green intruded in this diorama, dominated by bold monuments of concrete and steel; here and there a flourish of bronze or a sculpted relief harked back to a more organic world, though the cold shine of polished metal removed it all, elevating the city from places of soil and leaf ... or even from its own dark, crumbling roots of stone.

And, oh, the cacophony! Vehicles sped by with the roar of powerful engines, far noisier than any of Khashoggi's creations or the mechanical whir of automatons. On a nearby street corner, the clarion blare of a trumpet announced a busker entertaining passers-by for spare coin. Underneath it all lay the constant thrum of voices. Talking. Laughing. Shouting. Human voices in accents quite unlike anything heard in Babylon. Still, the voices buoyed all other sound, a perpetual undercurrent in the soundscape of a teeming metropolis.

Into this scene spilled Mustapha, Will, Meadow, Dique, Harold and Ackley Fahrenheit. The startling glitz gripped Mustapha by the heart, filling him with equal parts wonder and dread. The chill that took him forced his attention to Fahrenheit, whose face wore the chalky mask of one overwhelmed by what he saw. Mustapha wanted only to cling to the man in that moment in a desperate attempt to steady them both.

Will hauled Harold clear of the dim stair, delivering the dragonfly to a paved walkway alongside the street. He lay in a pool of light that shone down in sharp beams from beneath the awning of a theatre.

A sea of gasps and startled exclamations leapt from the throats of one hundred humans; one minute strolling the city streets on a balmy evening, the next witness to the strangest royal advance party in history. Not that any of the shocked faces swarming around registered any recognition of the beings at whom they gaped.

The commotion surrounding the newcomers drowned out

the dying rounds of gunfire from the dingy alley. Mustapha had sufficient presence of mind to realise that none of the weapon-toting gangsters had pursued them into the street. Numerous onlookers peered down the foreboding stair nonetheless, no doubt curious as to where the outlandish band had arrived from.

Mustapha's pointed ears burned, conscious as he was of the crowded ring of strangers staring at them. For a long moment, he stared back. Human faces — the haughty and the humble, the surprised and the suspicious, contorted in every grotesque arrangement of fascination — gawping at the cluster of bodies sprawled before them. The crowd dressed altogether unlike the humans of Babylon, or even of Phydeantum; more shirts than tunics, more jackets than cloaks. The men wore odd thin scarves, the women a degree more modest than the average Fae or Mer counterpart ... or anybody in Lady Antoinette's court.

They stared at Mustapha with his strange, elongated ears. They stared at the pixies as if they were characters from a book. But mostly they stared at poor Harold, like a science experiment gone horribly awry.

Blood trickled from the wound on Harold's arm, having saturated his sleeve. In front of the crowd, Will tore a strip from his tunic and wound it tight around the dragonfly's injured limb.

The dumbstruck cordon wobbled and broke, as a single figure pushed through the inner ring. A slip of a woman in clean white robes, with hair the colour of varnished blackwood bouncing in lush curls on her shoulders, and eyes of a matching shade. She appraised the group in a wide-eyed instant, the warm glow of awe — recognition, even — dancing across her petite features. Then she composed herself, smoothing her palms against her robes. She addressed Will.

'Please, good sir. I am named Sister Karen.' She seemed to think this might be of relevance to the companions. The swelling throng of onlookers kept their distance, shuffling their feet but saying nothing, many eyes darting back and forth between Sister Karen and the sturdy blond newcomer with his motley crew.

'Well met, Sister Karen. I am known as "Wagoner" Will. My friends call me Will.' He still crouched by Harold, who crawled into a sitting position with a dazed frown. Will glanced at Mustapha; the strangeling mouthed *Not now*. It might be best if the woman believed a fellow human to be the leader of such an odd assortment of beings. 'You are an Acolyte?' Will asked. 'The Order of the Unhomed?'

A hushed reaction whispered through the crowd. Nudges and murmurings arose, along with collected breaths of surprise. 'I am honoured by your knowledge of our Order,' spoke Sister Karen, a hitch in her voice and a flush in her cheeks. 'Our meeting is serendipitous. You must allow me to help you. We should ... move away from here. There is a place we can be safe. Your injured friend can be attended.'

She waved her hand, indicating some nearby place. It acted as an enchantment on the gathered humans, who parted to make way for her. Mustapha and Will hoisted Harold to his feet, then the group began to shuffle in the wake of the diminutive Acolyte.

'It isn't far,' assured Sister Karen, her voice somehow soft and strident at the same time. She glided along the pavement, still parting clumps of rubber-necked spectators.

Mustapha scrambled to catch up to her. He struggled to assimilate the myriad novelties his senses absorbed. To make matters more difficult, the pulsating drumbeat in his head now grew stronger almost with every step.

'What ... is this place?' he managed.

Walking beside him, Sister Karen turned her head and offered a half smile. She did not appear troubled – or even surprised – that the strangeling would be disoriented. 'You are in Mingo City,' she replied.

They took a corner, and a block later, another. *Mingo City.* Dazzling lights banished the darkling cloak of night, luring one deeper into a place of constant activity. A city that perhaps never slept. The sound of conversation and the throaty roar of mechanised carriages created an unbroken drone of sound. A gritty smell, like oil or smoke yet neither, hung in the air. And all around stood the forest of buildings, each one a Tower of Babel.

In a gap he saw them again: the giant, tapering candles; spires of a magnificent structure that had dominated the skyline as seen from the *Khonsu.* Sister Karen's zigzag path brought them ever nearer to it.

Soon, the weary group arrived at a plaza, a yawning space out of keeping with the dense cityscape in all directions. A single circular fountain dignified the area, burbling with a quiet voice. Despite the clearing, few people gathered; the glamour of city lights had drawn most, moth-like, to precincts of entertainment.

In relative tranquillity stood an enormous building, all buttresses and spires, reaching towards the stars. If the spires appeared as candles, then the structure beneath served as a wondrous and macabre birthday cake. Hundreds of tiny arched windows, in rows and florets, adorned every wall of the massive oblong construction. Sculpted figures threatened to leap from every corner. From within spilled a welcoming glow; not the stark electric ambience of the recreation strip, but a buttery gold that spoke of mineral light or ensorcelled flame ... or a fire in the hearth.

'It's ... astonishing,' murmured Mustapha. Clarity came to him in the instant he realised that the pounding beat had ceased altogether.

Behind him, Ackley Fahrenheit arrived, visibly shaking, with Meadow and Dique to either side of him. Will supported Harold at the rear. The dragonfly gritted his teeth, staring up at the grand façade before them.

'Welcome to the Church of the Sacred Twenty,' Sister Karen announced, gesturing for the companions to follow her inside.

CHAPTER TWENTY-FOUR

THE VOLUNTEERS

16 : 10 : 30

All the colours of the rainbow spilled into the Church of the Sacred Twenty, with the light of Anato filtering through a multitude of stained-glass windows. The Moon Goddess seemed to bestow her blessing on the hallowed space — luminous shards of every pigment danced with the flickering motes of a thousand candles.

A forest of slender columns stretched towards a vaulted ceiling, each column branching from a junction near the top, furthering the illusion of mystical trees. Mustapha's mind harkened back to the storied glades and copses of Petrichor, over which the ancient hamadryads watched.

The strangeling sat on a broad marble stair, facing an aisle polished to a high gleam, in a nave filled with rows of wooden benches. A handful of worshippers had made their way into the Church from the frivolous nightlife outside, each finding their own bench to perch upon, and contemplate the glory and mysteries at Mustapha's back.

Numerous Acolytes also made their way around the prismatic space. Some alone, some in pairs, the white-robed devotees brandished tapers, relighting extinguished candles in silence. Hunched shoulders and bowed heads kept their faces mired in shadow. Despite the festive colours, an air of gravitas filled the Church, made more sombre by the Acolytes' downcast vigil.

Fretful lines furrowed Mustapha's forehead. The company had spent a day in this place; resting, refreshing, reflecting. The Acolytes who welcomed them had insisted upon it. The strangeling felt he had much to reflect upon, though he also felt the gravitational pull of some inexorable force. His vacant eyes now studied the polished marble, the arboreal columns, the host of tiny flames, like dancing will-o'-the-wisps. The bitter gall of dismay formed in his mouth; he swallowed it down.

Against the odds, we made it here ... why must it all come tumbling down now?

Sister Karen appeared from a place beyond Mustapha's left shoulder, to stand at the foot of the stair in front of him. He knew she came from the Sacristy, where several Acolytes with basic skills in nursing and medicaments tended to the wounded Harold. Mustapha straightened, eyes brightening.

'Brother John got the bullet out,' she explained, 'but it was lodged deep. It shattered his exoskeleton going in ... I'm not sure how well it's going to heal.'

The strangeling slumped. 'Surely he'll...?'

'Hopefully, he will keep the arm ... but I'm not sure. Sorry ... I'm not very good at these things. Here,' she said, reaching within her robe and producing a parcel wrapped in muslin. 'I thought you might be hungry. Your companions are eating their way through the refectory. They tell me you have had a desperate voyage.'

'Thank you,' said Mustapha, accepting the parcel and unwrapping it. Within he found a portion of light, fluffy cake, packed with glistening cherries and a layer of toasted almonds on top. He took a tentative bite. The flavours sang across his tastebuds, almost distracting him from gloomy thoughts of a five-limbed dragonfly. 'I'm sorry we've darkened your beautiful door with this. Guns are … things we usually try to avoid.'

Sister Karen's reply came in feathered tones of empathy. 'Bear no shame, traveller. As you are aware, sheltering those who seek guidance and sanctuary is the very cornerstone of our Order.'

'A timeless vocation. Whenever there is suffering or greed, there will always be those who need guidance. And it is quite the sanctuary you have here.'

The Acolyte eyed him. 'You hold the word "timeless" in such casual regard. The Order has always considered Time one of the most powerful forces in the universe.'

When Mustapha returned her gaze, he found it full of curiosity, rather than reproach. 'I look around your Church and I speak to the other Acolytes, and I can see you have adopted the Pantheon of Rhye. The image of Onik graces a dozen works of art in this room alone. You can be sure: I revere the God of Time just the same as you. I meant only that the lot of mere mortals is unchanged; across decades, across millennia. You Acolytes have seen it for yourselves, undiminished for how long now? Hundreds of years?'

'One thousand years,' granted Sister Karen. 'Do you not believe that Onik could choose to undo the hurt of this world? That he could send us down another, more favourable path?'

Now the dark-haired waif seemed to test him, to probe his thoughts … and, no doubt, his faith. Mustapha took a mouthful of the delicious cake, savouring it with deliberate slowness. He swallowed. 'Perhaps he does. I would not doubt that it is within his grasp. But whatever his grand designs, he has seen fit to leave countless souls stranded – more and more of you, with every passing generation – as outcasts. Beyond the brink of this world. And now, without your High Priestess to give your own Order guidance. You still worship him?'

A sad flicker crossed Sister Karen's face, as the parry-riposte struck home. It lasted only a moment. 'The events that fill time are inconsequential to its passage. I do not blame Onik for the violence that plagues Mingo City, or that which plagues even this Order,' she replied in a level tone. 'The unrest between Aaronites and Michaelites has been a blight on our community since the very days of the Sacred Twenty. To learn that the Order itself is split into two factions surprises none of us. If Lady Mercy was aware, she chose not to act ... at the cost of her own life. We do not fret. It is perhaps through her sacrifice that you and your companions are here.'

Mustapha stroked his moustache, directing a vacant stare at the vibrant forest of columns in front of him. He recalled the whispered plea from the High Priestess to Timbrad. *Save me.* 'What became of the others? Brother Aaron? Brother Michael, and the rest?'

She shrugged. 'They returned. Sacrilegious violence broke out, here in this very room. We only finished mopping up the blood yesterday. They ... serve a penance, of silent seclusion.'

'All twenty of them?'

'All twenty.'

The strangeling pursed his lips. He kept his back to the Altar: the masterwork of sculpture and mason-craft that begged his attention – no, demanded his respect – just over his shoulder. Dominating the Church interior, the semicircle of polished bronze figures had torn the breath from all their chests as Sister Karen first led the company down the nave. Familiar and yet wholly new to them, the oversized figures basked in a pool of sanctified light, streaming down on them from a window above. Ten to either side, with the central two leaning over the Altar itself, frozen in attitudes of reverence.

The Altar — far too large to be used by humans as any kind of table — appeared misnamed; *sarcophagus* may have been more appropriate. On the lid of the huge stone casket, the relief of a twenty-first figure spread wings of a mighty span. *It's him again!* Meadow had cried, doubling over as if to vomit. Several Acolytes attended the companions then, offering the pale-faced pixie and his friends a room in which to place their belongings and rest. Mustapha alone chose to stay and contemplate the Church further, sitting on the stairs atop which the Altar loomed.

Now he rose to his feet, turning to face the prodigious sculpture.

So, these were Khashoggi's brave volunteers. Sent unknowingly, to sustain the wonder of Rhye ... and secure the legacy of the Prophet for all time. Well, what a legacy it has been. They set off to voyage the stars, and ended up birthing a community here. One that stayed undiscovered for an awfully long time. He studied them. The same faces they had seen carved from stone, in the gloom of the arcade. He saw the statues of Aaron and Michael — the original Aaron and Michael — named in stone, bowing over the entombed creature. They appeared nothing like the brooding Acolytes he had met back in Babylon, bearing their names.

Now that he looked closer, Mustapha wondered if he saw traces of rivalry in those lifeless visages.

His eyes fell to the casket, upon which a scroll was carved. It contained script; a poem of sorts. An ode to the volunteers, for whom the Order had been first founded.

A ship from out beyond the stars
Did find the Seven Seas,
The craft was lost, though they survived;
It brought them to their knees.
They yearn to journey home again
For here they don't belong –
They seek the final traveller,
A prophecy in song.

Twenty are the voyagers
Fabled in their story
Come from far across the void
Bound by oath and glory.

Three royals fight to hold the throne
A duke to watch them dance
Four are on an odyssey
To yet give peace a chance.
Five shieldmaidens on the rise
(a sixth behind the skins),
Four to keep the beat alive
And cast away their sins.
One to bring the power back
And one to bring the soul
One to serve the servants
As they all watch Time unfold.
We all watch Time unfold.

Twenty are the passengers
Twenty bravest souls
'Cross time and space to find this place
A gift for years untold.

Upon this land they found themselves
A long, long way from home
A strange new world, a foreign place
Their destiny unknown.
They wait an age, they bide their time
'Til hope has come and gone
The world turns cold, the light grows dim –
They seek their Promised One.

Behold: THE WINGED ONE.

An involuntary shiver seized the strangeling. There, atop the casket lid, a male butterfly looked ready to flutter aloft at any given moment. The artist had captured their subject with such finesse that Mustapha could read vivid emotion in the Fae creature's face. A certain bravado shone through, tempered by earnestness; yet beneath it all, in the quirk of a lip and the too-wide eyes, Mustapha saw insecurity. Self-consciousness. The desire to please.

'Wait,' he said. 'The Order can't have known that my friends and I were travelling in search of Mingo City …?'

'Not exactly,' replied Sister Karen, her eyelashes flicking downwards. 'A couple of things tipped us off, though.'

'Which were?'

'Chiefly, when our airship returned without Lady Mercy aboard. A brutal argument broke out, in which the aggressors revealed that … our original plan might have failed.'

'Hm.' Mustapha pictured the docking airship, the pomp and ceremony, and the massive crate with its inconceivable gift inside. 'What else tipped you off?'

The Acolyte did not answer immediately. Her eyes darted to the giant stone casket and the larger-than-life butterfly depicted on it. She looked back to Mustapha with head bowed and hands clasped.

'You are he, are you not … Lord?' she asked in a deferential tone. 'The King of Rhye?'

Somehow, Mustapha managed to keep his expression even, though his eyebrows rose a fraction. 'I am. At least … I think I still am. I'll admit, we hardly look the part of a royal entourage.'

Sister Karen offered a bashful smile. 'I knew it was you, Lord, from our first meeting. You are indeed noble of countenance, if it does not disrespect you to say so.

'The King of Rhye is known here in Mingo City, though we've not had the honour of your presence amongst us. Stories and songs from neighbouring Phydeantum tell of a seraph, bright as moonlight and blessed by the Pantheon, who brought an end to War.'

'I had long hair and a penchant for near-death experiences back then,' he mused, with a wry smile.

'Forgive me, Lord … you also had wings.' Sister Karen's eyeline drifted over Mustapha's shoulder, to emphasise the distinct lack of feathered appendages.

'I paid a high price to get us here,' he replied. 'Where is all of this leading to?'

'You're not supposed to be here.' The statement landed, plain and simple, like a sock to Mustapha's jaw. Fragments of a dream flashed in his mind, in which his own father had spoken the words. That perversion of reality, on the hillside below Two-Way Mirror Mountain.

You're not supposed to be here.

'Lady Mercy came to you in the good will of celebration,' the Acolyte continued, 'but also in the hopes of securing your help.'

Mustapha blinked. 'Yes, I do remember that. She lobbied for me to help create a home for the Unhomed. Or otherwise, to—'

'—Or otherwise to unwrite our history, such that the Sacred Twenty were never Unhomed in the first place,' the woman finished.

The strangeling turned a slow circle, arms spread wide. 'Is this city not "home" enough? Over a full millennium, your ancestors have built something truly remarkable here. The elder human in our party, Ackley Fahrenheit, gave deeply of himself to help me extend the frontier of Rhye. To bring this land – this wondrous city – back into the kingdom. Are you not "Homed", now? You belong! Congratulations!'

The Acolyte shook her head. Her face spoke of divine patience, underwritten with concern. 'Lord, *home* is more than bricks and mortar. It is a place of *belonging*. Yes, a civilisation has arisen here. But we do not belong – we exist, in a place that is neither Rhye nor Earth, neither Obelis nor the shared world of mortals. We have erected for ourselves a house, but remain disconnected from all.

'This is not the ending the Order sought. Prophecy speaks of a Winged One, who would enact a miracle, sending the Sacred Twenty home. To the place from which they came. But that isn't what we got.' She gestured with an open palm towards the casket. 'Here we still are, and a great peril besides. Lady Mercy intended *you* to go back ...'

'Back where?'

'Not where ... *when*. Well, both, really.'

Mustapha's eyes widened. 'She wanted me to go back ... in time? To Old Rhye? To meet the Twenty?'

'That's correct, Lord.' The bashful, through-the-eyelashes gaze now captured the strangeling with full force.

'The gate? The gilt door, with carvings all over it?'

'Yes, Lord. It is a portal. Back to Old Rhye ... the year 1739AG, to be precise. One thousand and ten years ago.'

1739. After Godsryche. Holy Onik.

For a full minute, Mustapha could not speak. His mouth hung ajar, ready for use, but no words formed. A cavalcade of thoughts, partly formed or incoherent, stormed through his head. At first the tumult produced only white noise that refused to be deciphered. He forced himself to breathe; to bring order, where insanity threatened to take over.

Slowly, he turned his head from Sister Karen to the enormous stone casket. Back to Sister Karen. Once again to the casket, with its lifelike rendering of a valorous butterfly.

'Oh. Oh … no.'

'The Door is but one of many,' continued Sister Karen, seeming glad that Mustapha had at last caught up. 'Gifts from Onik himself, to honour our worship. Lady Mercy delivered that particular Door to you, to help realise the prophecy … because, as you can see, our grand plan has failed.'

'Because you're still here?'

'And because … that's not you,' said the Acolyte, pointing now at the casket lid.

'It's supposed to be me?' Mustapha frowned.

'That is a contentious issue within our Order, and indeed all the people of Mingo City, Lord. It is fundamental to the rift between Aaronites and Michaelites. Some say that the Winged One was a seraphic figure, who died in ancient Rhye. Others say something different. That he returned to live among us. The question is a source of perpetual heated debate, driving civil unrest. It threatens the very—'

'Whoa – stop, stop, stop!' exclaimed Mustapha. His knees caved in, and he wobbled back to a sitting position on the Altar step. 'I need time to process this.'

'Time is something we don't really have, Lord.'

Mustapha fixed the Acolyte with a stare. 'That much, I can

understand. I used to have a conduit ... a way of communicating with the Pantheon. Now, all I hear is musical nonsense. Bells. Drumbeats. Does Onik still answer your prayers?'

'He does not. We assume he has forsaken us; perhaps as punishment for our failure. It is a grim portent.'

'Hm.' Kaleidoscopic thoughts gradually coalesced. To say he had a plan would be an overstatement, but Mustapha knew he had to keep moving forward. 'I need to gather my friends,' he said, rising to his feet once more. 'And then, you can tell us about this prophecy.'

Golden light emanated from each corner of the modest study, courtesy of electric lamps. Their posts, polished beechwood shaped in the likeness of idealised men and women, supported bold shades of coloured glass, echoing the stained windows of the Church proper. Other furnishings, elegant yet functional, served the purpose of allowing visitors to be immersed in the abundance of books, stuffing shelves that climbed to the cornice of two walls. A ladder, propped against one bookshelf, allowed the quest for knowledge to reach towards the high ceiling.

Sister Karen had not required the ladder. At eye level, she reached for a leather-bound tome like so many others. This one appeared well used and well worn. It rested, open, upon the tabletop around which the companions now sat. Young, nameless Acolytes had delivered a digestif of wine to each of them. The group now huddled around the weighty book save for Harold, dozing under the influence of a light sedative in the adjacent sleeping quarters.

'So, that's how Sammy the butterfly wound up on the lid of a coffin from a thousand years ago,' muttered Meadow, to nobody. He stared hard at the wine glass in front of him. There were no drowseberries in Mingo City. The offerings from the Church cellar tasted somewhat of cat's urine, according to the distasteful scrunch of his face. 'Is he … still in there? Please say no.'

'He is, yes,' answered Sister Karen. 'The Order keeps and protects his relics, an honour of the highest calibre.'

Meadow pushed his wine glass away and began studying his folded hands on the table. He said nothing more.

Dique leaned forward, clearing his throat. 'My question is this: What happens if we all stay put? Mingo City doesn't look ready to fall down any time soon. Can't we just leave it as it is?'

They had all examined the spidery script, the line drawings, the work of historians from centuries past. The fledgling civilisation had grown, somewhere in the wilds of Old Rhye. Over months and years, the encampment of the Unhomed had become a settlement. Eventually, scholars within the growing population recorded events that unfolded. Such histories, sparse as they were in those early days, suffered fragmentation in frequent times of internal conflict. Arguments had become fights, and fights battles, leading to doubtful retellings of old stories. As always, the victors recorded the tales and the vanquished went unheard.

Why nobody wandered out of the settlement, nobody knew. Or perhaps they had, but no such anecdote had been recorded. Likewise, nobody seemed to have stumbled into the isolated place, though a more sinister explanation existed for that.

The Order of the Unhomed guarded its secrets like hoarded treasure, forever locked in the vault of Time.

One postulate within the tome's pages regarded the fate of the spaceship itself. The contrivance that Khashoggi had made, to send his volunteers to the stars. The companions all knew where it had come to rest; or at least, where it had become manifest in the New Rhye of Mustapha's imaginings. But for one thousand years it had lain hidden, undisturbed, the focus of a chilling theory put forward in the leaves of that musty volume.

'We must assume that the spacecraft was rigged for detonation,' said Sister Karen. 'We cannot sit idle — Rhye as you know it is threatened.'

A tomblike silence met her words.

The threadbare histories seemed to agree on one aspect: A power struggle had erupted amongst the volunteers. Finding themselves stranded in a fantastical place, opinions were divided as to how they should proceed. Some favoured repairing their downed ship to attempt a re-launch. Others saw the lush and vital world around them and developed fanciful notions of staying. As the situation escalated, historians believed that the spacecraft could have been sabotaged ... or worse.

'Why must we assume that?' quailed Dique, his voice small in the still room.

'It's the worst-case scenario,' explained Will. 'The one that endangers us all, if true ... or if we disregard it. Sister Karen is right. And if it is set up as an explosive device, then the whole of Babylon is in danger.'

The pixie's face fell. He had never before conceptualised a weapon that could level an entire city ... let alone the city that most denizens of Old Rhye now called home.

Mustapha, seated beside Dique, reached over and slung an arm around his friend. The strangeling had no wife, no children. Will represented his whole private world; Will, who sat, hale and safe, across the table from him. Dique, on the other hand, stood to lose more than Mustapha could ever fathom. *Roni. The sextuplets.* He squeezed Dique closer, as if this could keep both their hearts from breaking.

From beneath a darkened brow, he levelled a glare like twin embers at the Acolyte. 'You told me there were other Doors,' he said.

'I did,' replied Sister Karen. 'The holiest of relics, crafted by the God of Time. They are safeguarded in an enclosure directly beneath our feet.'

She spoke in such a matter-of-fact way. The companions cast involuntary glances towards the floor.

'Where — or *when* — do the other Doors go?'

The Acolyte shrugged. 'I'm afraid I don't know. True knowledge of the Doors is granted only to the High Priest or Priestess, as well as the governing leader of Mingo City.'

'The President, you mean?' asked Will.

'Exactly.' She did not question how Will had come about this detail. 'For the past ten years, the President of Mingo City has been a man named Mephistopheles.'

'Perfect,' declared Mustapha, slapping the table. 'He's precisely the man we need to see. As you say, we're out of time. Where can we find him?'

It was Sister Karen's turn to glance downwards.

CHAPTER TWENTY-FIVE

INSANITY LAUGHS

14 : 00 : 05

Creatures spilled forth from Below like a cauldron bubbling over. Goblins dragged carts piled high with all the wealth of their family hoards, straining and complaining with the effort of pulling the weight of worldly possessions behind them.

Kobolds bore no such struggle, leaving with little more than the wild manes upon their backs. Full-grown kobolds held tight to the hands of their children, snuffing their forehead candles for them as they came squinting into the daylight.

Brownies skittered in rag-tag tribal clumps, unsure of their direction but glad to follow in the footsteps of those who exhibited a greater sense of purpose.

The sight of ponderous cave trolls lumbering beneath the arched doorway proved astonishing for many. The ungainly beings had clung to the deep darkness these past ten years, having no business in the sunlit kingdom.

A host of other warren-dwellers swarmed and scampered, dawdled and dashed: wights, slithering grootslangs, bauks and bluecaps. Troglodytes in all their forms spewed from the gritty underworld. There may have been hidebehinds, though nobody could be utterly certain.

Nothing quite like the Wilden procession had been seen in Rhye for the longest time, yet few cared for the exotic spectacle. Fear for their own lives preoccupied every mind. Only the question of fleeing or digging in heels mattered now to the denizens of Babylon.

Under the great pressure of stewardship, Minister for Security Leith Lourden had spread word throughout the populace of the ominous countdown. She still harboured hope that the impending disaster could somehow be undone, though that hope dwindled by the hour. An evacuation needed time. Dragonflies took the message to the far eaves of Eleuthervale, Hiraeth, Papilion and Arboria. Competent sylphic wings bore an urgent message to the distant havens of Ardendale and the Highlands. Anticipating a mass exodus from Babylon – from districts both above and below the ground – Trixel had advised Leith that the fringe provinces should also be put on alert. The movement of panicked creatures could not be predicted, but the forests and rural glens would no doubt take a substantial hit. Distant villages might strain under the influx of those abandoning their inner-city homes.

Warnings raced towards Governors Sharles, Flaye and Rintaaken in the Southern Provinces, and Crispin Crabapple in the Northern.

'Poor souls don't know which way to run,' said the fixie, casting a glum look down on the clogged streets below.

'I did the right thing, didn't I?' asked Leith, beside her. They sat together on the edge of the landing outside the King's Pavilion – the platform from which Mustapha would launch himself over the cityscape, once upon a time. Their legs dangled; far beneath them, crowds filled the labyrinthine byways criss-crossing Babylon. From this vantage they could survey the progress of fleeing citizens.

'You did the only thing,' assured Trixel. 'People need to be given the opportunity to escape danger.'

Leith gave a reluctant nod. 'I only wish we had time to organise something safer. There must be creatures getting crushed in the mess.'

Knotted throngs cluttered every square and plaza, as countless souls tried to thread in one direction or another. Making matters worse, a great number of Mer Folk had delayed returning to The Works and the sea beyond, following the death of Mher and the nightmare of the automatons. At last, they did retreat, though it came too late, leaving them to mill helplessly amongst the departing masses.

Not everybody clamoured in the streets. Tens of thousands of elderly, infirm, stubborn or disbelieving citizens heard the news and chose to remain steadfast in their homes. To make such a choice courted possible death, though many countered that to flee would bring them greater shame or uncertainty than the alternative.

Leith had called an emergency council of all Officers of Babel, ahead of breaking the dire news. Accompanied by Archimage Timbrad, Lance Sevenson and Trixel, she had fronted a briefing in which she outlined the plight that faced them, as well as the options available to all staffers. They could either collect their families and belongings and join the evacuees, or they could stay, as part of the effort to direct traffic and support those staying behind.

To her immense pride, the vast majority opted to stay. They maintained a stolid fealty to the throne of Mustapha and to the diligent leadership of those who had governed in his absence. Now they repaid that leadership in kind, giving to the city what could well be the final days of their lives.

Squads of pixies, sylphs, humans and Adept walked the streets, providing what assistance they could to a fearful public. Their presence did generate a degree of calm; though despite best efforts, there were still casualties. Smaller creatures did get crushed in the general panic that first ensued. Outbursts of violence and the turbulent flow of bodies left tribes and families divided. Riots broke out. Overloaded wagons were ransacked. Officers on patrol tried to quell the flares with minimal fuss, but an air of tension prevailed. Every tear-streaked face, every sleepless stare, conveyed the knowledge of a malevolent timebomb ticking somewhere beneath their feet.

In the aftermath of the announcement – while the city reacted and the mass exodus lurched into motion – listless energy drove Leith and Trixel together. At sporadic intervals they scrambled for one apartment or the other, or a vacated sitting room, or even a secluded pocket of the outdoors. They made frenetic love; a biting, grinding, hungry love, born of uncertainty and need. Wordless frissons of passion saw the pair grapple as if in the throes of combat. Primal moans tore from their throats, until their bodies parted, lathed in sweat.

The gnaw of anguish would follow the heated distraction of sex all too readily, returning them both to the horrors of the present moment ... until desire stole unbidden into them once again.

The desire for touch. For closeness, when all else threatened to unravel and fall apart.

Trixel hoisted her soft leather trousers and raked fingers through her tousled green hair. She surveyed their environs while the breathless sylph rearranged her own clothes.

Their latest tryst, in the verdant oasis of a community garden, stood little chance of being disturbed. In the Urban Quarter the streets now thinned; with the passage of mid-afternoon and the lengthening of shadows, fewer and fewer Babylonians straggled for ways out of the threatened city.

Across the way from their leafy concealment, a row of shopfronts lined the slanted hillside roadway. 'We should be in Babel,' said Leith, appearing by the fixie's side.

Trixel kissed her cheek, retrieving a rogue leaf from the sylph's platinum tresses. 'Of course. We *should* also be checking in with the engineers at the spacecraft—'

'—Which is what we are doing—'

'—and ensuring the passageways of Below are clear. We *should* be in half a dozen other places. Where should we go, Leith? We can do everything and nothing. Do you want to go back?'

Only a block away, the yawning gate leading underground sucked at Leith's attention. She chewed her lip, indecisive.

Everything and nothing.

My head is everywhere and nowhere.

A racket of creaking wheels on the road, ribald debate and the *clip-clop* of hooves broke the sylph's line of thought. The noise approached from the uphill direction, back towards the city centre. Leith and Trixel ducked behind the fronds, curious eyes locked on the thoroughfare.

'Hurry up, you louts! More treasures to be had along the way! Move along now ... you don't want to go hungry tonight, do you?' came a female drawl, vacillating between a syrupy lilt and a snarl.

Multiple guttural growls followed, protesting in time with the grind of cartwheels.

'Aw come on, ma'am! It's already so heavy!'

'Yeah, feet are tired!'

There could be no mistaking the grumble of swarthy Wilden creatures. On cue, a large wagon appeared on the road – the kind that would be hauled by a draft horse. With no horse in sight, this wagon rolled slowly down the slope, guided by a malignity of goblins. Atop the wagon teetered a huge pile of furnishings – chests, vases, trinkets and baubles that chinked and jostled with every bump.

'Tsk, tsk, tsk! Who wants to go without food or lodgings tonight?' The sing-song threat came from an overstuffed satyr – a woman, bearing a wide load of her own, wedged into tattered finery. One disconsolate *'We're gonna die anyway!'* got drowned out in a chorus of *'Shut up!'* from the lone goblin's fellows. Weaker rebuttals then dissolved into noises of general malcontent. 'Over here!' declared the satyr, gesturing towards the window of a merchant's closed shop. Through the glass, fine clothes, rugs and bolts of plush fabric beckoned.

In their leafy vantage, Leith rocked forward on her feet. 'Looters!' she hissed.

Trixel blocked her with a restraining arm. 'Just watch.'

With a mixture of sighs and groans, the goblins brought their treasure wagon to a halt. The front wheels were chocked, a lump of rock hurled and the *SCRASH* of broken glass signalled a new conquest of riches.

Again, Leith tensed, ready to descend upon the petty criminals; again, Trixel restrained her. 'What good will it do?' she said. 'Besides, they mete out their own justice. I'm telling you ... watch!'

A dozen goblins ferreted about in the store, returning in singles, twos and threes with the merchant's goods. One way or another, they jammed bolts of cloth into nooks and crevices on the overflowing wagon, or simply piled them high on top.

Then, they attempted to leave.

'Can't ... get the chocks out,' groaned one goblin, heaving on a rope tied around a block beneath one front wheel.

'Well?' leered the satyr, 'who wants a larger share of the spoils? Get and help him!' Several others went to work, straining on both chocks with a great display of overwrought effort. Alas, the wagon now appeared too heavy to be freed. Mutters and grumbles of *'Do your own dirty work'* and *'Give us a break, Big Fat Fanny'* peppered the goblins' chatter.

Eventually, the voluptuous satyr waded in amongst her downtrodden charges, swatting them aside. 'Bugger off then, you warty reprobates! Any lazier and you'd be horizontal! Here, I'll do it myself.' The slavish goblins stood aside, as she positioned herself downhill of the wagon, took up both ropes, and gave an almighty yank.

Nothing happened. Nothing, that is, until a goblin rushed in from either side and gave each wheel chock a savage kick, setting them both free.

Clear of any obstruction, the enormous wagon began to roll, gaining momentum with every revolution of the wheels. In the shadow of the rolling juggernaut, the satyr had no chance. It pushed her flat and simply kept rolling, bouncing over her bulk as if she were only a fleshy bump in the road. Agonised shrieks and wet squelching accompanied several rickety jumps the wagon made as it steamrolled her. The crunch of bone ended one inelegant cry.

This trauma may not have been enough to kill the satyr, though as she reappeared beneath the rear of the wagon, it became evident that some part of her – clothing or flesh – had become snagged on the undercarriage. It dragged her in its wake, once more gaining speed. A wandering smear of gore marked the wagon's brutal passage down the paved roadway.

Gobsmacked goblins froze to the spot for several heartbeats. Perhaps they failed to believe their fortune. After a moment they recovered themselves, realising that all their hard-won spoils also sat aboard the runaway wagon. With gurgling exclamations, they pelted off after it.

Leith and Trixel gaped at the macabre scene, then looked to each other.

'Well, there's an outcome,' said the fixie.

Leith's eyes were still wide. 'Is that what you expected to happen?'

'No. No, it is not.'

'Praised be to Lhestra ...?'

'Don't be silly. The Goddess of Justice must be preoccupied with bigger things, surely. No ... I'd say that satyr had it coming to her, pure and simple.'

The sylph stared at the bloody swipe on the roadway, a literal and figurative blemish on her ethical standard. 'You don't think I ...?'

'What would you have done? Spent the afternoon apprehending goblins and doing background checks on a satyr? Yes, you have law enforcement staff for that, but where are they? Hopefully guiding civilians beyond the fringe of Babylon, or else heading to the hills with their own families.'

'But ... I just—'

'Leith, I love you ... but we only have fourteen hours to save the city.'

'Save the city? I'm afraid the time for that may have passed, Minister Tate ... Trixel. We are in damage control mode, now.'

The sorcerous light at the bottom of the pit cast harsh shadows across the angles of Archimage Timbrad's face, belying the calm, consoling tone of his voice. He positioned himself on a low rise near to the foot of the spacecraft, co-ordinating a dedicated taskforce of Adept, Mer Folk and humans, who busied about the giant vessel.

'Damage control mode?' echoed Trixel, colour draining from her face. 'That sounds ... terminal.'

Timbrad wore a look of concession and regret. 'We altered course only a few hours ago. I sent a runner to inform you and Min – Leith. Perhaps he chose to abandon duty for a chance at safety.' He said this without the weight of judgement.

'Or perhaps he expected to find us still in Babel,' the fixie replied. 'Leith and I have been combing the streets, checking in with traffic control. The exodus continues, though there are many choosing to stay in their homes.' With her straight-backed stance, Trixel looked ready to defend their listless behaviour, though the flush of colour returning to her cheeks almost betrayed her.

The Archimage only nodded. 'The spacecraft is weaponised, as we feared. The countdown device will trigger it ... but the whole system is protected by safeguards of immense complexity. Physical locks, otherworld technology and potent wards intertwine, to ensure this device cannot be undone. Part of me is exasperated; another part knows only admiration. It is ingenious.'

'It's unholy,' countered Trixel.

Leith contributed nothing. With deepening dismay, she watched the ongoing labour and the determined faces of those who moved about the machine. Beyond the immediate activity, tucked in a shadowed corner, a cache of workers' rations formed a boxy pile.

At least two dozen figures still toiled in the abyssal pit. They studied the spacecraft, poking and prodding its grime-streaked innards, then spoke in tones too low to be overheard, scratching diagrams in the dirt. A collective shake of heads and the process began again. At intervals they turned feverish eyes towards Timbrad and the two women, or up the dizzying spiral stair.

They're torn between finding a solution to this nightmare and getting as far away from it as possible, thought Leith, offering a wan smile of encouragement.

Over the past two days, engineers had gained access to the device within the craft by removing panels of overlaying fuselage. A hole gaped wide, like a jagged wound in the side of a metallic behemoth. Inside the shell, amidst a dense array of pipes, cogs, cables, levers, buttons and switches, nestled an object of cold, black iron. Bundles of wires and cables disappeared inside it, at either end of its oval-shaped body. Some of these cables ran to the instrument panel, with which Leith was already familiar.

Upon the panel glared the mechanical countdown display.

All manner of attempts had been made to disentangle the fiendish contraption; to wrest it from the bowels of the spacecraft as a surgeon might resect a malignant tumour. Unnecessary components had been stripped away, now littering the cavern floor. Sheets of sickly coloured fuselage lay about like shards of an enormous eggshell. Sorcerers worked in groups of three to mould the discarded panels with theurgic fire.

To Leith's vacant stare, Timbrad explained that the Sorcerers were attempting to produce a blast-proof shield, using components of the spacecraft's own skin and some near-forgotten alchemical spell from the distant past. 'They dare not hope to prevent the blast, but rather, to contain it.' Trixel began asking him questions; the two may well have been in a different province. The Archimage went on to say that once the blast shield had been mounted, all the workers would leave the pit, by translocation.

Leith's attention wandered. The hulking shape on the edge of theurgic light held her gaze like a magnet.

Torr Yosef still stood, frozen in time, mutilated finger jammed in the strange keyhole. Everybody worked around him, as though he, too, were just another component of the machine. Sadness welled and an involuntary sob wracked her chest. To see a construct of such potent wrath forever fused to a creature of noble countenance – the last of a pious race – proved more than she could bear.

She formed the gesture of sylphic prayer with her fingers, as if she could commend him to the gloried mists of Obelis. *He said he had earned a soul. Does that secure him a place in the afterlife?*

Leith allowed her eyes to trace the dramatic lines of the golem's shape.

That stately skull, from which so many virtuous thoughts had sprung. Wise words and levity, in equal measure.

Is there no soul in wisdom?

The armoured shoulders, wide as a cart, that he squared in the face of battle.

Is there no soul in courage?

The legs like girders, that bore him forward even in the knowledge of his brethren's demise.

Is there no soul in perseverance?

His feet, now rooted in stone, looked every part as indelible as the cavern floor around them; heels planted firmly in his last—

What is that?

Leith had never needed to study the golem's metallic feet before, but from where she now stood, the small etching at his left heel showed clearly, caught in the glint of Sorcerer's torches. She moved closer, threading between the workers to crouch by Torr Yosef's lower limbs.

Only the size of a coin, the crisp lines of the etching had not – could not – be worn down on the untarnishable stellite; the same strange alloy that had withstood the brunt of horrendous metaphysical force, inflicted by the Adept. Yet there it was: a small 'M', in the centre of a seven-pointed star, itself enclosed in a plain circle.

A maker's mark? But how? The golems were birthed by ... Valendyne—

She called to Timbrad and Trixel. 'Here, what do you make of this?'

The Archimage strode over, White robes now soiled by a hem of filth. Trixel followed, curiosity writ on her elfin face. They knelt in the dirt beside Leith and examined the mark to which she pointed.

Thought tugged at Timbrad's brow for a moment before he answered. 'I've seen this before, but not for a very long time ... and only ever in books. Histories,' he said.

Leith twitched. She knew also where she had heard of it: the *HISTREE* section at the Repositree. 'What is it?'

'The Sigil of Marnis. The Pantheon can supposedly leave a mark upon items — usually relics, icons — they have blessed. I don't think one has been seen for an Age. This mark makes sense — by Mustapha's account, Yosef was given this shell at the New Dawn, forged by the Creator himself. Perhaps only Marnis could place an etching on it like that.' He continued to stare almost wistfully at the Sigil. A sense of wonder, even in the face of death.

A shadow stole across Leith's face. 'But if Yosef bore the blessing of Marnis ...'

Timbrad snapped out of his pondering, the same cloud darkening his handsome features. He finished the sylph's sentence. '... Then who could have possessed him?'

All three stared at one another, mouths agape, comprehension eluding them. The fixie first broke the terrible pause. 'What, in the name of Obelis, is going on?'

The arduous labour continued. Theories that flirted with

blasphemy would not negate the need to press on. Still, Leith's insides squirmed at the notion that perhaps Marnis himself had struggled to possess the golem. It seemed ludicrous, in light of everything her faith had taught her. She tried to bury the idea but her mood plummeted, reflecting the oppressive dark of the pit all around her. She felt the weight of the entire kingdom above.

Hours rolled on, with no concept of night or day filtering into the stygian depths. She knew from watching the countdown clock that on the surface far overhead, evening blanketed the land. A multitude of stars would paint the heavens, inspiring poets, guiding Astrologers, fuelling belief that every soul that lived and died, now dwelled in the Pantheon's embrace.

Except they wouldn't be. Poets, Astrologers, believers and dreamers alike would all be running scared, or else fortifying their homes, hunkering down in their own domains until whatever end came for them.

Leith slumped onto a nearby rock. The morbid thought prised open a door of grief within her. To cast out the nihilism she turned inward, only to find the blackness there, as well.

Failure.

She had failed to keep the Ball from descending into a chaotic mess, harming Ackley Fahrenheit. Failed to secure Babel and nullify the veiled threat of the Order. Failed to protect Lady Mercy from her killers. Failed to keep the Golden Gate safe from misuse. Failed to turn Trixel back from the voyage that almost ended her life. Failed to neutralise the automaton uprising, enabling Torr Yosef to reach his doom and destiny simultaneously.

Each failure a nail in the lid of a casket.

When the gentle hand fell on her shoulder, she did not register it right away. Clawing her way through a depressive murk, she saw the fixie beside her, violet eyes large.

'It's time, Leith. They've done everything they can.'

'Time ...?'

'Time for us to get out of here.'

The sylph peered about the cavern, frowning. She swept long locks away from her face, finding her cheeks sodden with the aftermath of crying.

The final work crew had constructed an installation about the foot of the spacecraft. It established a cocoon of sorts, enclosing the heinous device within it. The cocoon, shining a sorcerous blue, bore fenestrations to help disperse the energy of a great explosion. Through one of those windows, the face of the clock showed.

04 : 57 : 20

Leith gave her wings an instinctive *flaff*. She imagined rising from the pit, swooping through caverns with desperate speed, straining to create distance with the fixie in her arms. *I've done it before. I could always do it again. Maybe.* Then she cast her eyes around; at the Mer, the humans. *Wingless.*

'The Adept can translocate us out of here,' explained Trixel, in answer to Leith's sluggish mentation. 'There are enough who possess the ability. They don't need to take us far. Even if we only get as far as the surface, there is time enough for evacuees on foot to reach the city limits.'

The sylph gave a half-hearted nod. *We can get away. Away from the devastation, the destruction, the fear of death. Away to a brand-new start.*

Again.

What is left behind? Only memories. Memories of fallen champions. The failed vision of a perfect society. The spirits of so many, who stay in their homes and wait for death to come.

Spindly shadows danced on the rough-hewn rock walls.

Amongst them, the silhouette of a creature she knew. Clinging to the void. Biding its time.

It all makes sense now.

Through filmy eyes, she looked away from the flickering shape of destiny incarnate, at the remnant shell of Torr Yosef.

'I'm staying down here,' she said.

For a full hour, Leith bore the torrent of emotion pouring out of Trixel Tate. She had ever known the diminutive fixie to be effusive, but now she felt wave after wave of energy crash against her, like a hurricane driving whitecaps against a barren coast.

Trixel begged. She pleaded. She demanded, yearned and prayed. She reasoned and argued, until at last she fell to her knees, head buried in the sylph's lap, arms flung about her while she sat upon the rock.

Leith said few words during the tirade. Through limpid eyes she gazed about, taking in her surroundings and yet absorbing so little. From time to time, she would alight again on the face of her lover – *Oh, Trixel!* – and her heart would crumble all over again.

Timbrad paced. To begin with, he offered calm accompaniment to the torrid wash of Trixel's words. After a while he gave the fixie her head, walking the gritty floor in silence; though the strain of worry on his face deepened as time passed. Workers milled about, awaiting guidance, varying degrees of consternation painting their expressions. The Adept were running out of time to ferry everyone else a safe distance from the spacecraft.

'For the sake of those who are here,' said the Archimage eventually, sorrow deep in his august visage, 'we need to leave.'

Trixel rose, trembling, to her feet and brushed the dust from her clothes. 'And leave you shall,' she said. 'I will remain with Leith.'

Gasps sprang from the assembled workers. Renewed sadness

struck the party like a punch to the gut. Few could comprehend such a decision from one of the esteemed women, let alone them both. Timbrad set his jaw and gave a single nod. 'Though it wounds me, you have my heartfelt respect. Should the time come, move as far from the spacecraft as you can. If Oska still smiles upon us, the shielding will hold. Should you come after us, I will be taking these good folk into the north, towards the Highlands.'

He embraced each of them then; first the fixie, then the sylph. Leith shuffled into Timbrad's arms with a resolute eye and a smile that threw a fraction of her usual sunshine. 'Thank you,' she said simply.

Timbrad turned from them. 'Gather in, everyone,' he called to the remaining souls, who crammed together at the base of the pit. The Adept — those who bore the ability of translocation — ringed them, with outstretched arms.

Leith tuned out the arcane ritual. She heard the chanting of voices; a call-and-response that conjured an incandescent halo. White light intensified to a brilliance that made her squint. For an instant, she turned away from the spectacle. When she looked back, Archimage Timbrad and the entire working party had vanished. The aura faded, leaving only a swirl of pebbles and dirt that tumbled to the ground.

The two women sat alone in the vast gloom, pallid Mage-light dancing on the spacecraft and the silent golem.

'You didn't need to do this,' said Leith, staring at her feet.

'You know damn well I had to,' Trixel replied, not unkindly.

The great pit swallowed their words, making their voices small. Barely an echo bounced back to them. Without the incidental sounds of toil around them, a deathly quiet reigned, with only the menacing background hum of the spacecraft to fill it.

'Promise me one thing.'

Leith lifted her head. 'What is that?'

'Promise me we aren't going to spend our time discussing how guilty you feel, or how I shouldn't have stayed, or how we're both idiots for being here. I'll be a manuban's milkmaid before I live on another hundred years, while you get to wander off to the afterlife without me.'

Trixel had not smiled, nor had her words carried any humour. A severity pinched her features, as it had on the first day Leith had ever seen the fixie, at the Council of Rhye in Via. Yet as she spoke she carried away Leith's last remaining fears. They would be together and not a moment would they waste on remorse, or regret, or hopelessness.

'I promise. What shall we talk about, then?' asked Leith.

'We shall talk about the food all those workers left behind. I'm hungry ... and a fixie never holds vigil on an empty stomach.'

'You're the only fixie there is ...'

'Exactly. Therefore, I make my own rules.'

'Tell me ... is there anything a fixie *does* do on an empty stomach?'

Now, Trixel's face did flash a wicked grin. 'You know there is ... but for now, this *other* primal instinct prevails. Come on, Lourden, let's eat.'

They rummaged through cartons, sacks and pouches, appreciative to find loaves of rhyebread, cured meats and fish, a bushel of nuts and canteens of water. To their great pleasure, they also chanced upon two bottles of drowseberry wine.

'Food for days,' remarked Trixel.

'Too bad we only have ... what?'

'Three hours, give or take.'

'Only barely enough wine, then,' said the sylph with a grin, and both women bubbled up with laughter.

They attacked the food with voracious appetites, then settled down with a bottle of wine each.

'So ... what do you think became of the *Khonsu?*' asked Leith.

Trixel took a swig and wiped her mouth. With a faraway look, she replied. 'They weren't in a good way when I—' she frowned, '—when I went overboard. If we assume they survived the storm, their greatest obstacles were going to be themselves. That Mer crew was as solid as a rock. But of our company, believe it or not, the one who had his head screwed on the tightest was Ackley Fahrenheit. He seemed to know what was happening from the outset ... and was more lucid about it than even the Prophet.'

'And ...?'

'And Fahrenheit thought we were doomed.'

'Poor Ackley.'

The fixie took another sip. 'Oddly enough, he wanted nothing more than to try and push through. So little left to live for, but he wanted the voyage to succeed anyway. He had already forgiven Mustapha when I spoke to him last. He was ... hopeful. It was really rather sweet. He spoke about hoping to find gold at the end of a rainbow. I didn't quite understand him.'

For a time, the women enjoyed wordless companionship, just drinking the wine; each tried to find inner stillness in the dire complexity all around them. When they spoke again, they spoke of their successes, about the aspirations of youth and about their dearest friends. They spoke prayers, to those Gods and Goddesses who had helped them through their lives. For Leith, it pushed away the encroaching blanket of despair. She revelled in the warmth of Trixel's lean form snuggled against her, the pine-scented ruffle of hair against her cheek.

At length, Trixel gave a contented sigh. 'I love you, my huntress. Always.'

'And I love you, my qilin.'

As the clock whittled into its final hour, the pair shifted position, to sit with their backs against the blast shielding.

Eventually, the ensorcelled flames guttered and winked out, one by one, and the obsidian dark closed around them.

CHAPTER TWENTY-SIX

KING OF THE IMPOSSIBLE

02 : 00 : 00

Electric lanterns lit the descending stair of timeworn sandstone. Sister Karen led the company single file down a passage that in no way represented the architectural flair of the church above. An austere, almost brutal lack of adornment characterised the dark red interior; though at each turn of the stairwell, a recessed alcove or chapel marked the final resting place of a previous High Priest or Priestess of the Order. Mustapha felt as if he entered the gullet of a monolithic beast ... a beast that swallowed history.

Lady Mercy will never rest here.

He dismissed the maudlin thought. His immediate concern lay with Harold, dragged from a medicated sleep by the perceived urgency of their situation. Harold's face betrayed pain as he nursed his injured arm. The Acolytes had tended and dressed the wound and applied a simple sling, but each jolting downward step brought a grimace from him. He bit down on any complaint and refused assistance. Mustapha resolved to watch him closely anyway. The dragonfly had a tendency to fight his battles in private.

When Sister Karen revealed the entry to the sunken enclosure, nobody registered surprise. They almost expected to find it beneath the Altar. Mustapha, for one, would have been disappointed were it anywhere else. The wonderment came instead with the method she used to open the heavy portal door on the floor behind the Altar-stone.

She beat four times on a drum-like device ensconced behind the great casket. Meadow quirked his eyebrows, idly playing with the leather straps holding the war drum to his own back. Mustapha only pursed his lips, praying for the unrelenting *thump-thump-thump* in his brain to stay in hibernation. And so, it did.

As the hidden door in the Altar stage grated open, he clutched the camphor chest tight and peered down the now exposed stairway to hell. For an abstract moment, he feared they might find another spacecraft – another haunting relic of future past – in the bowels beneath the Church. He shook the irrational image from his mind, though at this point, almost anything seemed possible.

The Acolyte's footsteps fell with nary a sound as she descended the throat of the building. The soft clatter of boots, instruments and the heel of a cane followed. As one, the group tried to match their escort's soundless movement, as if afraid of rousing a slumbering monster.

Following close behind Sister Karen, Mustapha engaged her with a whisper. 'Does Mephistopheles live down here? I mean ... is this some sort of Presidential bunker?'

She replied without looking back at him. 'No, not at all. We descend to a place much older than the Presidency, which itself is a relatively recent office – barely half a century. The tombs around you, as you will appreciate, date back one thousand years.

'Nobody knows exactly where Mephistopheles lives — he seems to come and go without a clear schedule, always arriving where he needs to be at the appropriate time. He is determined to meet you down here ... he perceived that this is where your quest was always leading you.'

'He knew we were coming?'

'He did. It was he who requested that Acolytes scour the city in search of you. He seemed to know your party had arrived, but then lost track of you somehow. I am grateful for my good fortune in being the one to encounter you downtown.'

'How did he—'

'Nobody knows how he gains such knowledge. Nobody deigns to ask, lest they incur his ill will. There is an aura about him ... it is difficult to explain. But do not fear. He seeks to help you and is as excited by your arrival as are we.'

The assurance did little to quell the writhing discomfort inside him.

To his surprise the discomfort steadily morphed into something else the deeper they went. Just as nausea and hunger both gnaw at the stomach yet represent different things, he found that a curious pull drew him in the Acolyte's wake. A sense of connecting with something undeniable. The pang of imminent destiny.

'Are we almost there?' called Meadow from near the back of the file, with a trailing mumble about the longest staircase in history. Indeed, the descent seemed interminable; the stark red stone an endless well to the core of the earth.

'No,' returned Sister Karen, with a note of humour in her voice. 'We are completely there.'

Harold groaned in relief. The heavy breaths of Ackley Fahrenheit hung in the air. They had arrived upon a landing before a broad arch with a pointed apex. Mustapha noticed an insignia marked

434

the stone beneath his feet: the letter 'O', within a seven-pointed star, within a circle. Twin lanterns flanked the arch itself, casting a pool of light that welcomed the visitors. A much greater light spilled from the room within.

'Please,' said the Acolyte, indicating with a hand that they should follow her through.

The arch opened upon a gigantic cylindrical room; of a size to swallow Khashoggi's spacecraft, though no such contrivance sat within it. Mustapha knew in a heartbeat why the stair had plunged so deep, for the room, like the innards of a turret, rose for some twenty storeys overhead, vanishing into near darkness.

The strangeling stood agape. Rooted to the spot, his eyes roved with dizzying wonder about the room. While sparsely furnished, 'featureless' would be altogether the wrong way to describe it.

He did not know where to focus his attention.

Enveloping the enormous room were row upon silent row of circular galleries, climbing towards the ceiling. Linked in places by ramps, stairs or ladders, the galleries would not have looked out of place in a castle or fortress.

The Doors, however, belonged on another plane of existence.

Mustapha's mouth hung open as he stared, neck craned, at the divine gift of Onik to the Order of the Unhomed. Portals ran around each and every level. Evenly spaced, there must have been fifty Doors running the circumference of each gallery. He at once comprehended, yet remained baffled by, the sight that met his eyes. Some were smooth and silver, like polished steel. Other metals and alloys winked back beneath the glow of lanterns that illumined them from either side: copper, bronze, iron and gold. Despite their age, the metallic Doors showed no sign of rust or tarnish. Then came the jagged, angular Doors built of every kind and colour of crystal, like entrances to fantastical caves. Elegant

Doors of carved obsidian and milky white ivory stood adjacent to simple constructs of wood or stone. Then there were portals of other kinds – mirrored surfaces, improbable curtains of molten lava or liquid metal. One Door appeared to be made of parchment.

The turret itself had walls of rough-hewn stone. No mason or builder had done any more than fashion the crude well in the earth, in which the myriad Doors could be visited.

Sister Karen wore a serene smile as the awestruck companions clustered around her. 'Behold the Doors of Time,' she said. 'Praise be to Onik. Please be humble in the presence of these relics. Mephistopheles bids you join him at the table.' She turned and gestured to the centre of the room.

They had been so engrossed in the singular chamber that they had all but failed to notice the figure waiting by a large mahogany table, some thirty yards distant. Not so Mustapha. After absorbing the vast spectacle of the room, the man's presence had caught his attention, like a moth to a flame.

A dozen high-backed chairs circled the table. The figure stood from his chair as the companions slowly approached, drawing gasps from several of them.

Mustapha perceived a man of daunting height. He rose to reveal an attenuated frame at least a head taller than Will. A suit of funereal black with a matching waistcoat clad his form, in a style matching many of the gentry strolling the pavements high above. A candy-striped shirt and a ribbon bow tie of black velvet set him apart, as someone out of place ... or out of time.

His chalky white face had an equine length; a pointed, close-shaven chin jutted beneath a sharp nose with delicate moustaches curling wide of his cheeks. A slick of thin black hair swept back over his vast pate, completing a look of off-kilter elegance – a dandy from a macabre soiree.

Mephistopheles levelled a grin at the uneasy group, barring yellowish teeth.

'I thought the President was a man?' murmured Meadow. 'She's ... beautiful.' Mustapha overheard him, his skin immediately prickling.

'What are you waffling about?' said Dique, also in a hush. 'He's a man all right, and he looks like he stole and ate every wheel in my pa's cheese shop.'

With mounting alarm, Mustapha spun to silence them. His other companions all wore looks of bepuzzlement as they reconciled whatever they saw. 'Say nothing – any of you! Leave the talking to me. Something is not as it appears.' By then they had reached the centre of the room, and at the table, the enigmatic President of Mingo City.

'Welcome,' began Mephistopheles, 'to the land of the Unhomed. We are honoured to host the King of Rhye and his distinguished party.' He executed a low bow, without overblown flourish. 'Pray join me – there is much to discuss.' A slight lisp marred his otherwise refined diction.

The companions, swapping surreptitious glances, took places around the table, upon which sat a large carafe of blood-red wine and accompanying glassware. Harold and the pixies set their instruments by their chairs, but Mustapha placed his treasured box in front of him. Sister Karen walked around them, filling a glass for each of them. Then she disappeared back in the direction they had all come.

Meadow's expression suggested a hope that this wine was better than the one he had rejected upstairs.

Mustapha, flattening his palms on the table to keep composure, took the lead. 'Thank you for receiving us, Mr President. Uncertain of what we might encounter, we ... avoided any fanfare on our arrival.'

'Please, call me Mephisto. I have worn many a mantle, and the one named President is merely the newest of them. I do so now only under some duress. The people need me more than ever before, so I do as they require.

'Bear no regret over the mode of your arrival. Our city has a way of overwhelming the senses. The important part is that you came.'

'Sister Karen told us you have held office these past ten years,' Mustapha said. *Ever since the New Dawn.*

'That is correct.' Mephisto folded his hands on the table. His wine remained untouched. 'It has been both a challenge and a source of great pride.'

'Had you lived as one of the people of Mingo City prior to that? Are you from amongst the Unhomed?' Mustapha hoped his question might unearth some revelation about the man.

Mephisto chuckled — polite yet humourless. 'I come and I go. I travel abroad. Prior to the New Dawn, I found myself returning to the Unhomed with increasing frequency.'

Mustapha's brow furrowed. Will and the pixies all looked perplexed. Fahrenheit's dark glare created caverns of shadow for his eyes. Harold grimaced; his features drawn. 'And how is it that you travel, when all others who live here are stranded behind a veil of awareness?'

Mephisto cast his eyes about the expansive room and gave a vague circular gesture with one hand. His manicured fingernails ended in points. 'I am surrounded by ways out of here ... ways that most are not privileged to access. But often enough, I travel by boat. You might have seen our harbour of wondrous vessels, on your approach? Your own ship is quite a marvel.'

'Where do you go?'

'North and south of here, the continent extends. Townships and hamlets abound, where the Unhomed have spread their wings and emigrated away from Mingo City. To cruise the coast, hopping from one port to the next is quite the delight — a jollification, as a matter of fact! But when the mood strikes me, I travel east. You may have met the Phydeantines, yes? I walk amongst them as well, from time to time. Unfortunate lot … either starving or slovenly, with nought in between.' Mephisto shared these pleasantries in a calm and dignified manner, though a tension pulled at the corners of his eyes and mouth. Perhaps he sought to move on to other matters.

Mustapha almost missed the fleeting glitch. His frown deepened and his gut sank, as he realised that he had not been mistaken. For a brief instant, the outline of the man's form had become an indistinct blur … spectral, in fact. Just as quickly Mephisto appeared whole again.

The strangeling swallowed. The tabletop beneath his hands grew warm. Around the table, his friends sipped their wine or sat in silence; nobody else so much as flinched. *Did they even see it?*

'This is something I don't quite fathom,' he said. 'The veil … it is the edge of existence. Yet we now know the Unhomed have lived beyond the mind's eye. Many have even sailed — or flown airships — to Phydeantum and beyond. Lady Mercy brought her crew all the way to Babylon. How is that possible?'

'Ah.' Mephisto leaned forward, his expression turning glacial in the blink of an eye. 'That is precisely the matter we need to discuss.'

Again, Mustapha eyed his companions. Now some of them did shift in their seats, though one and all seemed content to stay on the sidelines of conversation. To speak up now would be to invite an icy rejoinder, from whatever creature they saw before them. Ackley Fahrenheit peered at the President, as if seeing someone he recognised, but doubting his own eyes.

Mephisto stood, towering over them. He began to wander back

and forth, slender hands clasped at his back. 'You all have endured a perilous journey. Perchance, did you encounter outlandish things? Unsettling things? Things that you, noble King, would never have imagined into existence?'

'Yes,' replied the strangeling. Images of Ogres, enslaved and tortured, raced through his mind. Byorndrazil, engulfed in cloud, lashing out with jagged forks of lightning. Goron, chained to a pike and wallowing in a filthy hole. 'Someone is punishing the Ogres.'

'Yes, indeed ... you may have even encountered some obstacles? Obstructions...?'

'Right again. There was a storm. For a time, our ship, was unable to move forward on the sea. To break free, I bargained with Adatar. It cost me my wings ... in fact, it cost me everything Ophynea gifted to me.'

'Impressive,' said Mephisto, fine eyebrows arching. For another blink his profile blurred, became insubstantial. An instant later, he appeared as solid as ever.

Mustapha grew impatient. The bitter gall of uncertainty rose in his throat. *I need answers.* 'Enough theatrics. You haven't answered my question. The veil — how does it work? What are you keeping from me? I want it all ... and I want it *now*.'

Mephisto rearranged his features, directing a sad smile at the strangeling; when next he spoke, his voice carried a new solemnity. 'The words that follow cannot be unspoken, good King. And once you know the truth, you and your friends are at the mercy of the divine.

'You play in the sandbox of the Pantheon, Mustapha. As you create a new Rhye, you also build for yourself a prison of your own design.'

'A prison? What do you mean?'

Mephisto glanced at the ceiling, as if distracted. When his

attention returned, he began a measured pace around the table. 'The veil – the edge of New Rhye as you have known it – has been a construct of your own imagining. You saw it as impenetrable, and so it was … mostly to you.

'The more you created, the more this gentleman learned fear,' he continued, indicating Fahrenheit with an open hand. 'Thus, the net drew tighter; the constraints more profound. But who has been pulling the strings? Who gave you the rope, with which to hang yourself?'

A flash of white light blinded him.

Nothing but white, all around.

Mustapha saw himself drifting in pure oblivion – untainted by War or Death, tinctured only by a desire to be reunited with his friends in a land reborn. Into that wistful dream came Marnis, the sound of music heralding his appearance. Marnis the Creator, in the guise of a dark-skinned youth, offering the seraph a burden of power and responsibility.

No, that's not quite right. Marnis never instructed me to recreate Rhye. He insinuated it, but he never spoke those words. Torr Yosef described the task … and I assumed the role for myself. I led myself into this. He recalled the God's departing words. *The Pantheon will watch over your progress, with keen hearts and open eyes.*

'You're saying I have been duped by Marnis,' said Mustapha. Murmurs of consternation now bubbled up from his companions, as they each sought to comprehend.

The strangeling pondered how the President of Mingo City could be so sure of everything he proclaimed. How he knew of their travails and their tribulations … how he could possibly have knowledge of the Creator's machinations. He resolved to demand an answer from Mephisto when a terrible sound broke the vaultlike ambience of the room.

A chthonic rumble agitated the ground beneath their feet. The table rattled in place; concentric ripples formed in the wine as glasses *tink-tinked* against varnished mahogany. Once again, Mephisto shot a glance overhead. This time, tiny trickles of particulate dirt fell from the distant ceiling. Fluttering motes of dust glinted in the light of two thousand lanterns.

'What ... was that?' said Dique, eyes wide.

'He knows, doesn't he?' said the strangeling to Mephisto. 'He knows we have figured it out.' Realisation dawned like a wave of nausea.

The Creator, who shunned the very first creatures birthed from his immortal will: the Ogres.

Once neglected by the God who had made them, and instead nurtured by the hand of Cornavrian.

Then liberated by the potent majesty of the Horn.

Now subject to cruel and relentless taunts.

The same Creator who waged a petty war with his twin brother Valendyne; then turned a blind eye to the golem genocide, saving only one to be a vessel for souls at the breaking of New Dawn ...

Mephisto replied with a grim nod. 'He has known the whole time, watching your every movement since you left the shores of Babylon.'

Mustapha palmed his forehead. *Those blasted kestrels!*

The persistent birds — falcons, by any other name — improbably following the voyagers across the Milky Sea. Coastal birds, far from their usual domain. *There were no nests on board the Khonsu, yet there they were ...*

'I should have guessed.' Mustapha massaged his temples. 'Marnis lied ... sort of. He told me that the Pantheon would be watching. But he really meant that *he* would be watching ... the Pantheon seem to have largely deserted us.'

Mephisto's frown spoke of disappointment. 'It maligns me to bear further ill tidings, but the Pantheon have, in fact, been with you – very near – from the beginning to this very moment.'

By reflex, Mustapha cast a bewildered look all about him. Perhaps he expected to see Gods and Goddesses parading on the many-tiered galleries above them, following the man's pronouncement. But instead, Mephisto gazed straight down at the tabletop.

At the camphor laurel chest.

'No...' Mustapha's disbelief wailed inside him.

'You may have been reluctant to peer inside, believing that you knew the precious cargo you held. I say this: You do not have to rely on my word, if you seek proof of duplicity.'

The strangeling found his fists clenched, balled against the now charred and smoking surface of the table. Prising them open, he grasped the chest and pushed up from his chair. His fingers fumbled with the brass catch; once, then twice. With a frustrated roar he tore at it, hingeing open the lid and upending the chest in his hands, in one exasperated movement.

Pitch black granules tumbled out, bouncing to a stop on the tabletop.

Nine of them.

NINE. Mustapha reeled in horror. His companions all leaned forward, counting the tiny remnants of the Pantheon for themselves. Will fixed the strangeling with a look of sorrowful sympathy.

Valendyne. Anuvin. Lhestra. Cornavrian. Oska. Floe. Augustine. Phydeas.

And Ophynea.

'Which grain do you think is which?' asked Meadow to nobody, and nobody answered.

Mustapha ground his teeth in despair. It mattered not — he had been lulled into a trap of his own making for the past ten years, and now found himself pitted against the Creator, without the Pantheon to help him.

Without most of them, at any rate.

A second rumble shook the room. Stronger and more sustained than the last, it brought rivulets of gravel pouring down on the party. Meadow and Dique were halfway under the table by the time the tremor abated.

'Why me?' cried Mustapha, over fading reverberations.

'He knows that you hold the key to thwarting his grand designs. You see, Marnis wants to reunite Adatar and Anato in the sky, to spite his loathed twin brother for all time.' Mephisto delivered his reply as if it were obvious. The simplest thing in the world.

The strangeling tumbled through a whirlpool of his own thoughts. *Did Marnis lure me here to the Doors of Time? Or have we made it to this point despite him?* It seemed unlikely that the Creator would place Mustapha where he needed to be, knowing that the strangeling could unravel his plans. *So ... did I overcome him somehow, to make it here?* He thought of the veil; the song he and Harold had used to bring it down. He thought of his bargain with Adatar.

His shoulders ached.

'Tell me ... do you hear the drums?' inquired Mephisto, jolting the strangeling out of his contemplation. 'Do they plague you, like a headache?'

'They do,' gasped Mustapha. *How...?*

Mephisto looked pleased. Relieved, even. 'Then you hear the call of Onik. The last of the Pantheon; the only one who could not be entrapped by the Creator. He sends you the relentless beat ... the pulse of the world. Through his blessing would you open a Door, traversing Time to accomplish your destiny.'

My destiny. 'That sounds a little vague,' said Mustapha.

Mephisto's smile spread into a wolfish grin. 'Your destiny is yet undecided … but was also determined a long, long time ago.'

Dissenting voices broke out around the table. Mustapha's bid for control over the confrontation slipped, as Will, Meadow and even Harold all vied for a moment to plunge their questioning barbs into the President of Mingo City.

Mustapha heard none of it. The spindle-limbed form of Mephisto glitched once more; in a terrible, breathless moment, Mustapha saw the man's true shape. The blood in his veins ran ice cold.

He understood then how Mephisto knew so much.

From the creature's gangling limbs with claw-tipped hands, to the bestial torso, one moment emaciated, the next an engorged bloat; to the hideous skull sprouting horns, and the maw filled with dozens of glittering teeth … Mustapha had looked upon this beast once before, and readied himself for the end.

The Two-Legged Death.

The agent of Valendyne, harbinger of one's demise; devourer of souls, conduit to the afterlife in Obelis.

'Do I die here? After all of this?' he asked quietly of Mephisto, drawing troubled and questioning looks from his friends. At the same time, he recalled the fractured message, sent to him by the disembodied voice of Ophynea.

Death is not the enemy.

I know that now, Goddess. Marnis aims not only to undo life in Rhye, but to destroy the balance of the cosmos itself. To disorder the seasons, and tease apart the threads of Time.

'You must make a choice,' answered Mephisto, 'but you must hurry. Even now, Marnis moves to unmake the very foundation of this place. Every one of you *will* die if he brings down these walls on our heads.'

'What must I do?'

'You must choose a Door and fulfill the task given to you by the Order. You must go back, and ensure the Sacred Twenty return to their home world. It is the only reality that leaves Marnis starved of the power he needs, to destroy you and bring his plans to fruition.'

'But ... Lady Mercy took the Door I need all the way to Babylon!' The implications of a monumental error caused Mustapha to sway on his feet.

'Find another Door,' suggested Mephisto, still wearing a toothy smile.

All the companions looked about them now. The birth of a new tremor threatened to cave the walls in.

'There are one thousand Doors in here!' cried Mustapha.

'To be precise, there are now nine hundred and ninety-nine.' The smile became a leer. 'But I can help you ... for a price.'

A price. A price! Always a price. 'What is it?' Pebbles rained down with a *sprinkle-clunk*. The floor heaved; the strangeling gripped the table, to keep from falling over. Glasses toppled and smashed, spilling wine like blood.

'Wear the Sigil of my Master,' said Mephisto. Twin argent flames burned in his hungry eyes. 'It will help you find the Door ... then, when the hour comes, I will visit you one final time.'

It all leads to this ... unless I can reverse history. Fate will always lead me to this place – this moment – unless I can send the Twenty home. He thought of the spacecraft, no longer buried beneath Babylon. *Will there even be a Babylon if I defy Marnis?* In the throes of the dilemma, he could no longer think clearly. *None of that matters. Everyone will live. Leith, and Timbrad, and Roni, and the sextuplets ... and maybe even Trixel.* With desperate eyes, he surveyed his friends. They had not seen the true nature of Mephistopheles; the harbinger of life's end, lurking beneath his façade. They watched him with growing concern as the groan of crumbling rock grew louder. More pervasive.

Nobody has to die.

'Do it!' shouted Mustapha, and flung his arm out flat on the table, palm upwards.

Mephisto leapt forwards with undisguised glee. A clawlike finger sprang out, slashing at the strangeling's exposed skin. Mustapha yelled, snapping his arm away; drips of silvered blood splashed to the ground.

For an instant he inspected it: the deep 'V', within a seven-pointed star, within a circle. He shuddered, dropping the arm to his side.

'It is done,' snarled Mephisto. 'You know me now, King Mustapha. You know I am in all places, at all times … and you are now marked, promised to my Master for eternity. May the speed of the Pantheon go with you on your journey … until we meet once more.'

Mustapha wasted not a moment. The sting of his new wound galvanised him, focusing his mind. He whirled, calling to his companions, who ducked and cowered from falling fragments of stone. 'Follow me – and quickly as you can! The stair to the first gallery is over there. We have to move!'

A rending sound filled the cylindrical space, as they made their dash to access the Doors of Time. Stones the size of a man's head began to fall. Then, with a thunderous *CRASH*, an entire ramp toppled from on high, landing not ten paces from the huddled company. Another chunk obliterated the table, throwing up a spray of splinters and a cloud of dust.

Amidst the chaos, Mephistopheles vanished.

CHAPTER TWENTY-SEVEN

THE DOORS OF TIME

00 : 27 : 00

Mustapha might have wandered the galleries for months on end, studying the Doors of Time. He could have opened each and every one of them, glimpsing vistas long forgotten, somewhere across the space between places. He would have been none the wiser, having not the slightest notion where he ought to be going or what to look for.

But now, with the Sigil emblazoned on him in mercurial ink, all hesitation left him. The wound guided him, instilling a fervour he dared not question.

The will of Valendyne compels me.

'Hurry! This way!' he cried, over the now constant rumble. It seemed to rise from the very thews of the earth. The floor cracked, ancient sandstone splitting and warping at crazy angles. The companions ran in zigzags, dodging the shattered rock as best they could.

He need not have urged them. Each in their own way hastened to escape the hail of debris from above.

Despite his injured arm, Harold fared better than the strangeling expected. With pained determination etched on his face, he engaged his wings and bounded forward in airborne strides.

Fahrenheit tripped on a jag of warped floor. Taking a side each, Meadow and Dique hoisted him to his feet, Dique rescuing his cane before it clattered into a widening crevasse across the centre of the room.

Hearts pounding and chests heaving, they achieved the stone ramp leading up to the first tiered gallery. There they found relative safety – for the time being, at least – as the overhead levels provided vital shelter.

'Where are we headed, Mustapha?' called Will, bring up the tail end of the fleeing group.

The strangeling paused, attuning his senses. Despite the ground-shaking noise around him, the forces within spoke louder. 'Up that way,' he replied, pointing at an oblique angle.

He sensed more than saw their intended Door. It beckoned to him from the fifth tier, at the far western limit of the wide, circular turret. He knew not where it went; only that it cast a summons he could not deny.

Spurred on by Mustapha's certainty – and, more than a little, by the desire not to die in a chasm, under a church, in a city at the edge of the world – his companions scrambled up the ramp behind him. Ackley Fahrenheit mustered a vigour rarely seen. Meadow and Dique brought their sprightly Fae energy to bear, though each shouldered an instrument they had no intention of shedding for the sake of speed. Harold clutched his slung arm close to him and forged ahead on quivering wings. Once atop the ramp, they began to run as fast as they could.

Rounding the first tier, they had the room's centre on their right side. Everything from pebbles to man-sized fragments of rock continued to fall. Mustapha considered the great volume of earth that must sit directly overhead; in irony it reminded him of the very cave-in that first revealed the Oddity. Perhaps this room would cave in, revealing a hole that showed the Church high above. The same rock fall would undoubtedly bring about their deaths.

To their left passed a procession of Doors. A solid slab of marble, engraved with an image of a Warlock coven. A green curtain of lush maidenhair fern. A simple wooden Door with a brass knob, so plain as to seem out of place. The strangeling flicked his eyes towards each; curious yet cursory glances. To where — to when — did they lead? It didn't matter — none of them were the Door he needed.

A quarter-turn around the circle, a stairway curved against the stone wall. It led through an opening to the tier above.

'We climb here,' said Mustapha.

As they ascended, booming, disembodied laughter filled the trembling air. A laugh that the strangeling knew: a malicious rebuke of his efforts, which had rung over a bellowing storm at sea. The Creator no longer disguised his voice. Ageless and imperious, Mustapha tried to imagine it coming from the youth in the vibrant robe, who had greeted him with benign charm at the New Dawn. It chilled him to the bone.

The startled faces of his companions darted in all directions. Will looked a question at the strangeling.

'Yes, it's Marnis. We have to hurry.'

On the second tier, they passed an innocuous iron gate, a Door of stained glass and another featuring a full-length mirror. One Door had a knocker shaped like a grotesque face, which called out to them as they hastened by.

'He's gonna kill youse all!' croaked the Door. 'You're never gonna make it … quick, through here!' When they ignored it, the Door warbled a laugh of its own. 'Ha! Youse are lost. Lost!'

Mustapha felt anything but lost. He knew gratitude, for the eerie force that drew him, inexorably, through the chaos. There came the call of Onik – the thundering drums, goading him on. But another undeniable energy stirred inside him – an energy that felt inherently his own. It danced and weaved around the rhythm set by the God of Time, like a melody of bells and voices. The notes welled up in his soul, forming chords, runs and arpeggios, buoying his flurried feet. With warmth in his heart, he recognised the thrilling puissance of the White Queen's tear.

The pearlescent gift of Lady Maybeth Giltenan.

His mother.

A vicious sting in his forearm yanked him back from his blissful reverie to the peril of the moment. The Sigil burned, both a promise and a warning. It too drove him onwards, his fate entwined with the fate of the land.

Love, Death and Time, acting as one.

Melody and rhythm, the essence of his being.

With swift and faultless bootsteps, Mustapha led his friends to that necessary Door – behind which lay concealed a destiny unknown.

A rickety ladder proved to be the only link between the second and third tier. A yawning gap marked the place where another ramp had torn away and tumbled to smash on the floor below. Will tested the ladder first, as the heftiest of the group; though several rungs protested with loud creaks beneath him, they held. The human leaned back through the hole to offer assistance to Fahrenheit, who came next. He declined with a gruff wave of his hand, instead passing up his trusty cane.

The pixies scrambled up after him. One rung cracked under Meadow's zealous boot, falling to splinters on the ground below. Mustapha sprang to catch him, but Meadow clutched an upper rung and completed the climb.

'After you,' said Harold to the strangeling with a wan smile. Mustapha studied Harold's face, usually staunch and reliable; now a hint of feverish light shone in his eyes. Mustapha suppressed a frown and instead simply nodded, hoisting himself onto the ladder.

As he neared the top, the walls imploded.

The entire turret seized with a deafening *CRRRACKLLLL*, great tearing cracks spiralling upwards like inverse lightning. Many lanterns shattered and popped, throwing sparks into the air. The walls bowed, as if the room were a cannister squeezed from without by a monstrous hand.

On the second tier the wall blew inwards, smashing the ladder to pieces. For a split second, Mustapha trod frantic steps in the air. With steel-trap reflexes Will grabbed for him, finding his unbranded forearm. Mustapha flung up his other hand, and a moment later the two embraced on the third tier.

'Harold?' Dique peered down through the dust-filled void to the level below.

The dragonfly's pale face appeared from the murk. He stood amongst the rubble of a ruined wall. He raised a good arm, tapping with the pincer on his battered helm. 'Head protection ... never leave home without it!'

'Do you need help?'

'No. Stand back – I'm on my way up!' Then he zoomed through the hole, landing amidst his haggard friends.

'How much further?' gasped Meadow. 'I don't know if we can handle another crunch like that.'

'We have to,' replied Mustapha.

'We need to,' said Fahrenheit.

'We will,' said Will.

'Why are we standing here, discussing it?' asked Dique.

They traversed the third tier as drunkards, for by now the entire turret shook. Several Doors had toppled and fallen, rendering blank and fractured stone walls behind them.

For the first time during their ascent, Mustapha knew true unease. *What if our Door is destroyed?* But still he felt the rhythm of Onik's call and the chorale of certainty rose within him. The Sigil of Valendyne prickled, urging and cajoling him.

May the speed of the Pantheon go with you.

They found the next stairway, oddly intact amidst the devastation. A portion of the fourth tier had collapsed upon it, but the companions picked their way upwards without incident. At first, they had to sidle their way along the curved wall single file, such was the sliver of stone still clear for them to walk upon. Once reaching the gallery, they skirted a scalloped hole. A fall from this height would prove fatal, perhaps for all except Harold.

As a group, they reached the undamaged stretch of the tier, pressing forward now with grim urgency. Another quake threatened, but the ancient structure held.

For Mustapha, the fourth tier passed in a blur. Dim lantern light filtered through a haze of dust. Even at this height it obscured vision; down in the pit, where Mephisto had greeted them, debris choked the air like a thick and cloudy soup. *Stop looking down ... our path still leads above.* A cough barked behind him, followed by a wince. *Harold.* Somewhere, wherever they were going, they would need to find help. Mustapha stumbled on now, tripping on fallen fragments of stone. Picking himself up, he moved forward once more.

The dogged company followed his footsteps.

Another stair, another precarious climb, and at last they set foot on the fifth tier. Silent relief washed over them all, too exhausted to give their thoughts utterance.

The triune force within the strangeling compelled him still. For the benefit of the others, he pointed along the final stretch. 'Just there, around the bend.'

As they walked, the trickle of gravel and grit continued, but the rumbling tremors subsided. No further cataclysmic quakes thwarted their progress. Their footsteps echoed in the empty air; they hoped beyond hope that Marnis had abandoned his assault.

Nobody believed for a moment that he had.

Without slowing, they hurried along the wrecked gallery. Mustapha knew all his companions' eyes bored into him, expectant. They passed a Door covered with some sort of beast hair. Another crafted entirely from silver; an elegant portal no wider than a cupboard door. Then—

An empty space.

'The Golden Gate was here,' he declared. They had encountered no other vacant position on their ascent thus far. Either an intact Door, or the ruins of a toppled one, had appeared at regular intervals around each gallery. They regarded the empty space as they rushed by, but nobody offered a word.

Several Doors later, Mustapha froze. Blood pounded in his veins, his temples throbbed and the Sigil at his wrist spiked with pain. The pixies, following too close behind, careened into him.

There had been many ornate Doors. Impressive feats of craftsmanship that reminded them of the artisan's deified status. Mustapha had come to realise that not only Marnis could create beautiful things.

The double Door, tall enough to admit a human without stooping and wide enough for two abreast, showcased a masterwork in carving. From the polished mineral surface leapt a diorama so vivid that the depicted scene may well have been taking place upon the very face of the Door, and simply stopped in time.

A mountainous horizon gave way to sweeping hills and a plain in the foreground, near the forested foot of the structure. From opposing hills flooded two armies. Archers, pikemen and warriors ahorse all raced to converge on the level ground, soon to become awash with the spillage of battle.

As if to emphasise the danger, the ardour and the bloodshed, the entire scene — the entire Door — had been carved from a piece of gleaming vermillion stone.

Cinnabar, to be precise.

Mustapha swallowed, his heart hammering. 'This is the one,' he announced.

'Are you sure?' questioned Dique.

He nodded. 'There can be only one, and this is it.'

Nobody challenged him further as they gathered before the ominous red portal. From the shuffles of feet and the rustling of cloaks, Mustapha knew they were as impatient as he to see what lay beyond.

'Not much left to do, then,' offered Dique with a shrug.

Mustapha agreed. There would be no time for ceremony. At any moment, Marnis might renew his torment. The strangeling stepped forward, placing a hand on each delicately curved handle — how smooth they sat against his palms! — and pushed down.

A gentle *click*, and the jamb cracked open. Mustapha pulled; without a creak, without a whine, the Door swung wide on divine hinges.

The scene that greeted them drew sighs and gasps from all. A place of rustic beauty, with serene hills rolling into the misty distance. Lush verdure adorned the nearest slopes; ash and oak, cherrywood and flowering myrtle, standing as nature's sentinels on a calm morning. A range of violet, white-topped mountains did march across the horizon, though there came no sign of raging armies.

'That's a sight for sore eyes,' said Meadow.

'Indeed, it is,' added Will, 'though danger can lurk within beauty.' He must have seen the look of trepidation on the strangeling's face.

Ackley Fahrenheit nudged through the group, his cane clacking on stone like a proclamation. His eyes blazed with the light of intent. 'Mustapha, my King,' he said, 'I would like to be first across that threshold.'

'Be my guest,' said Mustapha, standing aside.

Fahrenheit regarded the Door, but offered no hesitation. He did not look back at the world he left behind; it had given him only misery and confinement, the damning prison of fear. He no longer blamed Mustapha for his years spent as a hermit in Hiraeth. He now knew that Marnis sat at the terrible heart of their tribulations. The Door promised sanctuary from the evils of his predicament – no matter where it led.

Now, he wandered further from the place he had come ... of that, he felt sure. The distant memories of a gay promenade and a seaside idyll grew dimmer with each new twist in the thread of his life. Only one jewel shone bright in his mind, though even she receded further in his memory as he approached the portal.

The only way out is through.

He shrugged the cloak back from his shoulders, and with a bold chest and a clear eye, he strode through the Door.

Emboldened, Meadow stepped forward. He had never wearied of adventure, though his face grew less boyish and his hair more ash-blond with each passing year. The thrill of it drove his pixie heart and kept the twinkle bright in his gaze.

Yet bravado did not rule him in this moment. More, a sense of duty. Of owing. He thought of a young butterfly, so eager and diligent, that he had drafted from the Emerald Bar. That poor creature who had stumbled into a greater mischief than ever he had sought. The huge sarcophagus in the Church above, with its winged engraving, loomed like an accusation in the pixie's mind.

Wherever you went, whatever you did, Sammy ... we're doing this for you, too.

Meadow marched through the Door.

One image dominated Dique's mind as he made ready to follow in Meadow's footsteps: a vivacious brunette pixie, surrounded by six boisterous youngsters. In his imagination, the woman grew stouter, greyer, but ever more warm and homely. The children around her also aged; standing taller and straighter, more self-assured. One donned the garb of a Fae Knight. Another the apron of a publican. Still another, the greens of a forest steward ... and on it went, each one wandering out of the scene to fulfill their own lives, embroider their own rich tapestries.

At the end, only grey-haired matron Roni remained and Dique knew. *Just you and I ... and maybe a cosy little cheese shop.*

With unfaltering steps, he walked through the Door.

Harold gritted against the pain of his shattered arm. He could feel the worrying creep of infection in his blood, the sheen of perspiration on his brow.

His mind remained clear. His place would always be beside Mustapha, Meadow and Dique. The three had drawn him into their shenanigans years ago, his life irrevocably changed as a result. How shameful, for a dragonfly of honour to succumb to the allure of a thief's life.

Yet it had become so much more:

A journey to the heavens, escorted by a host of pterippi.

The gift of a sacred relic from a bygone Age.

Triumph snatched from the jaws of tragedy, in the battle-soaked foothills of Two-Way Mirror Mountain.

From petty crime to glory and fame ... all at the side of his dearest friends.

He only hoped they wouldn't leave a crippled dragonfly behind.

Harold stepped through the Door.

Will glanced at Mustapha.

'Go on, then,' said the strangeling with a wink, 'You go first. I've got your rear.'

The quip brought a smile to the wagoner's face. And so, he still thought of himself — a simple human, spending his life on the land, tending to the fruits of the earth. At times he felt out of place amongst the band of roguish Fae, though Mustapha would have none of it. He cherished Will with every word and gesture. Even when they fought, Will knew that his lover only meant to make their bond stronger yet.

Deep inside, Will felt his own greatest struggles still waited ahead. The portal beckoned and whatever lay beyond he knew he faced it with his greatest champion by his side.

Fixing the smile to his face, Will took a deep breath and passed through the Door.

A brackish snarl broke through the moment, rising to a heinous cry somewhere between a shriek and a roar.

Mustapha spun to face the way they had come. Back along the

gallery, settling dust still fell in a curtain swathed in lamplight. Particles quivered in the air with the ear-splitting bellow, and fresh runnels of gravel were shaken from the levels above.

Horrified, the strangeling watched as an enormous figure burst through the swirling dust, charging towards him along the tier. The loping form of the beast bespoke doom, with its twisted horns and hideous oversized maw. Forelimb claws reached out, ready to shred the strangeling to pieces.

'Not today!' shouted Mustapha. As the Two-Legged Death bounded towards him, he dived through the Door.

ALL DEAD AND GONE

00 : 00 : 00

Upon a beautiful daybreak, the infernal device within Khashoggi's spacecraft detonated.

For a fraction of an instant, the entire metal shell seemed to inhale. When it came, the exhalation released a devastating force on a level never before seen in Rhye.

A tiny seedling of immense power sparked within the device, blooming outwards faster than any mere mortal might comprehend. The shell of the great contrivance ballooned outwards; then, at the limits of its integrity, ruptured with a ferocious release of heat and light.

Within a heartbeat, the two women sitting at the base of the spacecraft ceased to exist. Their awareness winked out in a moment without pain or suffering, their very beings made memory like vapour rising into the heavens.

The burst consumed and exceeded the capacity of the sunken

pit at the roots of Babylon, overcoming the Adept's blast shielding as if it were made of paper. Explosive energy jolted the bedrock, raising the roof of that lowest cavern and continuing to rise with brutal prowess.

The intricate caves and networked passages of Below were blown outwards, untold volumes of rock heaved aside as if no more than dry kindling atop a fire. Few Wilden creatures had remained in folly to guard their homes; none survived, as angry conflagration destroyed everything before it.

Compression sucked at the topography of Babylon, before hills and dales alike bloomed upwards and burst open. The earth vomited forth the full might of the blast. Dire brilliance streamed from a thousand new faults and crevices that broke through the landscape.

At the surface, directly above the epicentre, the Tower of Babel seemed to warp – to *bend* – then the deafening squeal of overstressed steel and the bursting of glass marked a catastrophic fracture through the once elegant spire. The hanging gardens about its skirts were consumed in flame, and the structure itself spewed gouts of smoke. Babel settled for a moment at a precarious angle, before toppling over with a tortured moan.

Lance Sevenson remained in the Tower until the very end, and perished within its walls. He had sworn to serve Babel 'until the day it comes tumbling down', and that is what he did.

The devastation did not end with that moment. Rushing behind the initial explosion came the shockwave, an invisible wall of force that flattened everything it touched.

The avenue of gingko trees stood no chance. They fell like spilled matches, soon engulfed by fire. Townhouses and stately homes upon the prominence also knew no quarter, mashed to the ground as the wave rushed outwards at terrifying speed.

Splintered remnants of trees, roofs, monuments and other debris left in the streets took to the air. Flying scrap became deadly missiles in the sky. Flocks of birds flew for their lives with raucous screeching.

Anyone who remained in their inner-city dwellings felt the wave of death consume them. Bone-melting heat scorched through the districts of Above. The obliterating shockwave that followed sent the remnant shards flying in a wrathful wind.

From the chasm ripped wide in the middle of Babylon, an enormous cloud rose into the azure morning sky like the emerging crown of a hellish monarch. The roof of the cloud billowed upwards and outwards, mushrooming for miles and blanketing the blasted city. Even the rays of Adatar could not pierce that diabolical cloud, though none remained beneath to bewail the coming of darkness.

The blast rumbled outwards across the Bay of Marnis. Boats and ships were cast about as if by a giant's hand, then obliterated on the rippled surface. Waves surged against the tide, pushing as great rollers against the edifice of Levi.

On the city fringes, to the north, east and south, those who had fled Babylon looked over their shoulders in mute horror. At the gateway to the Highlands, Archimage Timbrad paused alongside a column of exhausted refugees. The garish yellow light from the explosion flashed across faces drawn tight in disbelief. A hot wind followed, blasting them with sufficient strength to cast the frail into the dirt.

The sonic boom and rumbling aftermath reached them last of all. Many clapped hands to ears. Eardrums burst and bled; the screams of deafened creatures fell on the muffled and ringing ears of others.

The cloud loomed higher, dominating the sky. A chill gust rushed in to replace the heat, though no wind could do more to freeze the heart than the sight of Babylon razed.

The city burned, the sky grew bleak, and a dark night of the soul descended on them all.

In the days after the blast, many evacuees died. An illness plagued their constitution, bringing cramping pain and terrible gouts of blood from every orifice. Nausea and fever wracked them, and the Apothecaries soon were overwhelmed by a foe they could not fend off. In dismal pockets of the land, agriculture made way for barrows and mass graves.

The sickness abated, but did not relent in entirety. Over weeks and months, the denizens of Rhye struggled to eke out their survival, even as Death tapped young and old on the shoulder at random.

A bitter, unseasonable winter caused meagre crops to fail. Toxic rain fell, making matters worse. The population dwindled, as starvation and depression claimed many more lives. Prospects of ever returning to the city dimmed, as those who remained lacked the skills, the resources or the determination to contemplate such a monumental task.

The site of old Babylon became a windswept wasteland, haunted by the derelicts of its grandest buildings.

Skeletal monuments to a King long gone.

One icy Saturday morning, nearly four years after the blast, a disparate knot of survivors huddled together on a stark hillside. They stood beneath a denuded tree, cold wind whistling all around. They would later argue which day truly ended the Age of Harmony: the day of the blast, or this very day.

After a brief but solemn rite, they lowered the body of Archimage Timbrad into the ground. His poor emaciated remains had been found not far from this place, after he had braved the elements in search of a lost group of children. The children they also found and buried alongside him, erecting a humble cairn upon the spot.

The Archimage had grown weak from protracted illness, unable even with his formidable power and inner strength to stave off the encroaching end. His theurgy waned, until he became little more than any other mortal man, ravaged by nuclear fallout.

A bitter wind howled. Grey sleet began to fall. At last, the mourners were driven back down the hillside to shelter.

With their departure went the last great Age of Rhye. When the winter finally passed, none remained to see the Grand Dance of Adatar and Anato or offer their melancholy prayers to the sky.

THE END...?

ACKNOWLEDGEMENTS

The saga of Rhye cannot be told without acknowledging the singular talent of the legendary Freddie Mercury. In similar fashion, the musical creations of Brian May, Roger Taylor and John Deacon continue to provide a near-boundless source of inspiration in realising this next part of our heroes' journey.

In the years since I began this passion project, it has grown to become much more than a one-man show. Fat Bottomed Boys, who bring the contemporary soundtrack of Rhye to life, are now a fully fledged band: I would like to thank Louis Henri Chambat, Thibaut Sergent, Christian Rogeaux, Julien Hatton and Nico Parquet for bringing my material so gloriously to life.

The land of Rhye was dreamed into existence, but Luc Hudson sees it as though he crawled directly into my head. For sensational cartography, graphic design elements and vibrant character art – as well as alpha reading from start to finish – thank you, Luc.

Thank you to my growing community of writers and readers, friends one and all: for the support and the motivation to get this done, and do a proper job of it. A specific thanks in regard goes to Erin Nightingale, for developmental editing this thing into its best shape.

Last but absolutely not least: gratitude to my very own Queen, Love of My Life, etc, Ebony; for believing and enabling me in this obsessive quest.

The show will go on!

GIMME THE WORKS

Open up your eyes and see
Within this Age of Harmony
Queen has joined us once again –
Go quickly now and find them, friends!

Author's Note: Many, many Queen references in *Metropolis* hark back to characters and places that have already been referenced in *The King of Rhye*. For simplification purposes, this Appendix will generally focus on <u>new</u> references only.

PROLOGUE: A WORLD SO NEWLY BORN

- Title – ref '39 (*A Night at the Opera*, 1975).
- The dawn of a new Rhye – hereafter called 'New Rhye' – begins with blinding white light and the jangling of bells – for this moment in time, I imagined the opening of Brian May's *The Dark* (*Back to the Light*, 1992).

- The story arc of New Rhye begins, of course, with creating a new world. The references will certainly become more poignant; but for now, let's bookmark it: *Is This the World We Created? (The Works,* 1984).
- A play on words calls back the musical link between Queen's second and third albums – the outro from *Seven Seas of Rhye (Queen II,* 1974) becomes the whistled intro to *Brighton Rock (Sheer Heart Attack,* 1974), being '*I Do Like to be Beside the Seaside'.*
- In a brief exchange between Mustapha and Torr Yosef, the golem pre-empts that his Lord is hearing the sounds of music in his mind. Alas, it isn't quite true, but *I Can Hear Music* (Larry Lurex, 1973) is the line almost uttered. Instead, Mustapha is hearing bells – The bell that rings / Inside your mind... from *A Kind of Magic (A Kind of Magic,* 1986).
- Central to New Rhye is Mustapha's seat of power, which ultimately takes the name of The Tower of Babel, from *The Miracle (The Miracle,* 1989). Mustapha blithely ignores Fahrenheit's warnings that this would be a terrible name to give his newly minted home.
- There is a passing nod to *Face it Alone,* the song fragment from The Miracle sessions, given a new life by Queen in 2022.
- The word 'metropolis' is used twice in this Prologue, and is the title of the novel. This is in reference to the decopunk masterpiece of the silent film era, directed by Fritz Lang. *Metropolis* was used as the stylistic inspiration for the film clip to *Radio Ga Ga (The Works,* 1984). As we shall see, Art Deco motifs and the theme of a new technological age, are present throughout the pages of *Metropolis.*
- Bear with me: this particular thread begins most tangentially, but grows in profundity as the story unfolds.

In 'The Golem's Prayer', Torr Yosef refers to 'mercy dreams'. As far as Queen references go, it is safest to say that this is subtle foreshadowing of the arrival of Lady Mercy – see *Hammer to Fall* (The Works, 1984). For any art historians out there – anyone who enjoyed learning about *The Fairy Feller's Master-Stroke*, as it was portrayed in *The King of Rhye* – I would point you towards *Mercy's Dream*, painted by Daniel Huntington. Not only is it an exquisite piece of art (much like the *Master-Stroke*), but the more you know about this painting, the more you will see its subject integrating with this tale.

PART ONE: WHEN LANDS WERE FEW

- Title – ref '39 (*A Night at the Opera*, 1975).

CHAPTER ONE: THE BELL THAT RINGS

- Title – ref *A Kind of Magic* (*A Kind of Magic*, 1986).
- A kobold sprints from the districts Below to the world Above, carrying an urgent message. 'Move over! ... I said, move over!' she cries; moments later, a helpful fellow Wilden creature helps to clear a path, shouting 'Hey, hey, hey! ... Clear the way!' in a reference to the lyrics from *Gimme the Prize* (*A Kind of Magic*, 1986).
- The main tale certainly begins in *The Dark* ... and here we see our frantic kobold running *Back to the Light* (*Back to the Light*, 1992). The streets aren't explicitly 'paved with gold', but Babylon represents Mustapha's Utopian vision.
- Upon delivering her message, the breathless kobold gives her name as 'Godgifu'. This is the Old English version of

Godiva. Now the details of the kobold's flight fall into place, and we see the story of a young woman who has run naked through the town while the populace is behind closed doors. Only one or two Peeping Toms have their shutters open as she passes. The reference belongs to *Don't Stop Me Now* (*Jazz*, 1978).

- We are introduced to Mustapha's inner sanctum, his quarters at the pinnacle of Babel. Within is an apparatus featuring a huge array of Windows. It is implied that this apparatus appeared without Mustapha imagining it into existence; its function appears to allow him to see hazardous or destructive events unfolding in Rhye. The motif of Windows here is important: the concept of portals in general features heavily throughout the story, with Windows being one half of this. The most obvious connection to Queen would be *Keep Passing the Open Windows* (*The Works*, 1984). This Mercury-penned song was produced for the soundtrack to the film *Hotel New Hampshire*. The first edition source novel, by John Irving, contained 401 pages; Mustapha's viewing apparatus features the same number of Windows.

- 'People on streets …' belongs to *Under Pressure* (*Hot Space*, 1982). This song is rich with themes that can be seen throughout the threads of *Metropolis*.

- It becomes apparent that Mustapha experiences auditory hallucinations. Or perhaps, telepathic communication from the Pantheon? *The bell that rings / Inside your mind* from *A Kind of Magic* (*A Kind of Magic*, 1986) serves Mustapha as the power of premonition, with a sinister edge.

the town of Crueladaville, a reference to the Disney Villain from the film *101 Dalmatians*, herself referenced in *Let Me Entertain You* (*Jazz*, 1978).

- Khashoggi murmurs 'Bijou of the sea' in addressing the undine, Salacia. A direct reference to *Bijou* (*Innuendo*, 1991).
- Khashoggi and Salacia are, as it happens, indulging in a *Seaside Rendezvous* (*A Night at the Opera*, 1975). The Prophet says as much, at one point. The pair engage in a lively dance upon the sand – one might imagine the mood of the song is the mood of their moment together.
- This chapter leans more heavily into the motif of machinery, technology and innovation than any part of the saga that comes before it. I aim to weave in the themes prevalent in *The Works* (1984) which, right from the first track *Radio Ga Ga*, presents themes of technological advancement. The centre of industry and innovation in Babylon, populated mainly by Mer Folk and Torr Yosef's automatons, is therefore named simply *The Works*.
- After the events at the climax of *The King of Rhye*, we are introduced once again to *Khashoggi's Ship* (*The Miracle*, 1989), here dubbed the *Khonsu*.
- Khashoggi boards the *Khonsu* and is met by two newly commissioned automatons. They don't have names, so give their serial numbers to introduce themselves. Those happen to be the publication numbers for the Studio Collection vinyl pressings of *The Works* (1984) and *News of the World* (1977); the former containing a track that pits machines against humans, the latter sporting a cover that foreshadows the 'machines vs humans' motif. Could it be a sign of things to come?
- Khashoggi renames the automatons – Mack (after

producer Reinhold Mack), and Mandel (after musician Fred Mandel, who played keyboards on record and on stage for Queen).

CHAPTER SIX: SECRET HARMONIES

- Title – ref *A Kind of Magic* (*A Kind of Magic*, 1986).
- People come from all over Rhye to visit the King in Babylon. Amongst them is Harold, arriving from Arboria. Here, it is a place of forests, if not a *Planet of the Tree Men* (*Flash Gordon*, 1980).
- Early in the chapter, Mustapha walks along a terrace covered by a massive overhanging fern garden – otherwise known as the Hanging Gardens of Babylon – ref *The Miracle* (*The Miracle*, 1989).
- Visitors arrive from out of the mysterious West, in an airship – an unprecedented technology in Rhye. A contingent of white-robed individuals disembark and their leader introduces herself to Mustapha as Lady Mercy (*Hammer to Fall*, 1984).
- Mustapha houses his Advisors and Ministers, and accommodates guests to Babel, in the Residential Parlour. This is a subtle nod to Freddie's party pad during the Hot Space Tour: known as the 'Presidential Poofter Parlour' (as opposed to Roger's 'Hetero Hangout').
- Lady Mercy discusses the Order of the Unhomed – an enigmatic society whose mission purportedly began one thousand years ago. This becomes important later, when we discuss the 'rage that lasts a thousand years' – ref *A Kind of Magic* (*A Kind of Magic*, 1986).
- Lady Mercy mentions the God of War's act of 'levelling a

mountain', referring to Anuvin's destruction of Warnom Bore in The King of Rhye. This evokes the lyric *Til the mountains crumble into the plain*, from *Innuendo* (*Innuendo*, 1991).

- The chapter ends with the pointed words: *The Show Must Go On* (*Innuendo*, 1991).

CHAPTER SEVEN: MUSIC AND LOVE EVERYWHERE

- Title — ref *The Millionaire Waltz* (*A Day at the Races*, 1976).
- We have arrived at the Ball — inspired, of course, by *Dreamers Ball* (*Jazz*, 1978). The scene opens on Leith Lourden — isn't she 'dressed so fine'?
- Arriving at the ballroom, Leith soon runs into her friends, who are worth specific mention.
  - * Meadow's cloak is 'shot through with reds, yellows, blues and greens', somewhat representing the sleeve of *Hot Space* (1982).
  - * Dique is dapper in 'his finest silver-grey dinner suit', thus encapsulating the sleeve for *The Game* (1980).
  - * Dique's wife is named Roni, after John Deacon's real-life wife Veronica. She is dressed in 'the yellow of melting butter, featuring … sunflowers and poppies'; hence, yellow detailed in red … just like the sleeve of *Flash Gordon* (1980).
- Harold is already there — Leith mentions that he has 'been fiddling about [on the stage] for hours already'. Meadow scoffs. This relates to an offhand comment from Roger Taylor about Queen's soundcheck habits. Brian would turn up early and take forever to get ready, whereas preparation took Roger little time at all.

- The band (minus Mustapha) take the stage, and soon a waltz begins ... what would a Ball be, without *The Millionaire Waltz*? (*A Day at the Races*, 1976).
- The lights blink out — and the true show begins. This next scene is written utterly to reflect the vibrant energy of Queen taking the stage during the *Live Killers* (1979) era: billowing dry ice, coloured lights and the thundering rhythm of *We Will Rock You (Fast)* (*Live Killers*, 1979) and *Let Me Entertain You* (*Jazz*, 1978).
- The pixies comment on Mustapha's evolving appearance. From the shorter hair he sports at the beginning of *Metropolis*, he also now wears a moustache. Meadow also retorts that he appears to have 'a tuber down his trousers'; Freddie once famously claimed in an interview that there was 'no hose' shoved down there ... everything on view was his own.
- Dique's Zither is amplified via a device he conceptualised with Torr Yosef, à la the beloved Deacy Amp.
- Mustapha joins the band with a searing vocal; their song, *Rock of Ages*, is a melange of many Queen moments.
  * The title is a borrowed lyric from *Brighton Rock* (*Sheer Heart Attack*, 1974).
  * 'It's time to go crazy' — *Let's Get Crazy* being a Roger Taylor solo track; or perhaps Queen's *I Go Crazy*, a B-Side from *The Works* (1984).
  * 'It's time for a show' — 'are you ready for a show?' ref — *Let Me Entertain You* (*Jazz*, 1978).
  * 'Stomp your feet and punch the ceiling' echoes Freddie Mercury's signature on-stage pose.
  * 'We'll play you the hits ... We'll smash it to bits' recalls Brian May's solo track *The Guv'nor* (*Another World*, 1998):

> *He'll play them hits, electrifyin' / tear you to bits, leave you*
> *cryin', cryin', cryin', yeah...*

*   The Fairy Feller is named.

*   *Don't Stop* (Us? or *Me*) *Now* (*Jazz*, 1978)

- The scrallin lights change from warm white to an array of red, green and gold, recalling the famous 'Pizza Oven' lighting rig pictured on the cover of *Live Killers* (1979).

- A true bacchanal ensues. Performers somersault across the floor, servers move about with trays balanced on their heads, and an odd performer hides beneath cold cuts of meat on a refreshments table. We're right there at the launch party for the *Jazz* album, New Orleans, 1978.

- Mustapha swings from the chandelier. It is widely reported that Freddie did this at one of Roger's birthday parties. It is also reported that he was naked at the time ... but we probably don't need to go quite that far.

- In the next passage, we see the evolution of a developing sapphic connection between Leith Lourden and Trixel Tate. In combing the discography of Queen, I came across a number of tracks in their mid-career period (approx. 1976-1982) that could be used to tell the story of Leith and Trixel. The first, epitomised in this scene, is *You and I* (*A Day at the Races*, 1976). It's a beautiful night; lanterns are swaying, music drifts in the darkness and a buoyant vibe fills the air. Romantic feelings are pledged. The relationship between these two women will be a prevailing story arc throughout *Metropolis* – we will revisit their tale with another song in a later chapter.

- A gratuitous mention of *No-One but You* (*Queen Rocks*, 1997).

- Trixel explains to Leith why she has been hesitant to let the sylph get close to her heart. She has lived for centuries, and may live for a long time still; the average life expectancy for a sylph is one hundred years. Trixel does not want the devastation of watching (another) love grow old and die. This mirrors the dilemma of immortal hero Connor MacLeod in *Highlander* (1986) – addressed in Brian's *Who Wants to Live Forever* (*A Kind of Magic*, 1986).

- Leith's reply ends with the line 'here we are ... living in a new world.' This is a hybrid/ mash-up line, incorporating phrases from the opening line of *Princes of the Universe* (*A Kind of Magic*, 1986) and *Machines (Or Back to Humans)* (*The Works*, 1984).
- The women dance ... to a waltz, of course, continuing the motif of *The Millionaire Waltz* (*A Day at the Races*, 1976).
- Leith and Trixel share *The Kiss* (*Flash Gordon*, 1980).
- The moment is interrupted by Archimage Timbrad, who bears ill tidings of concern for Lady Mercy. The High Priestess has whispered to him a message: *Save Me* (*The Game*, 1980).

CHAPTER EIGHT: THE GOLDEN GATE

- Title – ref *The Miracle* (*The Miracle*, 1989).
- We return now to the adventures of Sammy the butterfly, central figure in *Spread Your Wings* (*News of the World*, 1977).
- The previous chapter contained perhaps more Queen references than any other chapter in the entire saga. By contrast, 'The Golden Gate' holds almost no Queen-derived Easter eggs ... but it remains a pivotal moment in the broader tale, literally opening the door to a huge new story arc. Strange, how a minor character could create ripples that flow to much greater events later on. Perhaps

we call it 'The Butterfly Effect'?

- One incongruous item stands amongst the treasures of the Main Gallery: a bathtub. This references the bathtub in which Freddie reportedly wrote *Crazy Little Thing Called Love* (*The Game*, 1980).
- Beyond the Golden Gate, Sammy encounters a strange man in an unfamiliar scene. The man calls out and reveals himself, having been hiding in some bushes. This is a pivotal moment, in which the scope of the novel goes next-level.
  * The man is thin and wears white.
  * He has burnished copper hair and appears of indeterminate age; young-looking, yet wise.
  * He has a streak of blood running down one side of his face.
  * Something baffles Sammy about the man's eyes.
  * He gives his name as Tom.
  * These visual cues are intended to elicit the one and only David Bowie. References — the Thin White Duke, Aladdin Sane and Major Tom, as well as Bowie's eye condition: anisocoria.
  * One explanation for Bowie's appearance is a further reference to his duet with Queen in *Under Pressure* (*Hot Space*, 1982). Yet there is another, much deeper explanation, which will be explored throughout this book.

CHAPTER NINE: A TRICKY SITUATION

- Title — ref *It's a Hard Life* (*The Works*, 1984).
- The phrase 'news of the world' gets another look-in. Great

album.

- Throughout this chapter, Mustapha grapples with the devastating evidence that projectile weaponry – guns, specifically – have made their way into his crumbling Utopian worldview. Mustapha's aversion to guns can be traced back to his forced patricide of Bastian Sinotar in *The King of Rhye*. To the seraph, guns emulate much of what is evil in the world. The message is reflected in *Put Out the Fire* (*Hot Space*, 1982): 'People get shot by people / people with guns'.

- In this instance, the High Priestess has been shot and her murderers – the very Acolytes she arrived with – have fled. You could infer that 'Lady Mercy won't be home tonight.' Ref – *Hammer to Fall* (*The Works*, 1984).

- Lady Mercy's desperate message is again mentioned: *Save Me*. She may not have been naked, but she's certainly far from home.

- A kobold announces that the Oddity has been sufficiently freed from entombing rubble that it can be accessed for examination. Mustapha sets off with a small party to view it. We return once more to the subject of the Oddity, shortly after David Bowie's Major Tom has made an appearance. Could it be … a *Space Oddity*? Are the threads coming together yet?

- Khashoggi tells Mustapha that he built the strange spacecraft 'another world' ago … eliciting Brian May's solo album, *Another World* (1998).

- 'Twenty humans left Earth aboard this machine…' – they would be the 'score brave souls' from '39 (*A Night at the Opera*, 1975). Does anyone else get the feeling we're *Goin' Back* to the very prologue to *The King of Rhye*, here?

- '... long before you were born.' It was nice to slip in this elegant phrase, to remind us of *Father to Son* (*Queen II*, 1974).
- At the chapter's end, all the talk of stages, curtains and pantomimes is reminiscent of *The Show Must Go On* (*Innuendo*, 1991).

CHAPTER TEN: ACROSS THE SEA

- Title – ref *Sail Away Sweet Sister* (*The Game*, 1980).
- An early mention of *Flick of the Wrist* (*Sheer Heart Attack*, 1974), as Mustapha and Will share a spiky moment.
- Mustapha speaks of the futility of a king who sits on his throne and does little else. This references the lyrics of *Is This the World We Created?* (*The Works*, 1984): '*Somewhere a wealthy man is sitting on his throne / waiting for life to go by*'. Later in the same passage, Mustapha says 'I pray for answers and the Pantheon gives no reply.' He is starting to doubt that he still has divine support. *If there's a God in the sky looking down / what can he think of what we've done...*
- The next Queen track to tell the story arc of Leith and Trixel's relationship is *Sail Away Sweet Sister* (*The Game*, 1984). The lyrics and perspective of this track inform the scene of the *Khonsu*'s departure. Leith laments the knowledge that Trixel is boarding the ship, leaving her in Babylon.
  - * Leith is unconvinced by Trixel's shun, which is in complete contradiction to their candid, finely clad moment at the Ball. *It ain't no use in pretending / you don't want to play no more ... You're all dressed up like a lady / how come you behave this way?*

483

* The sylph's prevailing reaction is a wistful outpouring of love. *Sail away sweet sister / sail across the sea … My heart is always with you / no matter what you do / sail away sweet sister / I'll always be in love with you.*

* Leith shows a pang of regret at wearing her heart a little too firmly on her sleeve at the Ball. *Forgive me for what I told you / my heart makes a fool of me / you know that I'll never hold you / I know that you gotta be free.*

* The middle eight reflects what would be Trixel's response back to Leith. It is in keeping with Trixel being so much older, and with an unknown life expectancy ahead of her: *Hot child, don't you know you're young / you've got your whole life ahead of you? / And you can throw it away too soon / way too soon…*

• During the procession of voyagers, Roni walks alongside Dique, with their six children cavorting out in front. In reality, John and Veronica Deacon's six children are not all of the same age as Dique's; but for the sake of the story, it seemed a fun way to explain how the pair ended up with six children, when ten years earlier Dique had none!

• At the procession, Mustapha wears 'a flowing scarlet robe, trimmed in white and black, which fell to pool around his boots … Upon his head he bore a crown of gold with scarlet silk — elegant without bombast'. This is intended to reference Freddie's royal regalia from the Magic Tour, 1986.

• Mustapha also carries an armful of de-thorned roses, which he tosses into the crowd. This gesture was often displayed by Freddie at concerts throughout Queen's live career.

PART TWO: THE WESTERN WAY

- Title – ref *Hammer to Fall* (*The Works*, 1984).

CHAPTER ELEVEN: NO PLEASURE CRUISE

- Title – ref *We Are the Champions* (*News of the World*, 1977).
- In the chapter opener, the vast body of water to the west of Babylon is given a name: the Milky Sea. This references '39 (*A Night at the Opera*, 1975).
- We return to the *Khonsu*, and spend a moment with Mustapha and Dique together. I wanted to acknowledge the long-term friendship between Freddie and John, which ultimately resulted in share songwriting trends in the early 1980s (especially on *Hot Space*, 1982), and several shared song credits later on (notably on *A Kind of Magic*, 1986).
- The astute might notice a passing reference to Brian May's solo track *Last Horizon* (*Back to the Light*, 1992).
- Mustapha encounters Harold outside the cabin occupied by Ackley Fahrenheit. There is a much more blatant reference to *Friends Will be Friends* (*A Kind of Magic*, 1984).
- In the following scene, the group are sharing an evening meal in Khashoggi's dining room. The opening comment from Dique names John Deacon's song *In Only Seven Days* (*Jazz*, 1978).
- Reflecting Brian's love for astronomy, Harold indicates that the crew of the *Khonsu* can navigate with the assistance of the stars – this was also featured in *The King of Rhye*.
- Dique displays his interest in the burgeoning field of electronics, à la John Deacon.

- During the dinner conversation Mustapha stops listening, plucking grapes from a bunch he dangles over his mouth. This is reminiscent of a photo of the young Freddie on the inner sleeve of the debut album (*Queen*, 1973).

CHAPTER TWELVE: 'YESTERDAY' MOMENTS

- Title – ref *Drowse* (*A Day at the Races*, 1976).
- Leith takes a brief sabbatical, to visit the Repositree. On the way, she contemplates some of the conundrums of recent days. Amongst them, the disappearance of the butterfly, Sammy. After some deliberation she decides that *Sammy didn't get very far*, a lyrical play on '*You won't get very far*' from *Spread Your Wings* (*News of the World*, 1977) – the song which is very much Sammy's Theme.
- Through Leith's musings, we continue to explore the fate of the twenty lost voyagers, who are by now quite clearly the *score brave souls* who boarded the spacecraft in '39 (*A Night at the Opera*, 1975).
- *If every leaf on every tree / could tell a story that would be...* the inspiration for the Repositree comes from this one line, from *The Miracle* (*The Miracle*, 1989).
- Leith visits the Repositree to research the history of Nurtenan during the Age of Sovereigns. She hopes to uncover evidence of the Order encountering Khashoggi's lost twenty voyagers. She reads several leaves referencing the Brixton Wolds. This northern forest region is named after a district in south London, where the Brian May Band famously played a gig in 1993. This set was later released as a live album.

- One historian is named Galleo – a play on *Galileo* from *Bohemian Rhapsody* (*A Night at the Opera*, 1975).
- The region of Ardendale is named – a reversal of Dale Arden, Flash's love interest in *Flash Gordon* (*Flash Gordon*, 1980).

CHAPTER THIRTEEN: GUILT IN THE TIDE

- Title – ref *It's Late* (*News of the World*, 1977).
- Mustapha argues with Fahrenheit about his motivations for the voyage and for dragging Fahrenheit along. The human insinuates that he has seen several worlds ... and has started to miss his own home world, the Earth he knew. He has started to acquire a similar philosophical outlook as Khashoggi, as inspired by *Earth* (*Smile*, 1969).
- In that same discussion, Fahrenheit states 'There is no way back home', a line from *Leaving Home Ain't Easy* (*Jazz*, 1978). This same line will feature as an upcoming chapter title.
- Meadow and Dique spend time with the Mer on board the *Khonsu*, and discuss the ship's genius. Meadow describes it as 'the machine of a dream', borrowing the line from Roger Taylor's *I'm in Love with My Car* (*A Night at the Opera*, 1975).
- Harold engages in astronomy on board the *Khonsu*, much as his counterpart Brian May would.
- 'Those were the days ... all gone now,' reminisces Khashoggi slipping into depression. The line borrows lyrics from *These Are the Days of Our Lives* (*Innuendo*, 1991).

CHAPTER FOURTEEN: WATER IN MY BRAIN

- Title – ref *Somebody to Love* (*A Day at the Races*, 1976).
- The chapter opens with an exploration of the weakening of Will and Mustapha's relationship. It contains flavours of *Love of My Life* (*A Night at the Opera*, 1975), including an affirmation from Will that 'I still love you'.
- 'Mustapha still felt he had died a little inside' – a nod to Freddie's ode to the ongoing tribulations of romance, *Somebody to Love* (*A Day at the Races*, 1976).
- Another song about love, though this one is taken out of context: the line *Right until the ends of the earth* is italicised, being from *You Take My Breath Away* (*A Day at the Races*, 1976). The heavier exploration of love songs in this section signifies the shifting dynamic between two on-page relationships: the weakening of love between Mustapha and Will, and the forging of love between Leith and Trixel. Keep an eye on it!
- Mustapha muses that *We're all starting to lose our minds*. We're back to *Somebody to Love* (*A Day at the Races*, 1976), wherein Freddie sings about having water in his brain / no common sense / nobody left to believe... only some lines later, Dique will tell him directly that he has 'Water in (your) brain.'
- The pixies, for lack of something better to do, strike up a jaunty song. Amongst the lyrics are 'Everyone's going slightly mad', referencing *I'm Going Slightly Mad* (*Innuendo*, 1991).
- Mustapha appears on the Observation Deck, clad in a new outfit. It is designed to resemble something Freddie Mercury might have worn onstage, touring either *Hot Space* or *The Works*.

CHAPTER FIFTEEN: NO WAY BACK HOME

- Title – ref *Leaving Home Ain't Easy* (*Jazz*, 1978).
- Mustapha sings his incantation to the havens – BISMILLAH! – from *Bohemian Rhapsody* (*A Night at the Opera*, 1975).
- The reply is a booming, echoing laughter, such as that heard at the opening of *The Hero* (*Flash Gordon*, 1980). The lightning keeps the Flash Gordon motif going.
- The line *Got to set things to right* mirrors a line from *Fight from the Inside* (*News of the World*, 1977).
- Mustapha seeks an audience with Adatar, the Sun itself. Adatar grants his assistance escaping the storm, in exchange for a task: Mustapha must visit the nearby island, populated by a debauched people and bring them *Back to the Light* (*Back to the Light*, Brian May solo album, 1992).
- In Adatar's honour, Mustapha offers to (re)name their home 'City of the Sun' – and just like that, we're off to Sun City, as per Queen's controversial visit to South Africa in 1982.
- Banished from Adatar's presence, Mustapha is stripped of his wings and plummets towards the ocean. It is a scene reminiscent of the Icarus mythology, also touched upon in *No-One but You* (*Queen Rocks*, 1997).
- Following Mustapha's actions, the storm breaks; the clouds open to enable *One shaft of light that shows the way*, as in *A Kind of Magic* (*A Kind of Magic*, 1986).

CHAPTER SIXTEEN: REST YOUR WEARY HEAD

- Title – ref *Play the Game* (*The Game*, 1980).
- Sitting on the beach with Will, Mustapha laments that all of his choices have led to loss and despair. It is a sentiment reflected in *Too Much Love Will Kill You* (*Made in Heaven*, 1995).
- The companions first encounter 'two women with butterfly wings', not unlike the pair of winged virgins that adorn the Queen crest.
- The fairies welcome the companions to their home in Grandville Palace, referencing Jean Ignace Isidore Gerard Grandville, whose art features on the sleeve of the album *Innuendo* (1991).
- The Potentate-Elect of Grandville Palace is a woman named Lady Antoinette, a pompous woman derived from the personage of Marie Antoinette, famously referenced in *Killer Queen* (*Sheer Heart Attack*, 1974).
- The companions discover that the ruling class in Phydeantum are prejudiced against the 'half-breeds' amongst them. This mirrors the politics of apartheid South Africa in the 1980s, when Queen visited Sun City.
- The setting – where *the sun hangs in the sky and the desert has sand / waves crash in the sea and meet the land* is intended to represent the vast, sweeping imagery depicted in *Innuendo* (*Innuendo*, 1991); itself somewhat influenced by Led Zepplin's *Kashmir*.
- Smoking a plant known as riddle-reed is common in Phydeantum. It is a hallucinogenic substance. This quirk of the Phydeantines comes solely from a line in *Play the Game* (The Game, 1980): *Light another cigarette and let yourself go …*

- Lady Antoinette is very much a 'caviar and cigarette' kind of girl, as depicted in *Killer Queen* (*Sheer Heart Attack*, 1974). After appraising Mustapha, she declares 'tonight, he eats cake'.

CHAPTER SEVENTEEN: PLEASURE DOME

- Title – ref *Life Is Real* (*Hot Space*, 1982).
- The companions are welcomed to Antoinette's court with a performance. The song is languid, reminiscent of the increasingly lurid nature of Freddie's songwriting during the early 1980s. Likewise, the entire scene is layered in sensuality, debauchery and sex, a staple of the times for Queen.
- Incidentally, *Surrender* is the title of a Roger Taylor solo track from *Electric Fire* (1998).
- Meadow and Dique are uncomfortable, and wearing ridiculous period costume … much like Roger Taylor and John Deacon in the video for *It's a Hard Life* (*The Works*, 1984).
- Continuing this reference, Mustapha is dressed absurdly, looking 'like nothing if not a gigantic prawn', as described once by Roger Taylor.
- The stoush between Harold and Lady Antoinette – and indeed, the prevailing politics in Phydeantum more generally - is inspired by the lyrics of *Innuendo* (*Innuendo*, 1991): *While we live according to race, colour or creed / While we rule by blind madness and pure greed / Our lives dictated by tradition, superstition, false religion / Through the aeons, and on, and on …*
- Mustapha gains intel from a satyr, regarding the mysterious civilisation beyond the known boundaries of Rhye. The

satyr speaks of the enigmatic Mephistopheles, who rules a huge population of the Unhomed. Mephistopheles is the name of the primary villain in the video game *Queen: The Eye* (1997). He is also a demon in Faustian legend.

- The scene that concludes the chapter is somewhere between an orgy and a nightmare, fuelled by riddle-reed. It is a homage to the instrumental sequence from *Get Down, Make Love* (*News of the World*, 1977).

CHAPTER EIGHTEEN: WHISPER ONCE MORE

- Title — ref *Las Palabras de Amor (The Words of Love)* (*Hot Space*, 1982).
- The opening page is a reference to the lyrics: *Pressure / pushing down on me / pressing down on you, no man asks for / under pressure ... splits a family in two / puts people on streets*, representing *Under Pressure* (*Hot Space*, 1982).
- Torr Yosef's inner struggle is a reference to the back-and-forth in *Machines (or Back to Humans)* (*The Works*, 1984).
- Trixel, recovering in Babel, mutters 'This could be heaven', a line from *Heaven for Everyone* (*Made in Heaven*, 1995).
- The chapter in general embraces the wistful, hopeful tone of *Las Palabras de Amor* (*Hot Space*, 1982), which speaks of the fostering of love.

CHAPTER NINETEEN: THIS NIGHT AND EVERMORE

- Title — ref *Las Palabras de Amor (The Words of Love)* (*Hot Space*, 1982).
- This entire chapter — a battle between the automatons and flesh-and-blood denizens of Babylon — is a homage

to the May/Taylor track *Machines (or Back to Humans)* from *The Works* (1984), an energetic exchange between machine and human. A new film clip was released for the song in 2023, which fittingly shows automaton-like machines in a menacing montage. The chapter is otherwise clear of any more specific Queen references.

CHAPTER TWENTY: BLOOD AND SAND

- Title – ref *White Man* (*A Day at the Races*).
- The companions need to escape Grandville Palace. 'Hey you two!' says Meadow, before suggesting to his friends that they won't want to *Fight from the Inside* (*News of the World*, 1977).
- 'Gotta leave! Hurry, hurry, hurry!' cries Harold, referencing lyrics from Brian May's song *Dead on Time* (*Jazz*, 1978).
- 'Goron's alive?' explodes Meadow, in a fan-favourite moment borrowed from *Flash* (*Flash Gordon*, 1980).
- Goron looks up at the companions from his place of imprisonment. 'One great big eye focussed in their direction', in reference to *Ogre Battle* (*Queen II*, 1974).
- 'The game is up,' Mustapha says to lady Antoinette. *The Game* she has been playing is one of power and manipulation, at the expense of Phydeantum's 'half-breed' lower class.
- Things get nasty. 'You are no ruler, *Potentate-Elect* ... you are a despot. A fat sewer rat, decaying in a cesspool of ill-gotten pride.' The glorious put-down is borrowed from *Death on Two Legs (Dedicated To ...* (*A Night at the Opera*, 1975).
- Mustapha's latest vocal onslaught brings with it a new power. 'AYO!' he sings, reminiscent of Freddie's triumphant appearance at Live Aid.

CHAPTER TWENTY-ONE: SHIVER DEEP INSIDE

- Title – ref *You Take My Breath Away* (*A Day at the Races*, 1976).
- Trixel is in recovery. Leith risks a nap. When the sylph wakes, she finds the fixie has left a bouquet of twelve roses on her bedside – or *A Dozen Red Roses for My Darling* (B-Side to *A Kind of Magic*) (*A Kind of Magic*, 1986).
- Astrologer Mayhampton meets with Leith in the Upper Kitchen. The Astrologer had a brief cameo in *The King of Rhye*; here, he is physically described ... with the same frizzled white curls as Dr Brian May.
- 'Mercury has just entered Virgo,' declares Mayhampton. A blithe reference to Freddie and his star sign. It is also a cosmic arrangement that an astrologer might explain brings calm. Mustapha's future seems *written in the stars* – ref *Made in Heaven* (*Made in Heaven*, 1995).
- The relationship arc between Trixel and Leith reaches its zenith. The final Queen track I attribute to their building romance is *You Take My Breath Away* (*A Day at the Races*, 1976). In real life, it is understood Freddie wrote the song for his then-lover, David Minns; in Rhye, it is also a queer romance that drives the narrative. Leith sits on the bed composing her thoughts, in a rearrangement of Freddie's beautiful words.

CHAPTER TWENTY-TWO: AT THE RAINBOW'S END

- Title – ref *All Dead, All Dead* (*News of the World*, 1977).
- This chapter opens with the suicide of Khashoggi. Suicide was a theme of two Freddie Mercury songs (excluding the vitriolic use of the word in *Death on Two Legs (Dedicated*

To...) – *Don't Try Suicide* (*The Game*, 1980) and *Keep Passing the Open Windows* (*The Works*, 1984).

- Before discovering Khashoggi's act, Will and Mustapha share a tender moment, a strengthening of their bond. '(You'll) *Let Me in Your Heart Again?*' asks Mustapha, referencing the title of the revived track originally written for *The Works* (1984).

- Meadow and Dique are playing together on board the *Khonsu*, in recognition of the shift to rhythm- and-beat-influenced music on *The Game* (1980) and *Hot Space* (1982).

- Khashoggi's suicide note begins with the all-too-easy *Dear Friends* (*Sheer Heart Attack*, 1974).

- On the Observation Deck, Harold once again plays the Horn of Agonies. He sure isn't *Sleeping on the Sidewalk* (*News of the World*, 1977), but he's *been blowing his horn since he knew he was born*, and he *plays around as well as he is able!*

- The veil lifts, and the companions see land and a glorious city ahead of them. *Such a beautiful horizon / like a jewel in the sun* ... it could be *Barcelona!* (*Barcelona*, 1988; Freddie Mercury and Montserrat Caballe).

PART THREE: THE FUTURE OF YOUR WORLD

- Title – ref *Princes of the Universe* (*A Kind of Magic*, 1986).

CHAPTER TWENTY-THREE: THE SOUND OF THE BEAT

- Title – ref *Another One Bites the Dust* (*The Game*, 1980).
- The companions plan to make landfall. Mustapha dresses in plain white trousers and a matching sleeveless tunic, along with a studded belt. He is dressed as Freddie

Mercury at Live Aid.

- Mustapha has an introspective moment aboard the nautiloid launch. He ponders the nature of progress and its effect on his world – the subject of *Is This the World We Created?* (*The Works*, 1984).

- On making discreet landfall, Meadow remarks that he would prefer the 'dignitaries' approach', favouring glamour and luxury. No doubt Roger Taylor would have agreed, as the consummate rock star.

- 'No Turning Back,' says Dique, in reference to the track by John Deacon and the Immortals, for *Biggles* (The Original Motion Picture Soundtrack Album) (1986).

- 'Are you ready for this?' asks Mustapha. 'I'm hanging on the edge of my seat,' replies Harold; thus begins a lengthy sequence mostly inspired by *Another One Bites the Dust* (*The Game*, 1980). They enter the dark underbelly of the city as night falls, setting the scene.

- '*Simps of Aaron intoxicate our brains*' is a tangential reference to the lyric *Intoxicate your brains with what I'm saying* from *Flick of the Wrist* (*Sheer Heart Attack*, 1974); the words are written in red, as is the album title on its sleeve.

- *Do you feel like suicide, Michaelites?* uses the phrase from *Death on Two Legs (Dedicated To...* (*A Night at the Opera*, 1975). It is written in blue, as is the title of its parent album.

- A man walks warily into the alley, with the brim of his peaked hat pulled down low. The setting is quiet but for the crunch of his shoes on gravel. *Another One Bites the Dust* (*The Game*, 1980).

- The conversation between the gangsters – one a traitorous informant, taking a bribe – mentions rival gang bosses Leroy Brown and 'Big Mama' Lulu Belle, from *Bring Back*

That Leroy Brown (Sheer Heart Attack, 1974).

- A man with a Tommy gun emerges from a dark recess ... and out of the doorway, the bullets rip! *Another One Bites the Dust (The Game*, 1980). Worth noting is that a Tommy gun is also featured in Queen's gangster-inspired thrash metal classic, *Stone Cold Crazy (Sheer Heart Attack*, 1974). A gunfight ensues and one by one the gangsters fall ... *and another one's gone, and another one's gone / Another one bites the dust!*

- A busker plays a trumpet on the street. This fellow is almost certainly *Sleeping on the Sidewalk (News of the World*, 1977).

- Sister Karen of the Order of the Unhomed appears and offers to direct the companions to safety. She names their location Mingo City — ref *Crash Dive on Mingo City (Flash Gordon*, 1980).

- She leads the companions to the headquarters of the Order, a cathedral-style building that matches the description of La Sagrada Familia, the famed cathedral in ... *Barcelona!* (*Barcelona*, 1988; Freddie Mercury and Montserrat Caballe).

CHAPTER TWENTY-FOUR: THE VOLUNTEERS

- Title — ref '*39 (A Night at the Opera*, 1975).

- 'Brother John got the bullet out,' explains Sister Karen. This one is very oblique, but thus continues the revelation of the true identities of the Sacred Twenty (you will recall we have already explored the identity of Tom, aka Major Tom, aka David Bowie). 'John' here refers to John Lennon, assassinated by point-blank gunfire. Freddie wrote *Life is Real (Song for Lennon) (Hot Space*, 1982) in memory of him.

- Harold has been injured – a bullet shattered one of his arms. While not by a bullet, Brian May feared at one stage he may lose an arm to gangrene, in 1974. 'Hopefully he will keep the arm,' confides Sister Karen.

- The Acolyte gives Mustapha a portion of cake – a cherry and almond cake. A book published by Queen assistant Peter Freestone, detailing Freddie Mercury's favourite foods, includes a recipe for this cake.

- The pair again speak of the Order's history, alluding to *the rage that lasts a thousand years* – ref *A Kind of Magic* (*A Kind of Magic*, 1986).

- Mustapha and Sister Karen discuss the two factions that threaten to tear apart the Order – and are at the heart of criminal activities across the entire city. They are the Michaelites (named for Michael Jackson, King of Pop, with whom Freddie recorded several duets) and Aaronites (named for Elvis Aaron Presley, King of Rock 'n' Roll, who died in 1977, and inspired the massive hit *Crazy Little Thing Called Love* (*The Game*, 1980)).

- The following song contains not only Queen references – the Sacred Twenty are established to be the '*volunteers*' mentioned in *'39* (*A Night at the Opera*, 1975); it also contains a riddle, which suggests the identities of these individuals. In the pages of *Metropolis*, only some of the Sacred Twenty are given names. They are:

  * Michael Jackson and Elvis Presley, being two of the '*three royals*';

  * David Bowie, aka 'Tom', a '*duke to watch them dance*';

  * John Lennon, one of the four on an odyssey '*to yet give peace a chance*';

- Neil Peart, one of the 'four to keep the beat alive' (Peart was the drummer for Rush);
- Karen Carpenter, aka Karen, a *'shieldmaiden behind the skins'* (Carpenter was a drummer); and
- Delores O'Riordan, aka Delores, another *'shieldmaiden.'*

- The names of the remaining Volunteers are not given in Metropolis, though one may begin to guess at their identities.

- Sister Karen reveals that the Order wish for Mustapha to travel back in time to ensure the Twenty return to their home world, thus never impacting the history of Rhye. It looks like Mustapha's *Goin' Back* (*Larry Lurex*, 1973).

- Onik's gift(s) to the Order of the Unhomed were the Doors of Time — ref *A Kind of Magic* (*A Kind of Magic*, 1986).

CHAPTER TWENTY-FIVE: INSANITY LAUGHS

- Title — ref *Under Pressure* (*Hot Space*, 1982).

- The opening passage of this chapter, as with the title itself, is intended to evoke the lyrics to *Under Pressure*. Families are split. People are forced onto the streets. The very phrase 'Under the pressure of stewardship' is used, to make the point clearer. Doom awaits ... *people* (are) *on the edge of the night.* Leith and Trixel live as though they have only these days remaining to them; trying to fit in a lifetime's passion in less than twenty-four hours. *Love dares you to change our way of caring about ourselves / This is our last dance.*

- The looters appear with their wagon and the corpulent satyr Fanny ... Big Fat Fanny, to be precise — ref *Fat Bottomed Girls* (*Jazz*, 1978). How she has fallen from grace!

- 'Leith, I love you ... but we only have fourteen hours to save the city' is an adapted line of Dale Arden's dialogue, that appears in *Flash (Single Version)* (*Flash Gordon*, 1980).

- At the spacecraft, the inexorable countdown continues. A pervasive theme of the book — especially at this tail end of it — is that *Time waits for nobody...* ref — *Time Waits For No One* (Freddie Mercury, from Dave Clark's musical *Time*, 1986).

- Trixel and Leith ultimately stay behind at the spacecraft, when all others leave. (They've) *just got time to say their prayers* ... (They're) *just waiting for the hammer to fall.* Ref — *Hammer to Fall* (*The Works*, 1984). The threat of nuclear disaster reaches a crescendo.

CHAPTER TWENTY-SIX: KING OF THE IMPOSSIBLE

- Title — ref *Flash* (*Flash Gordon*, 1980).

- The companions finally meet with Mephistopheles in the underground sanctuary housing the Doors of Time. The enigmatic man has an appearance similar to the deranged villain in the PC game, *Queen: The Eye* (1997).

- Mephisto describes travel as 'a jollification, as a matter of fact!' The phrase is lifted from *Seaside Rendezvous* (*A Night at the Opera*, 1975).

- Mustapha becomes impatient with Mephistopheles, demanding: 'I want it all ... and I want it *now.*' Ref — *I Want it All* (*The Miracle*, 1989).

- Mustapha learns that he has been caged in a world of his own design, by Marnis. He is incredulous; one might imagine him saying 'I ain't gonna face no defeat / I just gotta get out of this prison cell / Someday I'm gonna be free!' Ref – *Somebody to Love* (*A Day at the Races*, 1976).

- The Two-Legged Death returns. Ref – *Death on Two Legs (Dedicated to...* (*A Night at the Opera*, 1975).

CHAPTER TWENTY-SEVEN: THE DOORS OF TIME

- Title – ref *A Kind of Magic* (*A Kind of Magic*, 1986).

- Mustapha, with the Sigil of Valendyne slashed on his forearm, has 'silvered blood' or bleeds '*mercurial* ink' after the cinnabar was transmogrified in his veins during *The King of Rhye*.

- The ladder is destroyed in a rock fall, leaving Harold to fly up through a hole to the next tier. 'I'm on my way up!' he cries, quoting the Brian May solo single. Ref – *On My Way Up* (*Another World*, 1998).

- The companions arrive at the necessary Door. Dique seeks certainty from Mustapha, who replies 'There can be only one'; a reference to the 1986 film *Highlander*, and a quote which can be heard in *Gimme the Prize (Kurgan's Theme)* (*A Kind of Magic*, 1986).

- Fahrenheit muses on the 'gay promenade' and 'seaside idyll', being the town of Brighton-Upon-Sea which he originally left alongside Mustapha in *The King of Rhye*. These are evocations of *Brighton Rock* (*Sheer Heart Attack*, 1974).

- As Dique prepares to pass through the Door, he contemplates his future (with Roni): *Just you and I ... and maybe a cosy little cheese shop.* Ref – the John Deacon-penned *You and I* (*A Day at the Races*, 1976).

EPILOGUE: ALL DEAD AND GONE

- Title – ref *All Dead, All Dead* (*News of the World*, 1977).

- The Epilogue contains almost no distinct references to Queen. Instead, it gives the reader a glimpse into a catastrophic 'bad ending' for Rhye, were a nuclear explosion (and resultant fallout) to be realised. It explores the horror in a passage that evokes *Hammer to Fall* (*The Works*, 1984), with the mushroom cloud as dominant imagery. Of course … as our heroes concurrently navigate the Doors of Time, they now face the challenge of resetting the timeline, creating an alternate reality in which this does not come to pass.

- The explosion itself might represent the blast that closes *In the Lap of the Gods … Revisited* (*Sheer Heart Attack*, 1974).

- As with The King of Rhye, the final line hints at one last Queen reference – we finish with the tragic lament, the *melancholic* finale of *My Melancholy Blues* (*News of the World*, 1977).

Is this our last dance…?